# THE ICARUS AFTERMATH

## THE SUNFIRE SAGA, BOOK 1

## ARIELLE M. BAILEY

Cover art: Mirriam Neal of The Art of Mirriam Neal » http://mirriamneal.com

Cover design: Morgan G Farris » http://morgangfarris.com

ISBN 978-1-7354713-0-3

*To Carrie Fisher*

*Whose legacy will be with us...*
*Always.*

*Never regret thy fall, O Icarus of the fearless flight.*
*For the greatest tragedy of them all,*
*is never to feel the burning light.*

~ Oscar Wilde

# CONTENTS

# AUTHOR'S NOTE

I've always hated it when authors or publishers put notes or introductions with spoilers in the beginning of a book. So any spoilery notes will be saved for the end of this book. This is just a quick heads-up.

YES, I have (seemingly indiscriminately) mixed the Greek and Roman names of mythological characters. This book and its characters called for me to use both Roman and Greek names, sometimes both for a single character, like Hephaestus Vulcan, and sometimes one or the other, like Ares. I've also mixed elements from Roman mythology in with all the Greek mythology. It was intentional and not done out of disrespect for either culture; quite the opposite.

In Greek, Crete and Cythira and various other C-names are spelled with the equivalent of our English K, which is one reason I've spelled them with a K here. I also did it to simplify pronunciation visuals.

On that subject, a quick guide to name pronunciation:

Talos = TALos

Koralia = KoRAYleeah

Mikon = MEEkon

Athanasia = AthaNAzeea

## AUTHOR'S NOTE

Xuthos = ZUUthos

Xantippos = ZanTEEpos

For more notes on the story, see the end of the book.

I hope you enjoy this adventure!

~ Arielle

# THE ICARUS AFTERMATH

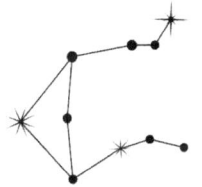

# CHAPTER 1

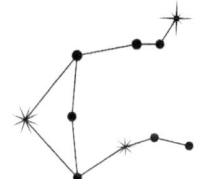

"**I**carus! The guns are hot!"

The shocked yell crackled over the radio, and Icarus yanked his fighter up, automatically scanning the guns on the side of the moonlit fortress below them.

"How can they be hot?" he snapped at his second. "They weren't supposed to be expecting us."

"How would I know?" Rhexenor said. "They're hot! I'm reading loading signatures everywhere."

Icarus was still scanning, lowering his fighter to see down the row of guns through the humid semidarkness of Krete's atmosphere. Nothing. Rhexenor must have seen wrong.

Wait.

There. In the center.

"Dammit." He yanked his fighter up, snapping orders. "Icarus to all fighters, get clear. This is a Red Order from your captain. Get clear now and return to base." He pulled the eagle fighter to the side and soared out of reach as the guns lit up one by one, yellow and orange and red painting the navy stones of the turreted wall. They had minutes—if that—until the firing sequences were complete and the barrage began.

There was a short burst of swearing from everyone and then silence as the fighters began to obey. They were rebels. They faced death every day. You got used to it, and you met it silently. That was the Code.

He counted the rising fighters as he flipped the radio to a different frequency. "Captain Sun to Base, Code Crimson Scarlet Vermilion. Abort the mission. General, abort the mission."

Seven fighters clear now. But too many still in range.

"Icarus, what's going on out there?" the radio operator asked crisply.

Thank stars it was his sister's voice.

"I don't know! They weren't supposed to know we were coming, but they did. The guns are hot. I'm aborting the mission." *Eleven fighters clear now.*

"Do you have the Key?" she asked, her voice still businesslike.

And then the first gun fired and a fighter went down in a blue ball of fire.

He swore as the dead woman's face flashed through his mind; she was a pilot from his third wing, under command of Xuthos. "Yes! Dad's team does. I can't talk. We're gonna get slaughtered if we don't get clear now. Icarus out."

Where was Rhexenor? He strained to check behind him. *There.* Right on his tail.

"Red Order, Red Order," Icarus repeated, his voice calm. He couldn't afford a panic now. "This is your captain. All fighters get clear of the fortress. Get clear now."

"We're trying!" That was Xuthos, hanging back to make sure the rest of his wing was clear.

A second gun fired, and two ships stuttered, others racing to their aid.

They weren't going to make it. There were still almost two dozen ships in range of the fire. These were new guns too, top-of-the-line shore defense batteries. Minos wasn't taking chances, not after Poseidon's last attack.

Icarus was going to lose most of his unit.

Unless...

There was one chance in a hundred to save them.

He was diving for the gap before he consciously thought, streaking in front of the guns, drawing their fire, shooting back.

There was a moment of horrified silence when his pilots saw what he was doing. Then a barrage of cursing, most of it from the leaders of his other two wings.

"Damn you, Icarus!" Rhex growled. "Don't do this!"

"Get them clear, and do it now. That's a Black Order, Rhex." He'd pull up when they were clear.

For a minute, he didn't think the gunners had recognized him. Then the shell trajectories changed, following him, and he grinned savagely.

"Took you long enough," he muttered. "What, Minos, couldn't find any young men to watch the defenses? Relying on half-blind grandfathers now, are you?"

Rhex swore at him again. "Get out of there, Icarus! You're too close!"

His second wingleader screamed at him too until her fighter spun sideways, bumped by someone else.

He risked a quick glance above him, counting the fighters still in range. "I can't get clear until you are," he said patiently, but he knew he was too close already.

He banked through another roll and lifted above four missiles that crashed into each other. The heat flared around him, but three more falcon fighters had gotten clear in the meantime. Only a few remained now, Xuthos defending them with his fancy flying and Rhexenor dropping down to back him up.

"Get clear!" he yelled again. The missiles were coming faster, more guns turning to focus on him. It was hard to blame them, really. He *had* taunted them pretty loudly, flaunting his distinctive fighter.

There. The last of his pilots was clear, Xuthos racing to join his wingmates and Rhexenor hovering to wait for his leader.

Heat blossomed around Icarus, scorching, burning his chest. He couldn't breathe, though he dimly realized he was tearing at the neck of his jacket to get more air. It didn't help.

Blue fire.

Red fire.

Fire everywhere, the same bright yellow as the sun, as his fighter.

*I'm sorry, General. I tried.*

*Talos. Take care of them. All of them. And her.*

*Melainis...my black swan...I'm sorry...*

Everything went black.

✝

"ICARUS IS DEAD."

The words dropped like heavy stones muffled in cloaks, thudding into the already tense silence on the starship bridge where the General had been waiting for the final mission reports.

A silence that stretched out, smothering, still, heavy.

"General?" the messenger said after a few minutes.

"Are you positive?" The woman wouldn't have dared bring her the message if she hadn't been sure, but...Icarus had died before, twice, and come back. This had to be another fluke.

"It's been confirmed. There are pictures of the wreckage." The girl stopped with a choke that turned into a cough.

General Athanasia looked up then. The messenger's face was streaked with tears, her auburn hair coming loose from its braid. Ianessa, the radio operator who had taken the last message from Icarus.

She blinked, trying to absorb the knowledge. Icarus of the bright blond hair and the blue-topaz eyes. Icarus of the quick mind and the bold spirit. Laughing, fiery, loyal Icarus.

"The guns were already hot," Ianessa went on, swallowing hard, forcing the words out. "He flew too close. He saved his fleet, almost all of them, but he..." She shook her head.

Icarus, her godson. Ianessa's foster brother. Leader of the Sunfire Squadron. Captain of their main fighter fleet.

There would be time to mourn him later. "And the Key?"

"He said Daedalus had it." Ianessa's eyes hardened.

"Well? Spit it out. Did we lose him too?"

"No, ma'am. He's vanished. We don't know where he is, if he's alive or dead. His team had to leave without him."

That was enough to bring Athanasia half out of her chair. "What?" She doubted he was dead—Daedalus was too canny for that. But maybe he was back in the hands of the Kretans. That could be catastrophic on so many levels, not least for the rebellion. But hadn't Icarus said they were clear of the palace earlier?

Ianessa watched her, waiting for something.

*Oh. That's right. Orders.*

Athanasia took a deep breath, pushing the grief to the side. It would have to wait. The Kallistratus Rebellion was potentially in more danger than ever right now, and it was up to her to decide the next step.

"How many pilots did we lose?"

Hand shaking, Ianessa held out a sheet of scrip with the tally. Rhexenor was dead, waiting too long for Icarus, the report said. Three other pilots were gone too. Several pilots were injured, none severely. The two remaining wingleaders had survived, but one had been badly wounded while trying to cover her wing's retreat.

Which was only to be expected from one of Icarus's pilots. They hated to leave anyone behind. This...how it must have wrecked them to fly away and leave their leader.

One other member of the mission was dead, their Kretan inside contact.

Looking up at Ianessa, the General said, "I'm sending for Talos. I'll tell him, but you'd better tell the rest of the Sunfires. Then send the news out to the navy, and assemble all the uninjured pilots for the debrief."

They had to be feeling pretty bleak. She needed to check on them...and they would need her too, even if only to reassure them it wasn't their fault.

"Ma'am." Holding her injured arms close to her body, Ianessa hurried from the room.

And for just a moment, Athanasia let her shoulders slump. She was alone on the command bridge, the radio operators and other mission support personnel working out of the larger bridge two levels below.

"Icarus is gone." She made herself say the words out loud. They tasted dry, but they brought her back to herself. This would leave a huge hole in the command force, one that would need to be filled immediately. She'd need a new fleet commander. The Kallistratus would have to shift bases, in case their location was compromised. And she needed to notify Talos, and Koralia...oh, stars.

Koralia.

Poor girl.

Athanasia's hands tightened on the arms of her chair as tears fell in a hot rush of grief.

*You firebrand. You saved them, but how am I supposed to keep them going without you?*

She let herself cry for just a moment, and then she wiped the tears away and reached for a com-pad.

They still had a war to win.

✦

SPACE WAS SO...HOMEY. Even when it was alive with missiles and explosions and racing ships of battle, nothing quite compared to the freedom and peace of being in a fighter, soaring through the darkness, the suns of various star systems bright glints around you.

Nothing.

Talos swung his falcon fighter to the right, double-checking the status of the wingwomen flying under him. With the inside information they'd just retrieved about Poseidon's little tiff with Minos and the Key Icarus was going after right now, they'd be rolling the Labyrinth back shortly. And then they'd sweep around the outer edge of the galaxy, gathering the individual rebel cells as they went, and finally push ahead with a concentrated assault closer to the center of the galaxy.

The olympian sons were about to meet their match.

His com-pad chirped once, then three times in quick succession, signifying a priority message. He reached for it with one hand, checking the identifying code.

The General.

But not a text. It was a live transmission.

He felt a little alarm as he put the fighter on autopilot. If Icarus had succeeded, it should have been a brief, automated message. For the General to message him personally…his fingers fumbled as he swiped the message open.

"Talos." General Athanasia looked straight at him, her face impassive, her eyes hard. "Report back to headquarters at once. The Key Mission has been aborted. We're down five fighters and two operatives, and Daedalus and the Key are in the wind." She paused and closed her eyes briefly.

The pause sent a chill through him. It meant bad news. *Very* bad news.

"Icarus is dead, Talos. I need you here."

No. He'd heard that wrong. It *couldn't* be. Not again.

He narrowed his eyes. "He…is this another joke, boss? It is, isn't it? That ass put you up to this so he could win this round."

But Athanasia wasn't laughing. She shook her head slowly. "No, it's real this time."

"Really? Because I get him wanting to prolong the joke after the last one I pulled. I mean, I kinda deserve it. And this really is a master stroke, but I'd have thought that—"

"Talos!" Athanasia didn't snap, but he felt like she had. He stopped and stared at her, seeing finally the heaviness in her gray eyes, the weary set to her head and shoulders, the tension in the way she pressed her lips together before sighing.

"It's real this time."

Still he hesitated. "He's died twice before, and it was real then too." But his voice was quiet, almost begging for hope.

"There are pictures of the wreckage and his entire fleet as witnesses. This isn't like the other times. There's no way—rational, accidental, or pure miracle—that he could have survived. Ianessa can confirm."

Ianessa. If Ianessa had the proof too…then there really was no hope.

"Okay," he heard himself say, the words distant. Then he shook his head. He couldn't let himself absorb the news yet. Not right now. "Do I need to tell the Sunfires?"

"Ianessa will. After you report in, I need you back here, Talos. Bring a squadron…" The video image wavered, and he remembered he was about to enter the planetary dead zone above his current base. Then it flickered back. "A squadron—your general will have the details."

"Aye, aye."

"I'm sorry, Talos."

"I know, boss. I know. I'll see you soon."

She nodded once and cut the transmission.

The ship shuddered as it entered the dead zone, and he grabbed for the controls, switching back to manual, easing the fighter through the radiation and down to the clouds above the surface. It was a procedure he could do asleep or bleeding out, which was fortunate, because that's exactly what it felt like he was doing.

Icarus had always been the better one at reaching out mentally to try to feel a person. Talos didn't have that talent, and though he'd been able to work on it when Icarus tried to teach him, right now he wished he did.

But even that wouldn't have helped. Neither General Athanasia nor Ianessa were known to make many mistakes. One on their own might, but not both together. Not when it came to Icarus.

*He's really dead this time.*

Talos broke through the clouds and hovered over the base, signaling to his wingwomen to land. His com-pad rang with an alert, and he opened it. It was a message from Ianessa to all the Sunfires, confirming Icarus's death. The chat started chiming like crazy as the other Sunfires demanded proof, but Talos flipped the pad over and lowered his fighter into the forest, landing in a clearing away from base.

He needed a few minutes alone.

The com-pad screeched now, and he turned it back over. Photos filled the screen, and then a short video. The proof of Icarus's death.

He forced himself to watch the video taken by a wingmate high enough to see everything: the golden eagle fighter diving toward the guns, Icarus taunting the gunners, keeping them busy until the rest of the fleet was clear, his second-in-command hovering behind him, and then...the fireball.

"You always did want to go out in a blaze of glory," he said to the empty air. Then he slammed a fist into the side of his seat. "So much for three times being the charm. What the hell am I supposed to do now, Captain?"

It never mattered how high they rose in the ranks or how many people they each led, Icarus was always The Captain to him and the rest of the Sunfires.

And now he was gone.

Tears burned his eyes as he punched the side of the fighter again. *You couldn't have had just one more miracle?* He wanted to swear, keep punching something, *anything* until Icarus sent a laughing video message proving he'd been joking.

But this was no prank. And he didn't know how to deal with this sense of utter loss and pain. He slumped back in his seat, staring numbly into the trees around him as grief and anger raged through him.

A while later—he didn't know how long—his radio crackled. "Base to Captain Talos. Sir, are you coming in?"

Blinking, he looked around him. Twilight was shading into dark. The base doors would be sealed soon, and any fighters still out would then have to stay out all night.

He hopped out of the fighter, grabbing his canteen. On the ground, he poured water into his hands and splashed it on his face, erasing all signs of grief, pain, and anger. Then he got back into the ship, fired it up, and rose into the air, heading back to base.

Grief would have to wait. First things first: get back to the General. Reorganize the fleet. And then go after Minos.

Krete wouldn't know what hit them.

+

"Is that all?"

"Yes, ma'am." The housekeeper shuffled the lists in her hand. "Unless you'd like to approve the arrangements for Aphrodite Venus's possible visit?"

Lady Skotia Koralia Melainis Nikephoros, First Daughter of Alalaxious Palace, threw back her head and laughed, a dry sound that appreciated the respectful teasing in the housekeeper's question. "You were handling her visits long before I was mistress here. I leave you to it." Besides, she planned to be far away if Aphrodite actually did visit.

The housekeeper's eyes twinkled as she gathered up the last of the thin, flexible black lists with white writing. "I think I can manage that. I'll see you at dinner, ma'am."

"Yes, indeed." Done with her household duties, Koralia turned to look out the window. It had been a cool morning, but the afternoon had turned hot an hour ago, and she didn't feel like walking out in it. Ares and Hephaestus Vulcan wouldn't be back for hours, and the palace was rather bare of warriors right now, so there were few people with whom she could spar. That left her without much to do at the moment.

The greenhouse, though. That would be cool, and there were always plants needing pruning or tending.

But as she headed toward the atrium and the hall that would take her to the greenhouse, a knot tightened in her stomach. Desolation gripped her, stopping her in her tracks.

Someone she knew and loved was in trouble.

Her fathers? Nah, they weren't that far away, so Ares would be back and shouting commands down the halls if something had happened. Servants would be rushing around.

So it couldn't be them.

And she hadn't felt her mother in years, so it wasn't her.

Couldn't be her brothers either. She didn't remember the last time she'd felt something from one of them, and they were always in danger anyway.

Her Amazon squad? Possible. But doubtful. They were on the Amazon homeworld and had been for a week.

Then her stomach twisted as the desolation grew like a black cloud slowly swallowing her.

*Icarus.*

The world faded around Koralia. She stared dully into thin air as static filled her mind, blocking out everything except one face.

*Icarus.*

*My sun.*

*No.*

Her com-pad beeped quietly, startling her so badly that she dropped it. Gasping in a breath, she became aware of her surroundings again—a lower-floor hall in Ares's fortress.

How long had she been sitting here? Based on the late-afternoon sunlight slanting through a window nearby, it must have been around an hour since she'd felt the shock.

A passing servant paused to see if she needed help, but she shook her head.

She dropped to the floor, gripping the pad tightly with her fingers before standing up again. Her mind screamed at her to hurry, to open the message and confirm bad news, find out what had happened to the rebel pilot, but she made her hands move slowly, deliberately. She didn't want to drop the pad again.

The notification blinked insistently, a live transmission, not a message.

She was running then, crossing the hall to an office and slamming the carved door closed behind her for privacy. Clenching one hand into a fist, she leaned against the door and twisted the pad with her other hand to open the transmission.

"Koralia."

"General."

The Kallistratus Rebellion leader looked exhausted and suddenly old. She peered out of the transmission, searching Koralia's face. "You felt it, didn't you?" she asked quietly.

"I felt...something. What...what is it?"

"He's gone. Really gone. There's proof, if you need it."

Slowly, she nodded. She didn't need proof, not beyond the blank darkness swallowing her, but she'd want to see it anyway. Not now. But sometime.

"What can I do?" she heard herself say the words, but they were automatic and sounded like the croak of a half-dead raven.

"Oh, Kora. As if you haven't done enough already. Nothing, little eagle. I'll be in contact."

Koralia felt herself nodding again and moved to switch off the transmission, but the General held up one hand.

"You won't...you'll be there when I call next?"

Blinking, she stared at the woman. "I...what? You think I'm at risk?"

"*Are* you?"

The words *you wouldn't be the first Amazon to follow her partner* hung between them, but the General did not say them.

Something slid down Koralia's cheek, and she put her hand up to feel it. Tears. She shook her head. "No, General. I'm not. Amazon word of honor. I'll be here."

Athanasia gave her one short, sharp nod, and then the screen went black.

The cloud was heavier, slowly numbing her senses. She needed to be truly alone, away from being disturbed. Flinging the office door back open, she hurried across the hall and up three flights of stairs to her room, almost tripping over her gown.

She didn't slam this door, just closed it quietly. Then she collapsed onto a thick rug in the middle of the floor, curling into a ball as she stared out the window at the harsh noonday sun.

The love of her life was *dead*.

# CHAPTER 2

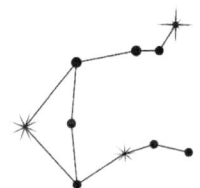

"I want his blood!"

The door to the command bridge couldn't exactly slam open, since it was automated, but somehow, Talos's entrances always made it seem like he'd flung double doors open to crash against the walls.

Athanasia sighed as she turned around from the navigation panel she'd been studying. "Hello to you too."

The fiery captain came over and bent down to kiss the top of her head. Then he paced away from her, stopping in the center of the bridge to put his hands on his hips and glower at her. "Our fighters never had a chance! They never even *fired*. *Minos* was the aggressor."

"Well, most kings don't take too kindly to people stealing their secrets. It's not like there was no provocation," she reminded him.

But he wasn't listening. Typical Talos.

"Spies can be shot or captured, fine. But this was aerial combat, and they hadn't attacked, and *he fired the first shot*. I want his blood, I want his commander, I want his gunners, and I want that fortress of his smashed to powder."

She sighed and let him rant. The only way to stop Talos when he was in one of his raging speeches was to smack him upside the head. That was Icarus's preferred method of handling his brother, but doing that now would inflame Talos further, because it would remind them both of their loss.

So she let him be and went back to plotting routes. No matter how many old shortcuts she mapped in, every single path to Outer Arms space had to go through Poseidonian space or Kretan space—and thus face the Labyrinth.

Since Poseidon had his own reasons for not wanting the Rebellion to succeed, they couldn't exactly go that way. And Jupiter had Inner Ring space far too well patrolled for them to try that route.

They were out of options. They needed the Key, the map to navigate the Labyrinth.

"So what's the plan?" Talos asked, spinning to face her again, his hands still on his hips.

"What?"

"The plan? For attacking Krete?" He frowned. "You did hear what I just said, didn't you? There are military precedents for a return strike, no matter what our people were doing there in the first pl—"

She shook her head to stop him. Oh, she'd heard all right. And he wasn't going to like the answer. "We aren't attacking Krete." She held up her hand. "Before you start blustering again, think for a minute. Whatever provocation Minos did or didn't have, we can't throw the fleet into a battle they won't win. He's re-fortified his entire coast, so either we go up against that or we face the Labyrinth itself. And we can't hit the Labyrinth without the Key. So unless Daedalus decides to drop back onto our radar, we have to get it another way."

"You still haven't found him?" His face darkened when she said his uncle's name.

"No."

He started to say something, paused, and then tried again, only to stop. She waited, silently hoping he'd see sense. She needed him sane and level-headed, not hot under the collar to rain retribution on Minos and Krete.

"So we leave Icarus un-avenged?" he asked at last, his voice bitter.

"Do you think I don't want vengeance too? But this is not a childish game of tug o' war. It's about bigger things. You know that. Icarus knew that. We're trying to pull the galaxy out of a civil war and give everyone a chance to know *peace*, not intensify the fighting. If we gather all our resources right now, we *might* just stand a chance against Krete." Athanasia shook her head. "But that's a huge *maybe*, and it would take weeks to get all our resources here, *if* we had a route around the Labyrinth, which we don't. And if we do take Krete, what then?"

He frowned but didn't say anything.

*Come on, Talos, think.* Sighing, she spelled it out for him. "We'll have lost so much of our fighting force that it will take months to recover. Poseidon might support us for taking care of Krete, but it has alliances with three olympian factions—yes, three now, and it's high in favor with Jupiter himself. You think they'll just let a reprisal go?"

He flung up his hands. "So we can't go up against them. Fine. Then what do you want me for?"

"Two things. I need a new fleet commander." He started shaking his head before she'd even finished the sentence. "Yes," she insisted, her tone firm before he could question or refuse to lead Icarus's pilots. "It has to be you. Despite your fever to annihilate Krete, you are the best person for the job."

Ignoring the jab, he asked, "How is Loxias not the better person for this? He's already friends with half the lieutenants here. Or how about Cleon?"

"Loxias *is* a great person for it, but he won't unite the more reckless pilots, especially not right now. Besides, his general needs him right where he is. Neither will Cleon, and he doesn't have the experience under fire that you do. And Rhexenor is dead." She stood up and walked toward him, putting a hand on his shoulder. "You *can* unite them, all of them. I'm trusting you to hold the reckless ones in check and shake the cautious ones up...but only a little! Don't push anyone too hard, not now." He didn't really need the instruction—with Icarus gone, he was the best fleet commander in the rebellion, and he'd always been better than Icarus at the more practical aspects of command anyway. But she still said it, because she had to have *something* to say, something that gave them both a chance to breathe through the reminders of Icarus that pulsed in the air around them.

Athanasia paused a minute and then reminded him, "Icarus would have wanted it to be you. You were always his chosen successor."

That broke through to him, as she knew it would. Talos had been stone-faced, but now he blinked hard, and she squeezed his shoulder. "Are you with me?" she asked quietly.

Closing his eyes, he breathed in and out a few times. "Yes. Yes, I'm with you, boss. Always. Of *course* I'm with you."

"Excellent." She bent back over the map. "I'm giving you Xuthos as a second."

"Xuthos?" His head snapped around to stare at her, and he frowned. "Can I ask why you're assigning me the only guy on base I can't stand?"

He could ask, but that didn't mean she would answer him. If he thought about it long enough, he'd figure it out for himself. "For reasons," she told him. "Very good reasons."

"Why can't I have Cleon?"

"Because as well as you two get along, he's still growing his backbone, so he can't push you back right now. I won't have you chewing him up too soon." She leaned back in her chair, waiting for the next question. He knew all the pilots in the fleet, and he'd throw every possible choice at her until he was satisfied with the answer or she stopped him. His knowledge of the pilots was a big part of why he needed to be the one to lead them.

"Tisandros?"

"Too much of a know-it-all. And too angry about Icarus. He'd have everyone out of control in no time."

Talos's eyes narrowed as he thought. "Lasthena?"

"She took hits trying to protect her wing and won't be back to full work for at least two weeks."

"Aren't there any Sunfires we can recall?"

That really was a last ditch stand. She raised her eyebrows at him.

"Yeah, yeah, I know, they're too important, they're needed elsewhere, I know." He glared at nowhere in particular. He was out of options now, and he knew it. Rolling his neck in a stretch, he huffed. "Fine. But what's number two?"

"Two?"

He came to lean on a console beside her. "You said you needed me for *two* reasons."

"Oh, yes. I think we might have a traitor somewhere, and I need you leading the pilots so you aren't interfering with the investigation."

"We *what?*" he exploded.

She almost smiled, watching the storm gather in his eyes again. *Out of the frying pan and into the fire.* It wasn't a laughing matter, but Talos could be dangerous when not reined in, and giving him another focus for his anger would help keep him in check, hopefully long enough for him to settle in and properly take charge of the fleet. He was a brilliant commander, but he'd just lost his brother and best friend, his constant companion since childhood. The anger was natural, and it had only been two days since the catastrophe, so it would take Talos a few more days to dial it back. She just had to keep him busy until then.

"I think we have a traitor in our ranks somewhere," she repeated. "But since I have a conference call with our generals," she pointed to a blinking com-panel, "Ianessa will have to fill you in." She squeezed his shoulder again and briefly rested her hand on his cheek. "It's good to have you back, Talos."

He nodded, distracted. Shaking his head like he couldn't believe what he'd heard, he left, storming down the hall to find his sister and demand answers.

Almost, *almost,* she could feel sorry for Ianessa having to deal with Talos's relentless questions, but the girl was well used to handling her foster brothers.

For a minute, Athanasia leaned back in her chair and stared out the window into the darkness of space. She wasn't looking forward to the conference. The generals would be going over the details of the Key Mission and discussing the next steps for the rebellion. Icarus's name would come up a lot.

Every time she thought about his death, it brought pain, like a red-hot cloak brushing her shoulder as someone went past her.

What she wouldn't give to hear Icarus laugh just one more time.

But for now, she had to strategize. She slid a touch-button up on the com-panel, and screens around her lit with the faces of her fellow commanders.

"Generals."

+

OUCH. Why was she so stiff?

Koralia blinked. The room around her was mostly dark, aside from the starlight streaming through the observation ceiling. She rolled over and winced as her elbow struck the floor.

*Oh. Right.*

She lay perfectly still for a moment while the truth crashed over her again. Icarus was gone. She'd come up here to cry, but couldn't, so she had just stared out the window, numb. She must have fallen asleep on the floor.

Slowly, she stretched, easing up into a sitting position. Supper would be over by now, but both Ares and Hephaestus would be worried if she didn't appear at least once before bedtime.

So she dragged herself to her feet, splashed water on her face, changed into an unwrinkled tunic, and left the room.

Walls of dark-golden marble veined in red were dimly lit by small globe lights set into the them, giving the effect of walking down a starlit canyon. This was normally her favorite time of day, when the inside atmosphere mimicked the night outside and a gentle calm spread through the fortress-palace Ares called home. But tonight it felt like she was submerged in an endless gray ocean with no sun to light a path, the current keeping her weightless as she drifted deeper.

It still wasn't wholly real to her. She knew Icarus was gone, but she couldn't make herself *feel* it.

Ares and Hephaestus weren't in any of the sitting rooms along the main halls, so she turned toward the library. It wasn't Ares's favorite place in the evening—he said too many ghosts haunted the shelves, and she could never tell if he was joking or serious—but Hephaestus could usually be found there.

Sure enough, she could hear both their voices when she turned down that hall. The double doors normally stood open this time of night, but now they were closed except for a small crack.

She paused, wondering if she should knock. *But is there anything they might be discussing that they wouldn't want me hearing? Unlikely.* As she drew closer, she tilted her head, listening.

"...doesn't count. She's been searching for purpose since she was fourteen, and the rebellion gives her that." Ares's deep voice sounded like he was arguing, but she knew he wasn't, he was just making a point.

"But Icarus gave her something else." Hephaestus Vulcan's tone was mild. "He was home for her in a way that we never could be."

"Because he wasn't just home or love. He was all of that *plus* purpose." Ares paused, and she heard a small sound like he'd turned around.

"You really shouldn't listen at keyholes, Melainis," Hephaestus said, swinging the door open and holding out a hand to her.

She shrugged but took it and let him pull her into the room. "You shouldn't talk so loudly if you want your conversation to be private, *Dad.*"

Ares grinned, his hawk-like profile sharp in the warm light.

The olympians looked at each other and then back at her, not pushing her to talk, leaving the first move open to her.

And she loved them even more for their patience: dark Ares, standing tall behind a desk, and warm Hephaestus, world-weary experience wrapped in kindness.

She couldn't bring herself to look them in the eye, so she stared at the map of the galaxy on the far wall. Glowing lights traced the location of each of the chief olympians, as well as any units of Ares's army.

"I kind of...hoped it was a nightmare," she whispered. "But it isn't."

"It isn't." Ares shook his head, and she didn't need to look at him to know he was frowning. "It's being blazoned all over the galaxy. Krete is absolutely Jupiter's favorite at the moment."

*At the cost of my Icarus.*

She didn't think she'd spoken out loud, but Hephaestus came up behind her and wrapped his arm around her, and she leaned into him.

The tears came then, and Ares crossed the room to hug her from the other side. Holding tightly to her fathers, she cried as anguish swallowed her from the inside out.

It felt real now.

†

KALLISTRATUS BASES WERE a close second on Talos's brief list of favorite places in the galaxy. They *hummed.* That was the only way to describe the energy that swirled through them. It wasn't chaos, not usually, just industry.

Everyone had their own job, and when that was done, there was always someone else to help with a different job. And in the rare moments when everything was actually done and there wasn't a battle to be fought or supply runs to make, there was always at least one room open for games or movies and drinking.

The rebels worked hard, but they played hard too.

Today, the hum was subdued, the cloud of Icarus's death hanging heavily over the base. The few people he met in the hallways nodded to him, but didn't smile. On a normal day, he'd have seen a dozen people between the command bridge and the offices two decks down, and all of them would be calling cheerful hellos or waving. But even the gangly teen slouching in a nearby doorway looked glum.

"Heirax." Talos paused, glancing over the kid. "Any idea where I might find Ianessa?"

The teenager looked up, and his face brightened a little, but his voice was somber as he said, "Hey! Yeah, two hallways down, third door on the right."

Heirax was an orphan whose parents had died thanks to their involvement with the Kallistratus. On any normal day, you couldn't get him to shut up. He practically bounced off the walls with excitement, racing between his assigned duties and arguing with one of the two young female orphans also on this base.

Icarus would hate seeing him this low-spirited.

But grief took time. So Talos just gave the boy a light punch on the arm and left, calling, "Thanks!" over his shoulder.

Ianessa's office door was plain gray, like everything on base. Why pre-fab panels didn't come in any other color, he'd never been able to figure out. Someone, probably one of the teen girls, had painted purple stars of different sizes on the door and scrawled a threatening message off-center, something about being dismembered if you disturbed the queen. He shook his head and knocked.

"It's always open for you, Talos, you know that," Ianessa's voice said from the other side.

"How did you—?" he asked, stepping inside and closing the door behind him.

"—know it was you?" she finished. "You're the only one who would dare stomp anywhere on General Athanasia's base."

*Not true. Icarus would have.*

He could tell she was thinking the same thing, and at the pain that rippled across her face, he dropped to his knees next to her chair and reached for her at the same time she held out her arms to him.

"He's really gone." She buried her face in his shoulder, and her body shuddered as she cried. "Talos, he's *gone.*"

He held her tighter, a few more tears falling to soak into the shoulder of her uniform.

A while later, he eased back. She'd stopped crying several minutes before, and his knees were starting to ache. With a deep breath, she wiped her face with her sleeve and was all business again.

"I suppose you came in here for a map of the base?"

"Among other things. How are the arms?"

She stretched both arms out slowly and rotated them, showing him. "Better and better every day. I can't lift them too high yet, and I have to walk like some weird mummy so no one bumps into me, but I'm getting there."

"Thank stars for that," he murmured. That was one bright spot in this sadness. For several days after the fighter accident that had shredded parts of her body, no one was sure she'd heal. The Sunfires had gathered by her bedside and not left for two days, until she woke up and was pronounced out of danger. That had been weeks ago—the last time he'd seen Icarus in person, actually.

"And you?" she asked him, searching his face.

"How do you think?"

She snorted, turning back to the computer screens in front of her. "I think you're ready to demolish Krete with your bare hands."

"Aren't you?"

"Yes. But we can't, and you know that as well as I do. I also think you came to me for news about the traitor since the General won't tell you about them because she doesn't want you tearing our bases apart trying to find them." Ianessa tipped her head back to smile at him.

"Actually, smartass, the General sent me to you because she had a conference call." He looked down his nose at her. "And, hello, did you forget that I have been commanding rebel troops for over a decade? I don't tear bases apart." Raising his eyebrows mockingly, he sat down on the edge of a control station nearby.

Ianessa snorted. "This potential traitor might have just killed your best friend. The man who was practically your twin. *Our* brother. You absolutely *would* tear bases apart, and there isn't a Sunfire or rebel who wouldn't help you...except me. Which is why I'm in charge of this investigation and you are the new fleet commander."

He groaned and tugged on his hair. "Yeah, with Xuthos as my second!"

She laughed. "At least you'll keep each other out of trouble."

Dropping his hands, he gave her a flat glare. "How do you figure that?"

"Oh come on, you'll be so busy being annoyed at him and stalling his ideas that you won't have time to go racing off on a personal vengeance quest...and that will keep *you* out of starting a mess." She wiggled the fingers of one hand, her substitute for a shrug. "At least, that's what the General is counting on."

He really should have expected her to be on Athanasia's side. Groaning again, he slid down the com station to the floor and leaned his head back against the equipment. "Look, it's not that I hate Xuthos. It's just that he can't hold a serious thought in his head for more than five minutes."

"And that he spends all his off-duty hours in prank wars," she reminded him, sounding like she was enjoying this.

"And chasing girls," he said, with a sour grimace. Okay, he'd forgotten just how much he disliked Xuthos.

She went to move one hand quickly and winced. He sat up, eyes sharp on her until she took a deep breath and let it out slowly.

"You sure you're not pushing it too fast?"

"Rich, coming from you. I'm okay, really. *Really*, Talos." Her tone was clear: *There are much bigger things for you to worry about.*

While she wasn't wrong, he made a mental note to talk to Loxias later. If anyone would know the exact details of how well she was healing, the Spartan would.

"As I was going to say," Ianessa continued, "you're being a little unfair to Xuthos. He also chases guys."

"Since when?" Startled, he looked up and saw that her eyes were twinkling. He rolled his eyes. "Chases them out of his way, you mean, when they get between him and something or someone he wants."

"Which won't be a problem for you," she said sweetly. "You've already flirted with all the girls stationed at this base. I think." She moved her finger in the air like she was running it down a list. "Hmm, there might be one or two..."

"You're just a burst of good cheer, aren't you?" Flopping back onto the floor, he shut his eyes, trying to think. She'd used the subject of Xuthos to distract him from somethi...*oh. Yes.*

He sat up so abruptly that he banged his shoulder on the com station. It hit right on top of an old bruise, but he didn't even wince, too focused on what she wasn't saying. "Stop being unhelpful and tell me about the traitor."

"Ah, there it is. I knew I couldn't sidetrack you for long." She scowled at the computer in front of her. "Thing is, I don't know much. None of us do. We don't even know if there *is* a traitor."

He looked sideways at her, not sure he'd heard correctly. "*What?*"

"Based on everything we knew, the fortress at Krete shouldn't have known

Icarus was there for another, uhhmmm, fifteen minutes minimum. Maybe someone slipped up, maybe someone was extra vigilant, maybe it was coincidence and they weren't actually waiting for our fleet. We don't know, but after something like this, it's routine to check for a traitor."

"Duh. I know that." He thought for a moment, sorting through the first part of what she'd told him. There was still something she wasn't saying, and he tried to decipher it.

*Athanasia.*

"That's all well and good," he stood up and came closer so she'd be forced to look up at him, "but the General wouldn't have warned me off the investigation if it was just a routine check. She suspects something is wrong... doesn't she?"

Ianessa's shoulders slumped. "Yes."

"Hmmm." If they weren't even sure what they were looking for, they could hardly blame him for doing a little looking of his own.

"Well, I'm sure you'll find something, if it's there to find," he said, patting her gently on top of the head, since he couldn't pat her shoulder. He was ready to be done talking and start doing.

He didn't think he'd fooled her, but she just smiled at him as he left.

Outside the door, he paused and poked his head back in. "And for the record, I don't think you go on a *quest* for vengeance. I think it's technically a *mission.*"

"Disagreed, but let's argue that another time. Shoo."

"Yeah, yeah, love you too." He banged the door behind him and stomped exaggeratedly down the hall until the junction, just to irritate her.

Not that he wasn't feeling annoyed enough for it to be real stomping. Meeting with Xuthos was his next job...and wouldn't *that* just be fun.

# CHAPTER 3

*He wasn't just home or love. He was all of that plus purpose.*

Koralia leaned forward, her arms resting on the railing of her balcony as her father's words ran through her head. The plain before her was golden with late summer grass, sparkling with dew that hadn't yet burned off under the rising sun.

They were right, of course. Purpose was the one thing her life had lacked for too long. Oh, she had goals. Jobs. Duties. But deep purpose that made you feel like your life mattered, like there was a reason for you to exist? Not so much. Not here on Akwila and not in her mother's palace—that had never brought anything but pain. Not even in Hephaestus's sprawling rock stronghold on Vulcani. True meaning had come into her life first with the Amazons, but even then, it wasn't the kind to hold her eternally.

It took a lot to cut through the loneliness of years. The bitter grayness of knowing you were valued but that you didn't really have a place that was *yours*. She was loved—loved very much—by her fathers, but even knowing they wouldn't trade her for anything or anyone didn't give her a place to belong. It didn't answer the question of *why* she was here.

People and relationships were what made life worthwhile, but even those had failed to give her life that final piece of purpose. She loved her fathers with all her heart. Her Amazonian sisters would mourn her if she passed, but aside from her fathers, no one had looked at her and felt that an irreparable hole would be torn in them and life would ever after be dark if she wasn't there.

A person could be given all the important jobs and duties in the universe and have so much family that they filled the galaxy from one end to the other but still not *belong*. And she hadn't.

Not until the Kallistratus and...and Icarus.

Joining the rebellion had finally enabled her to see her world clearly. She knew something was missing, but until Athanasia and Icarus had given her the map to the bigger picture, so to speak, she hadn't been able to define the lack, even to herself. So she'd flung herself wholeheartedly into the cause. Instead of her family blood holding her back, it had fueled her fight. After all, few knew better than she did how corrupt the olympians could be. How could they know, how could *anyone* know if they weren't raised with them, hadn't lived their life? The olympians were the ruling class, but there was a lot about their private lives that wasn't common galactic knowledge.

So the Kallistratus had given her grounding and purpose.

And Icarus had looked at her like no one else ever had. Oh, she was no stranger to admiration or interest, whether physical or emotional. Living part of the year in the palace of Aphrodite, she saw all kinds of love and romance. And as the daughter of three of the most powerful olympians, not to mention being a high-ranked Amazonian warrior and heir to at least one olympian empire, plenty of people had looked at Koralia with desire, fascination, or even love. She'd been courted by half a dozen men who seemed to want her for more than just her body, her influence, or her position, and had turned away a score of others who were more avaricious. As an Amazon, she hadn't had time for love or passion; as an olympian, she hadn't really cared.

But Icarus...he'd been different right from the beginning.

It had started as friendship, with bright laughter and camaraderie, and then it had grown into something more. He'd moved fast, too fast for her at first, but when he figured that out, he'd slowed down. Not backed off—Icarus didn't know the meaning of *back off*, but he'd given her the space she needed to see and trust that he was real, not playing with her and not only there for what she could bring him. And in the end, he'd given her a love so bright it dwarfed all others.

Something dropped onto her tunic, and she blinked, sending more tears sliding down her cheeks. She put her head down on her crossed arms and cried harder. It did nothing for the pain, but it was the only thing that even started to express the yawning abyss inside of her.

*What do I do now?*

She'd been asking herself that question for a few days now, ever since hearing about Icarus. Her rebellion assignment right now was simple: report back about the status of the olympian armies Ares trained. That could be done by any of half a dozen rebel adherents on the planet, and Koralia had already started to feel the drain of boredom. If Ares hadn't needed her to help train Theseus's army, she probably would have returned to the Amazons a month ago.

And now...she wasn't sure what to do, where to go. Her Amazonian generals would welcome her back with open arms, but they were in a lull right now and her restlessness wouldn't be any easier to deal with there than here. *Maybe it's better if I leave it all behind. At least for now.*

Yes. That's what she'd do.

Crawling back inside her room—because she didn't feel like standing up to walk—she retrieved the com-pad she used to contact the rebellion. Older than most, it was less easy to hack and had special security and encryption programs written into it.

Seeing Icarus's name at the top of the list of contacts made her want to curl into a ball and cry again, but she breathed deeply for a minute and opened Athanasia's name, typing a quick message.

*Could you use another fighter in any of your fleets?*

She didn't expect a reply before nightfall, but the General answered almost immediately. *Always. When should I expect you?*

*A week? Maybe two? I have to figure out transportation. Tata and Poseidon aren't exactly on great terms at the moment. Not to mention getting through the Labyrinth will be hard if I'm not on official business. I'll have to come through the Inner Ring. I'll bring my own fighter.*

*Inform me when you leave, and I'll make sure you have coordinates for our base.*

*Yes, ma'am. And thank you.*

*No need. As long as you come prepared to fight, you'll be doing us a favor.*

*I can safely promise you that.*

She put the pad down and wrapped her arms around her knees, thinking about her route through the galaxy to the rebellion. Even moving around between bases, the Kallistratus would have to be staying in the same general area, since they were cut off from the rest of the galaxy at the moment, thanks to Minos's new monstrosity: the Labyrinth which encircled his planet. Which brought her thoughts back to...

Icarus.

She shuddered and closed her eyes as more tears slid out.

But if she was going to be at the new base in less than two weeks, she needed to leave in the next few days.

Now she just had to tell her fathers.

. †.

DOWNSTAIRS, Ares and Hephaestus were in Ares's private office, but Koralia could hear them talking from three halls away.

Most of the olympians didn't know *how* to be quiet. Everything about them was loud, larger somehow. They weren't that much taller than most humans, and shorter than some galactic races, but whatever they lacked in stature they made up for in personality. Ostentatious palaces; clothes that were either elaborate or simple but luxurious; voices that carried; wild, teeming lifestyles; emotions freely expressed.

Even Ares, more minimalist than most of the olympians, lived in a palace where the furnishings proudly proclaimed he wasn't just a veteran general, he was also a prince. And Hephaestus was more moderate than many of his family, but he was still loud and only masked his emotions when he had an excellent ulterior motive, like a business meeting.

Hephaestus snapped at Ares now, and Koralia stopped in the middle of the hallway. This sounded like a real argument. She slid closer, straining to discern actual words. If they were arguing, they might not hear her coming. Not that it mattered if they did: if they hadn't wanted anyone to hear them, they would have engaged sound dampeners.

"She'd have to think about someone other than herself for that to happen. Uranus will freeze solid in the vacuum of space before then." That was Ares again, practically snarling.

Hephaestus chuckled, but it was a mirthless sound. "That metaphor's a little impossible and melodramatic, don't you think? How about 'Jupiter will stay quietly at home with Juno,' hmm?"

Ares grunted, obviously agreeing. "I'm not letting her see Koralia. Not this soon after losing Icarus."

"Hell no," Hephaestus agreed emphatically.

There was only one reason for *both* of them to be so protective of her. A sick shudder rippled down her spine and lodged in her stomach.

"I've got three new women wanting to take the Amazon entry test." It sounded like Ares was pacing the floor. "They probably won't pass, but Kora would be overseeing that anyway, and she can stay at the station there." His footsteps stopped for a minute and then continued. "I'll go with her. I have three armies I should check on. It's your turn to deal with her anyway, isn't it?"

"Since when? I dealt with her the last two times." Hephaestus slammed his hand down on...a chair? A desk? Koralia couldn't tell.

"She's *your* wife."

"Estranged *ex*-wife, thank you very much, and *you* slept with her! If anyone should deal with her this time, it's you. Someone has to threaten her about giving Kora any of her idiotic advice at the moment. And Hippolyta and Antiope aren't on planet to do it."

"I'm not staying," Ares insisted stubbornly. "I refuse." Dark bitterness layered his tone and sizzled the air around them. "I'd probably hit her if I saw her right now."

That *would* be a sight to see. Right outside the doors now, pressed close to the edge of the doorway, Koralia stifled a snicker. Some people just made you long to hit them, and her mother was definitely one of those people.

Hephaestus snorted. "What's unusual about that? Neither of us needs much provocation to want that. If you aren't staying, I'm not either." He sounded pleased. "I want to see how those new weapons for your project— what are you calling it, your Red Hammer Army?—are behaving."

"It's settled, then." Ares crossed the floor to the doors and flung one open, raising his eyebrows at his daughter. "How much did you hear?"

She grinned at him and shrugged. "Mother's coming for a visit, and you're both running away from her."

Hephaestus shouted with laughter behind her, and Ares's shoulders shook as he laughed too. "That's right, and you're coming with us."

"*We're* actually coming with *you*, but semantics." Hephaestus rose from his seat as Ares guided Koralia into the office, his arm around her shoulders.

In the full light from the windows, they both stopped abruptly, studying her.

"What is it?" Hephaestus asked.

Of course they'd figure out she had something to tell them. They were the ones who had trained her to know when to mask her thoughts behind a neutral facial expression, and they could always tell when she was doing it.

But it wasn't like she'd intended to hide this from them.

"Is there someone else who can give the women the Amazon test, Tata?" she asked, tipping her head back to look up at Ares. "I'm...I'm...leaving. Or I want to."

"To join the Kallistratus?" Hephaestus asked, his voice low.

"Yes." She frowned. "How did you—"

He crossed his arms over his chest and looked at her. "Oh, come. Icarus is gone, and you've been bereft for three days. You've always felt at home in the rebellion. You think we wouldn't have known that's where you'd head?"

Ares squeezed her, pulling her closer to him. "It's not a hard leap, firefly. It was either them or you going back to join Hippolyta and Antiope."

She smiled at the pet name, a wan smile. "I almost did. It would've..." *It would have dulled the pain a little more.* "But the Kallistratus won out."

"Nothing was ever solved by running away," Hephaestus said, and she nodded. He understood. They both did.

She couldn't run *away* from Icarus, she had to run *toward* the pain, the reminders. He was gone but the rebellion was very much alive and filling a void the galaxy desperately needed. That was where she could do some good.

"That's our girl." Ares clapped her on the shoulder approvingly. "And you won't be going empty handed. I've been clearing out Phobos's junk, and there are a dozen eagle ships and some falcons. Mostly blacks and greens, a few blues."

Her eyes brightened. The General would be thrilled to get the fighters.

Seating himself behind his desk, Ares looked at a schematic on the screen in front of him. "The tracking devices aren't active, because he was trying out that faulty cloaking system." His tone was offhanded, indifferent, as if it mattered very little to him. "I was just going to send them all back with Heph to rip apart or drop them on the recyclers."

Well, *that* was a lie. He wouldn't have sent them either place. Phobos had gotten those ships a few years back when he was trying to start an elite fighter unit. They were only lightly used, since Phobos had abandoned the idea after a few weeks and raced on to another project. And Ares didn't believe in wasting perfectly good fighter ships just because they were a little old. If he hadn't arranged to sell them to the rebellion himself, he'd have had an aide sell them on the black market, and they'd have eventually made their way into the hands of the Kallistratus.

"Thank you," she said seriously. "Thanks so much."

He shook his head and scowled at her. "I'm not doing it out of the goodness of my heart. I'm teaching Phobos a lesson about doing what he's told *when* he's told."

Sure he was.

She raised her eyebrows at him but he ignored it. "Okay, whatever you say, Tata. I still have to arrange transport, so I don't kno—"

Hephaestus tossed her a thin silver disk, and she caught it reflexively.

"No need," he assured her. "I need to head home soon anyway, and I have to stop off and hand Poseidon his new weapons for his Seasharks. The modifications aren't going to do what he thinks they will, but who am I to argue with a customer?"

"Especially when it's our esteemed uncle," Ares interjected dryly.

Hephaestus went on as if he didn't hear. "I can drop you near the border of rebel space. I'll have you there in two days."

She stiffened. "And how do you know where the rebellion is?"

Ares snorted as Hephaestus tapped her under the chin fondly. "Don't ruffle up. I'm the Lord of Fire. You think I'm not going to know where the biggest fireball in the galaxy is?"

She blinked and stared from him to Ares. She had always suspected that they knew far more about the rebellion than either let on, but it was one of those things they didn't talk about. Ostensibly, the silence allowed them all plausible deniability.

But now her dad had just admitted he knew exactly where the rebellion was and what it was doing. And Ares...he just *happened* to be cleaning out Phobos's storage complex this week? That was a lie. He knew...*they* knew...

They knew she'd be leaving, and they'd smoothed the path in front of her.

She blinked at them both and then laughed. It was a high, strange sound, and it ended on a half sob, but it was her first laugh in three days.

"I love you guys," she said, her voice husky. She wasn't going to cry again, she *wasn't*. She'd done enough of that for a year.

Flinging her arms around Hephaestus, she hugged him hard and pulled his head down for a kiss. Then she did the same to Ares, bending over him where he sat at the desk. "For some of the most dangerous men in the galaxy, you're not half bad at the father thing," she informed them.

"High praise indeed from an Amazon brat," Ares retorted. "Now go eat something."

"And it had better be more than a single pastry!" Hephaestus added.

"Sirs." She bowed and then performed the Amazons' double-salute before slipping out of the room and drawing a deep breath.

She had figured that her fathers would want her close still, not charging off into the danger that was the Kallistratus Rebellion. But no. They hadn't just understood, they'd given her their blessing, in actions even more than words. Her mother might be a thorn in her side, but she'd definitely been fortunate when it came to fathers.

Everything hurt still, but there was a gleam of something shining in front of her now.

Hope.

# CHAPTER 4

**X**uthos.

Of all the pilots on base, why did it have to be *him*?

Talos kept a running list of people he'd rather not work with. It was small, but Xuthos was in the top three, and there was an itemized list for why.

First of all, he was lazy. Talos hated laziness.

Secondly, it was difficult to keep him focused on anything for long unless it was a battle.

Thirdly, Xuthos constantly had a girl hanging off him, which was just annoying, especially when you were trying to get him to pay attention.

Not to mention he'd stolen the girlfriends of at least two of the Sunfires. They might have been casual girlfriends, and neither of his brothers held grudges, but Talos remembered.

Fourthly, Xuthos was prone to exaggerating stories until you had no idea where the truth actually lay. Sure, the Sunfires embellished their exploits sometimes—everyone did—but it was usually easy to see where the line fell between truth and fiction. Not so with Xuthos.

And to top it all off, he was too good at staying out of trouble. Normally, this was a good thing in the rebellion. But unfortunately, Xuthos's particular brand came with an irritating side effect: it was really hard to know when the man was lying about what he had or hadn't done on a mission. More than once, Talos had suggested hooking him up to a lie detector and making him dictate his mission reports out loud.

Icarus had laughed at that suggestion.

The other Sunfires didn't mind Xuthos as much. Brygos and Kynna actually liked him a lot, the little traitors. Icarus got along fine with Xuthos, but Icarus got along well with everyone, at least on the surface. Xuthos's laziness had irritated him and so did his disregard for the chain of command, but Icarus kept him in line by sparring with him regularly and handing him his ass every time. Somehow, that worked for them.

Not so much for Talos. He really wished he could have had his usual second at his side. Pelagon was sensible—a little unimaginative, true, yet steady and used to the way Talos worked. But with Talos changing bases, his former general needed someone else to lead her fighter squadron, and Pelagon was the natural choice.

Sighing, Talos trudged down another hallway. He'd been on base for a day and couldn't put off his meeting with Xuthos any longer. Heirax had said the pilot was in one of the lower fighter bays. Talos had checked two already, and both were empty. Stepping into a third, he jumped back as a rebel hurtled past him, aiming something—a gun?—at another person.

"Three hits in two minutes!" someone yelled from the other side of the bay, and there was a scraping sound and then a thud and swish as three pilots slid down an eagle fighter and ducked under it, pointing what looked like more guns under the fighter and toward the sound of more running footsteps.

Talos narrowed his eyes. "Xuthos!" he shouted across the room, flattening himself against the wall beside the door as he searched for the tall pilot he just knew he'd find at the center of this game. There he was, popping out from behind a falcon fighter on the far side of the bay.

Silence fell as swiftly as if a light had been turned out. The few pilots Talos could see tucked themselves into the shadows of the row of fighters, looking hesitant. Behind him, he heard someone else come into the bay, but they too stopped.

"Talos?" Xuthos kept his voice bland. "To what do I owe this pleasure, Commander?"

Commander? Talos gritted his teeth. Really? The pilot couldn't have picked a better or faster way to further irritate Talos right now than by reminding him of the promotion which had come about only because of his brother's death.

"What the zeusian blazes is this mess?" Talos demanded, gesturing to the dozen or so pilots now coming out from behind equipment crates and fighters.

"What makes you think I know?"

Not even two minutes in and Talos already wanted to punch him. "It's a chaotic mess in here. You're always in the middle of those. Now what are you all doing?"

"A battle," Xuthos said as if it was obvious. "Don't worry, we're using stun-guns. It's training." He shrugged, the gun in his hand sweeping a slow arc on the floor with his movement. "Honing everyone's reflexes. It's good practice." He smirked, the same expression Talos had seen set a roomful of people giggling.

But this wasn't funny. "In a *fighter bay?*" Talos wanted to reach out and strangle the pilot. There were at least two empty rooms for use as gyms on this base, not to mention an entire storage level. They couldn't have found anywhere else for this training battle?

"Why not?" Xuthos crossed his arms, a challenge blatant on his face. He had come closer, sauntering with long, easy strides, his head tilted arrogantly.

Someone sucked in a quick breath behind Talos, and he recognized the sound as Lasthena, Icarus's former third-in-command. She must have been the person who had followed him inside.

Talos pointed to each of the fighter ships in the bay and then jabbed his finger emphatically at the expanse of space beyond, seen through the windows high up. "Proper respect for fighters, that's why not," he snapped. "These ships are our lives. We don't gamble with them. Even a stun dart can do damage to the systems of one of these, to say nothing of a chain reaction if more than one hits something vital."

Xuthos snorted. "You Sunfires and your absurd fighter worship." He was on dangerous ground with that comment, and he knew it, for he rocked slightly forward on the balls of his feet as if balancing for a quick getaway.

Talos glared at the pilot. Xuthos was five inches taller than him, but in a match between them, Talos was sure he could beat the other man. For one minute, he was tempted to try it, to tackle Xuthos to the floor and again try Icarus's method of keeping him in line.

The impulse must have been obvious, because the rebels standing nearby eyed the door like they were going to make a run for it.

Then Talos bit his tongue and breathed in slowly. "I'd rather you kept all stun-gun battles out of the fighter bay," he said, his tone as neutral as he could manage. Raising his gaze, he included everyone in the request. "Please."

As one, the other rebels straightened up and saluted him. "Yes, sir."

For a minute, it looked like Xuthos would argue. But either he thought better of it or he knew better than to object right now.

"You've got it, Sunfire," promised Lasthena, coming out from behind him. Even for an Atlantida nymph, she looked shockingly pale under the lights of the bay. Athanasia had said the woman's injuries weren't too bad, but looking at her now, Talos wondered exactly what that meant. He'd check her medical file first chance he got. He didn't trust Lasthena to be honest about how much recovery she needed, especially since they were friends and she had an idea of how stressed he was right now.

"Go sit down," he ordered her, softening his voice and reaching out to take her by the shoulder and gently move her back in the direction of the hallway. "You shouldn't be on your feet yet."

Her grimace turned into a quick smile for her new commander and then morphed into a firm look at the pilots standing around. She moved her uninjured arm, pointing toward the door, and the pilots were quick to leave. After a quick nod to Talos, she followed them out.

"No stun-gun battles around the fighters," he repeated sternly, turning back toward Xuthos. "These fighters are far too important to risk an accident because a dart went astray or someone fell the wrong way and came down on a control panel."

"Sure, if that's what you want." Xuthos shrugged, as if it didn't matter one way or the other to him. "But you really should lighten up."

He really did want to get punched today. Talos clenched his hand into a fist at his side, reminding himself that a fight was the last thing Athanasia needed right now.

That was another thing that irritated him so much. Xuthos was so flamboyant all the time, like the rebellion was just a game. A fun adventure. He was almost as bad as an olympian.

The rebellion was so much more than a fun scuffle. It was a way of life, especially for the Sunfires. But getting into that argument with Xuthos again would be futile. He would just find some way to make it seem like Talos was being unreasonable.

And maybe he was. But he kind of had a good reason for it right now, didn't he?

"We fly a scouting mission at 0300," Talos said finally, wanting to be done with the conversation. "You, me, Cleon, and Tisandros."

Xuthos looked like he thought twice about what he was going to say and then said it anyway. "Not Lasthena?"

"Looking like death? I think not." Talos's iron-firm tone left absolutely no room for argument.

Xuthos shrugged again, saluted with a lazy cockiness, and loped toward the door.

Talos waited until he had left the bay before slumping back against a fighter with a groan.

This was going to be great. Just *fantastic*.

*Dammit, Icarus.*

.+.

"You mean there will be no central memorial service?"

Athanasia shook her head. "We can't afford it right now."

The red-haired woman on the other side of the screen winced. "I imagine that is going down well with the Sunfires."

That actually wrung a chuckle from Athanasia. "No, but you know them..."

"Oh, yes. I do." The other general raised her eyebrows. "At least half of them will be there anyway, however they have to manage it."

"Mmm, all of them," Athanasia said confidently.

"Really? It'll be hard for Siromos and Dione to make it."

True, but they'd manage it somehow. "If every single one of them doesn't show up to attend the memorial, I'll buy you a gallon of the finest blackberry tango wine you've ever tasted."

The other general laughed. "And if they do, I'll buy *you* one. You'll need it, dealing with them. Speaking of which... How's Talos holding up?"

That was a complicated question, but Athanasia just shook her head. "As well as we can expect. He's settling in and about to start running his pilots through maneuvers, getting them used to him and keeping them busy."

"Or keeping *himself* busy."

Athanasia conceded that with a wry smile. Talos never sat still, especially not when he was grieving.

"And that's my new fighter captain calling me. Don't tell Talos, but I miss him." The red-haired general gave Athanasia a long, serious look of sympathy.

"Thanks for handing him over." The General nodded to her friend. "Athanasia clear."

With a few quick taps, she finished sending off a report to the generals on the other side of the capital systems and leaned back in her chair, staring thoughtfully at the wall, dark in the station's artificial night. Her decision to hold Icarus's memorial now instead of waiting hadn't gone over well, but her fleet needed closure. She wished it could be different, that she could have brought together all or most of the rebellion generals and all of Icarus's friends for one service, but it was too dangerous right now. Hemmed in by the Labyrinth, Poseidon's territory, and Inner Ring space, they were pretty well cut off from the rest of the galaxy at the moment, so anyone who came would have to dodge imperial patrols all the way. And that wasn't worth the risk, not even to grieve together, as much as it would have helped ease everyone's pain.

Icarus's pilots needed to say their final goodbye soon and move on, or they wouldn't face the Kretan threat with wholehearted focus. There would be another memorial later, when more of the rebellion could gather.

At least Talos would be here for the near future. That would help the fleet…and her and Ianessa. And Mikon would be on this station for a while too. Not to mention Koralia, who should arrive in the next day. Apparently, Hephaestus had business in the general area, so her travel had been faster than she'd thought.

More likely Hephaestus had moved his entire schedule around to give his daughter what he knew she wanted but wouldn't request. He practically worshipped the ground Koralia walked on.

That was the thing about kids. They wrapped themselves tightly around your soul and stayed there. Athanasia had never had kids of her own and hadn't missed it, but the day Icarus and Talos had danced into her life and playfully pretended to shelter behind her—wild-eyed eleven-year-olds being yelled at by Daedalus for messing around in his workshop—they'd walked straight into her heart, never to leave. And a few years later, when the two young men, only fifteen, had walked onto her makeshift rebel base and volunteered to join the fledgeling rebellion, something about them had whispered *home* for Athanasia.

She probably should have sent them away, told them to grow up more first. But stars knew they'd needed her, needed a place away from Daedalus and his eccentric and controlling behavior and idiotic jealousy of Talos. He might be the galaxy's most brilliant inventor, but a great father he was not.

Besides, of all the rebels with her at the time, the two of them understood the rebellion and the reasons for it in ways few others did. They had grown up on Krete in the shadow of imperial power, surrounded by the excesses of high society.

Who was she to refuse them a chance to fight for what they believed? Especially when she'd been doing the same thing all her life, first spending twenty years with the Amazons and now almost as many with the Kallistratus Rebellion, guiding it as it grew from a dozen people in one room to several hundred people spread across the galaxy.

In the two boys, intense Talos and bright Icarus, Athanasia had recognized kindred spirits, the same fire that had animated her for twenty years. All the Sunfires had it—that incandescent spark that drew them to Icarus and Talos as inevitably as magnets and from them to Athanasia herself. They'd been fighting in the rebellion for well over a decade, and most weren't kids any longer—the youngest were in their mid-twenties now. Still, they swept through life and the galaxy like wildfires.

And even as a child, Koralia had displayed the same flame. Really, she and Icarus and the love they'd shared had been inevitable. The Sunfire captain could never have fallen so hard for anyone less problematic than the olympian Amazon. And no one other than wild, unexpected Icarus could have shaken Koralia fully awake.

*Together...* Athanasia shook her head fondly. Together, they had been as perfect as a glorious sunset at the end of a long and satisfying day.

*But all sunsets fade to night.*

It would be good to have Koralia here. Athanasia had been waiting a long time for that, to have the Amazon at her side again and to see her with the Sunfires. The loss of Icarus would make it fiercely bittersweet, but that, too, they could face together.

And at least she would get to see all of the Sunfires for a couple of hours at the memorial. Because of course Icarus's siblings wouldn't stay away. She could give all the orders she wanted and fume until she was blue in the face; they'd just smirk at her and come anyway.

Icarus had trained them well in when to break the rules. They would come.

Athanasia smiled to herself, looking forward to the crushing hugs, good-natured arguments, and brilliant energy that followed her adopted kids everywhere.

That blackberry tango wine was as good as hers.

✝

DEALING with lost comrades was hard, but facing betrayal was hell.

Talos rubbed his forehead, but the headache remained.

At least in death, there was finality. An end. The person was gone, and that was that.

With a traitor on the loose, you were constantly looking over your shoulder, suspicious of everyone and everything. The smallest joke someone made could have you on high alert, searching the people around you for a sign that they'd been the one to blab or slip confidential information to the enemy. The person who had condemned you and your fellow rebels to any of a dozen fates, most worse than death.

He stared unseeing at the wall, muttering and taking deep breaths so he wouldn't punch anything and wake someone up. The last thing he wanted was Athanasia hearing his annoyance and guessing what he was doing.

*Well,* he amended, *she probably already knows. But as long as I don't do anything she can specifically scold me for, we'll be good.*

Betrayal was much, much worse than losing people. Because you didn't only lose lives, you lost trust, and it took a long time to figure out when and where and whom you could trust again. If there was a traitor in the ranks of the rebellion, they needed to find them fast. Before they started to rip the Kallistratus apart from the inside.

Which is why he was currently sitting on his bunk flipping through personnel files long after everyone except the night watch had gone to bed.

He'd been over the list of files twice and couldn't see anyone who had reason to betray the Key Mission or the rebellion as a whole.

Talos *knew* most of the people on this base. Athanasia tended to keep the same core group of people with her everywhere she went, just like other generals. They were good men and women, people who had a personal stake in the rebellion and its success. There wasn't a man, woman, or child here who hadn't been hurt or harmed in some way by the overbearing power of the olympians, particularly the Jupiterians, and who didn't want it checked and some measure of peaceful prosperity returned to their individual home worlds or families.

There would have been no reason for anyone to betray Icarus.

Swearing, he punched his pillow, the blankets underneath muffling the sound.

"Damn your blaze of glory," he fumed. Icarus and his infuriatingly poetic end. It hurt to even think of it.

As poetic as his end had been, death wasn't. It was just cold and final and left brutal claw marks behind, wounds that seeped pain for months and years.

The first numb rush of grief over his brother had passed, transforming into anger. A hot fury that simmered every minute of the day, driving him to work harder, do better, win the war, make sure his best friend's sacrifice hadn't been in vain.

Anger was better than tears. Better than guilt. Better than grief.

"You were the golden one, you stupid bull," he said aloud to the empty room. "They followed you because they loved you. They'll follow me because of you, but that's not enough. They have to follow me for *me.* They have to trust me. How the hell is anyone supposed to live up to you?"

He couldn't. Daedalus had made that abundantly clear all through their childhood, and even though most of what he said was a lie, some of it wasn't. Both he and Icarus could lead. But Icarus had been born to set hearts on fire, and Talos was born to identify problems and fix them. He made grand speeches better than Icarus ever could, but the flashing grin that made people willing to throw themselves off a bridge or follow him into hell—that magnetic charisma was all Icarus.

It had never bothered Talos, because the two of them worked together so well and each filled their own place in the rebellion.

But now he was supposed to step in and lead the pilots—*Icarus's* pilots.

All because of a traitor.

*Probably*, he qualified to himself. Probably because of a traitor. They didn't have actual proof yet. He punched the pillow again. There were too many questions and not enough answers.

Aimlessly, he turned over another file. But a third time through them wouldn't give him answers the other two times hadn't, so he sighed and set the tablet aside.

Really, who would *want* to betray Icarus?

He was an intensely popular leader in the Kallistratus and a hero to most of the rest of the galaxy. His enemies either hated him passionately or respected him while wishing he'd meet with some accident and stop troubling them.

They'd gotten their wish now.

The more Talos thought about it, the more the idea of a traitor made sense. The Key Mission had been carefully planned for weeks. Talos hadn't even gotten to see many of the plans, in case the security protocols on inter-base communication weren't enough to protect the information. It was one of the best-planned, most top-secret missions the Kallistratus had carried out to date.

So what had gone wrong?

A sleeper agent planted by their enemies? Unlikely, given the rigorous mental testing Athanasia put rebels through before allowing them to join. Politically motivated? No, that just didn't make sense. So it was personal. But...again, no, he'd already been over that. Icarus was too popular for that.

Love? *Hmmmm.* He stretched out on his bunk, flipped his light off, and stared at the ceiling, mulling that over.

Icarus was an inveterate flirt. He'd had a girl in every port, or so it seemed, until he met Melainis. It was possible that one of the girls in the rebellion was heartbroken enough to betray him...but highly implausible. Icarus hadn't even dated any of the girls on this base, as far as Talos knew.

No, that just didn't make sense either.

He swore again, viciously. *I just need one answer. Just one, to be able to unravel the whole thing.*

But none came, and he finally slipped into the oblivion of sleep for a few hours.

# CHAPTER 5

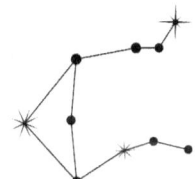

"**K**oralia! Welcome to rebel headquarters!"

The Amazon blinked, halfway into an Amazonian salute, as the General wrapped her in a warm hug. On the two-day journey to this sector of space, she'd spent a lot of time thinking about the rebellion and wondering what waited for her here. Being greeted by Athanasia herself wasn't on that list.

She'd also forgotten the General was so short. Well, short for a human or an olympian but tall for a Hyadean nymph, Athanasia's father's race. Koralia was of average height, but the general stood almost a full head shorter, which put her firmly in the category of petite.

But oh, did her hug feel good. Koralia squeezed her tightly, soaking in the love and understanding radiating from the small woman.

Athanasia patted her on the shoulder. "The memorial is in a few hours, but first, let's talk." She pulled back and turned to leave the bay, walking quickly.

Trying to look everywhere at once and listen to the General at the same time, Koralia didn't realize she was supposed to follow until Athanasia stopped and looked back at her.

"I assumed you'd want to jump right into work, but if you'd rather not, just say so."

Koralia blinked for a second before nodding. "No, no. I can't sit still right now. Please, I'd love to work right away."

"Excellent. Now come on." Athanasia waved impatiently and started walking again.

Koralia followed her through several halls, into an elevator and up three floors, and then onto a small bridge. Screens filled one wall of it, their steady hum comforting. Most of the consoles around them were dimly lit in low-power resting mode, and only one other person was in the room.

Athanasia dismissed the watch—a short, sandy-haired girl—and motioned for Koralia to come closer. "First of all, how am I introducing you?"

She blinked at the General, finally looking straight at her, seeing the extra lines around her eyes and the weary set of her chin. It had been months since they were together, and Athanasia shouldn't have seemed that much older, but she did. But then, grief tended to do that to people.

"I want to earn my place," Koralia admitted. "As me. Just Koralia the Amazon."

The General sat down and looked her over. "You're sure?"

"Yes." It was another thing she'd thought about a lot on the journey. "And I think it will be better if I don't talk about him," she said quietly.

"Nonsense." Athanasia's tone was brisk. "If you're thinking that people won't want to discuss him, that's temporary. Everyone is, of course, on edge right now, but people will settle down."

"I meant that I was...we were..." She couldn't quite bring herself to finish the sentence.

"Ohhhh." The General looked at her for a moment, thinking. "Yes. Maybe just for now. Not forever, mind you. People should know who you are. But for now, if it's easier for you, we'll just say you're an Amazon and an old contact of Icarus."

Koralia didn't understand why Athanasia thought people should know who she was, but she didn't feel like asking about it right now. So she just nodded.

"Now, about the Amazons," Athanasia said.

"Yes, ma'am. I talked to—"

"Hold that thought." The General tilted her head toward the door. Quick footsteps were coming down the hall, and someone burst into the room.

Curly dark hair, tanned skin, restless eyes, dressed like a pilot, and radiating energy so fiercely it filled the whole bridge. Koralia straightened automatically. She knew this man. Well, she didn't precisely *know* him yet, but she felt like she would have recognized him anywhere.

Talos. Icarus's cousin, adopted brother, and best friend.

"General, there are nineteen gorgeous new fighters in Bay 7. Where in all the galaxy beyond did they come from?"

"Her." Athanasia motioned toward Koralia. "Kora, meet Talos. Talos, this is

Koralia, a former undercover operative from Akwila, one of Icarus's contacts, and an Amazon."

Koralia smiled brightly at him. "It's good to meet you. Icarus talked about you a lot."

He had started toward her with his hand held out and a smile, but that made him pause. "You knew Icarus?" The smile stiffened, still present but off-center now.

"I did. I'm sorry for your loss."

He shook her hand quickly and dropped it. "Yes. The blue eagle fighter in Bay 7. That's yours?"

"It is."

His eyes narrowed. "What's your pilot rank?"

Koralia blinked. This *was* kind of how she'd expected to be welcomed: being grilled. She just hadn't thought Talos would be the one to do it. Wasn't he assigned to a different base anyway? He and Icarus didn't usually operate out of the same area anymore, something Icarus had hated but accepted as part of being a rebel leader.

"I'm not a crack pilot, if that's what you're asking, but I spent several years with the Amazons, so I'm at rank four." She'd been a three, but she hadn't flown fighters regularly for long enough that she wasn't sure she still qualified for that rank. Talos, she knew, was ranked ace, as Icarus had been. The other Sunfires all sat somewhere between ace and one. The best of the best.

"And may I ask where the fighters came from?"

Athanasia turned away, shaking her head as if she was exasperated, but she didn't stop Talos, so Koralia kept answering.

"The black market on Akwila. Lord Ares offloads old fighters there all the time." It wasn't exactly a lie; the fighters would have been headed to the black market eventually. Ares had just eliminated that step this time.

"Almost twenty fighters? At a single time?"

"Yes."

"You were an undercover operative. And you're here now...why? Was your cover blown?"

"No. My station observer was changed." It was a reasonable question, and he appeared satisfied with the answer. But he didn't stop.

"You were with the Amazons? Why aren't you now? As I understand it, to be *with* them is different from being trained by them. Almost no one leaves them, unless marriage interferes. Are you carrying a dark backstory?" The words were probing rather than mocking.

Oh, he had no idea, but right now was not the time for this conversation, so she had no qualms about stretching the truth slightly. "Not exactly, no. I left. Some of us do, you know."

He didn't like that, but he didn't have a comeback.

"Is there a problem?" she asked before he could find more questions. She didn't object to answering—suspicion was normal for anyone new coming into a rebel cell—but Talos had a strange edge to his voice, like he was looking for something in particular.

"I don't know. We've had reports of traitors attempting to infiltrate"—that was a lie, she could tell, but not much of one—"so these questions are just routine."

Also a lie, though she didn't understand why it would be.

"Ah. And of course, you can't take my word for it. I understand. I won't even try telling you that betraying the rebellion is the very last thing I would ever do." She smiled at him again, trying to lighten the atmosphere.

It didn't work.

He looked at her for another minute and then turned toward the other side of the bridge. "General?" He strode over to Athanasia, and they spoke in low voices for a minute, too low for most humans to have heard. But Koralia was olympian, so the words were easy to pick up.

"Where did she come from?"

"Akwila, didn't you hear her say it?"

*Did the General just roll her eyes?*

"She's a disgraced Amazon."

"There are a few Amazons who leave without being disgraced, Talos. I did. So did she."

"Well, you're different, General. I don't trust her."

Athanasia sounded like she was smiling at the underhanded compliment. "Of course you don't. You don't know her."

"About the traitor, I was thinking—"

But the General cut him off. "She isn't the traitor. And you aren't supposed to be anywhere near the investigation anyway. You don't have to trust Koralia, but I vouch for her."

Based on Talos's sharp intake of breath, the General didn't vouch for people often. As flattered as Koralia felt by that, she didn't really want to become the subject of an argument between Talos and the General.

But if Talos was irritated, it didn't show. "Yes, ma'am," he said. Wheeling around, he nodded sharply to Koralia, saluted the General, and left the bridge.

Athanasia sighed as the door swished closed behind him. "He's going to feel like an idiot when he figures out who you are."

Koralia wanted to laugh, but the encounter had left her with a hollow feeling. She hadn't expected Icarus's Sunfires to fall at her feet in welcome, but she had hoped she'd get along with them, that they'd give her a fair chance, that she could eventually talk to them about Icarus.

Athanasia came closer, resting her hands on Koralia's shoulders. "I miss him too," she said, her voice low.

And for just a minute, she clung to the older woman. Her fathers had been sympathetic, but neither of them knew Icarus the way she did or the way Athanasia had. No one but the rebels understood the depth of not just grief but wrenching void that followed the loss of their brightest leader.

Two small ships streaked past the window then in a blaze of green and blue, and the General let go of Koralia to check something on a screen. Then she laughed.

"Those kids never do what they're told." Turning around, she motioned for Koralia to follow. "You should see this."

As they walked down several hallways leading to a lower floor of the base, Athanasia pointed out key areas of the base and chatted lightly about the personnel present, until Koralia felt herself relaxing, letting go of the tension that had tightened her shoulders during the encounter with Talos.

"Most people think running a rebellion is long days of directing missions, pilots hardly ever leaving their cockpits, everyone constantly changing bases to avoid detection, encrypted messages that take hours to decode, and snapping out orders like gunfire," Athanasia explained, shaking her head with an amused quirk of her eyebrows.

Koralia grinned. "And here I thought it was you sitting in a darkened room, gathering reports from all your operatives and putting them together like a giant puzzle."

Athanasia outright laughed. "I leave that to my techs, and they sit in well-lit rooms. But some days *are* like that, everyone rushing from one thing to the next, missions constantly in and out, the techs and radio kids bringing me reports sent from people like you. Other days, it feels more like I'm the rabbit grandmother from that old tale, the one who lived in a shoe and had too many children." She gestured to the window overlooking a small docking bay.

Koralia stepped up and looked down. She counted ten people, all in the middle of an animated discussion. Some had flopped down on the floor on top of bags of supplies, others were perched on the two fighters in the bay, and the rest sat on boxes and crates nearby. "What exactly am I looking at?"

"Sunfire brats and their friends." Athanasia's voice was neutral, as if she knew how many memories they would evoke for Koralia.

Her throat tightened as she watched. The Sunfires: Icarus's elite squad of fighter pilots who now led their own fleets from various bases throughout the galaxy. The people she'd anticipated meeting as her future family.

Icarus had described them so vividly that she thought she could recognize some of them even without the few photos she'd seen. Talos was easy to spot, being hugged by two girls at once. A red-haired woman sat on a crate, her head tilted up as she talked to a dark-haired, broad-shouldered man. *Probably Ianessa and Loxias.*

For one second, she thought about listening in, but it would have felt wrong to her, hearing their conversation without being introduced. As an olympian, eavesdropping rarely bothered her, but...this family was different.

She was trying to figure out if the tall boy to the side was Scythe or Red Arrow when someone came down the hall toward her and the General.

"That's funny," a deep voice said. "I could have sworn you sent out a message saying the Sunfires were to stay with their generals and not come here for the memorial. Something about services on individual bases being safer than having everyone together in one place?"

Koralia turned around. The speaker was so tall that he dwarfed both her and the General. She thought she recognized the tone of his voice, but he stood too much in the shadows of the dim hall for her to be sure.

"I did." Athanasia gave the other person a wry grin. "Apparently, they didn't get the message."

"You mean they didn't listen." He chuckled.

"I'm only Rebel-Mom when they feel like it." Athanasia sighed in an exaggerated manner and rolled her eyes. Then she pointed to Koralia. "Xan, meet Koralia, Amazon-trained and my new aide. Kora, this is General Xantippos, my new junior commander and supervisory general of the youngest Sunfire. They'll be stationed here for a while."

She held out her hand, and he took it firmly but gently, long fingers closing over hers. The movement brought him into a little more light, revealing a man well over six feet tall, with wide shoulders. His skin was covered with short black, white, and gray hair—mixed together, it looked blue. Around his mouth and jawline, it changed into patches of black skin. Between his pointed ears, black hair hung braided to the middle of his back, and an aura of power clung to his long limbs and broad biceps.

Her eyes widened for a second, and then she assumed proper stance for greeting a kentauri: one foot in front of the other, bending her head first to the left and then to the right.

"My lord stallion."

A smile tugged at the corners of his mouth as his ears flicked forward, and he returned the same greeting, bowing low as to a superior. "Lady Amazon Antaineirai."

"Just Koralia, please." She tapped her shoulder where her Amazonian badge would normally rest. "I'm just a rebel here."

"Only if you will call me Xantippos."

"It would be my honor."

The formalities over, he turned to look over the bay below, and Koralia searched her memory, wondering why he seemed familiar to her. The kentauri produced some of the best war strategists in the galaxy, several of whom had worked for Ares. And there were many kentauri among the Amazons, but they were all women, of course. Blue roan coloring was only found in one or maybe two tribes of kentauri, which narrowed down the possibilities. Still...hmmm. No, she didn't think she'd actually met Xantippos before—she'd have remembered his striking face. *Maybe I've just met other stallions from his tribe?* That was probably it.

Then what Athanasia had said clicked in her mind, and she spun to look at the General. "I'm your new aide?"

Xantippos, perhaps sensing he wasn't wanted, bent his head to them both and left, gliding down the hallway with long, smooth strides.

Athanasia put a hand on her shoulder. "Yes. I need you more than you know. We might have a traitor somewhere. I need Ianessa to run that investigation, so someone has to take over running mission communications and training my new radio recruits. I reassigned the previous group to other generals, and this was supposed to be more of an observational post, giving me time to train more." She rolled her eyes. "So much for that."

Koralia just blinked.

"Well?" Athanasia said. "Tell me you don't have experience training communications staff."

"I..." Koralia closed her mouth with an audible click.

Athanasia waited, her eyebrows raised. "You were saying?"

"You know I do, ma'am," she said, her tone resigned. She had been running mission communications since she was eleven, first as assistant controller for a few years and then on her own. With Ares, with Hephaestus when he tested weapons, and then with the Amazons, where she'd run communications for some of Athanasia's missions.

She was used to jumping right into action. That was what you trained for as an Amazon. And while she'd expected some level of suspicion—you didn't get to be a rebel without it—somehow, after the scene on the bridge, she didn't think Talos would take kindly to a newcomer training recruits. And Talos's word carried a lot of weight with the rebels, as much as Icarus's had.

But Athanasia was still the boss.

"I'll be honored to serve wherever you need me, General," she said, bowing respectfully.

Athanasia cuffed her gently on the shoulder and chuckled. "None of that. Talos might take some time to adjust to you, but he does that to everyone. Just treat him like you do anyone else who challenges you. You'll settle in here soon enough, and I really do need you. So do they, even if they don't know it yet." Athanasia motioned for her to look back out over the docking bay.

The Sunfires were laughing over something, and the blonde woman turned to grab one of her brothers in a headlock, dragging him down to the floor. Koralia smiled as another brother grabbed both of them, dragging them back up to stand and shoving them toward the doors.

"You were as close to Icarus as any of them," Athanasia said quietly. "You all need each other. But yes, let them get used to you as a rebel first."

Nodding, Koralia looked back through the window. The Sunfires were climbing down from the fighters and straightening up from their seats, pulling on long red cloaks and filing toward the door. Ianessa paused to adjust her cloak and looked up, waving. For a minute, Koralia thought the gesture was meant for the General, but then Ianessa waved again, looking straight at her.

Startled, Koralia nodded, a short, jerky acknowledgement.

And suddenly she needed to be away from everyone. Just for a minute. It was almost overwhelming, being on Icarus's base, surrounded by his people, walking the halls he'd raced down on his way to missions, laughed through when he came back, and from which he'd texted her when he was on his way to meetings. Seeing his family.

"May I go to my quarters?"

If the General knew what she was feeling, she mercifully didn't comment on it. Instead, she snapped her fingers, motioning for a short, dark girl to come closer. "Mykali will take you. The service is in an hour. And Koralia?"

She looked up. Athanasia was smiling warmly.

"Welcome to the Kallistratus."

# CHAPTER 6

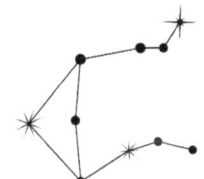

Talos hated funerals but loved memorial services.

Funerals were cold, heavy affairs. You couldn't smile, you couldn't hug anyone genuinely, and you absolutely couldn't make jokes without at least half a dozen people looking at you like you'd just committed sacrilege.

Memorial services? Those were a celebration of someone's life without feeling like you were weighed down with rocks. You could be sad and happy at the same time. You could laugh, give people real hugs, make jokes, and when your voice broke and you turned away, the other person would clap you on the shoulder or leave you alone, not smother you with doleful platitudes.

Icarus had hated funerals too. Death was hard; it hurt like hell, but having known a person and loved them was something to celebrate, not mourn. You could grieve loss without acting like a dying crow, Icarus had said once.

*He would have been so proud of this memorial service,* Talos thought, looking around him.

The entire population of the base was gathered in a large docking bay which had been cleared of all fighters. The eight remaining Sunfires stood in a body behind and to the side of Athanasia, their red mourning cloaks a vivid splash against the gray walls and floor.

"He died on his own terms," Athanasia finished. "And that's not something a lot of people can say." She let that sink in for a minute, then stepped back and motioned for Talos to take her place.

Loxias squeezed his shoulder, and Ianessa patted him on the arm before he strode to face the gathered rebels. The General sat down in the front row, next to the woman she'd introduced earlier. Talos paused for a second to wonder why the new girl was front and center—had she known Icarus that well?—and then took a deep breath.

"Icarus always wanted to go out in a blaze of glory."

More than one rebel winced, but Talos kept going. "He was my brother, and I loved him, but he was an idiot sometimes." A few people chuckled at that—probably pilots from Icarus's fleet.

"When we were growing up, he always said he wanted to do something glorious, something amazing. Who doesn't as a kid? And then we started running missions for the Kallistratus and tripping over these guys"—he gestured toward the Sunfires—"and it was like Icarus had found his calling. We were the firebrands, the kids no one was sure how to handle. Most of us were orphans, literally or practically. Without ever meaning to, Icarus became our leader, the soul of our bizarre, dysfunctional family. Although," he grinned, "*dysfunctional* is too nice a word for what we were early on."

Several people snorted.

"If we weren't blowing up things that weren't supposed to be blown up, we were getting into fights and taking on opponents twice our size." He shook his head. "We were *all* idiots. And that common ground is what kept us together, that and Icarus. In flying and training to fight the olympians, we found our purpose. And that would never have happened if Icarus hadn't said, 'Hey, I'm bored, let's find some fighters to steal and make an elite squadron.'"

The entire bay of people laughed now.

Talos gripped his hands together behind his back, nerving himself to say the hardest part. "I didn't have it easy growing up, and I spent my teen years being angry at everything in the galaxy. I wanted to do something that mattered, but I didn't know what. Icarus understood that, and while he couldn't make that better, he did make me a promise. He'd keep me alive if I would stay at his side, searching for purpose together." He paused and smiled, looking out at the stars beyond the bay. He wouldn't break down now. That could come later.

"When the war started, we knew it was our chance to change the future. And that's what Icarus lived for, every day for the rest of his life. The Kallistratus. Our mission to bring peace and justice back to the galaxy. And there is nothing in any reach of the galaxy that he would rather have died for."

He breathed in deeply. Several rebels were wiping away tears. Behind him, Ianessa was also crying, and Mikon was staring straight ahead, his jaw clenched tightly. The other Sunfires were somber, staring at the floor, and Siromos nodded to him as if to tell him to keep going and get it over with.

"If there was one thing he'd want us to remember, it was that he was the best pilot in the galaxy, not just the Kallistratus."

Everyone laughed again, and he grinned. "But also that our fight isn't over. It's still out there, still waiting for us. All of us. So let's get back out there and finish it."

Someone in a front row started clapping, and the rest of the rebels picked it up, row after row cheering—not him, but Icarus.

He dropped his eyes to Athanasia's, waiting for her reaction. She shook her head at him and smiled, the fond, half-exasperated smile they called her Rebel-Mom expression.

Briefly, his eyes shifted to the woman at her side, the new one, dressed in Amazonian armor under her red cloak. Her amber eyes were shining with unshed tears, but she was smiling, almost as if...as if she was in complete agreement with everything he'd said.

*Interesting.*

Then Ianessa was tapping his shoulder and everyone was moving toward the open bay doors, shielded against space, for the final salute.

Five missiles shot from the station and burst in blinding flashes of golden light. Then a single missile of blue exploded slowly: a signal bomb engineered to linger in the air.

"Alis volat propriis," an unfamiliar female voice said, intoning the words almost reverently and with an olympian accent.

*He flies by his own wings,* Talos silently translated and leaned around the General to see who had spoken. It was the newcomer, the flame-haired Amazon.

*Just how* did *she know Icarus?*

There was a moment of silence, and then the rebels echoed the farewell. "Alis volat propriis."

The last sparks of the blue missile died out, and Athanasia spoke the traditional ending to every death service, whether funeral or memorial. "From stardust back to stardust." After a few seconds, she added, "Audeamus."

Talos bent his head briefly, feeling Loxias grip his shoulder from one side and Ianessa slide her hand onto his other shoulder.

He was in charge of the Sunfires now.

✝

ICARUS WOULD'VE LOVED *that memorial.*

Koralia leaned back against a crate and stared at the ceiling. He'd have been especially pleased with what Talos had said and that his Sunfires had defied Athanasia's order to stay away.

Oh, he'd have beamed with pride over that.

Her chest ached. Her mother had insisted for years that heartache was a real thing and you could feel it physically. And Koralia had dismissed it, along with most of what her mother said about love. For a supposed expert on it, she was wrong often enough that Koralia had taken to ignoring all of her advice.

*But Mother was right about this.* It felt like someone had used her heart in a game of kickball. She supposed it would feel like that for a while.

"These aren't just fighters." An awed voice broke into her thoughts. "These are *weapons*. Tal, did you see them?"

She poked her head up over the stack of crates in front of her to see the speaker. He was tall, with curly auburn hair, and wore a short black cape over an old imperial olympian uniform. On most of the people of the base, it would have looked pretentious and ridiculous. He wore it like he was born to it.

"I saw them," Talos said, sounding annoyed at being interrupted.

"And you didn't think to tell me about them?" demanded the tall boy. His eyes narrowed, and his head tilted in a pout that would have looked childish except for the sharpness of his eyes and face.

Who was the kid? A careless grace sat on him, and his stance was familiar, but she couldn't identify him.

He glanced over her way, and she ducked back down, focusing again on the radio codes in front of her. Athanasia had promised to get Koralia settled into her new position later that day, so she was preparing herself. She could have done that in her room, but she wanted to immerse herself in the atmosphere of the rebellion, and a fighter bay was a good place to do that.

Talos snorted. "I was a little busy, in case you didn't notice."

"Oh, all right," the boy said, his tone grudging. "I suppose you kind of were."

She was starting to think *boy* was the wrong term, based on the depth of his voice. His face made it hard to judge his age, and children grew up fast these days. He could be anywhere between sixteen and twenty-six, but if she had to guess, she put him at twenty-one or twenty-two.

"Where did they come from?" he asked, seeming unbothered by Talos's irritation.

"New operative on base," Talos said shortly. "Ow." He spat a few inventive curses. "Mikon, would you stop drooling and get over here where you're supposed to be? I can't seal this back into place one-handed."

The tone was sharp, but the boy again didn't seem annoyed. His hands in his pockets, he strolled out of sight, over toward where Talos was presumably working on a fighter.

If Koralia had known he was in this area, she would have gone somewhere else to study. How long would it be until Talos recognized her? He and Icarus told each other everything and had for years. He had to know a lot about her. And would he still suspect her then? She would have, if their positions were reversed. If the rebels were looking for a traitor, she was a logical choice, not only because she was full olympian, but because she'd known Icarus so well.

For a minute, she thought about finding Talos and just telling him who she was. Having it out so the storm could burst and be over.

No, better to give him a chance to get to know her first.

"What's the new operative like?" Mikon asked, his voice practically bursting with curiosity. "What system is he from?"

"She." The word was muffled, and there was a sharp whine, like a piece of metal being cut, and then a slam.

"A new girl on base?"

Koralia almost laughed. His voice sounded the way she imagined a puppy's would: eager, questioning, innocent, mischievous.

"Don't get any ideas," Talos grunted. "No, not that way; twist it. I have to seal it separately or it won't hold."

Another screech of metal on metal filled the work area, and then silence until Mikon asked, "Why don't get any ideas? Is she older? Or married?"

Hissing sparks drowned out anything else Mikon said for a minute. Then the welder shut off and Talos said, "If that doesn't hold, nothing will. And, no, don't get any ideas because..." He paused, sounding like he wasn't sure what to say next.

Koralia froze, half wishing she wasn't there and half hoping to hear something that would make his attitude a little easier to deal with.

"...because she's an Amazon," Talos finished, as if it closed the discussion.

But it didn't, apparently, not for Mikon.

"So?" the boy retorted. "My mother's an olympian."

"Your mother is a she-devil who is to blame for everyone thinking you're going to go batstardust crazy and murder someone," Talos said, sounding distracted. Something thunked, like a crate being closed.

"Rude," Mikon said casually, "but fair."

Koralia wanted to laugh. It was the strangest conversation.

And then Talos's words clicked into place, and her eyes widened. Half-olympian, an air of careless grace, good hearing, his *name*. Mikon was none other than the youngest of the Sunfires, Icarus's little brother, the wild one, codenamed Scythe. He must have dyed his hair: he'd been blond in the pictures she'd seen of him.

"I can handle an Amazon," Mikon said, his voice and two sets of footsteps coming closer.

She risked another glance around the crates. The two stopped in front of one of the eagle fighters she'd brought with her, and Talos climbed underneath it, a scanning device in his hand.

His thoroughness wasn't surprising, but he wasn't going to find any tracking devices or bugs. Her fathers had made sure of that. They had told her that Phobos had stripped the trackers from the fighters, but she knew he hadn't. Ares and Hephaestus must have done it themselves, probably staying up late while she was sleeping.

"I really don't care who you chase, but leave this one alone," Talos was saying, ducking out from under the fighter and dusting his hands on his pants. "At least until I tell you she's clean."

Mikon stood up straighter, his posture radiating intense curiosity. "There's a possibility she isn't?"

Talos hesitated—she heard his breathing change—and ducked under another fighter. Moving very carefully, she eased further behind the crates so she could still watch but wouldn't be seen as they worked their way through the group of fighters.

"What aren't you telling me?" Mikon asked. He didn't sound annoyed, just persistent, as if he wouldn't let the matter drop until he had an answer he liked.

Little siblings were like that. 'Course, so were older siblings. Siblings, period.

"Would Icarus have told me?" Mikon asked hesitantly. She wasn't sure where the hesitation originated. Was it because he was pushing a boundary with Talos? Or some other reason?

Talos slid out and straightened again, sighing. He put a hand on Mikon's shoulder and frowned up at the younger man. "No, he wouldn't have. It's a security issue. Protocol. All new operatives have to be vetted first, even if they've been consistently active elsewhere. You should know this. Leave it alone, dammit, Mikon."

Talos's face turned toward her for just an instant, his eyes darker than usual. The look he shot his brother was half threatening, half tired, like he didn't have the energy for this battle.

She twisted a little so she could see Mikon's face. His expression crumpled, and he reached out and hugged Talos.

It didn't look like a younger brother comforting an older brother. She couldn't read emotions the way some olympians could, but their body language was expressive enough. Mikon held onto Talos like he couldn't stay standing without help, a younger brother needing his older brother to reassure him. The height difference between the two would have been comical if the moment wasn't so full of raw anger and grief.

Both of which she understood well.

The moment ended with Mikon pulling free, shaking himself like he was waking up, flipping his cape back over his shoulders to hang in front, and stalking away like he was on a mission. The sound of muttering drifted back to her as he left, but she couldn't make out the words.

Talos let out a shaky breath and collapsed against one of the fighters, gripping it to stay upright. He pressed one finger against the bridge of his nose in a movement reminiscent of General Athanasia. He looked exhausted, the weight on his shoulders too much to carry, like he was not only trying to stay afloat in an ocean but keep other boats afloat too—all in the middle of a raging storm.

She understood that feeling too, and for the first time since she'd arrived, she saw and felt the real Talos. The person Icarus had loved more than anyone else in the galaxy. The one Icarus would have done anything for. Not just the responsible big brother and rebel leader, but the human with a broken past who had loved Icarus fiercely and saved his life a dozen times.

The man hurting as badly as she was.

But then he shoved himself off of the fighter, swearing and growling something about enough weakness for one moment, and went back to scanning the fighters.

As quietly as she could, she eased herself up from her seat and, keeping to the shadows, slipped out of the other end of the docking bay, heading back to her room.

Leaving Talos alone to his grief.

# CHAPTER 7

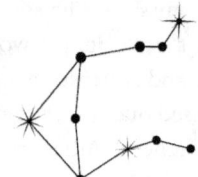

"Do we get to set the base on fire now? Please tell me we get to set the base on fire."

"We are not setting the base on fire." Talos hid a grin behind his hand and motioned for the next transport to take off. Then he glanced at Heirax. The teenager's look had turned speculative.

"If we set it on fire, there won't be anything to trace," he wheedled.

"We're not setting it on fire because if we're doing anything, we're blowing it up," said Xuthos, walking past with his arms full of extra munitions, which he dumped behind the seat of his fighter.

Talos snorted and shook his head at the pleading look Heirax sent him. "Still no."

"Spoilsport," Xuthos called from his fighter.

Talos ignored him, mentally checking his list of what still had to be done. This was the second base move the Kallistratus had made since the failed Key Mission. All the bases were still in the general vicinity of Krete, but by hopping around, they would hopefully throw off any tracers and keep the rebels safe from Kretan reprisals.

"Captain Talos?"

"It's Commander now, actually," he said, turning around to come face-to-face with Koralia, the ex-Amazon.

Not who he'd been expecting.

"Commander, then," she acknowledged with a slight tilt of her head. "May I have a minute? I have a question for you."

54

Before he could answer, Xuthos ducked out from behind his fighter and stopped short, eying the woman with blatant admiration. "Hellooo." He whistled and gave her his most dazzling smile. "I don't think we've met. I'm—"

"Not the time." Talos sliced sideways with his hand, frowning at his second-in-command. He opened his mouth to ask the Amazon what she wanted, but she cut him off.

"Yes, I know, you think I'm a traitor, you—"

"You think *she's* a traitor?" Xuthos leaned to the side, looking at Talos like he was losing his mind. "Why?"

"—and you don't trust me," Koralia went on, ignoring Xuthos and the other pilots now staring. "That's perfectly within your rights. You also don't like that I'm the new head of communications. But the General and Lieutenant Ianessa are already on the other base, and this is a priority communication, so I need to talk to you for a minute."

She tucked her arms behind her back and waited. She hadn't been rude, just factual, and he hated to admit he was actually a little impressed at how confidently and calmly she'd just spoken, especially knowing he was suspicious of her.

Xuthos whistled again but stopped at a look from Talos.

"Finish loading the fighters. We leave in twenty minutes," he ordered, hoping Xuthos wouldn't choose now to snap snarky comebacks.

He didn't, and Talos breathed a silent sigh of relief as the pilot took Heirax back into the base. Motioning for Koralia to follow him, he led her to the edge of the landing field, where they wouldn't be overheard by the rebels loading the last few transports and the pilots preparing their fighters.

"This just came in." She held out a thin sheet of scrip on which a message had been written in loopy but neat handwriting. "You managed the Kretan operatives for a while, right?"

Every time she said something that indicated how much information the General had given her, he wanted to wince. But he held tightly to his temper and nodded.

"Who is Ambrosia?"

He blinked. "She's dead," he said shortly. "In the Key Mission."

"Really?" She held out the scrip closer to him. "Because this says she isn't."

Snatching it from her, he scanned it. There, at the bottom, was Ambrosia's code.

*I'm alive, I'm safe, and my cover is intact. Awaiting orders.*

That was impossible. She'd died inside the fortress, just before Daedalus retrieved the Key, just before Icarus...

Throwing a suspicious glance at Koralia, who rolled her eyes, he lifted the scrip and read it again.

The words didn't change.

"She was our inside operative in Minos's palace," he said slowly, handing the scrip back to her. "We all thought she was dead. Daedalus saw her fall."

Koralia's neutral expression didn't change. "Someone was mistaken."

"Obviously," he said dryly. "What transport are you on?"

"Last one out, probably the one you'll be escorting."

"Get that to the General as soon as you land."

"Blast. And here I was planning to take a shower and attend a fashion parade first."

She smiled blandly at him, and he grimaced. Okay, he'd probably deserved that.

"Yes, well, fine." He spun around toward his fighter, but her voice stopped him.

"Talos?"

He turned back. "Yes?"

Her eyes held his gaze, hopeful but cautious. "Maybe we can go back."

He'd been thinking the same thing, of course. Back to Krete; attempt to get the Key again and make Minos pay.

Icarus would be avenged.

+

THE REBELLION FIGHTER pilots loved moving day. They got to do what they loved best: fly. Protecting the crew and equipment transports, scouting ahead, and doing the final flyover checks of both the old and new bases.

The techs and engineers hated moving day. They were always concerned over whether their gear was all going to arrive in one piece or be lost and what they'd have to cobble together to make do with.

And Athanasia just finished every moving day thankful if everyone arrived and all the equipment was more or less in one piece.

This time had gone so smoothly that she expected every minute to hear something blow up or someone come in screaming that something vital had been left behind. Especially since they'd gotten a later start than usual because she'd let everyone sleep in after the memorial yesterday.

But none of that had happened, and Koralia's news was the bright ending to a day that had been almost too good to be true.

After Athanasia read the message, she summoned Talos, Ianessa, Xantippos, and Koralia to the new radio room and read the message out loud.

"This changes things, right?" Talos paced, dodging around com stations and screens.

Athanasia tapped the radio record in front of her, looking for irregularities. There weren't any that she could see, but everyone on the Key Mission had been convinced Ambrosia was dead. Someone had really messed up...or there was a trick hiding somewhere.

"Is it really her?" Athanasia asked, scrutinizing the scrip again.

"It's her phrasing," Ianessa confirmed, and Talos nodded agreement. He pointed to it. "The way she writes the code—it's the same as she's always done."

Xantippos leaned over Athanasia's shoulder to read the message, his ears pointing forward. "All we have is Daedalus's word that she went down?"

"Yes," Athanasia said, frowning. "But since we still don't know where he is, we can't verify his report or ask what happened or—" She shook her head.

"Are we sure it isn't Daedalus?" the kentauri suggested.

Athanasia shook her head at the same time Ianessa said, "He'd use his own contact."

Talos directed a dark glower out the window in the general direction of Krete, and she watched him, waiting for one of his usual scathing remarks about his uncle.

But when he turned back, he just raised his eyebrows and asked, "How likely are the chances that she could have been our traitor?"

Trust him to cut to the heart of what they were all thinking. Ambrosia could have faked her own death, and now be trying to continue being a double agent. Athanasia studied the scrip again, hunting for any clue that might be hidden in the few words while the others continued to talk around and behind her.

"Suspicious, are we?" Koralia asked provokingly, looking up at Talos from where she sat.

"Always," Talos countered. "I suspect everyone. You aren't special, Amazon."

"Good to know, *pilot*."

The General rolled her eyes. It was hard to blame the girl for needling Talos after the way he'd been down on her, but was now really the time?

But then Koralia squinted. "Do you have a picture of this Ambrosia?"

"Why?" Talos turned to look at her while Ianessa moved over to a computer bank and began tapping commands into it.

She shrugged. "Just wondering."

Athanasia knew it was more than that, but Koralia wouldn't tell them unless she was sure of something. So she looked up and watched the girls, waiting.

"Found one!" Ianessa grabbed a blank sheet of scrip, laid it over the screen to pick up the image, and handed it to Koralia.

One look at it, and the Amazon stiffened.

"What is it?" Xantippos asked.

"Just a moment, please. Do you have any other pictures?" Koralia joined Ianessa at the computer. "Different hair color? Clothes?"

"Mmmm, here. And here." Ianessa pulled a few other pictures up, mostly of the girl at various rebel functions, like memorial services and victory celebrations.

"Yes, I see." Koralia bent over the computer and did a quick search, the screen filling with pictures, but Athanasia couldn't see who was in them.

"Lieutenant?" Athanasia asked, intentionally using her rank, a subtle reminder of the need to talk to those around her. Amazons were as used to operating independently as they were on a team, and Ares would have promoted that independence. But the Kallistratus didn't run like that. It was a team effort from the top to the bottom.

"Koralia?" she prompted again, when the girl kept staring at the screen. "What don't we know about her?"

She turned, folding her arms over her chest. "She's Ariadne. Daughter of Minos."

"What?" three voices exclaimed in shock: Ianessa, Talos, and Xantippos.

"Are you positive?" Athanasia asked.

Koralia grabbed a sheet of scrip, transferred another image to it, and handed it to Athanasia. "See for yourself."

It was from the society page of a galactic newspaper. A year old, it showed a young, dark-haired woman. Athanasia had to look closely before she could see the resemblance. The Ambrosia they knew was blonde with blue highlights, a radically different haircut, and clothes and makeup that changed her whole look. But when she looked closely, the features were definitely those of Princess Ariadne of Krete.

What a tangled web this was.

✢

"WELL, THIS COULD BE A PROBLEM," Talos drawled. He sensed the General rolling her eyes at his understatement, but he didn't turn to look at her. Instead, he stared down at the table, processing that information.

Their inside contact was Princess Ariadne. Minos's daughter. Kretan royalty.

How had they missed that?

"So we're all thinking she could be the traitor?" he repeated, looking around at the others in the room. He'd run the Kretan contacts before Icarus, so he'd known Ambrosia, and even met her face-to-face twice. She was pretty, with big brown eyes that looked up trustingly and the backstory that her family ignored her and she wanted peace for the galaxy and her conscience. He had liked her. She had adored Icarus, but most people did. Talos tried to think through her backstory. Were there clues they'd missed? Had he ever met the princess while living on Krete as a kid? He didn't think so, but it was possible. Still, it was so long ago. Even if he or Icarus had met her once, there were a hundred reasons why they wouldn't or couldn't have recognized her now, fifteen years later.

The General and Ianessa were both looking at Koralia as if she knew the answer to his question.

"How would I know?" The Amazon shrugged. "I don't know her that well. The last time I saw her, she was more than a little self-absorbed and selfish... well, kind of selfish," she qualified. "But I haven't seen her in two years."

"Some help you are," he said flippantly.

"Next time I'll make sure to infiltrate our enemies and learn all their plans before I join up," she retorted.

"If we could focus?" the General said, raising her eyebrows at him.

Which seemed a little unfair. Sure, he'd started it, but the girl had given back as good as she'd gotten.

Ianessa swept a screen clear and grabbed a stylus as the General motioned the Amazon forward and said, "Tell us what you know about the Kretan royal family."

He pushed himself back from the table to see her better—he still couldn't think of her by name yet. Until he was sure she wasn't a traitor, he would keep his distance.

She sat down and frowned at the floor. "They're all jerks?"

Low laughter ran around the bridge, and the tension eased a little.

"Besides that," the General said, smiling.

"Ariadne's a middle daughter. I know one other sister, and she's kind of bland—follows in Ariadne's shadow a lot. Minos is a—" She looked like she was searching for an appropriate word. "He spends half his time figuring out how to keep Krete mighty or make it mighty *again*, depending on the day. The other half of his time is split between dealing with his crazy wife, pissing Poseidon off, and presumably governing his planet."

"Crazy?" Xantippos leaned forward so he could see the girl better. "Literally?"

"Insane as a forming nebula," she said solemnly. "Or that's the last report I heard. I haven't been on planet in a while."

There it was again, the annoying, persistent feeling that this girl knew a lot more than she was saying. That she was hiding something huge. General Athanasia had accepted her, and she wasn't known for trusting people without reason; Ianessa too seemed to like the new girl and had no qualms about her training the new radio recruits, which was unexpected. But Ianessa trusted Athanasia implicitly.

Usually, he did too. But that was before Icarus fell.

"How do you know so much about them?" he asked, or rather demanded.

Her shrug seemed forced. "I'm an Amazon. I go where I'm sent, and that included Krete more than once." As if she saw the doubt in his face, she added, "Regular soldiers don't have the access to palaces and royal families that we do, in case you're still wondering how a lowly Amazon knows so much. We're allowed into a lot of rarified places."

He narrowed his eyes at her, and she looked back with a smirk tugging at the corners of her lips, clearly unconcerned with his opinion. It stretched into a contest of sorts, neither dropping their eyes until Ianessa snickered.

Irritation flaring up, he turned away.

"Satisfied?" Athanasia asked, her tone amused.

No, but he wouldn't say that, so he waved his hand in response.

"Koralia." Ianessa's voice held an odd tone.

He turned back around to see Ianessa looking at the Amazon with an intensity he didn't understand. "From what you know of Ambrosia—Ariadne —is it plausible she would betray her family and kingdom?"

"Yes." The answer came without hesitation, and the Amazon's face didn't change as she added, "She was alternately the star of her family and ignored by them." Koralia paused, thinking.

That tallied with what Ambrosia had given them as her life story, at least, the second part of it did.

"The Kretan royal family is weird," Koralia said. "The kids aren't exactly loved and adored above all else. They're just lauded when they're needed or when they do something about which Minos can boast. I can't really tell you why, but...yes, I think she would betray her family and kingdom. Yet that doesn't tell you whether she'd betray *you*."

Xantippos and the General looked at each other for a long moment, and everyone else held their breath, waiting. Talos forced himself to sit patiently as the silence stretched out.

Just as he was about to ask if he could take a team and scout, Athanasia turned to him.

"Who would you take?"

He grinned. This was why the General was his favorite commander. She didn't ask stupid questions, and she knew the people under her command. She didn't have to ask him to put a team together. She knew he was already doing that in his head.

"Mikon, Xuthos, Cleon, and Tisandros." His new command squad—to test them and adjust to working together—and his little brother, because the kid was sharp and having a Sunfire at his back was always a good idea.

And he just wanted to spend time with Mikon. He hadn't seen him in a while. Mikon had been scouting for Xantippos for many weeks, trying to get a feel for what other systems might be good places for the Kallistratus to establish bases.

"Do it." The General looked around, checking that no one else had anything to say, and then added, "Dismissed."

Grinning, he left the room with long strides. They were going back to Krete.

# CHAPTER 8

"You know, Icarus would be really happy to see you here."

Koralia's head snapped up so quickly she almost hit it on a nearby screen. Twisting away from it, she turned around to see Ianessa leaning against the doorway, and her eyes widened as she realized the Sunfire had spoken in a low whisper. With the distance between them, a normal human shouldn't have been able to hear the words.

Hellstars. Whatever Ianessa knew or thought she knew, if she had needed confirmation Koralia was olympian, she had it now.

Looking pleased at the reaction she'd gotten, the redhead came inside and pushed a button, closing the door and then locking it.

"True," Koralia said, keeping her voice neutral. "He did like watching his recruits at work."

Ianessa laughed. "Are we really going to pretend that's all it would have been?"

How much did she know? Koralia racked her brain for every interaction she'd had with Ianessa in the last three days. Had she said or done anything, aside from right now, that could have given away her identity? Icarus had said Talos knew the most about her and then Ianessa...but that didn't extend to her name, did it? Icarus had been almost fanatical about not using real names and normally referred to his family by their codenames. Not because he didn't trust her, but because they were almost always in places that could have had listening bugs hidden anywhere.

Besides, Icarus had always called her Melainis, not Koralia.

"Ah, so we're going to stay silent until we each figure out what the other knows. Or at least, that's *your* play." Ianessa sat down in front of one of the com panels and slid her finger up the touchscreen, engaging the sound dampeners. Then she smiled at Koralia again, a huntress bringing a deer to bay.

*Starstorms. I'm not getting out of giving her some answers.*

"How about we change tactics?" Ianessa said brightly. "I tell you what I know, and you tell me how you'd like to handle it. Don't worry, I'll respect whatever you decide. Especially until I know what your power is."

Koralia tried to breathe deeply without it being obvious. She felt for a chair behind her, pulled it out, and sat down. "Continue," she said in a monotone.

Ianessa folded her hands in her lap, looking more at ease with the movement than she had the first time Koralia had met her. She was healing quickly. *Good. Everyone was so worried.*

"You're Koralia Nikephoros, also known as Melainis and Black Swan, and the operative Icarus codenamed Katana."

If she knew that much…she also had to know just what Koralia had been to her brother.

But Ianessa's tone hadn't been smug, and that gave her hope as the other woman continued. "You're the daughter of Ares, and you're a *current* Amazon, not an *ex*-Amazon. You, like our general, are still counted one of them."

Now how could she have known that?

"And you were engaged to Icarus, practically if not formally. Meaning you have more right than most to be here, on this base, with our family."

The extra minutes had given her enough time to gather herself. "Fascinating story," Koralia said, her tone bored. "May I ask if you invented it all or if some of the more colorful pieces are from a galactic gossip site?"

Ianessa laughed, and the sound was genuinely humorous. "Oh, Kora—I may call you that?"

Koralia shrugged. "Sure."

"You're good, Kora. But I'm the Shuriken. I'm an ex-Hestonai. My sister and I *built* the rebellion's current communications and information division."

She had forgotten that. The Hestonai, usually called Hearthfire Priestesses, served as councilors to the Imperial Intergalactic Senate, advisors to Jupiter, and watchwomen for the political temperature of the galaxy. They were the first to know of uprisings and rebellions and the first to try to smooth them down through a campaign of information—which basically amounted to propaganda.

Once someone entered the Hestonai Order, they were bound to it for life. If you left, you rarely got far before you were found and executed.

But Ianessa had been lucky: she had Talos and Icarus on her side before she made her escape. And once those two put their minds to anything, no power in the galaxy could stand against them.

Ianessa's smile vanished for a moment, and a hard look came into her sea-green eyes, as if a bad memory had surfaced. It passed, and Ianessa pointed to the com-panel Koralia had been standing over when she entered. "I have access to Icarus's travel logs and have for years. And since I'm running communications while on recovery duty..." She lifted her shoulders a fraction of an inch. "I also have access to the logs of anyone passing through the nearby systems, coming here. You didn't come from Iskyra via Akwila, like Talos thinks—or would think if he stopped for a minute to consider it. You came straight from Akwila, first via an official ship registered to the Lord of Fire and then on your own."

The woman smiled, tipping her head to the side to gently shake hair out of her face. "Suffice it to say that I know who you are. You're actually doing pretty well hiding your blood, but the way you veil your emotions is so casual. Like it's old habit." Ianessa shook her head. "No one in the Kallistratus does it like that. Even our half-olympians don't."

There was more than one half-olympian in the rebellion? *I thought Mikon was the only one.*

Ianessa leaned forward, wincing when her shoulder brushed the edge of the chair, and rearranged herself until the pain eased. "When we do it, it's like..." she paused, searching for words.

Koralia did have an answer for that. "Like there's a hard edge underneath it all. It's born of desperation, out of months and years of being on the run, having been interrogated and learning the hard way not to let people know what you're thinking."

Ianessa laughed, sounding pleased as she pointed at Koralia. "That exactly!"

There was a pause, each waiting for the other to speak first.

"Anyway, I know who you are," Ianessa finally said. "But that's not a threat. I'm not angry at you or anything else you're imagining. Far from it. I'm guessing you haven't told anyone because you want to prove yourself." At Koralia's nod, she went on, "I'd like it if—when it's just us—if you could..." She bowed her head against the sadness that came into her face. "If we can be honest with each other. I've wanted to meet you for a long time, you know. He was so in love—he'd never been like that before."

Koralia's throat tightened, and she stood up abruptly. "I can't—" But the words choked off, and she dug her fingernails into her hands, trying not to break down, trying to shove the image of Icarus's face out of her mind.

"I know." Ianessa stood up and reached out, the motion tentative. There was a pain in her face so strong that Koralia sensed she needed comfort even more than she needed to give it. So she stepped closer and carefully brought her arms around the other woman, trying not to jar the still-healing wounds.

Ianessa leaned against her, hugging back.

After a few minutes she pulled away and looked expectantly at Koralia. "So? Can we be friends?"

That won her a smile. "Yes. Of course, yes. I'd love that. I've wanted to meet you too." She'd spent many an hour imagining Icarus's family and what they'd be like. Now here she was, and it was as much pain as it was fun.

"Excellent." Ianessa's smile was a little too bright, as if she was trying not to cry, but the approval in her eyes was genuine. "Even better, I get you all to myself for now, since I'm not going to tell Talos." For a minute, her smile faltered. "Maybe I should, but he's too caught up in...everything. Being angry and sad, feeling lost, having to step into Icarus's place not just in the fleet but feeling like he has to lead us too." She shook her head. "He's one of the best men I know—really—and he's usually good with newcomers and making them *feel* welcome even while he distrusts them until they've been proven. But he's not thinking straight right now."

"Some days, I'm not sure I am either," Koralia whispered, staring down at a nearby screen.

"You and me both, girl," Ianessa admitted with a tired sigh.

An alert rang through the radio room, pulling Koralia's attention back to her job. Talos's scouting team was ready to leave, and she needed to be on duty.

"Sorry," she apologized, turning back to Ianessa, but the other woman was already standing up again.

"No, no sorries. You have to work, and I need to start digging deeper into some rebels' backgrounds." She grinned. "But we'll talk soon. Don't I have stories to tell you! Don't let Talos push you around today, by the way." She motioned toward the com panel.

"Wouldn't dream of it."

"Good." Ianessa made her way toward the door but then paused. "Kora?"

"Yes?"

"It's good to have you here."

How could one feel like smiling and crying at the same time? "Thanks. It's good to *be* here."

Then the Shuriken was gone, and Koralia was bending over the radio to connect with Talos's team. But the day didn't feel half as gloomy now.

. †.

SOARING OUT OF THE BASE, headed toward the Labyrinth and Krete, Talos breathed in deeply. He'd been in a fighter yesterday, but it had been a week since he'd had a mission and he'd been going base-crazy. He flexed his hands over the controls and reveled in the feel of them, in the freedom of being one person in a small ship in the vastness of space.

"Coms check," he said over the radio. "We have a new coms officer, guys, so let's break her in gently." Not that his boys ever actually would, scouting mission or no, but he wanted to get under Koralia's skin right now, see if she'd crack.

"Many thanks for your unnecessary courtesy," a feminine voice said sarcastically.

Bull's eye. That had needled her slightly, but she'd risen to it.

"Ooooh, I think I recognize that voice," Xuthos said. "Am I talking to Talos's latest suspected traitor?"

He gritted his teeth. Trust Xuthos to not let that go. Sure, that's what she was, but did he have to be so blatant about it?

"That sounds about right. You're talking to Koralia, the newest rebel on base," she replied. "And who might you be?"

"Lieutenant Xuthos, second-in-command of this base's fighter fleet. Pleasure to meet you, Koralia."

"That's Lieutenant Koralia to you," Talos cut in, forestalling whatever flirtation Xuthos was about to start. "This is Talos, mission commander, formally checking in with my scout, Mikon." They didn't need codenames for a simple scouting foray.

"And this is base, formally logging your check-in," Koralia responded. It was unnecessary, since the com system would automatically have recorded it, but he didn't miss her taunting undertone.

He had to grin. The Amazon seemed to be good at one thing: pushing back as good as he gave. And wherever she came from, he appreciated anyone who could do that.

Tisandros and Cleon checked in, and Talos could sense Mikon impatiently waiting to speak.

Xuthos beat him to it. "And where do you hail from, Lieutenant?"

"You're a full-fledged Amazon, aren't you?" Mikon burst out, as if he couldn't stay quiet another minute. "A lieutenant means you're the second highest rank?"

"Third highest, yes. And you're the one they call Scythe."

"Yes!" He sounded surprised she knew that, and Talos rolled his eyes. All she'd have had to do was open Mikon's personnel file. Every good coms officer familiarized themselves with the members of any mission they ran.

Wait, had he just thought of her as something good?

Well, she would have had to be, if she'd been put in charge. As much as their trust in her made him uneasy, Athanasia and Ianessa weren't known for making mistakes with personnel.

But he still couldn't shake that her connection to Icarus had been something more than ordinary. He had almost asked her about it several times in the last few days, but he wanted to maintain the upper hand, which meant finding his information out from other sources and not confronting her just yet.

"You honor us with your presence, lady warrior," Xuthos said.

Talos cleared his throat audibly. "Can you please not flirt during a scouting mission? Bear half a degree right. I want to slide around the edge of the Labyrinth, if we can."

"Like you've never flirted during a mission." Xuthos snorted, following Talos's flight path.

"Not during a scouting mission." He checked his map and altered his course slightly. According to the last coordinates of the Labyrinth, this should angle them around the side, giving them a straight shot toward Krete. His instructions were to contact Ambrosia—or Ariadne or whatever her real name was—and record the exact location of the signal.

"I bet Mikon tells a different story," Xuthos said, not even trying to pretend he wasn't baiting him.

There was a pause, and Talos quickly reviewed recent scouting missions he and Mikon had been on. He couldn't recall any flirting, but half of those had been with Ianessa or Dione at mission ops, and who flirted with their sister?

Well, Loxias would occasionally flirt with Ianessa, but their relationship had always been closer to teammates than adopted siblings.

"I solemnly swear I have never seen Talos flirt on a scouting mission," Mikon said with exaggerated sincerity in his voice.

Talos's shoulders shook with silent laughter. Never *seen*—clever boy. Scouting missions meant people rarely left their cockpits, and when they did, it was usually in abandoned locations. Of course he couldn't have seen Talos flirting with anything—there wouldn't have been anything *to* see. *Hearing* was a different matter.

He flipped his radio to private coms. "Good to know you still have my back."

"Ianessa said I had to," Mikon said.

He couldn't see his brother, but Talos knew the words had just been said with a perfectly straight face and laughing eyes, and he grinned.

It was good having the kid back.

Someone snickered over the radio, and he remembered that private coms didn't mean their base officer couldn't hear them—it only blocked the other pilots from listening. Switching general coms back on, he shook his head. Koralia was getting a full induction into the rebellion and the Sunfires, that was for sure.

"Accelerate to crossing speed," he ordered. "And do so silently." An idea struck him, and he grinned. "Xuthos, you can chat up the new officer back at base. I hope she freezes you out."

Xuthos protested just loud enough to be heard, but all the pilots settled down to steady flying, and Talos relaxed back into his seat.

If he had judged Koralia correctly, she'd do just the opposite now. She'd let Xuthos flirt with her and maybe even return it, and that would give him the opportunity to see her in some non-professional moments. And maybe figure out who she was and why she bothered him.

He didn't really have information that proved she was anything other than what the General said: an ex-Amazon come to join the fight. If it wasn't for the fact that he was positive Icarus had been betrayed and positive it had been personal, not political, he'd even have liked her.

He couldn't prove anything, but he knew, somehow, that she was hiding a significant connection to his brother. And he would find the proof, if it meant he barely slept for the next month.

. †.

"Talos to Base, we're coming up on Krete now." He leaned to the side to study the blue planet.

Then his fighter hit what felt like a solid wall, something that sent it spinning and shuddering. He fought for control as the yells of his other pilots confirmed they'd just hit the same thing.

"What *is* that?" Cleon was demanding. He'd been flying rear and appeared to be only lightly hit.

"I don't know!" Mikon snapped, and Talos could practically feel him twisting around as he tried to see what was out there.

"The Labyrinth! We hit the shraking Labyrinth," Tisandros yelled, yanking his fighter up and back. "Where the hell did it come from?"

Koralia's voice came crisply over the radio. "Base to pilots, please report."

"We will just as soon as we have anything *to* report," Talos snapped. "We've hit some kind of interference that could be the Labyrinth." He hoped it wasn't what he thought it was. If they'd actually hit the Labyrinth, that could mean only one thing: it had been extended further into space than their last patrols showed.

"Talos to all pilots. Orient yourselves on galactic latitude seventy-five." Mikon was already doing it before he'd finished speaking. "Xuthos, take Cleon above the planet and around from its north to its south, Tisandros, follow me: we're going to circle it retrograde. Mind the gravity and stay far enough back that we're not pulled into orbit. Scan the—whatever this thing is —with active sonar and map it. Go slowly."

He eased his fighter to the left cautiously, reducing speed and alert for anything else that might suddenly rise up and hit him.

"There," Mikon said over the coms, and a green circle showed up on Talos's navscreen. "It stops. But...oh, no, it doesn't. Huh?" Talos could hear him slamming repeatedly on a button.

"Respect the ship!" He reminded Mikon sharply. "No hitting anything."

"Kretan scouting mission, Koralia to Scythe," she said over the radio. "Please hold. I think I can clear up your map on this end."

Mikon sounded pleased as he replied, "Yes, ma'am, Scythe holding."

How had she known that his codename was the way to get his attention? Talos shook the question away and focused on keeping the fighter steady through increasing gravity that had it shuddering, trying to pull it toward the planet.

"Try this," Koralia said, and their screens cleared to be replaced with a clean map. An orange line, signifying a live force field of some kind, ran in a three-quarters circle around Krete Prime...and looked like it might be starting to angle off to cover the other planets in the system too.

"So it does stop but then it starts again." Mikon said what they were both thinking. "What do we do now?"

"Stop asking questions so I can think," Talos said automatically. "And see if you can scan the capital fortress from here."

His scout was silent for a minute, and then he swore. "The guns—I think they're hot."

Startled protests and more swearing broke from the other pilots.

"Settle down!" Talos yelled. "We're too far out for them to reach us anyway, settle down." At least, he hoped they were. They'd had no intelligence of Krete being able to hit them this far out. And why would the planet need a security net around their system if they *had* developed longer-range weapons?

"This is Base, you are ordered to return at once. This is Base, you are ordered to return at once." Koralia's command was calm, but her voice wasn't.

He had no time to wonder about it, however, too focused on trying to navigate the gravity waves still attempting to trap his fighter. He'd never had this problem this far out from the planet. What was the Labyrinth doing to space here?

Frustrated, he turned his ship, waited for the rest of his pilots to gather, and headed for home, muttering.

They badly needed more information on how this thing worked.

# CHAPTER 9

our people waited for them when the pilots burst into the main bridge on the rebel base: General Athanasia, Lieutenant-General Xantippos, Koralia the Amazon, and Ianessa. Everyone else was gone, unusual for a main bridge in the middle of the day, but the General probably didn't want them overhearing this mission report. Or so Talos assumed.

"It's spreading," he announced as the doors of the bridge closed behind them. "The Labyrinth is spreading. If we want to try getting the Key again, we have to go immediately, as soon as we get a team together."

Before anyone else could speak, the Amazon spun around to stare at him like he was insane. "And how do you propose breaking into a fortress that's more heavily guarded than ever in...two days? Three at most? However long it takes them to close the gap." Her voice was sharp and almost defensive.

If she'd actually calculated the probable spread of the fortress and hadn't just guessed, that math was impressive. But he couldn't ignore her challenge. Straightening his shoulders, he turned so that he faced her head-on. "Obviously with careful planning. I assure you, Amazon, it can be done."

Her eyes had narrowed at his use of her title. Now her lips lifted in a half-smiling grimace that showed her teeth. "Tell me, pilot, did you ever hear of the Kidaon Fortress?"

"Who hasn't?"

"And do you know who finally infiltrated it?"

"Oh, let me, I know this one." Mikon came up behind him, and Talos could hear him grinning at the woman. "A crack team of Amazons, five years ago.

Got in, freed the prisoners, and put overload spikes in the whole system. Took the staff two years to get the fortress operational again." He stopped and cocked his head speculatively. "Was that you?"

"I was on the team. In fact, I *led* the team." She glared at Talos. "That base had six times the position advantages Minos has, not to mention probably four times the security. So believe me, I know a thing or two about infiltrating fortresses. This one might *look* easy, and compared to Kidaon, it might be. But Minos's people are all on the highest of high alerts since our last attempt. You won't get anywhere near that Key."

"Do you seriously think I don't know it'll be hard?" Arguing with someone in front of the generals and his pilots wasn't very professional behavior, but she was acting awfully smug for a newcomer. And that remark about the Kidaon Fortress was over the top. "Did you miss the part where I said *with careful planning?*"

"No, I just missed the part where you said you had *an actual idea* of where to get in or knew exactly where the Key was. What if it isn't even kept in the fortress anymore? I'd store it in the palace, if it was me."

"I can't argue with that," Ianessa interjected.

Talos threw her a glower. "Whose side are you on?"

She held up both hands and smiled, her eyes wide with fake innocence. "I'm a casual bystander."

"So am I," Mikon said quickly, and moved to stand next to Ianessa.

"Thanks for the support, fam," Talos said as sarcastically as possible. "And if you'd let me finish, Amazon, you'd see that I do have a plan, one that would keep casualties to a minimum."

"All right, quiet!" Athanasia's command ricocheted around the room. The General rarely needed to raise her voice, and when she did, it meant business. All of the pilots snapped up to stand ramrod straight. Mikon, Tisandros, Cleon, and Xuthos ranged themselves in a straight line, while Talos stood a few steps to the side of them, looking between them and the General.

"The next person to talk without orders will have my hand meet their face —hard. Koralia, I know Talos has a genius for irritating you, but please stop winding my best pilot up long enough for me to get this sorted out."

"Ma'am," she said, bowing her head like the General was a queen.

Which she was, in everything but birth. And even though he knew it was petty, the gesture annoyed him. That was *his* Rebel-Mom and queen, not hers.

"Xuthos, report," the General ordered.

"Yes, ma'am." He winked at someone, and Talos glanced sideways to see Koralia stepping up beside the general.

"No flirting," he grumbled, low enough that the whole room wouldn't hear but loud enough that Xuthos, standing next to him, *would* hear it.

Mikon, also hearing, snickered under his breath.

His second didn't look at him. "The Labyrinth now surrounds the far side of the planet. We could only get halfway around it before we were directed out into open space. But we did pick up a transmission. The signature matches Ambrosia's."

Ianessa handed a sheet of scrip to the General, who read the transcribed message aloud. "'I have the answer you need, but I'm running out of time. Meet me tomorrow.'" Athanasia looked up. "Hmmmmm."

"So a mission might not be necessary at all?" Ianessa wondered, sounding hopeful.

He understood that. She'd been on the radio for Icarus's last mission. She probably worried every time one of them talked about going back to Krete; she just didn't say it because she knew as well as anyone how important this was.

"Talos, report," the General said crisply.

"The Labyrinth is definitely spreading. They've extended it almost all the way around the planet, and their guns were hot. It looks like they're also extending it around the system."

Ianessa flinched, but the General and Koralia didn't, looking at the new map which incorporated the data from their scouting.

The Amazon traced the line of the Labyrinth and turned the map projection sideways. "You think the guns were hot to protect the planet while they close the ring? Or because Icarus spooked them?"

That was exactly what he'd been wondering, and he was a little disconcerted at how quickly she'd guessed that.

"I think maybe both. But we also picked up a transmission from the palace," he added. "Just as we were leaving. I sent it on. Did you get that one transcribed too?"

He expected Ianessa to take over, but it was Koralia who read aloud from a tablet in her hand. "'Attention, Kallistratus. I have information vital to the rebellion. Contact me with this code.'" She paused, scowling at it. "This is a royal code." She tapped the message and looked up. "If it's Ariadne, she's not going out of her way to be subtle, which would be weird after she's gone to such lengths to disguise herself."

Talos ran through a mental list of every contact in their Kretan spy ring, but couldn't think of anyone who might be in the palace aside from Ambrosia. She'd never used a royal code before, so why would she start now?

Someone bumped him slightly, and he glanced sideways. Mikon was rocking forward and backward on his heels, watching Koralia like she was an exotic bird that he was figuring out how to call to his wrist.

Just what Talos didn't need right now, the boy being smitten with another Amazon, especially this one.

The General pulled up a projection of Krete and motioned for the pilots to gather around it. Koralia input the reconnaissance information, overlaying the projection with colored lines: blue and purple showing the locations of the messages from the surface, green for the pilots' flight paths, and orange for Krete's defense batteries.

"But how can this be Ariadne if Ambrosia's transmission from the other side of the planet is also Ariadne?" asked Xuthos, pointing to the blue dot on the projection. "She can't be in two places at once, can she?"

"You don't have any other operatives on Krete?" Koralia asked, looking from Talos to the General to Ianessa.

"Three, but none in the capital," Ianessa answered for them, circling the projection slowly, studying it while she explained. "It got too dangerous, and Ambrosia—or whoever she is—was the last active one. We even told those three to go dormant for three weeks on either side of the Key Mission." She tipped the projection to the side for a minute and then replaced it right side up. "If Ambrosia *is* Ariadne, that explains why she didn't seem as concerned about getting caught. We thought she was just pretending not to worry so Icarus would think she was brave."

"Did she have a thing for Icarus?" Koralia asked, her voice monotone, eyes fixed on the projection.

Ianessa and the General looked at her and then at each other, like they knew something no one else did. Talos narrowed his eyes.

Why did everyone seem so full of secrets lately?

"I don't know. Talos?" Ianessa asked. She moved to rest her hands on the projection table but winced and straightened up. Mikon crossed the bridge to stand behind her, and she smiled gratefully at him before leaning gently against him, letting him support her.

They looked so alike at times, those two. Both auburn-haired—Mikon's darker than hers—and tall with pale skin and high cheekbones. Refined, beautiful…and deadly when crossed. Talos smiled at them for half a second, and they nodded to him.

Then he racked his brain, trying to remember Ambrosia and the few interactions he'd had with her before he'd handed the Kretan spies over to Icarus and headed off to Samatia to build its spy network. Most girls they'd known were infatuated with Icarus at one point or another, including a majority of their rebel spies; he'd stopped keeping track long ago.

"Yes, I think she did," he said at last. Which brought them back to the question of why Ambrosia—or Ariadne or whoever she was—would have wanted to betray them. And was it Icarus himself or the rebellion that had been betrayed?

"Damn Daedalus," he said aloud. "Just like him to disappear on us when we're in the middle of a mess."

Mikon snickered. "Roast him, Tal."

"I'd rather you didn't." The General gave Mikon a stern look and then extended it to Talos.

Talos returned a defiant look. "If he was dead, we'd have heard about it by now. Is he just sitting around down there, doing nothing? What is he *thinking?*"

The General sighed. "Maybe Minos caught on to what he was doing?" But she didn't sound like she believed it either. If anyone was too good to be caught, Daedalus was.

Seething, Talos kicked a nearby wall. "I hate that Icarus is gone too. There isn't a person on this base that doesn't. But Daedalus gave his word he'd try to get the Key out, and now we only hear silence? Bloody coward."

"Unless the palace transmission is him."

Everyone turned to look at Koralia, who had spoken. She shrugged and added, "What? He is the royal inventor, isn't he? Who else would be transmitting from the palace?"

"You've met my uncle?" Talos asked.

"Not exactly. I was in the room when he was talking to my general, if that counts. But that's not how I know about him."

*Icarus.* Icarus had told her.

She didn't say it, but everyone thought it, and Talos narrowed his eyes at her. Was it his imagination or did she avoid looking at him? Icarus didn't talk about his father to most people. But Talos still didn't recognize the woman—and he thought he'd met everyone Icarus had dated.

The General interrupted his racing questions. "We need to determine if we can take the risk of meeting with Ambrosia or not. Koralia." She turned to look at the Amazon. "Respond to the palace code. Use every scrambler we have, and send a message asking for clarification."

"Ma'am." Koralia moved over to a com station, and Ianessa went with her.

While they did that, Talos went back to studying the projection.

"Wait." He moved around the generals and over to a control panel. "The Labyrinth extends further out this way," he explained, redrawing the line of the force fields.

Koralia looked up and frowned at the red line he'd just moved. "Just what does the Labyrinth *do*? I still don't have a clear idea of that."

"I'm sorry." The General put a hand on Koralia's arm. "I meant to have briefed you."

He bristled. How dare the General apologize for not having briefed a new, very junior member of the rebellion in the midst of all the chaos of the past week?

To his surprise, Koralia looked just as fierce as he felt. "Don't, General, please don't." Her eyes flashed darkly for a second.

Athanasia raised an eyebrow, but didn't respond, just motioned for Talos to explain.

Grudgingly, he did so. "As near as we can figure, it's a force field blockade net with a series of paths and gates. If you're willing to pay a heavy toll, you turn off your sonar and are either guided or towed through with tractor beams. Krete's the gateway to a bunch of the settlements and systems beyond, and you can either go through them or—"

"Or risk nebulas and gravity wells and a score of other dangers beyond, which is how Krete became a major player on the galactic scene in the first place." Koralia nodded, her forehead furrowed as she stared at the map.

The door to the bridge hissed open, and Heirax slipped inside, holding what looked like a stack of inventory tablets. The General looked up and nodded for him to wait, so he stood back in a corner near the door.

"And because of being the gateway, he's blocked off all of this sector," Koralia said, slowly moving around the projector table, her focus on the map.

"Yes." Talos wanted to swear, slam something, or throw something, but that wouldn't help them right now.

"Including all of your bases in this area," she continued.

"Yes."

Athanasia zoomed the map out, pointing to the area now outlined in blue: rebel-controlled space. "We wouldn't be interfering, except that he's also blocked off a couple dozen poorer systems." She pointed to them, and they came alive as gray dots. "Poseidon's outer trading posts are too far for most of them to travel, but Minos just made it a lot more expensive for them to come to Krete for supplies. Not to mention cutting off most of the trade routes in the region."

"Which Poseidon does use," the Amazon said slowly. "Because they're less expensive. Hephaestus has used them in the past too, sending weapons to these systems."

Now *that* was a strange piece of information for her to know. He thought Hephaestus's routes were closely guarded knowledge.

"Amazon information," she explained in an aside, anticipating his question.

He was starting to think that she just used that as her standard answer, true or not.

"So they're trying to cut Poseidon off from those too," she deduced, still staring at the map as if it held some golden answer. "And everyone else is caught in the middle of this stupid war that Poseidon has had going on with Minos for almost thirty years."

As if he couldn't stand still any longer, Tisandros moved around Talos and closer to Koralia. "You Amazons certainly know a lot, especially things that could be useful to the rebellion. But you still refuse to join."

*Finally!* Someone else not just falling over the Amazon because she was pretty and sharp.

The atmosphere on the bridge shifted, unease tightening between everyone. The generals stood back, watching, and Ianessa ranged herself on the side of the Amazon, which made Talos frown again.

"They haven't joined *yet*," Koralia's voice was sharp-edged, "but that doesn't mean they haven't helped or that they won't in the future."

"Is that a promise?" Tisandros asked insistently.

She raised her eyebrows and drew herself up. Not that it made much effect against the pilot—he was pretty tall—but the glitter in her golden eyes did have him moving uneasily, backing off without exactly conceding.

"I would never promise for the Amazons," Koralia said, her gaze still boring into Tisandros. "But you should not so quickly dismiss their choice. Not everyone has the luxury of throwing everything away to join the rebellion." Her lips twisted in self-mocking. "Or the desperation," she added in a softer tone, dropping her gaze.

There was a very slight pressure in the air around the bridge, as if someone had pushed a wave of something toward them.

A sure sign that Mikon was agitated, his olympian abilities accidentally coming out.

"If we're *quite* finished playing 'question the new woman,'" the General's voice sliced through the tension, "I'd like to return to the discussion."

Koralia dropped back into herself, the glimpse of her Amazonian bearing gone. As if nothing had happened, she asked, "So what you're saying is that Minos doesn't care what his Labyrinth is doing to the trade or settlers in this region, no one can figure out what Poseidon is up to or what he's thinking, and neither Poseidon nor Minos seem to care one way or the other about what else is in this region?"

"That's about the size of it," Xantippos agreed. "But to be entirely accurate, we have reason to suspect that Minos is aware the main rebel leadership is headquartered here. And that he's more than happy to keep us locked up where we sit."

"We think he might be taking bribes to keep us here," Cleon volunteered, limping forward to join the discussion. He'd injured his ankle in the first mission to Krete. It didn't keep him from flying, but walking would be painful for another week or so. But at least he'd gotten out. Unlike...Talos cut that thought off.

Too many injuries, too many men giving everything for the cause. He withheld a sigh and looked back at the Amazon, who was staring at him, her face blank and eyes speculative. He raised his eyebrows as if to say, *What?*

"Krete is the gateway out of this sector. But this over here?" She pointed to the expanse of space that bordered the tiny rebel-held region and butted up against Krete and Poseidonian space. "This is no man's land," she said slowly. "Poseidon isn't as territorial as Jupiter, not when it comes to his eastern borders here. Remember when I said Minos is a little obsessed with making Krete great again or extending her greatness?"

He nodded, and so did the others around the bridge. Then his eyes dropped back to the map and he saw what she had seen.

"This isn't just defense of his system," he said, the words pouring out as it all came together in his head. "He's conquering! Starve out the systems here until they're happy to let him take over, and eventually send in others to get rid of us if he has to."

Talos wasn't the only one cursing Minos and Daedalus now.

"That's clever," Mikon said, his tone admiring. He didn't actually admire the hellish strategy, Talos knew; he just respected the tactical brilliance.

"But I still have a question."

The General gave Mikon a sideways smile. "When have you ever needed permission to ask?" Behind her back, she made a motion for Heirax to bring over what he was holding.

Talos had forgotten he was there. As everyone shifted to make room for the teenager to approach the General, he realized how stiff he was and stretched his neck to either side. *That's what I get for not sleeping enough at night.*

"The guns were hot the other day, and now they're still hot." Mikon shifted his weight from one foot to the other, cracking his knuckles as he frowned. "Maybe they're hot until he closes the Labyrinth net, like you said. But maybe not. Some of us"—he nodded toward Talos and Koralia—"are thinking it: did Icarus spook him? And if so, is he just going to keep them hot all the time now?" He looked at Koralia.

Talos had a moment to be annoyed that everyone kept looking to her for answers, but she shrugged, like she didn't know any more than they did.

Xantippos had been quiet through most of the discussion but he spoke up now. "Good question, but I'm not sure it matters."

"What do you mean?" Athanasia asked.

The kentauri general magnified Krete again and pointed to the boundaries of the Labyrinth. "They are extending the blockade into space, but they're also closing their planet in. Until it's closed in, their guns are going to take out anyone or anything that comes in. Maybe Icarus prompted them to keep them hot, maybe not. But any mission we send to Krete now is going to meet the same fate."

Everyone absorbed that for a few seconds, and Talos felt sick. He opened his mouth to say the thought that was reflected on Ianessa's face, but Mikon beat him to it.

"We *need* that Key," he said, and everyone murmured agreement.

The General looked at Koralia. "Any response from the palace?"

She shook her head.

"Xantippos." Athanasia stood up and retreated to the furthest corner of the bridge from the pilots.

For a few long moments, the two generals spoke quietly together, too low for Talos to hear and too far away for him to watch the kentauri's ears for clues. He could have asked Mikon to listen in, but he tried not to do that in front of anyone but Sunfires, which ruled this time out. Instead, he glanced around the bridge, focusing on his pilots.

Xuthos kept trying to catch the Amazon's eye to flirt with her, but she seemed completely absorbed in the com panel over which she bent. Cleon looked curious but tired. Tisandros just looked irritated, but he often did.

Mikon shuffled closer to Talos, moving behind him. He looked around and smiled up at the tall boy. Mikon's response was a half grimace that showed how exhausted he was.

"We're going," Athanasia announced as she and Xantippos rejoined them. "We'll take the chance that Ambrosia is still loyal and has what we need. We're going in at 0500 hours tomorrow morning. A small team will take a corvis ship to meet with Ambrosia while three wings of fighters hover, ready to distract the fortress."

It was a sound plan, and Talos immediately began figuring out how the fighters would execute it. The General usually left detail planning to her fleet leaders; her job was to coordinate everything. It worked out well, since only the best flew in her fleet—unlike other generals, she couldn't afford too many novices in her fighter wings. Not when hers was the foremost rebel fleet.

"Cleon will fly the corvis ship, and Xantippos will go because I want a senior officer there in case something goes wrong. I need a volunteer to go with them, someone who can ask Ariadne if she's heard from Daedalus."

"I will." Ianessa spun around in her chair.

"Hell no," Talos said, at the same time the General shook her head.

"Permission denied," she said firmly. "You're not healed enough for active duty."

"I'll go." Mikon stepped forward, his eyes gleaming with excitement.

Talos rolled his eyes. Young hothead. "I need you in a fighter," he argued, shooting the idea down. "And your Kretan is...piecemeal, to say the least." Brilliant scout and charmer that Mikon was, the team needed someone who could speak the language well. Talos could, of course, but he'd be in space, commanding the fighters. And somehow, they were shockingly low on base personnel who spoke fluent Kretan.

"Mine's good." Heirax came forward, waving his hand tentatively, like he knew he was about to be scolded.

Talos had forgotten he was there.

"Absolutely not," two voices said simultaneously: Ianessa and Xantippos.

"I can do it!" he insisted stubbornly. "You know I speak Kretan as well as a native! I've run messages before. I'm just meeting her and taking a Key from her. And asking her one question. How hard can it be?"

Talos stayed quiet. He didn't object to using the teenager, but he knew Athanasia tried not to send her teen orphans into dangerous situations, if she could help it. They were the next generation, and someone should be alive to carry on after them.

Ianessa leaned over to speak to Koralia, who was looking confused. Talos could just make out the whispered words. "His parents were observers on a planet east of here. He ran message drops for them all the time, between them and our rebel contacts. It's how we could establish our bases here in the first place, somewhere to regroup after the Thisios tragedy."

"Please, General," Heirax said, his hands gripping his belt, his knuckles white with determination.

She sighed. "You're so young, and we could be dealing with a traitor."

Abruptly, the teenager swung to face Talos. "How old were you when you started fighting?"

Exactly the question he didn't want to answer. He'd been fourteen, if you counted the random things he and Icarus had done before leaving Krete for good and joining the General. "Young," he admitted, wanting to laugh. The kid had guts.

"How old were you?" Heirax asked Mikon next.

"Answer that honestly, and I'll…" Ianessa hissed in Mikon's ear, and Talos ducked his head to hide his grin.

"Uhhhh…" Mikon looked between Ianessa and Talos. "Olympians age differently from humans," he said finally.

Clever boy.

"You?" Heirax demanded of Xuthos.

The pilot shrugged. "Seventeen or so."

Heirax narrowed his eyes and turned to Ianessa.

"Young," she responded without being asked.

"That is not fair," the teenager complained. "You all *know* you weren't that much older than me. General?" he asked Xantippos.

The man grinned. "Young."

Heirax's eyes darkened, but he bypassed General Athanasia and looked at Koralia. "You're an Amazon. How young were *you* when you started fighting?"

Eyes widening, she darted a quick look at Ianessa, who shrugged, and then at Talos himself. She looked so reluctant to answer that he just knew it was going to be some outrageously young age. But he said nothing either, and she finally looked at Athanasia.

"Well?" The General sighed, the word half expectant, half resigned. "Don't tell me you've forgotten how curious the galaxy is about Amazons. Go on, give them a look behind the scenes. Answer the boy."

Koralia swallowed. "I was…helping my commanders, er, run missions when I was nine." She flushed a little and hurried to add, "But like the olympians, Amazons have different conventions."

Xuthos whistled, long and admiring. "The Amazons let you run missions that young?"

She shrugged and stayed silent, taking a step back, distancing herself from the group. Her red-and-tawny-yellow hair fell forward over her face.

That was a clear evasion. What was she hiding now? Did Amazons really start their kids that young? And if so, did that mean she'd been *born* an Amazon, not inducted in? Was that why she wasn't disgraced for leaving?

But Heirax was speaking again, so Talos put the questions away for later.

"Am I not allowed to risk my life along with everyone else? I'm young, but I believe in this cause, I believe in what we're fighting for. It's just a simple meeting."

Silence fell. Talos kept his eyes on the General, who shook her head after a minute and chuckled.

Everyone relaxed.

Athanasia raised her eyebrows at the teen. "Very well. You do have just as much right to risk your life as the rest of us do. I have faith in your ability to do the job. You may go. But"—she held up one finger and pointed sternly at him—"you'll follow every single thing Xantippos says to the letter or you'll be barred from mission teams for the next six months."

He looked like he was barely restraining himself from cheering.

*Were we that crazy about it when we got started?* Talos wondered, but he already knew the answer. They'd been worse, racing through the galaxy like death wasn't real, stealing operatives from Jupiter's most inner circles, like the Hearthfires, and the galaxy's most notorious armies, like the Spartans.

The General stood up. "Heirax, Mikon, Tisandros, Cleon, you're dismissed. You'll be brought in for the team briefing at 0430 hours tomorrow. Get some sleep."

They left the bridge, Mikon hanging back until Talos looked at him and nodded. But his younger brother was watching the Amazon. Mikon had always had a fascination with Amazons, and it looked like this time would be no different.

Talos sighed and turned to his second, but Xuthos had crossed the room to stand next to Koralia.

Was everyone on base obsessed with the girl? One would've thought she was part siren, not Amazon.

*Actually. Maybe she is.* That would explain the draw. Talos lifted his head and looked at her over the map projection, considering her build. Naaaah, she was attractive enough but too round and full for a siren. They tended to be ethereally striking rather than pretty, long and thin with sharp angled features. Otherworldly, not solid, as the woman opposite him.

He was less and less sure that Koralia had anything to do with the traitor, but she was still hiding something...something *big*. Mikon—and Xuthos—would be better off staying away from her until he figured out what.

But since his youngest brother rarely did the sensible, logical thing, he probably wouldn't start now. And Xuthos? The day he didn't chase a pretty girl on base, Talos would personally check him into the infirmary for blood tests to see if he'd been poisoned or his mind had somehow been hacked.

"Let's keep it simple," the General was saying, and Talos dragged his mind back to the briefing. "Get in and get the Key. You pilots provide distraction. Zero hour is in eleven hours from now, people. Get some sleep."

"And hope like hell the gate's still open," he muttered, saluting her. "Audeamus."

"Hope...and pray," the General agreed emphatically. "Dismissed."

# CHAPTER 10

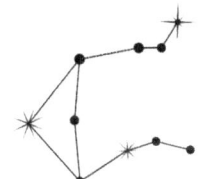

"**S**o."

Koralia looked up at Mikon, who was leaning against a wall in the hallway, and paused awkwardly. After that briefing, she felt like she needed an hour to herself, just her and the stars. But he looked like he wanted to talk to her, so she gave him a friendly nod.

"Standing guard or waiting for me?" She kept her tone light.

He grinned. "Both." Swinging around, he fell into step with her. "You knew Icarus?" The words burst from him as if he'd been waiting for a long time to say them.

"I did." She liked the Scythe, what little she'd seen of him so far, but she didn't really want to talk about Icarus again. Not right now. Not after that briefing.

But he rushed blithely on, seeming unaware of her reserve. "Wasn't he just the greatest?"

"Weeellll," she dragged the word out. "He did have a tendency to snicker in serious situations."

Mikon burst out laughing, his eyes bright. "You did know him well!" he exclaimed. "Ianessa was the one who finally broke him of that, her and Loxias. She's always been the big sister," he confided as they turned down another hallway leading to the communications rooms.

"The one to boss everyone when they need it?"

"Oh yes. I rarely need it, but Talos does. And Brygos. He needs it more than anyone and doesn't get enough of it." He glowered suddenly, and she couldn't tell if it was joking or real irritation. He cracked his knuckles, looking like he wanted to punch someone.

Okay, probably real irritation then.

"Every family has those, the responsible ones and the wild ones." It was a lame reply, but she wasn't sure what else to say to this kid who had gone from sunlight to thundercloud so swiftly.

"I wouldn't know." He snorted, and a smile chased the glower from his face as if it had never been there. "I'm an only child, or I was until Talos and Icarus found me and took me to the Sunfires."

"Olympians don't have a great track record with motherhood," she said, her lips twisting cynically. She should know.

He turned to stare at her, but they'd reached her destination, and she went into the communications room. Some way, somehow, she should be able to find a clue as to who had sent the second message, whether it was Daedalus or whether someone else was setting a trap.

She didn't expect for Mikon to follow, but he did, still staring at her as if he was trying to see inside her mind.

"You know some olympians," he said wonderingly, as if amazed and delighted at the same time.

He was such an odd mix of looking innocent and sounding old. Which, she supposed, was another side effect of having an olympian mother. It was the same for most olympian children, including her, though her fathers assured her that she'd never actually succeeded at the innocent look, despite her best efforts.

"How many?"

"What?" She looked up and froze at the intensity in his face. "What?" she repeated.

"How many olympians do you know?"

"I'm an Amazon," she reminded him. "There aren't many of their palaces I haven't been in over the years, from Juno's to Persephone's. Although she's actually a decent mother." Hades's son had thought so anyway.

What was it about this boy-man that made her ramble on? It wasn't that he looked safe—he didn't. So striking that he was actually beautiful...a mix of confidence, curiosity, and hard-edged anger...his emotions close to the surface, volatile and swift to change. There was nothing in any of that to make her feel more like talki—oh. *Ohhh.*

She smiled slowly. "You have just enough power to make people feel more comfortable about talking to you, don't you?" she asked, her hands resting on her hips.

He blinked at her for a few seconds and then burst into laughter again, high and bright. "I like you," he announced. "You're my new favorite person. Aside from Icarus and Ianessa, of course, and Talos. But please never tell him I actually like him. It'll go to his head."

She grinned and made the olympian symbol for locked lips. "You have my word."

He dropped down onto the floor, crossed his legs, and looked up at her. It was disconcerting, especially since she was trying to focus on analyzing the transmission.

Finally, she looked at him. "Is there something I can help you with?"

He shrugged. "I just like watching people work sometimes."

"Ah." She looked down at the message and applied another filter, hoping to narrow down what area of the palace had sent the transmission.

He sat there, watching, and she felt herself grow stiffer. *Relax, Kora. He isn't hurting anyone.* It had just been so long since anyone had seen her work.

Something beeped, and he pulled out his comdisk and glanced at the screen. "Oh." With legs as long as his, standing up should have looked ungainly, but he somehow made it look graceful.

"I, uh, have to get to the mess hall for supper." He looked sheepish. "Ianessa is bossy about that."

"Big sisters," she commiserated.

"Are you coming?" Bright-blue eyes searched hers, catching her gaze and holding it. Where Icarus's eyes had been blue topaz like the seas of his native Krete, Mikon's held a gray edge and an undershade of indigo, like the waters of Kythira. And she suddenly wondered what he looked like when he was truly furious.

She shook her head, pulling out of her musing. "Not yet."

His lips turned down, not quite pouting but close. "But you'll be at the radio tomorrow when we fly?"

"I wouldn't miss it for half the galaxy," she assured him.

His eyes narrowed even as he grinned. It was an olympian saying. He looked like he was about to ask another question—one she wasn't sure she'd want to answer—but to her relief, the radio crackled with an incoming report.

She shrugged apologetically, and he nodded, giving her a shy grin before leaving.

With a deep breath, she sank further into her chair, looking out the window for a moment while the report finished. The Sunfires she'd met so far were...surprising. Icarus had talked about them constantly, so she felt like she knew them, but really, she knew more *about* them. Things that had happened. What they'd done. Who was the wild one, the reckless one, the ruthless one, the kind one, the bossy one. Meeting them in person was, naturally, different.

Like Talos. She'd known that he was a suspicious person, but until that intense gaze of molten brown was turned on her, it hadn't felt completely real. Mikon she knew to be temperamental, but she hadn't expected him to be so friendly. Or Ianessa to be so interested in getting to know her.

It was a special kind of bittersweet ache, meeting someone's family after they were gone. Especially a family you already kind of liked and were prepared to love. But without the person who first made them all real to her, there was a hollowness, a throbbing reminder of what was missing.

It might not have hurt so much if Icarus hadn't felt larger than life. He was like an olympian in that respect. *Which just figures. Like I could fall for anyone else.*

Talos also reminded her strongly of Icarus in that respect, even shadowed and half on autopilot, like he had been since she met him. He and Icarus were so different in many ways, but some things they shared: a charisma that made them natural leaders, quick thinking, and an attitude of reaching toward life with both hands, grabbing hold and not letting go. Every time Talos walked into a room, she felt like wincing. Icarus had talked about him most of all, and it felt wrong to see him without Icarus—at either her side or his. *And*, she admitted to herself, *it hurts a little that he's so suspicious.* It would have hurt more if she hadn't known it was necessary. Talos hadn't gotten to be one of the leaders of the Kallistratus by being a trusting fool—and neither had Icarus, for that matter.

She smiled to herself, remembering how long it had taken her and Icarus to trust each other after they had first met. He'd been all golden smiles and edged banter until they'd worked out their partnership, which had started with her reporting events in the entire sector. Then her post had been changed and she'd reported to him on the Jupiterian armies sent to train with Ares, while he had told her the details of where they were being sent and how they were being used.

The memories rushed over her like a tidal wave. Broad shoulders, heavy eyebrows, flashing eyes that were as caustic as blue flame. A laugh that made you feel as if everything was all right in the world. Rough words that covered the depths of his affection for his family. Gentle, whispered words against her hair, lips hot on her skin...

She choked the thoughts off, forcing herself to breathe slowly against the gasping sobs that wanted to come. *In. Out. In. Out.*

No. Now was not the time to think about him. She couldn't go there without feeling like she was being ripped open again. It was too soon still.

It might always be too soon.

With a long sigh, she turned back to the radio in front of her.

"SOMETHING IS STILL MISSING," Koralia said half aloud to herself as she left the radio room an hour later and headed to the mess hall. She'd done everything she could think of to find out more about the message but had no more answers than at the beginning.

And no Amazonian or olympian knowledge that gave her any clue either. She'd never known the Kretan royal family well, aside from Ariadne, and they were more like acquaintances than anything approaching friends. The opposite, in fact. The world of olympian universities was cutthroat and wild and bizarre sometimes, and she'd met too many people there who she'd rather forget. Ariadne was one of them.

But everyone changed, or had the potential to change, and maybe the once-spoiled brat daughter of Minos had too. Without concrete evidence to the contrary, she couldn't urge the General to stop the mission tomorrow. But every time she thought of it, she itched to call in Amazon reinforcements, layer the planet with fighters, and protect the rebels.

That power wasn't hers anymore.

So she sighed and went back to pondering the message from Krete.

A few hallways away from her destination, Talos came out of an office and stopped abruptly when he saw her.

"Hi," she said cautiously. She didn't feel like an argument with him right now. Fortunately for her, he seemed tired too, even more shadowed than usual.

"Hi," he said, sounding just as cautious. "Any luck?"

"What?"

He pointed to the message she still held in her hand.

"Oh! No." She folded it up and shoved it into her pocket, frowning. "I'll try more later."

He nodded once, like he wasn't sure what to say next, so she motioned down the hallway. "I'm going to eat."

"Me too." He started walking toward the mess hall, and she fell into step with him.

It felt strange walking side by side, but it would have been awkward to trail behind him or speed up so she was ahead of him. He'd catch up to her quickly if she tried that anyway, so she kept pace silently.

As they approached, Mikon's voice floated through the hallways. "Okay, okay, listen. He just *looks* like the nice one of us. He's actually the worst of all the Sunfires. He never listens to orders, he's always trying to show us up, and he lies with a smile. Every story you've ever heard of female nymphs being calculating and deceptive? He beats them all hollow."

She glanced at Talos, wondering which of the Sunfires Mikon meant, but he had his head down as if the floor was fascinating.

Mikon continued, his voice smug, like he was thoroughly enjoying himself. "I don't know if any of you have ever been to Dythalsi, but it's a hub for producing energy. Power plants cover three-fourths of the planet's surface. When you break through the clouds of the atmosphere, you're met with a thick fog, and when you get below that, it's just gray buildings everywhere."

"Get to the point," someone called—Ianessa, she thought. The room was full of people-generated background noise, but it had sounded like the redhead's voice.

"I'm setting the stage," Mikon retorted over chuckles and snickers from his audience.

Koralia grinned. It was impossible not to like the youngest Sunfire.

"Our mission was simple." It sounded like Mikon clapped his hands together. "Go in, blow up this specific block of factories while it was night and no one was there, and get out. Talos must have gone over the plan five times on base and then again in space on our way there. So what does the *nice* brother do?" He snorted indignantly. "As soon as we dropped into the atmosphere, our coms went down. Dione had made a special effort to get us coms that wouldn't do that there, but they went down anyway, and when we broke through the fog, half the factory was already crackling with circuit shorters. That little thug had gone and done it all on his own and shorted out our coms intentionally!"

His voice was a combination of outrage, exasperation, and offense, and she laughed.

"What's so funny?" Talos turned toward her.

"His story." She motioned in the direction they were going.

"What?"

"Mikon's? About some time"—cold horror started to sweep over her shoulders as she realized what she'd just done, but she forced herself to finish —"when one of you upstaged him on a mission."

Talos was staring at her as if something had clicked into place for him, and she cursed herself violently.

Now she knew how flies felt when trapped by a spider.

"That's some good hearing." He grinned at her, but there didn't seem to be any malice or suspicion behind it. "No wonder the General has you on radio."

"Yeah. Uh, thanks."

Had she imagined his triumphantly knowing look? Maybe he was just distracted.

Either way, he kept going and so did she, turning the corner as Mikon's voice came closer and closer and the lit doorway of the mess hall loomed ahead.

She wanted to turn and see if Talos was watching her from the corner of his eyes, but she didn't dare give herself away any more. It was hard enough stifling her impulse to turn around right now and go to her quarters. Or the compulsion to stop him now and have it out—tell him who she was.

But no. She didn't want to go there yet, and he didn't need the distraction.

*Maybe you just don't want Icarus's best friend to be disappointed in you,* a tiny voice whispered. She ignored it, focusing again on the conversation in the mess hall. One Talos could also hear now, based on the way he was smiling.

"Like you didn't do the exact same thing half a dozen times," Ianessa was telling Mikon in the bored tone of an older sister.

"That's not the point!" Mikon protested. "The point is that everyone thinks he's the sweet one, but he's just as devious as the rest of us. And sometimes just dumb. Who picks Red Arrow as their codename anyway?"

Red Arrow—he had to be speaking of their second youngest brother, Brygos. Icarus had said he and Mikon fought a lot.

"Well, being able to do half the mission on his own *and* fritz our coms was pretty impressive," Ianessa said in a neutral tone.

"Don't defend him!" Mikon demanded, exasperated. "He went off orders! And caught it from Talos too, which served him right."

"Because you *never* do that," Ianessa said, sweetly malicious.

Koralia was almost at the doorway now, and Talos's comdisk sounded off: one long beep, then five chimes in quick succession, and then another long beep. He paused to pull it out and grinned at the screen.

Grateful to get away, she slipped into the brightly lit room. Twenty or twenty-five rebels sat around in various stages of eating, all of them watching Mikon, who stood in the center of the room.

He looked up, and his eyes sparkled at her. She nodded and proceeded to the side of the room to load a tray with food. When she was done, she didn't join Ianessa or Mikon, instead ducking into a chair at an empty table in one corner and spreading out the message scrip to look like she was busy. She didn't *feel* like eating, but then again, she hadn't felt like touching food in a week. If she could just get through the meal quickly, she could escape back to the radio room or her quarters and keep distracting herself with work…and hope Talos hadn't figured anything out from her slip-up.

Although…would it really be so bad if he figured out who she was?

What was he going to do anyway? He couldn't kick her off the base, and he would hardly turn the whole base against her—that wasn't his style, even if he did hate most olympians. And she had no proof that he did.

*Probably.*

"Red Arrow says he wouldn't have done it if you hadn't swept half the cliffs mission before we caught up to you," Talos said, sauntering into the room.

Koralia looked up quickly and then dropped her eyes. If he was going to look over toward her, she didn't want to see it.

"How does he know what I'm saying?" Mikon demanded. "Did you tell him?"

There was the sound of a scuffle, and she looked up again to see Mikon pulling away and Talos reaching up to ruffle his hair.

"'Course I didn't tell him," Talos said. "But he knows anyway." He headed to the other side of the room and started loading a tray with food.

There was a long pause while Mikon, still standing in one place, looked along the ceiling as if for cameras and then through his audience. Then he clapped a hand to his pocket, yanked out his comdisk, and flipped it on.

"That damned scum!" he exploded, eyes narrowed. "He bugged my com, didn't he? I'm gonna kill him, I'm gonna *kill* him."

"Keep that up and the General is going to revoke your swearing permit," Talos teased.

"I don't care. I'm gonna kill him!" Wheeling around, Mikon stalked out of the room, leaving Talos, Ianessa, and half the room laughing. Including Koralia.

Talos finished getting his food and joined Ianessa at her table. They bent their heads together, and whatever it was they were talking about looked serious.

Koralia intentionally didn't listen in.

Finishing her food quickly, she slipped back out of the mess hall and slumped onto a seat in an auxiliary radio room, which she'd picked because it would be empty all night. Exhaustion spread through her, and she really should go to bed, but...no. Between thinking about the Sunfires, seeing Icarus every time she laid down, and this message mystery, she wasn't likely to sleep for long anyway, and she could be more use here.

With a groan, she shifted to be more comfortable in her chair, dropping her head down on her crossed arms.

Maybe she'd just close her eyes for five minutes.

Or ten...

.✝.

"Koralia?"

She came awake at a touch on her shoulder and blinked groggily, lifting her head, almost bumping into someone bending over her. Startled, she scooted the chair back.

"Sorry, didn't mean to scare you." The blurry shape in front of her resolved into Ianessa, her hands down by her side in a non-confrontational posture.

"What are you doing in here?" Koralia asked, her voice thick with sleep. She cleared her throat a few times. "I thought you'd be asleep."

Ianessa sat down in a nearby chair. "I should be, but I can't." She stared out the window, not speaking for several minutes.

Just when Koralia had started to think they'd sit in silence until one of them awkwardly left, Ianessa sat up straight, clasping her hands in front of her.

"I keep thinking about his final flight," she whispered, staring at the radio panel in front of them. It was dark, but the artificial starlight filtering through the room cast her face in a soft gray glow. The look in her eyes was so familiar that Koralia ached. It was the same feeling she'd been trying to push away since the moment Talos had insisted on going back to Krete.

"They're going back there tomorrow. In just a few hours. And you can't stop wondering if...if it'll be different this time," she said, her voice so low it was almost lost.

Ianessa nodded slowly, and something glimmered on her cheek.

Tears.

What must it have felt like to hear his last words? The moment of his death had been bad enough for Koralia, and she was several sectors away when she felt it. Being the one to sit there and *hear* your foster brother dying on the other end of the line... That was an extra kind of hell. No wonder Ianessa was glad of a break from the radio room.

She stretched one hand out, sliding her chair closer to Ianessa, who took her hand and held it. "They aren't going to the base," she said. It was a far reach for comfort, but she felt like she should say something.

"I know." Ianessa was still whispering, and Koralia wondered if it was because she *couldn't* talk any louder. Sadness and fear did that to you sometimes. Weighed you down so heavily that you didn't have the energy to even talk.

"Talos will be careful," Koralia said, trying for a different kind of comfort. She didn't actually know that...except that as she said the words, she realized it was the truth. Hotheaded and impatient as Talos was, he was also fiercely protective of his family and his fleet, and he'd be especially careful after Icarus.

"He will." Ianessa spoke a little louder now, closer to a normal tone. "All the same," she smiled at Koralia, "I'm glad you'll be at the radio instead of me."

"So Talos and I can yell at each other when he thinks I've gotten his coordinates wrong or when I think he's about to do something stupid?" she said, and this time, her voice stayed light.

"Precisely."

They laughed together, and then, wrapped in the silence of understanding and sadness, they sat and watched the defense buoys blink their pattern of safety until the rest of the base began rousing for the mission.

# CHAPTER 11

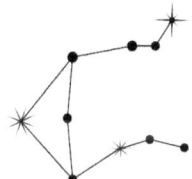

"I've double-checked everything, boss!" Mikon hollered from halfway across the bay full of fighters. "Can I go now?"

"Triple-check it!" Talos called back. "And no, you can't, and you already know that, so stop asking me stupid questions!"

"Yes, Mooooom." Mikon snapped an elaborate salute he'd picked up from some Jupiterian recruitment video and went back to work.

Talos knew Mikon only nagged him to cover his own impatience and nervousness, but there were days it was just annoying anyway. They had fifteen minutes still until they were supposed to leave, and every second was wearing on him. He wanted to be in the air, getting this done. The meeting was set, and Xantippos and Heirax and Cleon had left five minutes ago, since corvis ships were significantly slower than fighters. The fighters didn't even need to leave until the other ship was nearing the outer limits of rebel space. They'd catch up in no time.

"Commander?"

What could she want right *now*, right before departure? He turned to look below him and then slid down the nose of his fighter to land in front of the Amazon.

She held out a chip, like one that would augment a scanner. "Our techs worked something out that they thought might enhance the ability to scan the Labyrinth. I don't know if it'll work," she added hurriedly. "But I thought...maybe..."

"Thank you." He took it and dropped it into his jacket pocket, hoping it worked. Just in case the other part of the mission failed—

Nah, he wasn't even going to think like that. They'd get the Key.

Someone strode into the bay and stopped short. Then they whistled.

*Xuthos.*

"Come to see us off, Amazon?" the pilot asked, giving her a glance of approval before starting his pre-flight checks. "They do say that a kiss from a beautiful woman brings good luck on any flight."

She rolled her eyes, and Talos almost laughed at how unimpressed she looked.

"They also say it distracts one," she replied, "and I'd rather not run that risk."

"I'd be willing to run it, and since I'm the pilot, isn't my opinion what counts?"

"Hmmm." She shook her head. "Somehow, I don't think General Athanasia shares that perspective."

Talos had noticed before that where he and his siblings called Athanasia "the General," Koralia tended to say "Athanasia" or "General Athanasia." Maybe it had something to do with where and how she'd known the General before. Were Amazon warriors on a first-name basis with their generals?

"She doesn't have to know," Xuthos drawled.

But Koralia acted like she hadn't heard, her gaze back on Talos. "I just wanted to give you that," she said. "Fly safely, Commander." With a shrug, she went to leave.

"Wait," he said quietly. She paused, but didn't turn back around. "Please?" he added.

Slowly, she faced him and raised dark eyebrows. "Yes, Commander?"

Why had he asked her to stay back? He wasn't sure, except that it had something to do with what he'd realized last night and that he wanted this tense dance between them over with. He needed to know if she was the traitor. He needed to know how she'd known Icarus. Why she was here with the rebellion. He was no expert on Amazons, but he did know that few ever left them once they'd been sworn in.

"You're hiding something," he began.

Her eyes hardened. "Yes. I am." She clipped the words out.

He was doing this badly, but he was in too deep to stop. "It's hard to trust people you know are hiding something."

A blink was her response. "Hate to break it to you, Commander, but most people are hiding something. Can you tell me there's nothing *you're* hiding right now?"

This really wasn't going the way he'd planned, not that he'd actually planned it. And what was it with her use of his title? "No. I can't. But you're hiding something big. And I just wanted you to know that's why I'm—" He shrugged.

"Fighting with me all the time?" Her voice was mocking, but her expression wasn't.

"Yeah."

She looked at him for a moment and then took a step closer until only a few inches separated them.

This close, he could practically feel the leashed tension coiling around her, simmering behind her deep amber eyes.

"I *am* hiding something big. But I swear by Icarus I mean you and the rebellion no harm."

*By Icarus.* Had she just... She'd really just said that.

"Come back alive," she almost snapped at him and spun around, her back straight as she left the docking bay.

Well, that hadn't been helpful at all. If anything, it had made things worse.

She was attractive, he had to admit as he watched her walk away. That was part of the problem. Secretly, he enjoyed the rise he got out of her—loved having her attention focused on him. Icarus could date girls of all kinds, but Talos's type was specific and rare: he liked girls who gave as good as they got, who didn't fume over being questioned, who didn't take offense at being challenged, and who weren't intimidated by his position or his intensity. Who weren't after him for his name or authority.

Damn it. He couldn't let himself be distracted right now. *You're about to lead a mission. Focus.* He turned back to his fighter to complete his pre-flight check.

"Can you quit antagonizing her long enough to give me a shot, Commander?" Xuthos complained. "Unless..." He looked Talos over speculatively. "Unless this is your new method of flirting?"

"I'm not your competition," Talos said shortly as he climbed into his fighter and strapped in, double-checking all his instruments again. Xuthos could have the Amazon and welcome.

He inserted the chip into his scanner and waited for it to initialize. Everything showed green just as the countdown clock hit zero. Three wings of fighters soared into the blackness of space, Talos leaving last and flying above and slightly behind the wings, adjusting to the heavier drag on his ship. He preferred falcon fighters, but for this mission, all three wingleaders flew eagles.

Checking the formation of his wing and the position of the other two, he nodded in satisfaction and settled in for the the fifteen-minute flight to the outer boundaries of the Kretan system.

With nothing else to distract him, he kept going back to his conversation with the Amazon.

*I swear by Icarus.*

Whoever she was, she knew how much Icarus had meant to the rebellion. Not that it was hard to figure out, but she'd also known how much Icarus meant to *him* personally, unless he'd misunderstood the sharp intelligence in her eyes when she'd said it. Sure, most people in the rebellion knew he and Icarus were close, but the way she'd said it—it was like she knew there was no more sacred thing to swear by.

Who the hell was she? Since the first day he'd seen her, he'd felt like he should know.

Insanely good hearing marked her as olympian or mostly olympian. Amazonian could've meant she came from anywhere—they based their ranks more on skill than birth. But she seemed to have been with the Amazons for a long time, since childhood, so she was probably born to an Amazon. And a born Amazon could easily be part olympian, since the Amazons had close ties with more than one high-ranking olympian, especially Athina and Ares.

And he could only think of one olympian Amazon who would have known Icarus so well.

She couldn't be Melainis. No. That was unlikely. If Melainis had come on board, someone would have told him. In fact, he couldn't think of any reason she herself wouldn't have come straight to him if she'd arrived on station. She knew all about him, Icarus had made sure of that. And he'd never given her any reason to suspect she wouldn't have been welcomed with open arms.

He tried to remember what Melainis looked like. Talos had only seen one picture of her at some masquerade she and Icarus had attended, but he distinctly remembered dark hair and a proud tilt to her head and shoulders. Koralia didn't have those. She was flame-haired: dark-red and brown shading to warm-red and orange and then flaxen tips. And she didn't walk like an olympian. She walked like a warrior, wary but graceful, well-balanced and ready for action at any time. She didn't look like most olympians either—they tended to be all sharp features and arrogance, lazy smiles and smug eyebrows, carelessness wrapping around them like an invisible cloak.

She'd been so defensive over them going back to Krete. And if she wasn't the traitor—which he hadn't ruled out just yet—then that left some other reason. Like remembering how the last mission had ended. Did she think he didn't remember? Didn't care?

Icarus was *his* brother, great stardust.

If she *wasn't* Melainis, that left some other Amazon who had known his brother. Since Icarus had dated a grand total of three ex-Amazons, that still wasn't much to go on. But Talos was pretty sure one of the three was dead, and he didn't think the other two were actually in the Kallistratus, at least not anymore, so that narrowed it down a little.

*I should have thought of them sooner.* He was slipping up, and Icarus would have been disgusted. He'd look up the women when he got back to base.

But that still left Koralia. *She couldn't be a long-lost cousin or something, could she? Nah,* Icarus would have told him. *And she doesn't have the looks for it.* He and Icarus couldn't have looked more different, for all they were cousins, but still. Koralia was *too* different.

Maybe she was the daughter or sister of an olympian Icarus had crossed at some point. That was a long list, given fifteen years of fighting with the Kallistratus.

He still couldn't have said why he was so sure there was a woman and love involved in Icarus's death. After all, there were a dozen reasons why someone could have betrayed Icarus.

"Coming up on Krete now," Mikon said over the radio.

Talos took several deep breaths, centering himself in the here and now, the mission ahead of them. They only had one shot at this.

The mysteries would have to wait.

.✝.

"Coming up on Krete now."

Koralia acknowledged Mikon's transmission and marked the mission report at the side of the com screen.

In the new base, the radio room was next to the command bridge, so she could look across and see Athanasia waiting before the radar screen that told her the progress of the mission: red lines for the fighters, yellow for the diplomatic ship that carried the people set to retrieve the Key.

So much was riding on this mission.

"All right, flyboys and flygirls, listen up," Talos said, his voice coming clearly through the radio. "The last time you did this, it didn't end well. It's going to be different this time. Our mission is simple. My wing protects the rendezvous. Tisandros and Xuthos and their wings strafe the opening of the Labyrinth for two reasons: to distract the fortress and to test the current boundaries of the force field."

His voice turned hard. "If I see any of you going off on a personal mission of vengeance or anything else stupid, you'll be removed from the fleet imme-diately and not allowed back."

*Ouch.* Koralia tried not to grin. Hard, but fair. There was no room for personal heroics on team missions, and the Sunfires were legendary for their discipline—which obviously extended to the squads and fleets they commanded.

"Icarus took his fate in his hands when he came out here," Talos was saying now. "He knew the risks, and he paid the price to save most of you flying with us today. If he were here now, he'd tell you two things: focus on the mission. Complete the mission. And that's exactly what we're going to do."

He paused and then said, "For Icarus."

"For Icarus!" the rest of the pilots cheered.

"For Icarus," Athanasia echoed. "Keep your wits about you, pilots, and I'll see you soon."

"Ma'am!" they replied in unison.

"Cleon to Base, we can see the other ship now."

"Base to Cleon, roger." Koralia set the countdown timer. If the mission took longer than twenty minutes, the pilots had been instructed to pull the plug.

"Xuthos, go," Talos ordered.

For a few minutes, all she could hear was the sound of torpedoes being launched and the dull screeching and thudding as they slammed into the walls of the Labyrinth and detonated.

"This is heavy kickback!" Xuthos yelled. "Keep back further, guys."

The sounds of pilots strafing the Labyrinth continued for several minutes, until Koralia wanted to scream, hating that she didn't have visuals. What was happening with Xantippos's team?

A steady hum came from a screen to her left, and she swiveled to look at it. The scanner on Talos's fighter had kicked in, sending data about the Labyrinth.

The strangest data she'd ever seen. But maybe a tech would understand it.

"Hit them again, and this time try the red bombs," Xuthos was ordering his fighters.

The radio crackled for a few seconds, there was a buzz, and then the channel cleared with a click. "Cleon to Base, we're clear now and we have the Key."

A cheer went up from the fighters and the personnel on the bridge.

"Base to Cleon," Koralia said, relieved, "acknowledged." She looked over at Athanasia, who smiled and nodded.

"Bring them home."

"Base to all units. Good job. Get back here, everyone."

"Roger, Base," Talos said. "Tisandros, drop your wing around the corvis and stay there all the way back to base. Xuthos, form up to—"

"Commander, there's something weird happening!" Mikon exclaimed.

Koralia clenched her hands at the alarm in his voice, tension spiking through her. *Get back. Get away from Krete and get back here.* She leaned closer to the radio, trying to hear. Around the bridge, everyone froze, listening.

"Is that...glowing letters?" Talos asked. "Galactic Common letters?"

"That's what it looks like. And it's...Icarus's name!" Mikon yelled, surprise crackling through the words.

Shivers ran over Koralia's neck and down her back, straight to her wrists. She gripped the side of the com station to still her shaking. *Icarus's name?*

There was a mutter from Talos that she didn't catch, and then he said, "Where?"

"On the walls of the Labyrinth."

"Xuthos, take my wing back with yours," Talos ordered. "General, I'm breaking off to investigate. Mikon, stay on my tail."

"Commander!" Athanasia snapped. "Focus on the mission. We have the Key."

Koralia took a deep breath. *No, General.* They couldn't come back now. They needed to know what was happening.

"I *am* focusing, General," Talos said, "but part of this is getting more information about the Labyrinth, right? This is weird, and I'm going in for a closer look."

"Is it really worth the risk?" Athanasia asked.

"It's Icarus's name, General."

There was no arguing with that, so Athanasia sighed in resignation. "Be careful."

"Always, General."

Athanasia snorted, but Koralia didn't even grin, too focused on the radio.

She stared at the mission screen as the red dots marking the two fighters moved closer and closer to the purple line of the Labyrinth. The other group of red and yellow dots was well clear of Krete now, except for one wing that seemed to be moving awfully slowly, its leader hanging back.

Xuthos, based on the fighter signature, waiting for his captain.

"It's like water," Mikon said, fascinated. His voice was distant, like he was speaking through interference. "Like waves."

"There's an opening," Talos said. "Down and left. Stay on me."

Koralia flipped every clearing switch on the radio, but the last words were barely distinguishable.

"Commander, this is Base. I'm losing you." She waited. The red dots were were on the purple line now. The radio started to crackle. Icarus's name pounded over and and over in her head.

"Commander Talos!" Koralia kept her voice calm. "I can't hear you. Say again?"

"...blue and green...like seaweed..." The words were drowned out by white noise.

*No. Not again.* Krete couldn't take more Sunfires from them. Swiftly, she twisted all the dials to maximum reach and disengaged every lesser security protocol that could be blocking the signals.

"Talos? Mikon?" she tried.

Silence.

She spared a quick glance for the rest of the bridge. Athanasia looked grim, and Ianessa was staring, white-faced, at the map from which the two red dots had just disappeared.

*Talos, you stubborn idiot, don't make us lose you too.*

"Talos, report," she said again.

Still nothing.

"Damnation and thunderfire, Talos, if you don't report right *now*..."

And then even the static faded as the radio went dead.

# CHAPTER 12

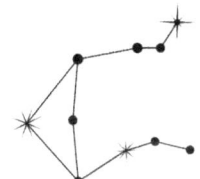

I

t's like jelly, was Talos's first thought as his fighter lightly bounced off a
wall to his left. He flashed his lights, signaling to Mikon to hold up, and
they hovered, looking around. As far as he could see in every direction,
force fields shimmered in lines and waves. From the outside, the Labyrinth
looked like white marble veined with green and blue, but only if you could get
parallel to it at just the right angle to look across it. Inside, it was like…hedges
and walls on the bottom of the ocean. The waves of the force fields undulated
with seaweed-like lines, and what looked like coral stuck up at corners of it.
Buoys maybe? Signal lights? And straight ahead of them, Icarus's name
painted in red on one of the force fields.

What the hell did it mean?

As they watched, one of the force fields shifted. Talos swung his fighter up
to avoid the wave coming toward them.

*Mikon.* He slewed around in his seat, hunting for his little brother. There,
right behind him; he was safe for now.

Talos would rather not have brought him in, but Mikon was the best of the
best when it came to investigation. Plus, he needed a wingman, and they
knew each other better than any other pilots on base. The rebellion won over
him wanting to be a protective older brother.

As they stared, the letters changed, glowing yellow now, making the
outline of a bull's head.

The radio, which had been dead since they'd crossed into the Labyrinth, flared to life with a squeal so loud that Talos instinctively twisted his head sideways and hunched down, as if his shoulders could protect his ears.

He hit the switch to log the incoming transmission, but didn't stop to read it because the symbol was changing again, this time to purple letters scrawled in an unsteady hand, this time in the Kretan language.

**Follow. The. String.**

**Safety.**

*String, what string?*

He looked around, hunting high and low. Nowhere did he see a string or anything that even resembled one.

Then Mikon's fighter bumped ever so slightly into his. For a minute, he thought it was unintentional, but it happened again.

Twice was a message. There was something his brother wanted him to see, and he had to look down to find it.

Angling the nose of the eagle ship down, he searched the force fields below them.

*There.* A purple line pulsed off to their right, going in the direction of the exit.

Before he could figure out what was the safest way to turn around, Mikon's fighter dove in front of him, flipped upside down, and rolled sideways so he was upright, facing the opposite direction.

Fancy flying, yes, but also the best maneuver to turn around in such a tight space without slamming into the force fields again. They'd survived one brush with them. Who knew if the next would be so forgiving?

Talos copied the dive and roll, bringing his ship up behind Mikon. New letters appeared in front of them, still glowing, still unsteady but badly spelled now and even more crooked, as if the person wasn't used to writing. He squinted, trying to read it.

**Ggo. Fsast.**

*Go. Fast.*

Mikon's ship rocketed away at full speed, and Talos followed. The purple pulses grew fainter for a minute and then stronger. Force fields shifted toward and then away from them as they swung through hairpin turns, down halls, and up slopes.

It was the strangest flight he'd ever been on.

Then the purple line disappeared.

Mikon hovered in midair, having come to an abrupt stop, which took real skill at the controls. He'd improved since the last time they'd been on base together.

The line blinked back on, and they started flying again, twisting through a long tunnel of only green and then through a large circular space of blue.

The light went out again, and Mikon's fighter slowed, but Talos had seen a break in the force fields rushing toward them and flew faster—dangerously fast—as he slipped under Mikon and streaked for the exit. His brother would follow.

Then they were in open space and much closer to the planet of Krete than when they'd entered the Labyrinth. Alarms blared over their sensors as Krete's defenses engaged, firing straight at them. But they were going too fast and were away before the guns had even gotten off five shots.

"That was so much fun!" Mikon was grinning, waving at him through the windows in the fighters.

Talos's head snapped back at the sound. The radios were back in working order, and the yell had come through loud and clear. Too loud.

"Talos? Mikon? Come in, this is Base, repeat, come in." The voice sounded calm but edged with concern. "Where are you? We've been trying to reach you for twenty minutes."

*Koralia.*

He almost felt sorry for scaring her, but not quite. "Talos to Base, we're out, we've got news, we're coming home."

"Good," a new voice snarled over the radio: Ianessa. "Because I'm going to kill you as soon as you get back here."

"Not fair!" Mikon protested. "We got out, we're safe, we're coming home. You aren't supposed to kill us unless we're not safe."

"I'm going to kill you for scaring the ever-shining-stardust out of us," she snapped.

"And I'm not sure I'm going to stop her," the General said. "So you'd better make sure your story is a good one."

Talos grinned as they cleared the Kretan system. Two wings of fighters appeared, hovering in space. Xuthos's...and the rest of Talos's own wing.

"I thought I told you to go back to base?" he said into his radio, close enough now to see Xuthos.

His new second snorted and flipped him off. "Someone had to drag your sorry ass back to base if you cracked up."

Talos snorted, and together, they streaked home.

This would be one hell of a debrief.

✝

ATHANASIA KEPT her eyes on a screen in front of her, trying not to show her staff how worried she'd been when the Sunfires had disappeared. One of these days, Talos's luck was going to run out. She just hoped that when it did, it was many years from now.

The bridge doors slid open, and Xantippos, Cleon, and Heirax stepped in. Before she could speak, footsteps raced down the hall, and Talos and Mikon slid in with the other wing commanders.

"You three"—she pointed at Talos, Mikon, and Xuthos—"stand over there." She indicated a corner with a stern look. She wasn't actually going to punish them, but it would do them good to sweat it out for a few minutes. It was one of the few ways she could keep any kind of order with these hotheads.

"And when she gets done with you, I'm going to choke you," Ianessa fumed under her breath, and Athanasia smiled. Ianessa would take care of making sure Talos and Mikon knew how scared they'd been.

"Heirax, well done." Athanasia held out her arms to the teen. He came to her quickly and bent to hug her. Then he stepped back and held out his hand. A silver disk, its case embossed in blue, rested there.

"It's the Key! We've got it now." He bounced on his feet with excitement.

"I've checked it," Xantippos confirmed before Athanasia could ask. "No obvious traps."

"The *Key*, General," Heirax repeated, his eyes glowing.

"Thanks to all of you brave souls." She smiled at Xantippos and then Cleon before squeezing the teen's shoulder.

Heirax offered her the disk again, but she shook her head. "Why don't you do the honors?" She led him to an empty data station and stood aside, motioning for him to insert it.

There was a rustle around the room as Koralia, Ianessa, and the command staff crowded around the terminal, and the pilots in the corner rearranged themselves so they could also see. It was a testament to their discipline that they didn't move from where she'd directed them to stand.

Almost reverently, Heirax removed the silver data disk and inserted it into the reader slot on the station. It whirred, paused, whirred again, and the screen started to flicker. Everyone leaned closer, waiting for the first glimpse of the map that was their ticket to breaking Krete's stranglehold on this sector of space.

The screen buzzed a few times, black crossed with lines of white, then silver and yellow, and then green as the station initialized the disk and prepared to load it. Green lines changed to blue, and the screen darkened again, pulling up the information.

Athanasia smiled to herself, eyes gleaming at the thought of the map to the force fields that had frustrated them for nearly two months. She could hear her staff holding their breath like wire stretched tightly...

The data station exploded, sending plastiflex flying from the screens with a loud screech.

Instinctively, Athanasia ducked and pulled Heirax behind her, shielding him from the worst of the mess. When shards and control chips stopped flying, she lifted her head, looking behind her for the personnel who had been standing there.

"Everyone all right? Anyone injured?"

Xantippos had covered Ianessa, and Cleon and Koralia appeared to have pulled other personnel away, so no one had been badly hit. Talos, Mikon, and Xuthos had leaped across the bridge and were now checking people over, guiding them to step out of the mess without cutting themselves.

The General stared at the smoking wreck of the data terminal and tried not to sigh out loud. So it had been a trap after all.

One more hope gone. At least the explosion didn't seem to have affected the rest of the bridge stations.

Someone's growl drew her attention back to her people, all of whom were now clear of the mess. Talos and Mikon looked positively murderous, and Heirax seemed about to burst into tears.

"Well. That's that," she said, with an encouraging smile for the teenager. "Back to the drawing board. At least we know who our traitor is now."

"I don't understand." Heirax sounded very young and lost. "I'm sorry, General. I failed."

"*You* didn't fail." Talos seethed. "Those treacherous Kretan bastards are at fault for this, and this time, *this time*, they will pay. There's no way this could be called collateral damage."

"Language." Athanasia frowned at him. There was a time and a place for swearing, and right now when she was trying to keep control of the bridge personnel wasn't it.

"But he's right," she added, mustering a smile for Heirax. "You didn't fail. We're closer now than we were, because we have information now that we didn't have then." Even if it didn't *feel* like they were any closer.

*First Icarus, now Ambrosia or Ariadne or whoever she was.* That reminded her...she looked around for Koralia. The girl was standing behind Heirax, one hand on his shoulder.

"And don't you blame yourself either, Koralia, or you, Ianessa. Neither of you could have predicted this." Shaking her head, Athanasia backed carefully out of the mess of plastiflex and control panels. "It was a trap. I'm just glad everyone is safe."

"We have one possible option left." Talos distanced himself from Ianessa.

So whatever he was going to say was probably going to get him smacked.

"When we were in the Labyrinth, we both received a transmission." He jerked his thumb in the direction of Mikon. "It's coded. But maybe..." He sighed and rubbed his forehead. "Maybe it'll have some answer. It could be another trap, but what if it's not? We were guided out, so maybe whoever did that... Well, we need to decode it right away. But the encryption looks high. We'll probably need Dione." Already he was thinking ahead to their next step, making plans before everyone else had fully absorbed the mess on the bridge.

"Yes, I want to hear all about this," Athanasia said, making her way toward him. And she needed to ask Heirax whether Ambrosia had said anything about Daedalus. "But first, let's get everyone out of here."

The techs stayed to clean up while her command staff filed out, their steps heavy through the gloom that had settled over them. So only a few people were left in the room when the sound of choking filled the bridge.

Athanasia turned just in time to see Heirax and Xantippos collapse, bodies convulsing as their faces turned blue and froth bubbled from their lips.

✝

IF ATHANASIA COULD BE SAID to have a gift for anything besides organization and rebellion, it was instinctively knowing when something would be unsuccessful.

Millions of people all over the galaxy thought the Kallistratus Rebellion was doomed to failure, that it would eventually burn itself away and die out. Athanasia knew better.

Most of the fledgling rebellion had looked at her in horror when she'd allowed Icarus and Talos to join them and even go out recruiting. They said it was futile, that there was no way two teenagers could properly recruit for a war everyone knew was going to take years. They were convinced the boys would get themselves killed—at best—and get all the other rebels killed—at worst. But Athanasia had seen in Icarus and Talos the perfect pair to inspire hearts and minds across the galaxy.

Several years later, when she had proposed splitting up the Sunfires and sending them as companions to the highest-ranked generals in the rebellion, her advisors had told her it was pointless, that the Sunfires wouldn't be able to fight well that far away from each other and that their effectiveness was because of their close unity. Athanasia had disagreed. And she'd been right, again.

And right now, she knew the fight for Heirax's life was in vain. On the battlefield, she would already have called it and sent the doctor to save someone they could still save. But they weren't on an active battlefield, and she couldn't bring herself to say the words any more than the doctor seemed able to stop working over the still-shaking body of the boy.

The teenager was going to die. Whatever poison he'd been given, it was spreading too fast. His youth was no advantage now, or maybe it was his human biology—nothing was helping.

Xantippos would be okay, the doctors thought, and that at least was good news, not just because he was a friend but because she needed the kentauri general on a strategic and practical level.

Heirax had barely said three words since he'd been brought here an hour ago, convulsing and calling out for Athanasia. He'd opened his eyes a few times, searching for her face and relaxing when he saw it. So she stayed, even though she needed to start containing the aftermath soon and decide their next move.

But she could afford a few minutes to stay with a dying boy. And even if she couldn't, she would have anyway. Anything she could do to make it easier for him.

The doctor's gaze met hers, and she saw resignation there before he went back to making Heirax as comfortable as possible.

Icarus's death she could not have predicted. No one could have. That's part of why it had hit so hard. But as much as anyone *could* prepare for unexpected deaths in war, they all *had*, so his death was still easier than this.

For all his height and eagerness, Heirax was only fifteen. The same age Talos and Icarus had been when they'd started, true, but he'd always seemed younger. Maybe it was his face, which looked twelve. Or the shy energy in his eyes. Or the sense of loss he carried under every smile.

So young, and she'd let him go to his death. It had been necessary, but that didn't make it any less painful.

Athanasia felt the moment he died. His hand was already limp in hers, but she felt the life leave him, the soul going on to wherever souls went after death.

Ianessa slipped in right then, looking around for an update. Athanasia didn't look up, but from the corner of her eye, she saw the doctor shake his head, and the Sunfire left again. She would carry the news to the others in the base, at least the important personnel.

*Only the dead have seen the end of war,* a philosopher said once. It was one of those sayings that seemed simplistic and obvious at the same time, even inane, but took on meaning the more you thought about it.

Icarus and Heirax knew peace now. Not that Icarus would enjoy that. He was born to battle as much as to breathing. But Heirax? Wherever he was, whatever afterlife existed, she hoped he was laughing with his parents again and enjoying the end of his war.

Athanasia held the teen's hand until it grew cold. Then she crossed his arms over his chest, kissed his brow, and turned to walk out of the medbay.

She had another hero to bury.

✝

KORALIA STARED at the wall outside the medical chambers, mindlessly tapping signal codes on her thigh. Athanasia hadn't yet left the bedsides of Heirax and Xantippos. Koralia and Ianessa had stayed close, passing orders from the General to techs and other personnel. Rumor had it they might be moving base again, in case Krete—or whoever was out for their blood—now had their precise location.

Talos had taken a team of techs and pilots to comb over all the fighters for anything that might have been planted on them in the battle. He'd reported an hour ago that the ships were all clean, but it was impossible to tell if the corvis ship had been bugged or had poison planted anywhere else on it. Regretfully, Athanasia had given the order to eliminate the diplomatic ship. Talos and Xuthos had towed it out into space and blown it up, returning just a few minutes ago.

Ianessa slipped out of the medbay, her face gray with exhaustion and pain.

"Heirax?" Koralia asked.

Ianessa shook her head, tears gathering in the corner of her eyes. She blinked them away and cleared her throat. "General Xantippos will probably make it. The doctors still aren't sure what the poison was, but they're working on it. The most anyone can say for sure is that it was on the disk. They were the only people to handle it, aside from the Kretan contact."

"At least General Athanasia didn't touch it," Koralia said. She felt cold-hearted saying it, but facts were facts and to lose Athanasia would have been catastrophic.

"Thank every benign spirit there is," Ianessa agreed sincerely. "The General asked Xantippos about Daedalus. Ambrosia apparently swore she hadn't heard from him." She rubbed one hand over the back of her neck, trying to ease out knots. "I need to make sure Mikon doesn't kill anyone or spontaneously combust. Can you find Talos and update him?"

"I'm not..." Koralia started to say. *I'm not sure you want me to do that; this is Talos and me we're talking about.* But the exhaustion on Ianessa's face had her nodding. "Go chill Mikon. I've got Talos." It was the least she could do.

"Thank you. And tell him to come up calmly. I don't need him riling Mikon back up."

"I'll tell him."

*And hope he listens.*

# CHAPTER 13

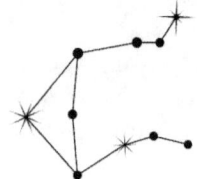

Walking the gray halls toward the docking bays, Koralia tried to shake off the weight of Heirax's death and the guilt that nagged at her stomach. This was war, and there was no room for "if only." You took the hand dealt and you did your best. If your best wasn't good enough, the victors wrote history and you mouldered in dust.

And that she would fight against, for the rebellion. For Icarus. And now for Heirax.

She found Talos alone in a smaller docking bay, slumped on the floor, his arms resting on his knees as he stared at his fighter. Trying for unobtrusive and knowing she failed, she sat down too, not close enough to crowd him but not so far away that they couldn't talk.

"Well?" he said, weariness heavy in his voice.

"Xantippos will live, they think. Heirax…didn't."

He swore softly, and she heartily agreed.

"Ianessa is with Mikon now and said to please be calm when you come up."

He nodded, one sharp downward movement of his head, and she stood to leave.

"Don't go yet," he said, the words no more than a whisper.

He wasn't talking to her, was he? She looked around, but no one else was in sight. Maybe he was talking to himself or speaking of Heirax—a natural expression of grief or frustration or something.

She kept going, heading toward the door.

"Melainis."

The name stopped her in her tracks like a hand around her throat cutting off her breath. Dread slowing her, she turned around. He'd stood up and was looking at her in a way far different than ever before. Appraising, understanding, his eyes roamed her face like he was reading something there.

"It is you, isn't it?"

She nodded, her gaze not leaving his, waiting for an outburst of...whatever he was feeling now.

A faint smile full of pain and remembrance flitted over his face and then was gone. "You're not what I expected," he said, his gaze traveling to her hair and back to her face.

"You aren't either."

He nodded. They both started to speak at the same time, but he stopped and motioned for her to go first.

"I'm sorry. I should have told you," she admitted. However he'd acted when he met her, she should have trusted what she knew of him from Icarus. She should have been a little less proud and a little less eager to prove herself and just been honest.

"Would've saved us both some headache," he agreed. "But I know why you didn't. And I should've seen it sooner."

The tightness in her chest and throat began to ease. "We're not exactly at full brilliance right now," she tried to joke.

"Yeah," he said, and the weight of worlds hung in the single word. "That we aren't."

There was so much pain and grief in his voice that she reached out and squeezed his shoulder. He covered her hand with both of his, and then pulled her closer until she was in front of him and he was gathering her into a hug, holding her tightly.

Koralia leaned against him and wrapped her arms around him, feeling the jagged hole that bled Icarus inside of him as surely as it did her. He held her like he understood everything she didn't say about the golden-haired hotshot they had both loved.

She knew part of Talos's story. Abused as a child by his own mother, then constantly belittled and mocked by Daedalus out of jealousy for his own son. Icarus had been the one to shield Talos and then take him away from Daedalus and Krete. Icarus had never needed to say anything for her to understand how tight the cousins were. Almost like twins.

Icarus hadn't just taken Koralia's heart with him when he died, he'd taken Talos's too, in a different but no less painful way.

Talos's shoulders lifted and fell as he breathed deeply before he stepped back. A smile was his only acknowledgement that he was grateful for the hug.

He let go of her and held out his hand formally. "I usually hate the whole "let's start over" thing. I'd rather learn and move on than pretend to start over. So let's just go forward better."

"I'm on board with that," she said, taking his hand.

He squeezed hers. "I'm Talos Sunfire."

"The man Icarus loved most in the galaxy," she added softly. "And I'm Koralia Nikephoros, known to most people by a name I'd rather not say, Koralia to the Amazons, and Melainis to Icarus and the rebellion."

"His black swan." Talos's grip on her hand tightened for a moment, she thought in sympathy. "The woman he loved most in all the galaxy. And a full-blooded olympian."

He'd said the last words so low that any human in close hearing range wouldn't have been able to hear them.

"Yes. Is that going to be a problem?" Her eyes narrowed in challenge. This was the real test. Accepting her for Icarus's sake, she'd always expected. But could he accept her and who she was on her own merit?

"No. Not for me. Have you *met* Mikon? If olympian prejudice existed in any of us, Icarus beat it out of us...and then that little brat charmed out whatever was left."

She couldn't help smiling. "I can see that."

His hands came up to clasp her shoulders. "Welcome to the Sunfires."

That was too much, and she had to swallow several times before she could whisper, "Thank you."

He dropped his hands and turned away for a minute. She thought he too was mastering himself. When he turned back, he looked like the Talos she had first met: hard, shadowed, in control of himself.

"You look different," he observed.

"I do?"

"Hmmhm. Your hair." He nodded toward it.

She put one hand up to it. "Oh! Amazon death custom. Usually they dye it in shades of blue, but I thought he would..."

"He would've," Talos agreed. "He would definitely have approved."

Nodding, she shoved hair back from her face, eyes narrowing. "Tell me we're going to find whoever did this—Icarus and Heirax and all of it."

His expression filled with dark promise. "We're going to annihilate them."

That wasn't exactly the answer for which she'd been hoping, but it would do. Ariadne or not, whoever had just poisoned their people had attacked them. It was tantamount to a declaration of war, and the rebellion did not back down from bullies.

If they wanted a fight, the Kallistratus would give them one.

✝

KORALIA. Melainis. The love of Icarus's life.

Talos was still trying to absorb it. He really should have seen it before, but that wasn't what was still fitting together in his head. It was all the pieces that Icarus had told him now meshing with all the pieces he'd already seen for himself.

Plus the little problem of his tiny attraction to her. That was the easiest thing to handle. Dead or not, she was still Icarus's, so he stifled the attraction ruthlessly. Betray his brother he would not.

"I need something to eat," he told her, and she nodded, walking alongside him as they went to leave the bay.

"I hope you know this means I won't stop arguing with you," she said tentatively.

He snorted. "Wouldn't want you to. And Icarus..."

"Icarus wouldn't want me to either," she agreed. "I know."

"I like a girl who can give as good as she gets." He almost kicked himself, but after all, there was nothing wrong with the word *like*.

He went to switch off the lights but paused. Someone was coming in, stomping and swearing.

Mikon burst through the door and carefully closed it behind him so it didn't slam. Then he kicked viciously at the nearest pile of crates, sending them flying to crash into others.

"Damned damn Kretans," he said, and Talos would have laughed if he hadn't been worried. Mikon only fell back on standard swear words when he was so furious he could hardly think. Usually, he used olympian profanity or invented his own.

As enraged as he was, it could take him a few minutes to notice them, so Talos stepped into his path, forcing Mikon to look up and see him.

He stopped abruptly, focusing on his brother with the intensity of a laser. "He's dead," he said in a half-strangled, husky tone. "He's dead, Tal."

"I know," Talos said, trying for a neutral tone. If he didn't sound sad enough, Mikon could go over the edge of fury, but if he sounded too sad, Mikon might break down and scream. Neither was a good option at the moment, not with him trembling on the brink of losing his self-control. Violent rages had been the only way his mother ever listened to him, and they still came forcefully to his surface in times of great emotion. They never ended well, and sometimes Mikon needed a helping hand to stay level.

"Why must peace come at so great a cost?" Mikon asked, anguish bleeding through every word. "Death is such a high price to pay."

"And yet," Koralia whispered, "they paid it willingly, and to take that from them is to rob them of their joy in sacrificing themselves to make a better world."

Mikon turned toward her, his mouth opening and closing as he searched for words. "I hate it," he said at last. "I hate death."

Koralia held out both hands to him, palms up, a mute invitation.

*Be careful!* Talos wanted to yell, but she looked like she knew what she was doing.

*After all, she* is *olympian*, he reminded himself. If anyone understood volatile tempers and rages, she probably did.

Mikon took her hands gently, his long fingers swallowing hers.

"I think you hate loss more than the death," she said. "Don't you? It is not death itself, it's the absence they leave behind."

Staring at her for a long minute, Mikon thought through that. His hands tightened on hers, and Talos started forward, ready to caution him and pull him back, but Mikon turned his head and smiled. "I'm okay," he told Talos. "I'm me again."

He slid his arms around Mikon, hugging him hard, partly for comfort, partly to feel for sure that the rage had calmed again.

It had, and Mikon rested his head back against Talos's but didn't let go of Koralia's hands.

"I hate loss then," he said with a huff of resignation. "It's all bloody...awful."

"Yes." It looked like Koralia was returning the pressure of his hands. "Yes, it is."

As if a sudden thought had occurred to him, Mikon pulled away from both of them and looked from one to the other. "Why were you two in here together? Were you lecturing him?" His eyes shifted to Koralia, and Talos wanted to groan.

"No, I was...giving him the news," she said cautiously.

"Oh." For a minute, Talos thought his fury was coming back, and then Mikon's shoulders slumped.

He needed a distraction until the rage was quiet enough that he could be sad without being in danger of exploding. Talos looked at Koralia over his brother's shoulder. He didn't dare even mouth his question silently. Even if she could lip-read, Mikon's hearing was good enough that he would be able to tell what Talos was doing, and if her answer was no, it could set off the very mood he was trying to help.

So he raised his eyebrows and motioned toward Mikon.

And she nodded in answer.

Taking a step back, Mikon scowled first at him and then her, his eyebrows low. "What are you talking about?"

"Me." Koralia pointed to herself. "I'm…I have something to tell you."

He leaned forward, as eager as a child. "What?"

"I'm…"

She hesitated again and looked at Talos, but he didn't have any more idea of what to say than she did. It was probably better to just get it done and over with.

"She's Melainis," he said quickly, his tone blunt.

Mikon blinked and then folded his arms over his chest, tilting his head to study Koralia like he hadn't heard correctly. "She's who?"

"Icarus's Melainis?" Talos tried again. Had Mikon forgotten the name of the woman Icarus had been in love with for over a year?

"Ic—" Mikon choked the word off and whipped around to stare at Talos and then back at Koralia. He advanced on her, studying her with such intensity that Talos wondered how she could stand so quietly under it.

"You're Melainis? *Icarus's* Melainis?"

She nodded.

Mikon threw back his head and laughed.

Talos grinned, relaxing. If Mikon was laughing, he was well on his way back to full control.

"You're her!" he gasped, when he stopped laughing. "Oh my stars. You're her. Oh, wait until I…wait a minute. I have to tell them. Brygos and Kynna will never never top this. Even Siromos won't." He yanked out his comdisk and spun it, locked a combination in, and began furiously typing.

Confused, Koralia looked at Talos for an explanation.

He obliged, unable to stop grinning. Mikon was right: the other Sunfires wouldn't top this for a long time, and it would be hilarious for months. "He got to meet you first. He'll crow over them for a long time. This is a triumph to crown all triumphs."

"Really? But it was pure chance."

Snorting, he shook his head. She had a lot to learn about Sunfires. "Doesn't matter. That's how this works."

Mikon finished typing, dropped the comdisk back into his pocket, and flung his arms around Koralia in a hug. Then, keeping one arm around her shoulder, he pulled her down to sit on one of the crates he had just kicked over. "We're going to be great friends," he announced. "Holy sh—" He choked the curse off, and Talos knew another moment of worry. What had alarmed Mikon now?

But Mikon just leaned over to stare into her eyes. "This means...you're *olympian*, aren't you? You're full olympian."

And she smiled then, brighter than Talos had ever seen, understanding blazing through the dust and grime that still clung to her skin. "Yes."

Mikon threw his arms around her again, hugging her harder than before. When he pulled back, his face was almost blinding in its delight.

"It's good to meet you," he said, respectfully inclining his head.

"None of that." She shook her head. "Please. You know what it's like."

"Don't I!" His eyes started to gleam, and Talos sighed to himself. From anger to glee to mischief: Mikon was fine now.

"We're soooo going to be great friends. And you can use your even better hearing to—*you can hear through closed doors*, can't you?" At her nod, he rushed on. "I can't. But now, you can tell me what people are planning. We will be the most feared duo on base."

Pinching the bridge of his nose, Talos shook his head. "Really, Mikon? Really? That's what you're thinking about right now? You just met her, and you're trying to convince her to help you play pranks?"

Since he was a child, Mikon had possessed one very specific expression the Sunfires called his "haughty olympian" look. It was at once condescending, dismissive, and offended. He still used it from time to time, and he pulled it out now, looking down his nose at Talos. "She's olympian," he said, as if that closed the argument. "She understands these things."

Talos groaned out loud. "Oh stars, here we go. He's going to overuse your kinship to death, I warn you. Which reminds me, there's something I have to tell you. Mikon, go stand over there."

Squinting in suspicion, he did as he was told, but he crossed his arms and glared at Talos.

"One thing you have to know about being a Sunfire." Talos leaned close, speaking in a low voice. "You are *absolutely* allowed to smack the younger ones. For you, this includes everyone from Siromos on down to Mikon. Technically, since you were...because of...well, seniority"—he couldn't quite bring himself to interject Icarus back into the happier mood of the last few minutes —"you can smack Loxias and Ianessa too, but they almost never need it."

She looked at him like she wasn't sure whether he was teasing or not.

"I mean it," he added seriously. "That's the way the Sunfires work. Seniors get to smack the juniors."

"I think smacking him would be rather like smacking a puppy," she teased, looking over at Mikon, who grinned. His hearing meant he'd missed none of the exchange.

Now if Talos had said that, Mikon would have stuck his tongue out at the very least and probably tackled him. But for this girl, he just grinned.

There really was no justice in the galaxy some days.

"He left out one part," Mikon added, coming back over to them. "Your seniority means you get to smack him too. Really! Ask Ianessa."

Talos didn't particularly want to admit that, but he could hardly do anything else in the face of Mikon's honesty. "He's not entirely wrong."

But she just shrugged, amber eyes sparkling in a face that tried too hard to look innocent. "I think we have that covered already, if you look at our track record."

Mikon shouted with laughter, and Talos grinned at her.

"Good point."

The door opened again, and Ianessa poked her head in. Silently, she looked at each of them in turn and raised her eyebrows. "Can I take this to mean everyone is on the same page now?" she asked. "Everyone knows she's Melainis, and we're all good?"

"More or less," he told her, his tone of voice promising they were going to have a Conversation later. How could she not have told him this?

"Let's do just that," she answered the unspoken promise. Her tone said she had a few things to tell him, probably smackdowns over the way he'd treated Koralia. "But right now, the General is ready to go over your Labyrinth experience, so if you could all move up to the command deck?"

Mikon was first through the door, and he kept looking back to check that Koralia was coming too, until she caught up to him and walked at his side.

Talos stayed just long enough to flip off the lights before following them. For the first time in a week, his shoulders weren't tight at the sight of the Amazon. A little annoyed at himself for not seeing it sooner, irritated at Ianessa for not saying anything when she figured it out, but mostly just relieved that the truth was out.

With the mystery of Koralia solved and the identity of the traitor clearer, he could fully focus on the biggest problem still ahead of them:

That thrice-stardust-cursed Labyrinth.

# CHAPTER 14

To test their commitment and resolve, new Kallistratus commanders were always asked one thing before they took the command oath. *What do you think the hardest part of this job will be?* The answers usually came back to one of three things: sending people into battle knowing some wouldn't come back, delegating to sub-commanders, and prioritizing missions when you wanted to save everyone.

None of which were true for Athanasia. She had been directing missions for decades. Things like delegating and prioritizing and sending people out to die were as familiar to her as making battle plans.

The hardest part of being a Kallistratus commander for her was keeping everyone else balanced after a big loss. Restraining those who impulsively wanted vengeance, encouraging those who were sunk in sadness, and giving everyone their own time and space to grieve, all without losing sight of their core mission—breaking the oppressive stranglehold the olympians had on the galaxy.

Icarus's loss had been the most devastating in recent years. If ever there was a poster child for the Kallistratus, it had been him. He'd built so much of their fighter fleet himself, with the support of the Sunfires. In many ways, he had been the other half of the rebellion's leadership, and now that he was gone, the weight was all on her. Talos and Koralia, when they pulled together, would help and could physically and mentally shoulder what he had done. And the Macedonian generals were a highly capable bunch. But no one could ever truly replace Icarus when it came to inspiring people.

And now on top of that, the rebels had to deal with the triple-slam of Heirax's death, the betrayal of Ambrosia, and another unsuccessful Key retrieval. Not to mention radio silence from Daedalus.

They badly needed a win.

Athanasia was so tired. Tired of death, tired of fighting, tired of getting up every day to figure out a better way to defend their people or take the fight to the enemy.

As the bleakness closed in around her, she reached for the medallion around her neck and removed a datachip from the back, inserting it into the table. It flickered to life, showing a long second of blackness before breaking into several moving figures. The camera panned over nine people before focusing on one group at a time. Athanasia eased back in her chair and lost herself in watching.

A tall kid with curly auburn hair, looking younger than his thirteen years, was lying back on a table, his legs up in the air as he tried to balance a short, tan-skinned girl with dark-purple-and-blue hair. She tumbled to the tabletop, and he sat up with a frown. She waved her hands, explaining something. He nodded and lay back, adjusted his position, and then lifted her into the air again. She stayed balanced better this time and gave a thumbs-up to someone out of frame. Mikon and Dione, the youngest Sunfires, always ready for silly stunts.

A tall, wide-shouldered satyr in his mid-teens sprawled across a sofa, cleaning laser pistols except when he paused to sneeze. In-between, he rambled in a slightly hoarse voice about how it would be safer to kill Heracles than imprison him. It was a well thought out argument, but no one appeared to be listening, except the person holding the camera, and they muttered something that sounded like "never letting you loose near him." Siromos, the most violent of all the Sunfires but still with a good head on his shoulders.

An older teenage girl with red hair sat cross-legged in a comfortable chair, mumbling in another language as she leaned over a book resting on her knees. After a minute, she looked up and across the room, and the camera followed her gaze to where a dark-haired boy close to her age was jumping off a railing onto the sofa. He bounced back up and looked at the redhead. She shook her head and held up two fingers. Looking disgruntled, he dashed up the stairs to try the leap again. Ianessa, always keeping Loxias balanced.

Two people dressed in hooded, voluminous cloaks moved through the room, depositing drinks by everyone and then leaping up to perch on a tall wardrobe which wobbled slightly but stayed standing. They gestured to each other, and the music volume increased suddenly.

Mikon and Dione each took a sip of their drinks and then gagged, shouting retribution, at which the cloaked people threw back their hoods and laughed. One blonde girl, one dark-haired boy. Brygos and Kynna, the daring duo.

All of it was being ignored by a pair of human boys, one husky and blond, one slim and dark, as they grappled in one corner of the room. It was hard to tell at first whether they were choreographing a ridiculous dance or sparring, but eventually it was obvious that they were working through fight moves. However, still weak and shaky on their feet, they kept falling over, and then one would inevitably start tickling the other.

Icarus and Talos, the leaders of the misfit family.

The video had been taken the week the Sunfires had come back from a planetside mission with a bizarre virus. The few who hadn't gotten sick on the planet itself caught it from their siblings on the way back. Athanasia had grounded them to base and had stayed home to make sure they actually rested and didn't sneak out of lockdown. Midweek, she'd needed to go off base to meet with an operative and asked Xantippos, a fresh recruit at the time, to stop in and check on them. The laughter he'd heard when he entered the door had made him pull out his camera and record this video.

When she got home, she'd sent them all back to bed, but she'd kept the video and had carried it with her ever since. It had become her lodestar, a thing she could pull out when she needed a shot of hope or a reminder of why they did this.

Like now.

The door of the command bridge slid open, and she barely had time to shut down the disk and replace it in the medallion before Talos, Mikon, Ianessa, and Koralia entered. Despite the recent tragedy, Mikon's footsteps had bounce and Talos and Koralia looked a little less strained than they had a few short hours ago.

*Ah, so they sorted themselves out.*

"You told him?" she asked.

"He figured it out." Koralia came toward her. "What's next?"

*What's next.* The mantra of the Amazons, always looking forward, never behind. To a fault sometimes but helpful right now.

Athanasia pointed to the chairs around the small briefing table in front of her. "Sit down."

Talos sat down on her left side and Koralia on her right, while Mikon claimed the chair next to Koralia, leaving Ianessa to sit across from Athanasia.

"Okay, tell me about the Labyrinth." She folded her hands and looked at Talos.

"Well, it's spreading, as you already know." He frowned. "And it doesn't respond well to conventional weapons. You said try, and we did. None of our bombs and torpedoes could penetrate it or even seemed to do any damage."

All of which the Kallistratus had already suspected, but it was good to have it confirmed. "And inside of it?"

As he and Mikon described their experience inside, one thing kept sticking out to her. "Obviously, Icarus's name was a ploy to draw you in. But once inside, you were guided back out." There was no reason she could think of to do that. "You said there was a message sent to both of you? Is it identical?"

"Yes." Talos brought out a datachip from his pocket and went to slide it into a terminal on the table. Then he hesitated. "Do we have a tablet reader nearby? If this self destructs, I don't want to blow the whole table up."

"Thank you for having at least that much sense today." She gave him a wry smile as Ianessa handed him a tablet.

But the tablet took the chip fine, so he slid it out and inserted it into the table terminal so they could all read it. Well. *Look* at it anyway. It was written in a language Athanasia couldn't read.

"What is it?" Mikon asked, staring at it, his head twisted to the side as he tried to puzzle it out.

"It's old. Ancient, I think, but nothing I recognize." Ianessa tried to run it through the translation algorithm, but nothing changed.

If not even an ex-Hestanoi recognized it, it was *rare*. Athanasia glanced at Koralia, who shook her head. "I don't recognize it either, but I agree, it looks ancient."

"It looks vaguely familiar." Talos squinted at it. "But I don't know why. Maybe it doesn't mean anything? What?" he added when they all looked at him. "The whole thing was like some hybrid of a trap, a dream, and a game. Maybe it's just a random confusing thing that happened and doesn't mean anything."

"Men." Ianessa rolled her eyes.

Athanasia raised an eyebrow at him, and he grinned at her. "Okay, fine, I think it's significant too."

"Now that we have that settled..." Athanasia leaned back in her chair, trying to think of whom to contact about the message. The Kallistratus didn't really have scholars. She knew some who didn't mind working with the rebellion, but it would take far too long to contact them through back channels.

"It would help if we at least knew what it was," Ianessa said, sounding like she was thinking out loud. "Maybe a deeper search on Krete's ancient languages will give me something."

While Ianessa cycled through search results, Athanasia observed each of them, trying to gauge their level of battle readiness. Xantippos would be down for at least a few days, recovering from the poisoning. Which, more than anything, had made it clear that they should expect an attack from Krete. So she needed this team at their best.

Of all of them, Koralia was the one whose readiness she didn't question. Athanasia had been frustrated before at how often Koralia's entire identity appeared to be wrapped up in being an Amazon, but at least she was predictable, especially when it came to battles and war. The Amazons were never not ready for a battle.

Talos looked ready, but then, he always did. He could be bleeding out on the floor from a knife wound to the stomach and he'd still be ready to lead or fight a battle. Weariness lined Ianessa's face, but not so much that she couldn't focus, based on her careful attention to the search she was running. So she was good for a little longer. Mikon...Athanasia studied him as well as she could without being obvious. When he'd arrived on base for the memorial, he'd moved like someone in a dream or underwater. The last two days had seen him coming out of that to where he seemed like his old self. But it was only on the surface, she could tell. Underneath, it was like he'd lost himself, floundering and drifting along, half alive. Poor kid. Icarus wasn't just his big brother, he'd been Mikon's mentor too.

*Time.* It would take them all time to find themselves again.

"I think I have something. It might be called Linear?" Ianessa tested the last word out slowly.

*Linear.* The name wasn't familiar. "How old is it?" the General asked.

Ianessa kept reading in silence for a few minutes, her brow furrowed in concentration. "I think it's...five thousand years old?" She looked up at the rest of the table and spread the results onto pop-up screens around the table. "Spoken by the...notaurians?" she read out loud. "I'm not sure about that name."

Notaurians. That rang a bell for Athanasia, but it would take her a few minutes to sort out why. She only remembered impressions: sun-warmed fields, dust, laughter, a slow pace. An Amazonian mission many years ago, perhaps?

"Apparently an ancient race from Krete, believed dead," Ianessa continued. "Talos? Kora? Ring any bells?"

"No." Koralia shook her head. "I've never heard of them, I don't think. But I've only been on Krete two or three times."

Talos snapped his fingers and pointed at Ianessa. "I have it. An abandoned temple, when we lived by Matala. That's where I saw something that looks like this."

A terminal chimed, and Athanasia felt like sighing. It was a reminder that she had a meeting with other Kallistratus generals in half an hour. That was another thing no one told you about running a rebellion: there was never enough time to get everything done without racing from one thing to another. Some crisis constantly hovered, needing to be discussed or averted or handled.

Trying to wrap up the meeting before the generals started calling in, she noticed Mikon hadn't said a word for a while, his head bent as he slouched in his chair. Had he gone to sleep? It wouldn't be the first time he'd slept through a meeting.

"Mikon?"

He looked up. "Yes, Mom? I mean, General?"

Talos snickered, and Koralia looked curiously from Mikon to Athanasia to Talos.

Athanasia loved it when they called her *Mom*, but this was a meeting. "Are you awake?" she asked him with fond exasperation.

"Me? Yeah, just," he waved a comdisk in the air, "doing stuff."

Which meant he was talking to his siblings. "Taunting Brygos can wait, please."

"Yes, ma'am." He'd long ago stopped asking how she knew exactly what he was doing when she couldn't see it.

"And I think I've seen something like this too." Talos tapped his screen and flipped it around to show everyone a blurry image of a tall person with horns. And maybe head tails? The picture was too blurry to tell for sure.

"Where?" Athanasia asked.

Koralia and Ianessa leaned forward to examine the picture more closely.

"Well, the White Mountains for one, when I was maybe nine or ten? We were on vacation. Daedalus said it was a trick of the forest light." He rolled his eyes. "And again in...Cy-Inthia maybe?" He closed his eyes, trying to picture it. "I'm not sure. Somewhere in one of the Outer Arms. Five or six years ago, when we were looking for the base Siromos is at now."

"I've seen one too," Mikon said, drumming his fingers on the table as he thought. "In a city. I was little, and so were they. I don't even know what city, I just remember that kind of face and that they were taller than me."

"What a feat." Talos snickered.

"Well, it was, even then," Mikon said factually, leaning back in his chair.

Ianessa's fingers were moving swiftly over the keyboard, tapping, circling, and sliding. "Let me see if I can find a clearer picture."

"Wait, so this means...they're still alive?" Koralia shook loose hair out of her eyes, gathered it up, and tied it behind her head. "These notaurians still exist?"

An ancient race that was not so extinct—one that not even Ianessa knew much about. They would need outside information on this. Athanasia couldn't think of any contact they had who would be able to help, but they would need to find one.

"Anyone know someone who might be able to translate this? Someone who won't tattle to the olympians, obviously. Someone who could do it quickly and won't need weeks of testing their loyalty first or an elaborate subterfuge?"

"Aw, but I like elaborate subterfuges," Mikon complained.

Punk. She arched an eyebrow at him, and he slid down in his chair, smirking.

Talos and Ianessa were obviously coming up blank, their heads bent over lists of contacts.

"I might know someone," Koralia said. "It's been a while since I saw them, but they may be able to at least tell us where to go for more information."

"Great. Talk to them, please. Ianessa, keep working on finding out as much as you can. And Koralia?" The Amazon didn't look up, so Athanasia repeated, "Koralia?"

"Yes, ma'am?"

"Now that we know who the traitor is, I'd like you to—what is it?"

Grimacing, Koralia held up her tablet. "I'm...not sure. This message just came in, marked priority and using Ambrosia's code but *not* signed. It says 'If you haven't met with me yet, do not. Repeat, do not. It's a trap, repeat, it's a trap.' But it came from the palace, not her last transmission location."

The brief silence that fell over the table was marked by Mikon putting his head down on the table with a gentle thunk and groaning. "Why can nothing be simple?"

"I don't believe her," Talos said. "Too little, too late."

This wasn't the first time Athanasia wished Icarus had kept more records on his contacts. Secrecy and security were important, but notes about his informants would sure come in handy right now.

"And we're sure it's not Daedalus?" Ianessa asked, looking around.

Low-voiced swearing from Talos answered that.

"Hey, wait. I have an idea." Mikon picked his head up and leaned back in his chair, looking completely at ease. If Athanasia hadn't banned them from putting their feet up on the table, that's exactly what he'd be doing right now. "Why don't we just take a scouting mission down to the surface? Y'know, go in disguise, look around a little bit, hang out in the marketplaces, see what we can find, then come back up here? Wouldn't take more than a couple hours."

"Huh. That's not actually a bad idea." Talos straightened up, staring at the table as he worked through the details in his mind.

It would've been a *brilliant* idea, except for one thing. "Precisely how do you think you're going to get through the Labyrinth?" Athanasia asked, raising her eyebrows at both of them. "You do remember that thing, don't you? Big blob of techno space jelly or whatever you boys are calling it? Blocks off Krete to the outside world? You can't get in without clearance?"

Talos and Mikon shrugged like it didn't matter.

Sunfires. She shook her head. They went through the world convinced that they could *make* doors if there were none to be found.

What the General didn't expect was Koralia's pleased smile or for the Amazon to say, "It's a great idea, and I have just the answer to the Labyrinth. We take your idea"—she pointed at Mikon, who flashed her a grin—"and we go one step further."

"Okay, I'm not sure I like the sound of *that*," Talos said. "But continue." He crossed his arms, ready to be convinced.

"I'm olympian, I've been to Krete before, and I've met Ariadne. Let's use that."

Talos was shaking his head. "I definitely don't like the sound of this."

"Let her finish," Ianessa insisted.

At the same time, Koralia asked, "Whyever not, O Master of Spies?"

Mikon tipped his head toward her but kept his eyes on Talos. "Yeah, why? You spy; why can't she?"

"If you get caught, we'll lose one of our most valuable assets." Talos hesitated, but no one even blinked at the word. "And you'll blow a war wide open. The daughter of Ares on Krete spying for the rebels?" He laughed, a short, sharp sound. "Better if one of us goes."

"Huh, he has a point too," Mikon said thoughtfully. "We'd hate to lose you so soon after we got you. That's just bad stewardship."

"She's not a *thing*, you bonehead." Ianessa rolled her eyes at her youngest brother.

Athanasia eased back into her chair, settling in. She still had time before the generals called; she could afford to let this play out.

Besides, it was shaping up to be highly entertaining.

"Guys?" Koralia held her hands palms up and looked briefly at the ceiling, sighing in exasperation. "You think this will be my first spy mission? Give me a break. I won't get caught."

Pointing at her, Mikon said, "And that's also a great point. I bet you're a magnificent spy."

At this point, he wasn't even trying to be helpful, he was just stirring the pot to see how far he could go before Talos snapped at him. Athanasia suppressed a laugh.

"Thank you, Mikon," Koralia said pointedly.

"My pleasure." He sent Talos a smug sideways glance, which his older brother ignored.

"How would you do it?" Talos challenged, his gaze intense on Koralia. "Names, times, places, procedure. How?"

"Hephaestus has mines to the west of here, beyond settler space. That's the excuse I used to get here, that he was checking out the mines. So we run with that story. It's only been, what, a week since I arrived? I can say I was on my way home from there and felt like stopping in at Krete."

"I like this more and more," Mikon commented, his fingers lightly tapping the sides of the table as he focused on Koralia.

She gestured in the air. "Dad—Hephaestus—will either send me a ship from his nearest settlement, or if I'm lucky, if *we're* lucky, he's still at Poseidon's palace. I get on board, fly to Krete, and ask permission to visit. I doubt they'd refuse me."

"I sure wouldn't, if it was me," Mikon interjected, earning an eye roll from Ianessa and a warning to *hush* from Talos.

Talos was frowning. "You don't have to prove anything to us," he snapped suddenly. "You don't have to do this to prove you're good enough to be here."

That sparked fire in Koralia's eyes. "This again? I thought we were over this," she snapped. "Hear me, Talos, this isn't some stupid posturing dance, and for once, would you get out of big brother mode? I'm a bloody *Amazon*—"

"Minus the blood at the moment." Mikon snickered.

"—and as much as I'm glad to meet you, and as much as I understand you feel responsible for all of us"—she pointed from herself to Ianessa to Mikon —"I've seen as many battles as you have, if not more."

Her voice softened for an instant. "I know he left them to your charge. I'm not trying to…" Pressing her hands together, she sighed. "I'm not trying to be a brat. Unlike someone else." She sent Mikon a teasing glance, and he beamed as if she had complimented him. "But I was born with certain advantages, and if we can't use those for our good, what use am I?"

Athanasia almost beamed with pride. The girl had come a long way since her turbulent teen years of hating everything and everyone connected with her heritage.

"She's right," Ianessa said.

"Definitely right," Mikon agreed. "Besides, she has super hearing, and I can make people talk. We'll make a fearsome duo." He looked immensely pleased with himself, and Athanasia settled further into her chair, waiting for the rest of the storm to break.

It didn't take long.

"You are absolutely not going with her. No," Talos said, shaking his head at Mikon.

"Excuse me? It was *my* idea!" Mikon tended to look like he was an easy-going kid, but that was a lie. His moods came and went as quickly as any olympian and covered a heart of iron. Outraged blue eyes flashed at Talos, and he leaned forward, ready to argue his point.

"An idea you were joking about and expected us to reject," Ianessa said without looking up from what she was reading.

"Still my idea!" Mikon crossed his arms over his chest, his face dark.

"No, not happening," Talos insisted. "You would definitely start a war."

"I would not!" Equal parts offended and outraged now, Mikon stood up, like he couldn't stand to sit another minute.

"You start wars every day just for fun, hello?" Ianessa pointed to the comdisk he still held.

Mikon tossed the disk onto the table. "That's *family*. It's different. I'm not going to start a war with Krete. And anyway, how can I start a war that's already been started?"

Ah, there it was. Athanasia had wondered how long it would take him to get there.

"And Koralia is an *Amazon*," Mikon emphasized. "She's used to missions like these. I'll just be backup."

"She's used to doing them alone as much as she is with a team," Talos countered. "What makes you think she needs your help?"

"Family sticks together." He brought it up like it would clinch the entire thing, but Ianessa and Talos just rolled their eyes.

"Shut up, Mikon," they said, sighing in exasperated unison.

Time for Athanasia to take a hand. She leaned forward in her chair. "If I could have your attention?"

Silence dropped over the table, and Mikon sat back down, scowling.

"Look at the symbol on the walls of this room."

Obediently, all four of them looked around at the rebellion emblem painted onto the walls. There had been an argument once over whether to display it anywhere so publicly, because anyone who came along after the rebellion left a base would know exactly who had been there, but someone had overruled the objections for this base and liberally decorated the bridge in multicolored compasses with the Kallistratus torch through the center.

"And on my shoulder."

Four sets of eyes focused on the pin she wore, the same design shining in silver over dark blue.

"And now look back at me."

As one, they lifted their heads to focus on her face and chorused, "Yes, General!"

"Very good. Koralia, you'll go to Krete. You'll have three days to discover whatever you can about Ariadne and Ambrosia and the notaurians. Try to find Daedalus too. At the end of that time, you'll return here, unless you give me a convincing argument for why I should let you have extra time there. Xuthos will go with you as bodyguard."

"All due respect, General, I don't need a bodyguard," Koralia objected. "I travel without one all the time."

Patiently, she raised her eyebrows at the girl. "As an Amazon or the daughter of Ares, yes, you do. As the daughter of Hephaestus, yes, sometimes. Sometimes not." She noted Koralia's rueful flush with satisfaction. So she and her father *did* still argue about that. "Xuthos was raised on a system close to Vulcani, and I believe he even trained in one of the self-defense schools on Vulcani for a while. He looks the part, he can act the part, and you'll keep him in line so he doesn't say anything stupid." Which was rather a tall order, but Koralia could handle it.

The Amazon didn't look happy about it, but she nodded. She'd follow the orders.

"Talos," Athanasia continued. "That leaves you with your preferred command squad. You'll be running active defense of the base. The Kretans, or some of them, apparently think they're ready for open war with us. Let's not give them a chance to surprise us."

"Ma'am." He saluted her.

"Ianessa, you're on research for both the Labyrinth and the notaurians. The new radio operators you and Koralia have been training—how soon will they be ready for consistent active duty?"

Ianessa thought for a moment. "Two days."

"I concur," Koralia said, nodding.

"Good. It'll take us that long to prepare for this mission anyway." Glancing at Mikon, she said, "I'm recalling Brygos to this base, because I want him helping us with the Labyrinth."

"I have to get off base then," Mikon said, looking slightly panicked. "General, please..." He broke off when she held her hand up.

"Just what revenge did you take for him bugging you?" Ianessa whispered across the table.

"Not telling," he muttered.

"Children," Athanasia warned.

"Yes'm," they said, but whether they meant "yes, Mom" or "yes, ma'am" was hard to know.

She rolled her eyes and kept going. "Mikon, for the next two days, you'll be on scouting duty with Talos until he gets the new duty rotations figured out. Then you'll be going with Koralia as her pilot—"

The look Mikon gave Talos was unbearably smug.

"—and I'm sure Koralia can come up with a convincing backstory for you."

The Amazon looked speculatively at Mikon, whose eyes gleamed with anticipation.

"An old friend of mine, I think," she said, one finger tapping her lips. "Half-legitimate son of someone Ares knew."

"That part's easy," Mikon remarked, but he didn't sound annoyed, just intrigued.

"And we've been kicking around the galaxy together as spoiled rich olympians for a few months."

He grinned. "Even better. But what were you really doing?"

Koralia raised her eyebrows at him and shrugged. "Training armies for actual spoiled rich olympians."

"So you were training armies and I've been fighting a war, but we're going to pretend we've been living the high life." His smile was bright with mischief. "This is going to be so much fun."

"Oh, great spinning stars." Talos frowned, looking between Mikon and Koralia. "This is the worst idea ever."

Ianessa laughed, propping both elbows on the table and then wincing. Athanasia started to dismiss her to rest, but Ianessa's eyes were still twinkling at Talos as she dropped her elbows. "Oh, don't even try to pretend you wouldn't be all over the idea if you weren't the one staying home.

He grinned. "Well, yes. But since I *am* the one staying home, this is going to be a nightmare."

"The mistrust," Mikon said, his tone resentful.

Athanasia arched one eyebrow at Talos. "Is that a reflection on my decision?" She matched her tone to theirs, the joking a mask to disguise the sadness they were all trying hard not to show, not right now when they needed to focus.

"Never, ma'am," he assured her.

"Now that we have that settled..." Athanasia looked around the table, waiting until they were all looking at her. "Put together the details, and I'll go over them later tonight. And, Ianessa, report to the medbay for a checkup either tonight or tomorrow." She had been healing fine, but Athanasia had seen her wince several times in the last two days and wanted their doctors to double-check the wounds. *Better to be sure now than sorry later.* "You're all dismissed."

All of them stood, saluted, and made their way to the door. Koralia paused behind her to lay her hand on Athanasia's shoulder and squeeze it, a mute communication. *Thank you, I won't let you down.*

Athanasia reached up to rest her hand over Koralia's. *I know.*

If it was anyone else, she'd have had to be more involved in the next steps, but three of them were Sunfires, used to operating more or less on their own. She could send them off to make plans and only double-check them before giving the go order.

And if anyone in the galaxy was used to operating more independently than even the Sunfires, it was definitely Koralia. Her fathers adored her with all their hearts, but between their palaces and the palaces of her mother, she'd grown up early. Earlier than Athanasia would have wanted any child of hers to grow up, that was for sure. Koralia hadn't lied to Heirax: she had been running missions from a very young age. Some with her fathers—who didn't know any better than to take her with them—and others with the Amazons.

The perks of being the daughter of the Lord of War included early access to the warrior order. Fortunately, the Amazonian generals had loved the moody eight-year-old and welcomed her into their ranks. They treated her as their personal doll until she was old enough to seriously train, and then they took her on as their pet project. Koralia had been spoiled by them, in fact.

*There are far worse fates than to be the adopted daughter of a bunch of women warriors.*

Athanasia had been a seasoned warrior when Koralia joined them, and the two had forged a close relationship that still remained strong. Sometimes it was more like an older sister and a younger sister, or an aunt and a niece, but usually, it was closer to adopted parent and child. Koralia had been the first of her adopted children—before Icarus and Talos even.

They would both have been very different women without the Amazons.

Athanasia smiled as the door closed behind her kids. If anyone could take on Krete and win, it was them: the Sunfires and the Amazon and her.

# CHAPTER 15

"This is going to be so much fun," Mikon repeated, as they made their way toward their quarters to begin planning.

Koralia glanced up at him beside her and smiled. Icarus had talked about his family a lot, but especially Mikon. He adored his feisty little brother, who had changed the attitudes of all the Sunfires toward olympians. In some ways, she'd pictured a younger boy. She couldn't remember how old Mikon was or if Icarus had even said, but after being around olympians all her life, she could tell one thing: he was no teenager. In height *or* years. He was built like Apollo and Poseidon, at least in stature, towering half a foot over her. His father was said to be human, but Mikon looked full olympian, which would back up their cover story on Krete. And with looks like that, he'd be the perfect distraction, keeping attention focused on him while Koralia looked for the information the rebellion needed.

He was right, this *would* be fun.

"What's your power?" Ianessa asked behind her, and it took Koralia a minute to realize the question was for her.

"My...what?" She turned around, pausing for a minute before continuing to walk in a sidestep.

"Your power? Olympian?" Ianessa gestured to Mikon. "He makes people feel comfortable talking to him. And he's only half-olympian. You're full. So what's yours?"

Oh. *That*. Her second least favorite thing to discuss.

"It's...nothing special." She shrugged and faced forward again.

"Really?" Mikon said, obviously curious. "What does that mean?"

She shrugged again, wishing she was anywhere but here right now, having this conversation. "It's not important. Yours now..." She nodded toward him, trying to turn the subject. "Yours is useful. When we get to Krete, I'm thinking—"

"Oh no. No." Talos, walking behind Mikon, reached out and caught her shoulder, turning her around. "You don't get out of answering that easily."

All three of them looked at her, their faces expectant.

*Well, hellstars.*

"I amplify loyalty," she said quickly. Better have it out and done, so she could see the suspicion on their faces and get it over with.

Mikon's gaze sharpened, and he focused more closely on her face. "You can make people feel loyalty to a leader?"

She had expected suspicion and mistrust and irritation but not excitement. "Ye-e-es," she said slowly.

"Why in all the stars of Belus would you not use that?" Talos asked, and at his tone, she turned to see him watching her with eager calculation. "That's... we *need* that."

"I've never used it on you, any of you." She almost tripped over the words in her hurry to get them out, needing them to know she was nothing like her mother, that she wouldn't use her abilities to manipulate them. "And I swear I never used it on Icarus either."

They stared at her, blinking.

Ianessa was the first to speak. "Why would we think that?"

For just a second, she closed her eyes. *Of course.* They were *his* family. Why would their reaction be any different from his, no matter what Talos had thought of her when she first came on board?

So she just shrugged again. "Most people assume we use it on everyone," she said quietly.

"Most people...or most *olympians* think that?" Ianessa asked, sea-green eyes narrowed shrewdly.

She didn't even need to answer that—they saw the truth in her face. Olympians mostly, the world to which she had been born, mind games and exuberant living the order of every day. Where you used the power you were given and everyone figured everyone else was using their power. It was a joke to them, the ability to influence others.

Mikon reached out tentatively, like he wasn't sure the touch would be welcome, and set his hand on her shoulder, squeezing gently, barely any pressure at all but enough to say he understood.

Talos gripped her other shoulder, and Ianessa took her hand. For a few seconds, they all stood there, letting her feel the sense of family they carried with them as an invisible cloak.

Then Talos and Ianessa stepped back. Mikon removed his hand but still stood close to her, and she felt him holding back a wave of something that wanted to crash forward. She recognized the familiar restraint, something she lived with every single day: his power wanted to be used right now, but he wouldn't let it. She looked up at him and nodded quickly, acknowledgement of his self-control.

His answering smile was bright as sunlight on a spring morning.

Then she looked at Talos. He was the hardest to read, because she knew his trust had been abused the most of all of them, even more, perhaps, than Mikon's.

"Sorry. I just...I thought... This world is so different from mine," she said, her voice low.

"Welcome to the fun side of the galaxy." Ianessa smiled. Then her gaze turned serious. "So let me see if I have this right. You can't actually *create* loyalty, can you?"

Koralia shook her head.

"And you can't amplify something that *isn't* there, right?"

"I can't."

Talos crossed his arms over his chest and took up the questions. "And it is not permanent, just a sort of...temporary thing that gets people through until it grows more naturally for them?"

She nodded. "Like a bridge."

"But it's not mind control of any shade, right?" Ianessa asked, and Mikon snorted.

"You know we can't do that," he said, his tone almost irritated, but Ianessa glowered at him and he shut up.

"It's not mind control," Koralia answered. "No. I just...I only amplify what's already there. I nudge them, so people feel more willing to trust each other. Most people..." She hesitated and then nodded at Talos. "Most people innately *want* to trust...trust their leaders, trust their people. It's just the getting there, pushing through any initial inhibitions or just doing it. And that's what I help with."

Talos's eyes lit like he'd figured out something important. "You have been since you were little," he said quickly. "You weren't just running ordinary missions with your fathers or the Amazons, were you? Your abilities—that was part of it, wasn't it?"

She smiled then, feeling more relief seep through her. He understood. "Partly. Mostly I was learning to control it back then. Hours and *hundreds* of hours of practice until I could give a speech or a command without ampli-fying anything. And my generals broke me of inappropriate use pretty early on." She grimaced, making the Sunfires laugh. The last whispers of tension dissipated like fog on a morning breeze, and they started walking again.

"No inappropriate use at *all*?" Mikon sounded disappointed.

"Well." She glanced around the hallway, but no one was in sight. "Maybe once or twice. When someone was...needed a lesson."

They all laughed again, and the sound was so full of home, from Mikon's bright laughter to Talos's snickering, that it almost made her ache.

"Well, all this has told me is that there is no reason for you to not be using your abilities here," Ianessa said, as if the conclusion was obvious. "Especially when the rebellion could really use that power."

Koralia had thought of that, but she still hesitated. The rebellion fought against the olympians, against the imperial monopolies that made their lives worse. She knew some rebels just condemned everything olympian out of hand. Wouldn't her power be included in that?

Not for this family.

The thought warmed her through.

They had arrived at Koralia's room, and everyone stopped in front of her door, heedless of blocking the hallway.

"You know one of the family mottos of the Sunfires?" Talos asked her, his eyes serious.

She nodded, but before she could repeat it, Mikon spoke.

"Identify your power, control your power, use it for good," he said softly, almost chanting the words. In the way he said them, she could feel what they had done for him, his self-worth that had been smashed into the ground by his mother.

"Use it for good," Talos repeated, his voice deep. He was the one who had founded that motto with Icarus. The first one Icarus had defended from the injustice that was adults making life hard for children because the children were talented. "We don't fear yours any more than we'd fear his." He tipped his head toward his youngest brother.

Mikon and Ianessa nodded, their agreement clear.

"So when you get back from Krete, we'll talk about it," Talos said, a ques-tion and a promise wrapped into one.

"We will," she agreed, answering the unspoken question. "And...thanks."

She stayed only long enough to see their smiles before closing her door.

+

SITTING DOWN ON HER BED, Koralia leaned back against the wall, focusing on slow breaths in and out.

Why the Sunfires still surprised her, she didn't know. After all, she had known Icarus. Known him with a depth that she knew he gave few others. He had opened every reserve to her in the end, and she'd seen the molten core that had led him to stand against bullies from a young age, from his father all the way up to the olympian sons themselves. Few had the courage or the sustaining fire to challenge the Jupiterians for more than a few years, let alone over a decade, but Icarus did, and any who followed him would have to have fire of their own, not just loyalty to his.

It was no wonder the rebellion still kept aflame, with them at its core and Athanasia at its head. It would burn until it restored justice to the galaxy or until every last member was dead…and then the memory of it would still kindle hearts ablaze.

That was the legacy of the Sunfires.

A legacy that she'd been welcomed into, wholeheartedly, no reserve, no holding back. It was almost too much to absorb.

So she just smiled, blinked back her tears, and pulled a tablet from the shelf next to her cot. She could think about that later; right now, there was a mysterious message to be translated.

The process of reaching her contact took several minutes and involved seven different codes and security re-routes, so neither party could be tracked. And that was presuming the other girl's location hadn't moved in the year since she'd given Koralia this set of codes.

Typing in the final code, she leaned back and closed her eyes, waiting for the screen to clear. And preparing an explanation for why she needed this information.

"Hello? Kora? Hi!"

With one final deep breath, Koralia sat up, opened her eyes, and nodded to the girl on the other side of the screen. "Chryse."

She looked good. Then too, she always looked good, even on days like this when she was tousle-haired and sweaty and dirty, like she'd been working on a house. A loose blouse open at the neck filled slightly with a breeze, and blonde hair draped artfully around her sun-bronzed face, as if it had been styled that way instead of falling there during work.

"How are you?" Koralia asked, wondering how the girl would react to being interrupted in the middle of what looked like a busy day. She didn't usually enjoy that.

If she was annoyed, Chryse didn't indicate it. "I'm good. Busy. We've had several new waves of refugees the last few months."

So she probably *had* been working on a house. Koralia nodded. "Makes sense. I heard that the rebellion is falling back a little. They've had some setbacks."

Chryse's eyes softened. "I heard about Icarus. I'm sorry."

Koralia wasn't sure what to reply—how did you answer that?—so she just nodded again. "Thanks."

"I assume this isn't a social call," Chryse said.

Safe assumption, given that Koralia rarely just called someone up to talk, and certainly not when she had to go through that many layers of security. "No, I have a question I hoped you could answer. This originated on Krete." She pushed a button to transfer the coded message. "I was wondering if you would know what language it is or know someone who might know, if you don't. I don't need an answer today, if you need a little time," Koralia added.

"Krete," Chryse mused, while she waited for it to come through. "Ah. I see. Good for you."

With those three short sentences, Chryse had indicated that she knew Koralia was with the rebellion now and she wished her well.

Koralia tipped her head in thanks.

Chryse bent over the connection on her end, her brow furrowing as she read. The message must have arrived.

"I don't need time; I can tell you right now that's Minotauri." Chryse sat back so Koralia could see her face, see how surprised she was. "You got this from Krete? Recently?"

"A day and a half ago. Minotauri? Is that related to Notaurian?" Koralia pronounced the last word hesitantly.

"Yes and no." Chryse shook her head, tucking her hands under her legs and leaning forward, the way she always did when she was going to expound on something. "Notaurian is an old and incorrect term. The singular for their race is minotaur and the plural is minotaurs. The language is called Minotauri. It's a derivative of Linear A. I can't read this, but I have people who can, right here with me, in fact. Do you want a translation now?"

"Yes, if you please, as soon as you can manage. We're..." How much should she even say? Chryse would not betray the rebellion, but Koralia needed to keep things concise because of time constraints. "We've got a time-sensitive situation on our hands."

"I'll call you back as soon as I have a translation."

"Thank you." She paused and repeated. "I mean it, *thank you.*"

"Pffft, no problem."

Chryse cut the connection, and Koralia let out a breath she didn't realize she'd been holding.

She had expected that Chryse would know a way to get a translation, but she hadn't expected that it would be so fast or so handy. Still, she didn't let herself relax, scribbling notes about what Chryse had said so she could show Athanasia later.

Minotaurs. Minotauri. Someone in the Labyrinth or operating it had deliberately lured the rebellion pilots in just to send them that message. That didn't mean it wasn't a trap, but whoever was behind it had gone to a lot of trouble to send it when they could just as easily have broadcast the transmission the same way Ariadne had hers. So it was a desperate cry for help, or it was an elaborate trap. Given that it was in an ancient language and the way they'd gotten it, her instinct bet on the former.

When Chryse called back, she leaped right in. "This is an older form of the language, like Archaic compared to Modern Olympian." She paused until Koralia nodded. "But we have a few refugees here who knew enough of it to give you a good translation. I'm sending it through now."

"Thank you. How many on Krete speak it, this Minotauri?"

"Oh, almost no one outside their race. Minotaurs are bilingual—they learn Kretan as children, so the Kretans never had a reason to learn Minotauri." Chryse's lips twisted ruefully. "*And* the Kretans rather consider it beneath them."

Well, that fit the Kretans she knew. Arrogant elitist snobs as bad as olympians, without the sense of humor that made many olympians tolerable.

"These minotaurs," she asked Chryse, "they're a native Kretan race?"

"Yes. You—when were you on Krete last?"

"Four years ago? Maybe six? It's been a while."

Chryse looked off into the distance as if she was trying to calculate. "So you wouldn't have been there when they started... Well, all right, the short version is that they've lived side by side with Kretans for years. They're very tech savvy, and Minos has decided to use that for his—" She gestured in midair, seeming at a loss for words.

"Quest for galactic power?" Koralia suggested.

Chryse's expression was halfway between a grin and a sneer. "Yes, that. He's basically enslaved them and forced them to create the Labyrinth. That's all I know. Your message is actually the first time anyone here has heard from Krete in a while."

Koralia nodded, and the tablet lit up with the translation message coming in. "How many are there?" she asked as she read through the message.

"What?"

"How many minotaurs are still on Krete?"

"About five hundred, I think."

That was too many for the rebellion to airlift from Krete, and Koralia noted that fact in her report for Athanasia.

Pondering, Chryse added, "Yeah, five hundred sounds right. We got the first refugees two years ago, and there was a steady trickle for a year or so. It stopped abruptly five months ago, and that was the last we heard anything. They've never been a large people group, but their numbers have decreased in the last decade."

That was...Koralia tried to reckon it in her head. Five months...so the refugees would have stopped arriving about a month or two before the Labyrinth began to be a threat to the rebels.

"Somehow, I get the impression Pasiphae is involved," Chryse said. "Or was involved."

"Pasiphae? She's insane, or so the report goes."

A defensive edge entered Chryse's manner. "And I work with what society calls 'monsters.' Maybe she's mad, maybe she's just misunderstood."

Koralia inwardly sighed. "No offense was intended," she said, her voice neutral. Chryse had always been defensive of her work. "Is there any way you know of that we can contact the minotaurs? Any special...meeting place or way we can visit without drawing attention?"

Chryse's expression said she regretted being so defensive, but she, like Koralia, just kept going. "I don't know. Let me see if I can get one to talk to you." She turned aside and motioned someone over, giving them a message in an undertone too rapid for the video to pick up.

Sitting back down, she said, "Most of them are really quiet and don't talk about their home. And we have mostly children and older people—everyone they could get out."

"Was Minos's slavery that bad then? Not that all slavery isn't bad, but..." Koralia racked her brain for anything she'd heard about Krete in the last few months, aside from the Labyrinth. Surely if the king of Krete was practicing slavery on an extensive scale, even internal to only his planet, someone in the galaxy would have heard of it and word would have gotten to at least the rebellion, if not the Amazons or Athina.

There were laws against slavery in this galaxy. Why was nothing being done?

Chryse responded with another crooked smile. "I don't know. They're a family-oriented people, and the most I can get out of them was that Minos took what they loved and used it against them. And like I said, it seems Pasiphae was somehow involved, but they don't hate her the way they do Minos, whatever her role was."

This just got stranger and stranger. Koralia sighed, making more notes. Three days might not be enough time to find answers.

"Yes?" a mellow voice said.

She looked up, back into the screen at a new face.

"This is Ladika," Chryse introduced. "She helps with our teaching programs."

"I am honored to meet you," Koralia said formally, bending her head the correct angle to acknowledge an introduction to an equal. The minotaur woman was short, shorter than Chryse, from what Koralia could see. Her skin looked fawn-colored at first, but when she looked closer she realized it was gray hair mixed with chestnut. The woman's rectangular face tapered to a wide mouth and full lips set over a square chin. Oval ears sat on top of her head, and in front of those, small horns angled a little to the outside, curving slightly over the ears. Head tails that looked to be about two inches in diameter sprouted from the base of her horns and hung down her back.

"It is good to meet you," the woman said slowly in Galactic Common, her accent heavy, melding the words into each other.

"I am sorry if I have interrupted you," Koralia said, slowing the words so they were more intelligible to a non-native speaker but weren't slow enough to be condescending. "Your people have reached out to us, and I would like to know where on Krete I should go to contact them. If there is a safe place."

The woman looked like she was working through that, turning it over in her mind. At least, that's what Koralia would have said if the woman was human, olympian, or several other galactic races. But she wasn't sure that facial interpretation held true here. Maybe Ladika was getting ready to tell her to leave the minotaurs alone.

"The queen's garden," the minotaur said in her slow, mellow tone. "Go there. Do not be caught."

Koralia grinned. "Queen's garden, don't get caught. Thank you, madam."

The woman lifted her hand—which looked like it had only three wide fingers ending in triangular nails—to her chest and bowed a little. She said something to someone off camera and walked off, graceful despite her age.

Chryse came back into full frame. "Aren't they just the most *amazing*? They've been through so much, but they're still loving and kind and the most helpful people you'll ever meet."

"I believe you." If Koralia hadn't already been looking forward to scouting around on Krete, she was now. "I have to go, but many, many thanks for all your help."

"Oh sure. And hey, some of the linguists here have been working on a translation program for Minotauri. I'll send it after we're done. It'll take a while to come through. It's only about ninety-five percent accurate right now, and you have to go through three steps to get to Galactic Common, but this way you'll have something there."

"Thank you," Koralia repeated. "The rebellion is grateful."

Chryse waved that away.

"I will inform you if we make any headway with the minotaurs and slavery," Koralia added.

"That would be great. And Koralia?"

"Yes?" She paused with her hand over the switch that would end the call.

"Be careful."

The words sounded odd, like a hidden warning or like Chryse wanted to say more and didn't know how. Koralia filed them away and nodded.

"You too."

Chryse's smile was the last thing she saw as she cut the connection and leaned back to think about the information.

*

# CHAPTER 16

"Is everyone clear on the plan?" Athanasia looked around at the table of rebels. "Mikon?"

"Do what Koralia says." He grinned at Koralia, who tried to keep her expression serious while she rolled her eyes at him. "And keep my eyes wide open. Ask about the minotaurs if I see any. Pretend I'm a lazy rich kid who is curious about everything."

"The curious about everything part is right on," Ianessa remarked in an aside to Koralia, but gave Athanasia an innocent smile when the General looked at her.

"Good," Athanasia said. "Koralia?"

"Find out everything I can about the Labyrinth and the minotaurs while pretending to be Daddy's little girl who is interested in making an alliance with Krete over the Labyrinth technology. Keep it just vague enough they can't claim false pretenses later. See if Daedalus is there or anyone knows where he's gone. And try to establish a minotaur contact."

"Excellent. Xuthos?" The General turned to look at him.

"Watch their backs, send message bursts trying to locate the palace contact, and remember that Lord Hephaestus hired me to guard his daughter."

Athanasia wished she could be there to see *that* play out, especially since Koralia had been known to "lose" her bodyguards ever since she was thirteen and told Hephaestus she was too grown-up for them. If Xuthos managed to stick with her for three days, Athanasia might just have to give him a promotion of some kind.

"And if anything goes radically wrong or for some reason you need to get out of there fast?" She asked all of them but looked at Xuthos, who hated asking for help.

"Text a code crimson scarlet to you," Koralia said, pointing in the general direction of the radio room, "and you'll send a code to Hephaestus, who will send a priority transmission to the Kretans, recalling me."

"And Xuthos, you've memorized the Minotauri transmission from the Labyrinth?"

He stood up and recited, "Kallistratus Command: I and my people are ready to fight the war with you if we can get off Krete. We have all the secrets of the Labyrinth and many more. Our contact is in the palace. A patriot."

"Word perfect," she praised him. He smirked and sat back down. "And your command structure?"

"Koralia, me, Xuthos," Mikon said, his eyes gleaming with eagerness.

Athanasia didn't miss the smug look Talos gave his second. Those two.

Xuthos sighed dramatically. "The indignity of being under a kid."

"Hey, I'm not that young!" Mikon retorted. "I'm technically older than you."

Xuthos looked him up and down in a way that implied he very much doubted that.

"I am," Mikon insisted.

"Sure, but when it's converted, you're younger, aren't you?" Xuthos wasn't giving in that easily.

Mikon scowled and didn't answer.

"And you won't have a problem with finding a suitable wardrobe?" Athanasia double-checked, looking at Koralia.

"None," she said confidently. "I have a few gowns with me, and as long as Dad is sending a ship, extras will be more than provided."

Hephaestus *was* still at Poseidon's palace, to their relief. When he'd received Koralia's message, he had contacted her at once and sent a small ship that now waited beyond the base.

Athanasia hoped his aid wouldn't come back around to bite them. Hephaestus might be Koralia's father, but he was still one of the twelve Supreme olympians. Koralia's loyalty to the Kallistratus had been proven over and over already. Her father's...that was an unknown factor.

"Explain that one to me," Xuthos said, crossing one leg over the other and leaning back, his eyes drifting appreciatively over Koralia.

That was another thing Athanasia would be sorry to miss: Xuthos having every opportunity to pursue Koralia. Being an active Amazon didn't give you much time for a social life, so Koralia had never dated much, nor had she ever been very interested in a long-term relationship...until Icarus. And Xuthos had made it his personal mission in life to date every attractive single woman he knew. If this mission wasn't so serious, Athanasia would be cackling to herself at the thought of how it would go down.

Fortunately, Mikon would be more than willing to tell stories when he got back.

Koralia acted like she didn't notice Xuthos's admiration."It's just the way Dad is. See, Ares, he doesn't care. He doesn't *mind* dressing up and being formal, but if we're out and about in the galaxy and he wants to stop in and see, say, Apollo, he just does it. Even if we're in battle fatigues. He even visits Hestia like that, possibly the only person brave enough to do that." She snickered.

Athanasia made a note to ask her about it later—she didn't think she'd heard this story.

"But Hephaestus?" Koralia continued. "He prefers to be adequately dressed in any situation, so his ships carry every kind of outfit from full formal wear to casual. Armor hangs side by side with elaborate robes."

"Aren't those the same thing?" Talos quipped.

Koralia looked at him, and her lips twitched sideways in amusement. "Okay, sometimes."

"Very well." Athanasia took charge of the conversation before they got too distracted. "You leave for Hephaestus's ship at 0500 hours. Xuthos and Koralia will get as much sleep as they can while Mikon pilots, looping around so it looks like you're coming from the mines. Hephaestus contacted Krete for you, and your arrival is timed for 1800 hours tomorrow night."

That would give Xuthos and Koralia time to do some careful looking around in the evening while Mikon caught up on sleep. The rebels were racing the clock here, and everyone knew it. They had to pack as much fact-finding into three days as they could.

Everyone was looking at Athanasia expectantly, and she sighed to herself. She was just putting off the final moment.

"Audeamus," she said, standing up and resting her hands on the table.

"Audeamus," echoed the rebels. One by one they rose, saluted her, and left the room.

The mission had officially begun.

✝

ONE OF THE SUNFIRES' most lasting mission traditions was the night-before drink and talk. Koralia had excused herself from it tonight, and they didn't push her. Ianessa and Mikon had started without Talos, since he'd been reworking the defense patrol rotation and waiting on the last of his scouts to come back from a patrol of their warning buoys.

So his siblings were already through one—small—round of half-strength hyacinth nektar and into their second when Talos joined them, swinging his leg over the back of a chair and sitting down beside Ianessa. She handed him a glass of nektar, and he tossed it back.

"Feeling pretty good about the mission?" he asked Mikon.

"Sure." Mikon dropped his voice and leaned closer. "Is there anything else I should know about?"

"Mmm." Talos downed a second glass of nektar. "No. Just come back alive. And I know Xuthos doesn't irritate you much *now*, but he might after you've spent a few days in close quarters with him. If, at the end of the mission, you feel like leaving him on Krete, you can't. That's all. Got that?"

Mikon's grin spread slowly. "Don't leave Xuthos behind. Yes, sir."

"That's our boy." Talos reached out and ruffled his hair. Mikon leaned into the touch, and Talos hugged him with one arm. "And please don't insult any Kretans to their faces," he added as an afterthought.

Mikon heaved a dramatic sigh. "Take away all my fun," he griped.

Standing up and heading for the door, Talos paused. "Well, *I* don't much care if you insult them or not, but it would leave Koralia a mess to clean up."

Mikon blinked, considering that, then rolled his head to the side and glared at Talos. "You did that on purpose," he accused.

"Guilty." Of course Mikon wouldn't intentionally create a mess for Koralia —he liked her too much. "See you tomorrow morning, Scythe-brat."

Talos whistled to himself as he left the mess hall. He didn't worry about Mikon, not for a second. His brother was smart and savvy—he wouldn't make a mess. Talos had other quarry tonight. Xuthos had left the mess hall a minute ago, probably heading to his quarters to pack.

When he knocked on the pilot's door, Xuthos opened it manually instead of voice activating it.

"Figured I'd see you before morning," Xuthos said. "You want to come in?" He gestured to his quarters, and Talos entered, standing casually near the door while Xuthos moved around the small room, sorting his mission kit into his bag.

There was very little use in trying to intimidate Xuthos. He stood half a head taller than Talos, as tall or taller than anyone else on base. He also had an air of joking ease that was difficult to dent. So Talos crossed his arms, leaned back against the doorway, and waited. He wanted the pilot's full attention for what he had to say.

Finally, when it looked like he was nearly done packing, Xuthos dropped his backpack on his bed, leaned back against the wall, and propped one foot up behind him. "Let's get this over with. If I do anything to Koralia, they'll never find my body. If I do anything to Mikon, they'll never find my body. If I mess up the mission, you'll execute me by firing squad. And if I get myself caught, you'll only come after me because you have to, and then you'll make sure I get shot in a non-lethal place during the rescue."

Talos laughed. "Not even close. If you do anything to Koralia, you're on your own. I am not getting between an Amazon and her prey; I don't care how good a pilot you are or how useful you are to the rebellion."

Xuthos grinned, folding his arms, his stance mirroring Talos's. "Self-preservation over team spirit? Why am I not surprised?"

"I'm all for team spirit. But you aggravate an Amazon and you are on. Your. Own."

"I'll keep that in mind."

He'd better. "Good. If you do anything to Mikon, he's more than capable of taking you out on his own with one hand tied behind his back, no matter how much self defense or hand-to-hand combat training you've had."

Xuthos looked mildly surprised at that, which was enormously pleasing.

"If you mess up the mission"—Talos continued ticking off the points Xuthos had listed—"the General will hang you out to dry, and I'm not taking that bullet for anyone." Well, he would for any of the Sunfires, but that went without saying. And even then, Talos would think long and hard about it first. One didn't step in front of an angry General Athanasia without careful thought.

"But you were right about getting caught."

"Well, that's something." Xuthos raised his chin in challenge. "So if you didn't come to tell me any of that, why did you come to see me? Special last orders?"

"Nah, that's the General's job. I just came to say that when you think of antagonizing Mikon—and you will—remember two things: he's half-olympian, and he's a Sunfire."

Xuthos snorted, pushed off the wall, and went back to packing. "So he's got a whole family of Sunfires who will come after him? No one in the rebellion *ever* forgets that."

Was there a bitter undertone to that? Talos couldn't tell.

"No." He waited until Xuthos looked up, and then he smiled slowly, savoring the puzzled look that came into the other man's face. "That means he was personally trained by Icarus."

Xuthos's eyes widened, no doubt remembering the numerous times he'd sparred with the Sunfire leader.

Talos gave him a jaunty salute. "Audeamus."

.+.

KORALIA HAD EXPECTED that Talos would find her sometime that night, so the knock on her door was no surprise.

"Come in," she called, not looking up from the linked belt she was rolling to fit more snugly inside her pack. Hephaestus made the most gorgeous chain-mesh belts that added armor-like flair to an evening gown, but they were a pain to pack in a way that wouldn't tangle them. She'd once had the knack of doing it quickly, but it had been a few years since she'd done it often and she was having a hard time remembering.

"Have a seat," she invited, with a quick glance over her shoulder. "I thought I'd see you."

Talos unfolded the camp chair leaning against the desk and sat down. "I told Xuthos that if he got in your way, he was on his own."

She snorted. "Do you think he will?"

"Nah."

That was good to know. Xuthos was the team member she knew the least, and she wasn't terribly comfortable going into this mission without knowing him better, especially since he'd be posing as her bodyguard. But the time for preparation was over, so she'd have to deal with it.

"Are we *sure* Ariadne or Ambrosia or someone down there isn't going to recognize him?" She knew she was overthinking; they'd already gone over that detail in planning meetings. But this was her first mission with the rebellion, and she'd met these people barely a week ago. She didn't worry she couldn't handle it—Amazonian operations were often sudden and didn't leave much time for preparation—but the women warriors trained closely together all the time. They *knew* each other with a familiarity she didn't have here. Any information Talos could give her that would help her feel more comfortable with her team would be welcome.

Talos rubbed his chin. "I really don't know. I believe him when he says he doesn't remember ever meeting her or seeing her. He has an excellent memory. And she was barely on base—she usually met me or Icarus elsewhere. It's plausible that he was never around at the same time she was."

Koralia stashed the now-folded belt in her pack and sank down on her cot, rubbing her forehead. "I'm just trying to...put it all together."

He nodded, understanding softening the hard lines around his eyes.

"What else should I know about him?" she asked. From where she sat, she had to look up to see him, so she scooted to the end of the bed, facing him with only a short distance between them. "What can *you* tell me about him? Besides the fact that you two don't get along."

He looked gratified that she'd asked. "Well, he's good at thinking on his feet and flying by the seat of his pants. He kept this fleet together and got them home after the disaster at the Battle of Stratonikeia a year ago, when Icarus and his second were wounded too badly to organize the retreat."

"Ah. Okay." *I remember that mission...and how long it took for him to recover.* She crossed her legs underneath her. "How come he isn't on watch lists somewhere? He's been a rebel for years, hasn't he? He's got to be around our age."

He nodded, leaning forward and resting his forearms on his knees. "A year or two younger, I think, yes. And he's not on a watch list somewhere because he's got a genius for staying out of *official* trouble. He's the worst for pranks and chasing every girl in sight and showing off and never being serious, but he's crazy talented at not getting caught. It's weird."

Weird or not, that would come in handy. "Good to know."

"Yeah. Xuthos talks a big game but he's capable—the General wouldn't have anyone in her fleet who wasn't and neither would—" He swallowed and hurried past the name they were both thinking. "And he's loyal, you don't have to worry about that."

Slowly, she raised her eyes to his, wishing they didn't have to talk about how many ways this mission could go wrong. "Sometimes the most loyal people are still the ones to betray you in the end."

Brown eyes blinked closed for a moment and then opened again, holding hers steadily. "I know," he said quietly, his voice barely above a husky whisper. "But not him. You don't have to worry about that. I'd stake a lot on it."

She reached out and gripped his hand for a minute. "That's good enough for me."

His smile was faint but warm.

"Mikon is what you really wanted to talk to me about, isn't it?" she guessed.

Hesitance settled in his tone. "Yes."

"So talk. What should I know?"

He ran his fingers through his thick dark curls, rumpling them. "His mother...you know about her, right?" At her nod, he continued, "She was a mess. She only ever listened to him when he would go into a rage and scream at her. It took years for him to learn to control that. He's good at it now," he added hurriedly. "Don't think he isn't. But you saw him a few nights ago. His temper can be dangerous." Talos stared at the floor. "And you're going among a lot of luxurious idiots who will remind him of olympians. And he has to mentally go back to that place too, in order to play the part. Plus, he hates Daedalus for what he did to Icarus and me. Just..." He looked up, and his gaze locked with hers, burning with concern and the weight of love for his brother.

"I'll be careful," she promised. "I grew up on Akwila. Olympians and humans and other races going into rages isn't exactly foreign to me." She winced; she hadn't meant for that to sound flippant, but he looked relieved.

"You did really well calming him the other day. I'm not worried he'll get you into trouble, just...just watch him?"

"You have my word." She moved closer and reached out again, sliding her hands over his and holding them. "You don't have to do this alone," she whispered. "I'm not Icarus and I never will be and I can't take his place, but..."

"But you're *here*," he murmured. "And you know war, and you know what it does to people, and you know what Icarus was to the Sunfires and what he left me with." He turned his hands so he could clasp hers. "Thanks."

She didn't have any response to that, just a nod.

He stood up, and she rose with him, walking the few steps to the door. Before he pushed the button to open it, he turned to look at her, and before she realized either of them had moved, his arms were around her and hers were around him and he was holding her tightly.

Embracing Talos felt different than the other Sunfires. Mikon hugged with a warmth almost at odds with his exuberance. Ianessa was comfort personified. Talos was fire and iron, both things she had known from birth. He felt familiar, the intensity in his veins the same that had run through hers all her life.

When his arms loosened, she pulled his head down and kissed his forehead. "I'll take care of him," she repeated. "We'll both come back."

Talos nodded, one short, sharp movement, and then he was gone, striding quickly down the gray hallway.

She closed the door and leaned against it. "We're trying, but we miss you, Icarus," she whispered to the small room. "Starfire, how we miss you."

+

THE NEXT MORNING'S goodbye was short, to Koralia's relief. She was more than ready to get the mission started. Talos flew her, Mikon, and Xuthos out to Hephaestus's ship in a shuttle and helped carry their bags over.

Running his hand through Koralia's hair when he hugged her, Talos whispered in her ear, "Come back safely, and don't leave Xuthos behind, even if you want to."

"Noted," she teased him over her shoulder as she went through the hatch to her father's ship.

Behind her, he hugged Mikon hard, which looked comical because Mikon was taller by five or six inches.

Then Talos shook hands with Xuthos, and as soon as all three were standing on Hephaestus's ship, he was gone, detaching and spinning away to return to base.

They were on their own now.

# CHAPTER 17

"You are approaching the border of Krete. Hover and send your entrance pass. Repeat: hover and send your entrance pass. Do not proceed without authorization. Your ship will be harmed and so will you."

Koralia checked the time and smiled. They were right on schedule.

"Couldn't they have gotten a less annoying electronic voice?" Mikon complained, pushing the button to send their authorization and flopping back into his seat.

"People wouldn't listen as well if it wasn't annoying, I think." Xuthos dropped into the co-pilot's seat and kicked his feet up on the dash, ignoring the annoyed look Mikon gave him.

"Probably not," Koralia agreed. "Xuthos, please put your vest on. I'm not a fan of leaving things for just before the ship's door is about to open." She arched an eyebrow playfully at him to soften her tone.

"Ma'am!" He snapped ramrod straight and went toward a side bench where he'd left his outer armor.

"I'll be right back," she told Mikon. It was time to dress for her role.

In the back room, as she pulled the long black gown over her head and hooked up the intricate copper belt, she sighed in relief that she was appearing as Hephaestus's daughter. She'd never have been able to wear her mother's styles without someone helping her into them. Vulcani makeup styles were simpler too. This way, it took only a few minutes to dress.

"Proceed at one-quarter speed until you have cleared the gates. Repeat:

proceed at one-quarter speed until you have cleared the gates. Then you may land at platform three." The electronic voice was speaking again when she stepped out, fully gowned and shod and ready to meet Krete's royal family as an olympian.

The ship began to move again, sliding slowly forward. There was a ripple in front of them, like sunlight glinting blue and green off water, and then nothing. They didn't even feel anything as they passed through; the planet was suddenly before them.

"So that's Krete." Mikon leaned forward. "Shining jewel of the Kaptara Sector."

"Shining pain in the ass," Koralia said in an undertone.

Startled, both men spun around to look at her. Mikon's eyes widened, flickering up and down as he took in her outfit, and he gave her a slow, approving smile.

Xuthos whistled, but when she looked at him, his face was straight. "Magnificent, my lady," he said, standing and bowing.

She gave him a cool nod, slipping back into her olympian manners as easily as breathing. "Mikon?"

He blinked and seemed to realize he'd been staring at her. "Yes?"

"Pilot?"

"Right, yes." He swiveled his chair around and closed his hands over the controls again.

"And, yes, that's Krete." She put one hand on the back of his seat. "It's like someone put a clawed hand down on a plate of solid land and shattered it like glass, scattering the shards over the surface of the planet to solidify in the ocean where they fell."

Mikon stared at the vista opening up below and tipped his head back to see her. "That's...I never thought of it like that, but that's exactly what it looks like."

She lifted one shoulder in a half shrug. "I can't take credit for it. It's what Antiope said when we were here last."

"Antiope," Xuthos repeated, sounding impressed. "Even *I* know that name."

Koralia looked at him. She hadn't intended to name-drop. "She was just a warrior to me," she said. "One of my generals, and hard as nails on me."

"Ah." Xuthos was looking at her again, his eyes traveling down her simple gown and gauzy shoulder cloak to the belt at her waist and lower to the heels that brought her closer to his height.

For just a second, she wondered if she was going to have a problem with him. Would he be able to remember he was supposed to be her bodyguard here and not her social equal?

She hoped so.

The ship settled gently on the landing platform, and Mikon powered it down. Collectively, they all took a deep breath. Through the door that was now sliding open, they could see a few people stepping off a land shuttle to meet them.

Xuthos moved to stand in front of her, and Mikon stepped up beside her, his hand sliding down to grasp hers and squeeze it quickly before he let go and slouched lazily, looking his part to perfection.

Darkness was swiftly falling as they left the ship, Xuthos staying one step in front of her while Mikon lounged at her side. Crashing waves could be heard in the distance, amplified through the dusk that softened yet projected all sounds. The landing platforms were lit softly with blue lights, except theirs, which was brilliant with red and yellow lights.

"Lady Skotia, darling!" A slim, brown-skinned woman came toward them with hands outstretched, dark hair falling in ringlets around her shoulders and navy gown flowing around her...practically falling off her shoulders.

Some things never changed.

"Ariadne." Koralia allowed the Kretan princess to clasp her hands and returned the grip, modulating her strength so it wouldn't crush the other girl's hands. "What a pleasure to see you again."

Ariadne stepped back and looked over the rest of the rebel party, and Koralia forced herself to breathe normally. This was the crucial moment. Would Ariadne recognize anyone in her group, even through the temporary Vulcani tattoos that covered half of Xuthos's face and the arrogant smirk Mikon wore?

Apparently not, because she just nodded to Mikon and cast Xuthos an admiring look before hooking her arm through Koralia's and pulling her around the ship toward the palace, waving away the small shuttle that had brought her. Koralia was glad; the walk was not a long one, and she wanted a chance to look around. Xuthos fell into correct bodyguard formation, to the side and slightly in front of her, while Mikon dropped behind them, looking around eagerly, taking in the planet.

"It's good to have you back," Ariadne was saying. The words sounded rehearsed, but Koralia couldn't tell if they were false yet. "Are you very tired?"

"Not yet. Do you still take dinner late here?"

"Oh yes. Dear Father refuses to change it." Ariadne rolled her eyes. "You must dine with me in my rooms tonight. We can eat with the family tomorrow."

Perfect. That would give her a chance to make some discreet inquiries.

The landing platforms were a modern material—non-skid and all-weather

—but the pathways between them were traditional stone, red-orange in color, fitted together expertly and curving around platforms as they led the walker to the palace. Which was as beautiful as she remembered, navy stone rising before them, pillars accented with light yellow, seashell white, and the same red-orange as the paths. Circular white motifs marched around the borders of the stone walls, which somehow looked graceful instead of blocky.

"Your palace is so beautiful," she told Ariadne sincerely.

"Isn't it? A little *dull* inside, but..." Ariadne blinked and, as if remembering the proper formal acknowledgement, added, "We are gratified by your appreciation."

*Not as glib as she once was. Unless she's just tired?*

The inside of the palace glowed with red and yellow lights. Decorated in a lavish, coastal theme, walking through it felt like being underwater, their way lit with coral-colored lamps in brackets on the walls.

Ariadne showed them to a large suite with several rooms.

"My chambers are down the hallway to the right, around the bend, and two doors down," she told Koralia. "Come find me as soon as you've washed. We'll eat and catch up. Don't worry about dressing," she called back over her shoulder as she left.

Xuthos snickered, and Koralia sent him a stern look. "Get your mind up off the floor."

"This is perfect," Mikon said, walking to the far windows of the antechamber and looking out. "We're over a garden." His eyebrows drawing into a frown, he looked quickly at Koralia. "Do you think she knew we wanted that?"

"Voice down until scramblers are up," she reminded him in a whisper. "And we're going to assume that she knows more than she seems to, but putting us here probably isn't part of that. This is one of their top guest chambers, and I am an olympian."

"Perks of traveling in style." He grinned at her.

"Precisely." She turned, taking in the layout. It was starkly simple, the antechamber leading to four rooms, one sitting room and three bedrooms, each with a bathroom. On the other side of the antechamber, a pillared balcony overlooked the gardens.

"My lady." Xuthos bowed, indicating the largest of the bedrooms.

"Good form," she praised his bow, patting him on the shoulder, and Mikon snickered as she walked into her room and closed the door.

When she came out a few minutes later, having washed the non-existent travel dust off, Mikon was lounging on the balcony, watching the dying twilight. Xuthos waited nearby, stripped down to indoor armor, lightweight but impenetrable mesh one could barely feel the weight of, she knew from experience.

"Oh good, let's go," Mikon said, coming back inside. He looked like he'd dragged his fingers through his hair in an attempt to straighten it.

"You aren't going anywhere," she reminded him. "Sleep."

His face darkened.

"Please?" she added. "I need you fresh tomorrow, especially because she's probably going to keep me up half the night."

"Fine." He threw himself into one of the chairs in the antechamber. "I'll sleep. But only if you first tell me why they call you Skotia."

She grinned, too amused to be annoyed. "It's my birth name—my mother's name for me, and the one I grew up with. I only started using Koralia about five years ago."

He nodded, his brow furrowed in thought. "Five standard years or five olympian years?"

"Standard years. I almost always reckon in them anymore."

"Me too," he admitted.

The sooner she went to Ariadne, the sooner she could start looking for the information they needed, but she lingered, enjoying the dark that wrapped around the rooms, lit only by a few candles now, and the camaraderie that existed here.

"You will sleep while I'm gone?" she asked after a few minutes.

"I'll sleep, I'll sleep." He huffed. "I said it."

"Good. And behave." She winked, which won a smile from him. "Ready?" she asked Xuthos. His answer was to salute and square up behind her.

With a last encouraging look at Mikon, whose glum look she steeled herself to ignore, she swept out of the room and down the halls to Ariadne's chambers.

✛

"Come in, come in!" Ariadne called from behind the servant who opened the door.

Koralia entered the antechamber and paused, taking in her surroundings. Through one doorway, she could see a small table laid for two with luxurious couches on either side. Through another, servants were airing out a bed.

"I won't need you," she told Xuthos, her tone normal, just loud enough to be heard in the other rooms. They'd discussed it already, and she had planned to send him out halfway through the meal, but she could see Ariadne was ready for a long chat, and it worked as well or better to dismiss Xuthos now.

His eyes widened, caught off guard, but he still managed to sound bored when he said, "Now, my lady, your father wouldn't want me to leave you."

Talos was right, he was quick on his feet.

With effort, she kept a straight face. "I'm in the royal palace of Krete. What do you imagine is going to happen to me here? Now go." Standing on tiptoe, she leaned in to whisper, "Go look for the garden and...you know." *Send word to base that we've arrived.* She arched her eyebrows, silently reminding him of his job. The signal might not get out through the Labyrinth, but he needed to try anyway. She patted his cheek, just distant enough to be dismissive without appearing condescending. That had never been her style and would have been a red flag to anyone, even Ariadne, who hadn't seen her in years.

His jaw clenched under her hand, despite his amused smirk, and it took her a second to realize that the alarm in his eyes was real, not faked. He honestly thought he'd be leaving her in danger.

Obviously, he'd never spent time around the royal families of the galaxy. Krete could be a seething hive of traitors and she'd still be safe the first night. Guest Custom demanded it.

"I must insist, my lady," he tried, but she patted his cheek again and then waved him off.

"Go."

Reluctantly, dragging his feet and looking back multiple times, he left.

"Loyal," Ariadne remarked, standing in the doorway of her dining room.

"Yes, and new." Koralia sighed as if it annoyed her. She followed Ariadne into the dining room and sat down on the couch opposite the doorway.

*Take it slow. Ease her in.*

"He's not actually from Vulcani, is he? He doesn't look like it. His skin is too light." Ariadne sounded a little too interested in the pilot, and that worried Koralia until she remembered that the princess had always had a sharp eye for a good body.

"No, from nearby." Koralia leaned back as if she couldn't care less. "And younger than Father usually hires, but he was down on his luck. And I thought I'd try someone more my age for a change."

"Really..." Ariadne looked speculative. But the princess didn't question further, just said, "Well, when you tire of him, send him my way. I could do with someone handsome for a change. Father's latest hires have been rather plain."

Xuthos was handsome enough, Koralia supposed—tall and dark-haired, with tanned skin and narrow, angled eyes. But trust Ariadne not to even *ask* about his fighting or guarding abilities. Koralia refrained from rolling her eyes. Yet another thing that hadn't changed.

"Have you talked to any of our old classmates recently?" Ariadne asked, stretching out on the couch and daintily lifting a few grapes to her lips.

Their old classmates. The arrogant half-olympians and royal children from around the galaxy, including several Jupiterian sons, all alumni of one of Belus's most notable colleges, which catered specifically to planetary royals and half-bloods instead of full olympians. Koralia hadn't officially attended the school—she'd only been there as aide to a few Amazons who were running a summer training camp—but the other students had counted her as one of them in some bizarre twist of reasoning that had always baffled her.

Probably something to do with her lineage. If they could claim her as a student, it raised the prestige of their school. Which was why they also claimed one of Apollo's sons had attended there, when in fact he'd only been there for a weekend event.

"No," Koralia answered, settling herself more comfortably and starting to eat. "No, I've been busy."

"Yes, I heard, the Amazons!" Ariadne sat up. "Have you been traveling a lot?"

"A fair amount off and on." She could feel herself slipping more and more into olympian speech patterns as she settled into the atmosphere. The nobles and galactic royals, including Krete, had always aped the olympian lifestyle. Thank stars she was only supposed to be here for three days. Any longer than that and she'd start to choke on the opulence and formality she had left behind in her mother's court.

"Please tell me about it!" Ariadne exclaimed. "You know how I long to travel."

That was possibly the first time she'd felt genuine emotion from the princess since arriving. Koralia made a mental note of it. "I'd be happy to, but I warn you, the stories will get long, so let's catch up on everything else first and then I'll tell stories until you beg me to stop."

Ariadne's eyes were shining with anticipation, making her look closer to actually pretty, instead of a petulant, plain princess. "Let us, then. Who is the gorgeous cub you have with you now?"

How Mikon would snarl at being called a cub. He was more like a full-grown wildcat. But she kept that to herself and shrugged carelessly. "He's a half-blood, connected on the Apollonian side somewhere. We met at a dinner of Dad's, and we've been kicking around together for a few months. He's fun and not a bad pilot, which helps me. Tata and Dad have had me looking into several things for them while I'm on temporary hiatus from the Amazons."

It wasn't too much information to give all at once. Listing what they had been doing lately was standard olympian practice, a status symbol. Koralia had always found it boring, but it served her purpose tonight, so she played it out just as she'd seen countless cousins do.

"Lucky girl, not just one, but two handsome men around you," Ariadne said with relish, biting into a piece of meat as if it was something else.

Koralia rolled her eyes. "Eh, sure. Remember, I'm from Akwila. I'm used to warriors of every shade and height."

Ariadne sighed with envy, and Koralia barely restrained her irritation. She sipped from her wine glass, paused, and took another sip.

"I had forgotten about the unusual tang your wines have."

"Oh, that." Ariadne waved her fingers dismissively, numerous rings clicking together. "The sea air. Sometimes I long for a clear wine, but Father says there's no need when ours are so superior to anywhere else."

Based on her tone, Ariadne wasn't very fond of her father. But hadn't she always been more of a mama's girl anyway? Koralia couldn't remember; too many years had passed.

"I imagine it grows tiring after a while, but my dad might just want to import some. And speaking of my fathers, they're interested in some of the advancements Krete has been making lately." There. She'd made her play. She reached for more fruit, waiting.

Ariadne wrinkled her nose. "Must we talk business now? You have days to do that."

That, too, was standard olympian practice. Introduce business, to assure your hosts you had a legitimate reason for being there, and then be begged to wait.

"My pleasure. Now tell me about your family. How is your father?"

"Too busy," Ariadne said shortly, but Koralia could tell the irritation wasn't directed at her.

"And your mother?" This was what she really wanted to know, and hopefully, Ariadne was relaxed enough to tell her something of importance now. Pasiphae had been rumored to be crazy for over a decade and many knew it, but since Koralia hadn't been on Krete in a few years, the question wouldn't sound odd.

"She's been unwell." Ariadne sounded a strange mix of sad and scornful.

Well, that was...something. "I'm sorry to hear it."

"Perhaps she will be well enough to see you for a few hours," Ariadne said, but her voice was doubtful under the fake tone that was back.

"And yourself? Weren't you working on your priestess ranks?"

"I was. Am. I'm third rank now."

"Congratulations."

Ariadne shrugged that off too, leaning forward, her eyes fixed eagerly on Koralia. "Now. Tell me all about your travels with the Amazons."

So Koralia spun tale after tale of her travels and wars until the lights flickered low. Not until dawn began to pale the sky did Ariadne release her to go back to her room and collapse in sleep.

✝

"ANY WORD FROM THEM YET?"

If Talos asked that one more time, Athanasia might ban him from the bridge. "None yet, aside from the message that said they were about to go through the Labyrinth."

"Sorry." Talos sighed, sitting down heavily in a chair as if he couldn't stand up any more. He had to be exhausted—he'd barely had any sleep the previous night, he'd been reorganizing duty rosters all day, and now he was pulling up maps to review again, as if it was a vital thing that couldn't be left until tomorrow.

Ianessa was no better, hardly leaving her station all day and looking up at every com alert, but at least she was combing through article after article on Krete and Kretan history. That would benefit them more in the long run than Talos's re-running of maps and Labyrinth boundaries.

Athanasia would give them one more hour and then she'd boot both of them to bed and go herself. Koralia knew what she was doing. They needed to be patient and trust she would be in contact as soon as she could.

Another com alert rang through the bridge, and they stiffened, their heads up and their eyes fixed on the com screen with burning intensity. But it was Brygos, letting Athanasia know he was coming as fast as he could and would be on base in twenty-four hours.

Talos and Ianessa resumed work, and Athanasia shook her head.

It would be a long night.

# CHAPTER 18

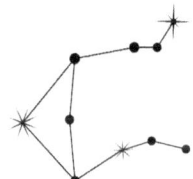

**K**oralia was woken by shouting: Mikon's voice, harsh and angry. As she fought her way out of the bed—she really hated thin, filmy sheets—she tried to make out individual words but couldn't. Yanking on some clothes, she did manage to figure out he wasn't actually shouting; it just sounded like it.

"So make something else up then!" Mikon was growling when she strode into the sitting room. He had Xuthos pinned to the wall, his arm across the pilot's throat, not hard enough to choke him but enough to hold him still. He glanced up at Koralia when she entered, and his eyes were pure fury.

He'd gone into a rage so soon?

"What's going on?" she pitched her voice low and unconcerned, like it didn't matter to her that Xuthos was flat against the wall and looking worried for his life.

"He"—Mikon jabbed a finger into Xuthos's collarbone—"told a servant that he was sneaking around the gardens for a rendezvous with you."

"Had to," Xuthos gasped out. "Suspicious!"

"And you couldn't have thought of *anything* else?" Mikon snarled. "She just lost Icarus!"

Xuthos's eyes widened even more, if that was possible, and he tried to turn his head to look at Koralia. "You're...*her?*"

It was *way* too early in the morning for this.

"Mikon, please let him go." She tried to put firmness into her voice without too much command. It was hard to tell how angry Mikon was at the moment, and the last thing she needed was to make it worse.

"The bastard needs a good beating," Mikon said, not moving.

"And trust me, I will handle it. For now, please let him go." When Mikon still didn't move, she added, "I don't want to make it an order."

Reluctantly, Mikon released him.

The instant he was free, Xuthos scrambled away from the younger man. "It was the best reason," he tried to explain. "And the only one they'd really beli—"

"Not now," Koralia cut him off and pointed to the door. "Out. I believe you, but we'll talk about it later. Go for a walk or something."

He lingered, worried eyes on her.

"I'm fine, and I'll *be* fine, but not unless you go," she hissed at him. "I'll find you after."

He left, and she waited until she heard the outer door close behind him before she turned to look at Mikon.

He was facing away from her, his hands clenching and unclenching, his shoulders heaving.

"Hey," she said gently, walking around him so she could see his face. "Hey, it's okay."

"It's not okay," he snapped. "He just made the story up without even consulting you—you, the other person involved. *And* the mission commander!" Indigo fire flared hotter in his eyes.

*What to do, what to do.* She tried to think. Talos had given her the background for Mikon's rages but no specifics for how to handle them. Then she remembered the docking bay.

"Hey," she said again, taking one of his wrists and leading him over to a sofa. She sat down, but he resisted, standing still and glaring out the window.

She slid her fingers under the edge of his sleeve until two fingertips rested over his pulse point. With her thumb, she stroked his wrist and the back of his hand, mindless circles and shapes, back and forth.

For a long, long moment, she feared it wasn't working. Then his pulse started to calm slightly and the tension in his muscles began to seep out.

She held back a sigh of relief and kept going until he dropped to the floor at her feet. At first, she thought he'd fallen, but then he leaned against her knees and looked at her.

"He should've asked you first," he seethed. "He should have."

"Mmhmm." Reaching for his other hand, she clasped it, holding both his hands now and waiting until more tension had left and he was relaxing against her.

"He had no right," Mikon muttered, but the anger was gone, and what remained sounded more like...grief?

Then she remembered his words. *She just lost Icarus.*

"It's okay to miss him, you know," she whispered.

Mikon nodded, leaning into her. With a deep, shuddering breath, he put his head down on her knees and cried.

Anger, she was ready for. But she hadn't prepared for this, and she stiffened, unsure of what to do besides continuing to hold him. Wrapping an arm around his shoulders, she stroked his head, her fingers smoothing through his auburn curls.

Weirdly, it didn't feel like comforting a child. Just two friends, grieving the same person, matching black holes inside them. Talos's pain felt different, further shaped by the responsibility on his shoulders, but Mikon's—his was pure grief. Much like hers.

It was over in a few minutes, and he sat up, shaking the tears out of his eyes and pulling away. "I'm me again," he said gruffly.

"I know." She patted the seat next to her, and he sat down, a bit awkwardly at first, but then he leaned against her and wrapped his arm around her shoulders, pulling her against him.

They sat that way for several minutes—breathing in the late-morning breeze, silently enduring the pain that hovered around all of them these days, and soaking in the comfort of a friend to share it.

"I need to go talk to Xuthos," she said finally, pulling back to look at Mikon. "He was right, it is a good idea and a great cover story." Especially since she wasn't known for sleeping with her bodyguards. With any luck, Ariadne would think she'd fled here to keep the affair secret from her father.

Mikon looked rebellious.

She put a hand on his shoulder. "Can you trust me?"

He tilted his head, studying her. "Only if you agree that if he steps out of line, I get to punch him."

"*If* he steps out of line, you can punch him, but only *after* I say so. Understood?"

"Understood." He vaulted up off the sofa and held out his hand to pull her up.

"Good." Once on her feet, she let go of his hand and shoved him toward the door. "Now go get cleaned up, and make sure to wear a white tunic."

"Why?" He stopped in the doorway and looked back at her.

"Because you're going to see Ariadne, and it adds to the illusion that you're connected to Apollo."

He eyed her, his mouth quirked to the side, but she thought the expression was more him not being sure he *wanted* to be connected to Apollo than doubting her word.

While Mikon got ready for the day, Koralia went to find Xuthos. He was waiting outside the door of their suite, and he stood quickly when she came out.

"Listen, I'm sor—"

She stopped him with a shake of her head. "No, *you* listen. Let's walk." They could have talked on the balcony, but Mikon would have overheard them there, and she needed privacy for this conversation.

"Milady Skotia." A servant came around a bend in the hallway and dropped into a curtsy on seeing them. "Her Highness is awake and ready for breakfast now, if you are."

*Blast it.* This conversation would have to wait. "Inform Princess Ariadne that I'll be there in fifteen minutes, GST." She thought Krete used Galactic Standard Time, so the extra information might not be necessary, but she couldn't remember for sure and she didn't need misunderstandings this morning.

The servant hurried off, and she pulled Xuthos back into their suite. Crooking her fingers, she motioned for him to bend down, and he did, angling his head so she could whisper into his ear. "It was a good story, and we'll use it. You did well. Just don't push it. And as much as possible, keep your hands to yourself when we're around Mikon."

He turned so he could see her. "Because of Icarus?" he asked, keeping his voice low.

She nodded.

"I'm sorry," he said quickly, his eyes dark and serious. "I had no idea."

She raised her eyebrows, reaching up to braid her hair loosely. "Why would you? If it would have changed your story, it's a good thing you didn't know. Nothing else you came up with would have been as believable as this. I'm not bothered—it's a mission. Like Icarus would say, we have a job to do. Let's get it done."

He didn't have a response to that, but she could feel his eyes following her as she went into her room to change.

+

"HOW UNDER SKIES do you contrive to look so fresh?" Ariadne greeted her when Koralia appeared for breakfast, one hand in Mikon's arm and Xuthos walking at her other side.

"Warrior hours." Koralia sat down on the couch closest to Ariadne so Mikon wouldn't be forced to sit right next to the princess.

Ariadne blinked, like she wasn't sure if she was being made fun of or not, and shrugged. "So you're Ky," she said, turning to Mikon.

It was the name they'd assigned Mikon for this mission, because it was simple and easy to remember.

Koralia darted a quick look at him, but he responded as if used to princesses. "And you must be the Princess Ariadne. They didn't tell me you were so captivating."

Ariadne trilled a high laugh, delighted.

Mikon continued to charm her throughout the meal and even persuaded her to take them on a garden tour afterwards. Since the Ariadne that Koralia remembered preferred the city streets to the gardens, this was a feat.

Leaving the palace, they stepped out into muggy air that just managed not to be oppressive because of the breeze blowing in off the sea. Koralia cast a quick eye toward the sky. In most places, this level of mugginess would signal an approaching storm, and wouldn't *that* just make their job interesting today. But Krete's sky shone bright blue with only wisps of clouds.

Ariadne led them quickly through the shrubbery and flowers, pointing out unusual plants and notable sculptures. *The visitor's tour,* Koralia thought with a curl of her lip. She would much rather have walked slowly and enjoyed the greenery, but Ariadne apparently didn't believe in that.

When Mikon became absorbed in an elaborate fountain, Ariadne came and slid her arm around Koralia. "You naughty girl!" she said in what she probably thought was an undertone. "So you finally learned to take full advantage of your bodyguards." Ariadne wiggled her eyebrows. "Ky told me about you and Xuthos."

"Well, I won't get to enjoy it for long if you talk about it so loudly that anyone can overhear." She shot Ariadne an annoyed glance, and the princess made an "oops" face. Not even a full day into this assignment, and Koralia was already wishing it was over.

"Don't worry, I won't tell anyone." Ariadne giggled, patting Koralia on the arm. "But I want to hear *details* later."

Details were exactly what she wasn't going to get, not if she begged the entire time they were on the planet.

"And this is the queen's garden," Ariadne continued in her tour-guide voice. "My mother is but the latest in a long line of queens to call this beautiful place home."

Koralia turned in a circle, raising her eyebrows. *Now this, I like.* The rest of Krete's palace gardens were showy and ostentatious, obviously created with display in mind. The queen's garden was more natural, like it had been a labor of love over many years. Unexpected twists brought them into patios where fountains tumbled or ponds sparkled, and at one end, there was a short maze passageway between tall hedges. It was true beauty, as opposed to the false grandeur of the other gardens.

"Oh! I'm sorry. Are you okay?"

Koralia was hurrying toward Mikon before he'd finished speaking, wondering what he'd gotten himself into now.

A minotaur girl stood in front of Mikon, the two of them looking at each other with wide eyes. She was dressed in the belted mid-length tunic common to Kretan servants. Her head came up to about the middle of his chest, her skin was red-brown speckled with white, and her horns, ears, and head tails were short.

A teenager maybe? Koralia had no idea how to guess the ages of minotaurs.

When the girl noticed Ariadne, she ducked her head briefly and bowed to Mikon, mumbling something in a tone that sounded apologetic before she hurried off.

Ariadne frowned, and for just a flash, Koralia saw the arrogant superiority she suspected always hid behind the empty-headed front. Mikon hurried to explain.

"It was my fault. I didn't see her. I made her fall; don't blame her." He kept his eyes on Ariadne, not looking at Koralia. He was playing his part well, knowing better than to chance a look at her or Xuthos.

"Hmff." Ariadne sniffed.

"Who was that?" Koralia asked curiously.

"Mother's little *pet*." Ariadne sneered the last word.

"Pet?" Koralia didn't have to pretend to sound horrified.

With a disdainful sniff, Ariadne turned away. "Servant, supposedly. But she might as well be a pet or toy the way Mother always wants her near. The," Ariadne used a Kretan word unfamiliar to Koralia, "could do with more manners. She should've kept her eyes on the ground as soon as she stood up."

Mikon shot a look behind Ariadne to Koralia, a disgusted glance that spoke volumes about what he thought of Krete's prize princess.

Ariadne walked quickly, an annoyed set to her shoulders and hips as she led them from the gardens. Was it worth annoying her further to try and get information?

At this point, yes, it was. The minotaur girl could be just the person they had come to find, the patriot who was supposed to be in the palace. *If* the message was genuine.

"I've never seen one of—what exactly *is* she anyway?" Koralia asked, walking on Ariadne's other side.

"Minotaur." Ariadne sniffed and shook her shoulders like she was trying to get rid of a buzzing fly. "They're from the other side of the planet, off some of the larger islands. They are a backwards people, mostly gardeners and farmers. Mother has them working here, and a few have some magic gift with defense tech, so Dad keeps them around."

*Gardeners?* The queen employed them as gardeners? Had they built this one? Koralia tried to look subtly around at the garden Ariadne was hurrying them out of. The layout resembled a maze in more ways than one, but simple enough that getting lost was unlikely.

Maybe she could venture one more question. "And your mother likes them as servants too?" She made the question sound faintly mocking, projecting an attitude of superciliousness about a mad queen's idiosyncrasies.

"Servants...and more," Ariadne said cryptically. "It's too hot for gardens today. Let's go swimming."

"I like where you're going, but I have something even better," Mikon said. "Swimming *races*." He raised his eyebrows at Ariadne in challenge. "If you're up for it, princess."

"Me? Did you forget I *live* here? Surrounded by ocean? I swim every day, Apollonian; you won't be able to keep up with me." There was that annoying laugh again.

Koralia would rather have stayed in the gardens, but maybe swimming would put the princess in a better mood.

While Ariadne was giggling up at Mikon, tipping her head in a way she thought coy, Koralia glanced quickly at Xuthos and raised her eyebrows. Had he managed to find a good spot to meet later?

He answered with the barest of nods.

That was one thing done then. With no more reasons to linger, Koralia turned toward the sparkling sands of the beach, following the sound of Ariadne's annoying voice.

✝

"TAL, WHERE'S THE GENERAL?"

Talos halted and turned back to look at Ianessa, who had ambushed him from an office on the command deck. "How should I know. Haven't you been on base all day? You're more likely to know where she is than I am."

"Well, I don't, and I need her, because I've just found something that could

165

blow this whole mission wide open for us. In a good way," she added when his eyes narrowed. "Though I don't know if you'll agree."

"Show me." He held out his hand for the scrip she was carrying.

"Ah, ah." She pulled it away and held it behind her. "Aren't you on your way somewhere?"

"Yeah, a debrief that will wait a few minutes. Now what do you have?" He sidestepped around her and tried to reach the scrip, but she was just faster than him and evaded his grasp.

A door closed down the hall, and the General's voice asked, "Shouldn't you two be working?"

Talos rolled his eyes. "I *was* going to debrief my patrol pilots, but she won't show me what she found, so now I'm stuck."

"I was waiting for you," Ianessa told Athanasia sweetly, dodging around Talos to show the General what she held.

"And why do I care that Queen Pasiphae of Krete supposedly had an affair some twenty-odd years ago?" The General looked up from the scrip and raised her eyebrows at Ianessa.

"Look at the next article. It was supposedly with Daedalus."

"Impossible," Talos scoffed. "He'd never."

"I don't know, it sounded kind of convincing," Ianessa said. "And it was right around the time Pasiphae's madness started."

He shook his head. "No, you don't get it. Daedalus barely even looked at a woman the whole time I lived with them. Seven *years*, Ness."

"Maybe because he was carrying a torch for the queen," Ianessa countered.

Talos wanted to laugh, but he made himself stop and think about it. Daedalus and Pasiphae? Yes, his uncle was in and out of the palace at all hours, but he was the royal inventor—there was always something needing his attention. At least, that's what he'd told Talos and Icarus. Was it possible that Pasiphae had been one of those 'things'?

No.

Couldn't be.

Not Daedalus, the man so dedicated to science that he could barely remember what day it was. Talos and Icarus had tried for three years to get him interested in a woman—any woman, hoping it would distract him from bullying Talos, and it had never worked.

There had never been the slightest sign that Daedalus had any feelings for Pasiphae other than annoyance when she wanted him to build her some new and outlandish invention.

"No way," he said again, more decisively. "It's just a rumor."

The General pursed her lips, thinking. "I agree—it's just not likely from

Daedalus. But send it to the ground team," she said, handing it back. "Maybe they can use the information anyway, to distract people if nothing else."

"Right away." Ianessa turned around to go back to her station, calling over her shoulder. "If I'm right about this, you don't get to argue with me for a month!"

"In your dreams!" He called back. Since the General was going in the same direction he had been before Ianessa waylaid him, he spun around and walked at her side.

"Koralia will take care of them, you know."

Startled, he looked down at her, ducking slightly to see into her eyes, since she only came to his shoulders. "Huh? Oh, yeah, she will. I know." He did; he just couldn't help thinking about them constantly, wondering what was happening on the planet. Had Mikon and Xuthos punched each other yet? Had Koralia gotten any good intel?

He wished he was down there with them. Even with all the horrible memories it would have brought back—Daedalus's envy, the gray days of his early teens, the final straw for him and Icarus—he wished he was there, sharing in the adventure and the danger.

Athanasia shook her head and poked him in the shoulder. "Stop. Worrying," she told him firmly. "They're going to be fine, and they'll find something. And stop wishing you were there; I need you here. Now go debrief your pilots."

Laughing, he wrapped his arms around her in a quick hug. She patted his shoulder and stepped into an elevator, probably heading for dinner. He should get some too, but that could wait until after he talked to his pilots.

He continued down the halls, whistling now. Athanasia was right, they'd be fine.

But he still wished he was with them.

# CHAPTER 19

**W**hatever the faults of its rulers—and they were many, as she was discovering—Krete was one of the most beautiful places Koralia had ever been. At least when it came to the ocean. Water so blue it was almost unreal, truly golden sand mixed with sand that was actually white and not some shade of eggshell or gray, and gentle waves that literally glittered in the sun as they washed the shore.

It was no bad way to spend an afternoon, especially when there wasn't much intelligence gathering she could do at the moment.

She spun around in the water, loving the weightlessness. All was forgotten: the need for information, the annoying princess, the hunt for a traitor, the worrying reports about enslaved minotaurs, the crawling sensation that Krete was even worse than they had suspected.

A laughing shout from Ariadne drew her attention. Mikon had just sped beyond her in another race. For all her boasting of being fast, he'd outstripped her in every single race since they started. And yet the princess kept challenging him.

Koralia snorted. Ariadne wasn't even *trying* to win at this point, she was obviously just enjoying the show.

Not that she could exactly blame the princess. Mikon was a striking boy. Koralia had kept a close eye on him all day, knowing how irritating the royal family could be. He seemed fine with the attention so far, despite Ariadne being rather vulgar a few times, but the instant he stopped being okay with it, she'd make up some reason to take him and Xuthos back to their suite.

Ariadne being annoyed because she was shut up on the planet instead of being allowed to travel was her own business; it didn't mean Mikon needed to put up with the girl's aggressive clinginess.

"Are you sure you aren't from Poseidon's lines?" Ariadne gasped, shaking water out of her eyes and climbing onto a rock, where she posed like a mermaid. "You swim like it."

"Better for you that I'm not," Mikon quipped. "Aren't you enemies with Poseidon?" Then his eyes widened in horror that he'd committed some social blunder.

"Ah, yes, but that's half the fun," Ariadne called back. "You'd be forbidden!"

The girl was a total idiot.

"Gotta say, the kid's doing great," Xuthos said, swimming up beside her. "She's starting to make *my* skin crawl, but he's taking it in stride."

"A real accomplishment, making you uncomfortable," Koralia teased, letting herself drift into slightly shallower water where her feet could touch bottom.

He followed her, keeping only a few inches between them, more than close enough for her to feel the heat of his body. She let him. If anyone looked over, they would think the rumors about them were true.

Ariadne squealed excitedly, and Koralia looked over only to roll her eyes. Mikon had been swimming underwater and had just emerged a good way out to sea. At this distance, she could see why Ariadne was so enamored. He did look like a son of Poseidon as he floated in water up to his neck, his curls dark and the water glistening on his upraised arm as he waved to her.

Idly, she wondered if it was possible that Mikon's father had been more than human, someone from the Sea Lord's lines. Icarus hadn't known. Come to think of it, she still didn't know who his mother was either. Icarus had said that was for Mikon to tell her. She knew the woman was an olympian, but that could have meant any one of a score of women.

Questions for another day, when they weren't in enemy territory.

She returned the wave, smiling, and sank back into the water. It had been months since she'd had a lazy afternoon like this. It felt good.

"I meant what I said," Xuthos spoke from behind her.

"Yes?" she said distractedly, still watching Mikon. Ariadne was a good swimmer and was fast catching up to him. The princess wasn't above using the excuse of deep water to have her hands where they didn't need to be, and while Mikon could take care of himself, she suspected that he would also grit his teeth and endure something he didn't want if he thought it would help the mission. Koralia wasn't about to allow that.

169

Then she realized he was laughing and darting away from Ariadne, turning it into a game.

Ah, he was a smart one.

"What I said earlier? I am sorry."

She blinked, bringing her attention back to Xuthos.

"What?"

He grinned. "And here I thought one benefit to having a fake affair with you would be that I got some of your attention." His voice was light, but it felt forced, like he was worried she would take it the wrong way.

"The life of a mission commander never allows for singleminded focus," she returned, matching his light tone. "Why are you sorry?"

"If I made you uncomfortable. You know, with the new cover story."

Her eyes narrowed until she realized what he was trying to say. "You didn't. Don't worry about it. Like I said, it's a mission."

He paused, looking torn between taking her at her word and not believing her. "Is it hard for you?" he asked, leaning closer and then glancing around like someone might have overheard.

Unlikely. They were a ways from Ariadne and too far for Mikon to have heard. The four of them were the only ones out in the water today. But Minos could have listening devices anywhere, so the caution was good.

"Is what hard?" she asked. "This?" She leaned back against his chest, resting her head on his shoulder, angled to look up at him.

Xuthos gulped, his arms coming up automatically to slide around her before he froze.

She smiled and moved back. "Is it hard to have to act this out? No. I'm used to this." *This is war. War is easy.* But she didn't say that, keeping their conversation to vague allusions. "But am I going to continue this when we're back at base? The answer is no." Holding her hand over his shoulder, she said, "May I?"

He nodded, and she lowered her hand to touch him, but instead of pushing off of him, she shoved him backwards. He stumbled and went down, scrambling to regain his balance.

When he came back up, she was waiting for him, her arms folded and eyes challenging. "More questions still?" He was being surprisingly considerate, but the more he thought about Icarus, the more likely the name was to slip out.

And here on Krete, that could be a very bad thing indeed.

Not to mention Icarus was the last person she could afford to think about right now, here on this planet that had been his home, with the people who had killed him.

Grinning, he crowded closer to her. "I don't know." He sobered, but his eyes glinted. "I'm okay with anything as long as you are."

"Careful..." She drew the word out, treading water in a loop around him, listening to the sounds of an approaching swimmer. "That is a broad invitation, and I'm good at creative interpretation."

His laughter rang out across the water. "And they call *me* the shameless one."

Before she could respond, something slammed into Xuthos, tackling him into deep water.

*Someone*, rather. "And sunk!" she called out cheerfully. "Well done, Ky!"

Sputtering, Xuthos emerged at the same time Mikon twisted in the water and came up for air.

"You heard him coming!" Xuthos accused her, shaking water out of his eyes.

With a careless shrug, she put on her most innocent face. "It's a gift."

"It's a something," Xuthos growled, grabbing Mikon in a headlock and dragging him under the water. Caught off balance, it took the Sunfire a moment to struggle free.

"Now *this* is a perfect afternoon," Ariadne trilled, swimming up next to Koralia and standing back to watch the men wrestle.

Koralia wouldn't go that far, mostly because of the princess herself. Without her, it would have been.

It was still a rare *good* afternoon for them, mission or not.

✝

"THAT WASN'T as terrifying as I thought it would be," Mikon announced, checking to make sure their door was tightly closed behind him.

"Speak for yourself," Xuthos said, shedding his vest and belt. "I thought Minos was going to burn holes in Koralia with the way he was staring at her. Was it just me or was he leering?"

"He was definitely leering. It was disgusting." Mikon bristled.

"You're young enough to be his daughter!" Xuthos set one gun down on a table nearby but kept the other on him.

"Creep," Mikon agreed.

"That was normal," Koralia finally responded, trying to untangle her circlet from her hair. She had been careful putting it in, but it had still gotten twisted somehow. And it was one of the simplest ones she owned, so how did that even *happen? Stupid elegant jewelry.*

It would be easier if she wasn't so tired. She had forgotten how exhausting it was to keep a conversation going with Minos. The man jumped around from topic to topic, speaking like he was an authority on everything. Probably because he was in love with the sound of his own voice. Or just because he loved sounding like an omniscient god.

*Ugh.*

Hands slid over hers, taking the circlet from her. Mikon, based on his height and the long fingers now working gently to untangle it.

"Normal?" Xuthos demanded. "What do you mean *normal*? Minos leers at everyone?"

"I revise myself; he's psycho," Mikon said.

"Would both of you please remember that you are in the palace of the man you are blackmouthing and keep your voices down?" Koralia sighed. *These two, honestly.* "Minos has slept around since the birth of his third child at least. He's pretty much infamous for it. Yes, he leers at everyone."

Mikon finished untangling the circlet and handed it to her. "No wonder Ariadne doesn't respect him."

A snort was her only response. He wasn't wrong, but there was far more to Ariadne's attitude than just that.

"Thank you," she told Mikon, holding the circlet up. "Get some sleep."

He made a face. "Not again. What are *you* going to do?"

She looked at him, trying to decide how much to say. He'd been all right with Xuthos for most of the day, once he had understood what was going on. He could handle the truth. "We have a rendezvous to keep up our cover—oh, and fire off the daily report."

"So you get to go out into the gardens in the beautiful moonlight and I don't?"

"One, it's not moonlight; there are clouds." They'd rolled in during dinner, which she thought fitting. "Two, as long as you're careful and sensible, you can sit on the balcony."

Mikon crossed his arms and pouted. There was really no other word for it —he, a grown man, was pouting. She wanted to laugh, but with an effort, she kept a straight face. Sighing dramatically, she held up her hands. "I'm sorry, really I am, but I can only carry on affairs with one person at a time right now. Fighting a war, you know, there are sacrifices. Cutbacks."

Mikon threw back his head and laughed, and behind her, Xuthos joined in. Pleased at getting them to lighten up, she left them to their amusement and went to her room to change into something more suited to a midnight garden rendezvous with one's lover.

When she came out, the two men were standing with their heads together, talking in low voices. They stopped too soon for her to catch any words and smiled admiringly, their eyes traveling down the royal-blue gown.

She stopped in front of them and pointed back and forth from one to the other. "Should I be worried?"

"Probably about him," Mikon jerked his head toward Xuthos, "but not me."

"Hey," Xuthos protested mildly. "You're the kid here. If she should worry about anyone, it's you."

"Forget I asked." She shook her head, walking toward the door. "Let's go."

At the doorway, she turned and put a hand on Mikon's shoulder. "You'll go to bed?" He looked so young in the glowlights—scarcely more than a teen— and worn out, the hollows of his face reflecting the shadows in the room.

He caught her hand and kissed her fingers playfully. "I'll sleep soon...*if* you leave the big sister bossing to Ianessa, O commander."

"No promises, but I'll see what I can do." She smiled, patted his cheek, and left, Xuthos at her side. Quickly, they stole down the hallway, peering around corners in an elaborate display of secrecy. Once outside in the gardens, he took her hand, and she walked closer to him, leaning on his shoulder. It was easy—he was tall but not so tall that it was uncomfortable. She heard his breathing hitch for a few seconds before settling again.

"Tell me," she said, before he could decide to pull her closer or anything else she didn't want, "how many of these midnight assignations have you had in your life? Fifty? A hundred?"

He laughed quietly, the sound exultant in the rising night breeze. "You overestimate me. My assignations tend to happen in the middle of the day just as often as at night, and I've only ever had a few in a garden. And none with an Amazon."

"Ah, then I have plenty to teach you."

He grinned down at her. "Ready and waiting."

She tugged him down a different path. Something, she didn't know what, but *something* was abroad tonight; a faint clicking on stone came from the direction of the queen's garden. By circling around to it via a different route, maybe they could surprise it, whatever or whoever it was.

In one shadowed hedge corner, Xuthos pulled out his transmitter, engaged the security that would hopefully prevent them from being discovered, and sent a quick report to the rebellion. Then they moved on, keeping to the side of the stone paths, ready to turn and face anything that came up behind them.

The clicking sound had stopped by the time they reached the queen's garden and ducked inside, staying under the spreading branches of the trees as they surveyed the area. It was clear.

Xuthos looked at her, a "what now" expression, and she shrugged. "Do nothing, I guess?" she murmured, sitting down on a bench while he leaned against the hedge.

"You know he has a crush on you, right?"

Koralia glanced up and slid down the bench so she could see him in the near-dark. "Who?"

"Mikon."

"Oh. Yes, I know. Just like I know you'd have been all over me except for one thing." She meant for it to be light, something to be shrugged off, but Xuthos turned away abruptly, and she clenched her jaw.

"Icarus," he said, his voice hard. Not angry. More like...sad.

The moment stretched out around them, too serious, too tight with emotion. "Or I'm an Amazon and that scares you a little," she joked.

He chuckled, and she breathed a sigh of relief as the worst of the tension broke.

"No, definitely Icarus," he said, turning back to look at her. "He'd rise from the dead just to kick my ass for annoying you."

"He wouldn't have to. Talos and Mikon would take care of you before he could." She tried to smile, but it twisted, and she sat for several minutes until she could speak without her voice breaking.

"Yes, Xuthos, I know how you boys feel. And I also know that you channel your aggression into relentless flirting, but you'll be careful with me, not because of Talos and Mikon, but because you have one tiny noble spot in that rogue heart of yours, and I managed to touch it." She smiled then and held out her hand, which he took, lacing his fingers through hers. She didn't feel the same way he did—his pulse jumped when he touched her but there was no answering thrill for her. Still, the human contact was grounding in the night breeze that whispered around them, hinting at secrets and dark mysteries.

He squeezed her hand lightly. "Can't we explore a little? Ariadne rushed us through so fast earlier."

She arched an eyebrow at him. "If we were really having a fling, would you spare any time for exploring?"

He looked her over, but she could tell it was more for effect than because he really had to think about it. "No. No, I definitely would not."

"Fortunately for you, *I* would. I love exploring, and doing it with a handsome pilot makes it even better."

Grinning, he pulled her up off the bench. "If I had known you were this good at flirting, I might have gone with some explanation other than an affair with you. You're dangerous for my heart."

"No, you wouldn't have," she said, tugging him along behind her. "You'd never have passed up the opportunity to torment the Sunfires like this."

"True," he agreed.

A low scraping sound echoed abruptly through the garden. Xuthos's hand tightened on hers, and he moved to stand in front of her, but she sidestepped him. Amazons stood beside their allies, not behind. Besides, the odds were high that she was the better hand-to-hand fighter of the two, for all of Xuthos's training.

The sound was coming from the small maze at the far end of the garden. Ducking into the shadows of the hedges, they crept in that direction. Just before she entered the maze, Xuthos put a hand on her shoulder. It was hard to see his face because of how dark it was in this part of the garden, but he leaned closer.

"Are you armed?" he whispered.

That was a stupid question—rebels never went anywhere without a weapon, so he really should have guessed that Amazons didn't. She didn't even bother answering, pulling away and going deeper into the maze. "Come on. I want to know what they're hiding."

He kept his hand on her shoulder as they went inside, flattening themselves against one wall and creeping along in short steps. As they came to each bend, Xuthos peered around it, and they didn't move on until he said it looked clear. It was a simple maze—too short to need memorizing. Almost like someone had wanted to play at going through a maze without any of the complications that came with a real one.

They were almost to the center now, and from there it was only a few short steps to the exit.

*Click, click.*

It was the same sound from earlier, and it came from a dead end off to their right.

And then a surprised grunt.

Slowly, ready to leap in any direction, she turned around, feeling Xuthos do the same thing.

A low half wall separated them from the dead end. A few seconds ago, the space had been empty, but now a tall figure stood there, staring right at them.

It took her several seconds to realize it was a minotaur. At least six feet tall, she could see the outline of horns and ears, but the clouds had grown thicker and nothing was visible except its silhouette.

"Hi," she said in Kretan. "We mean no harm." She repeated the words in Galactic Common.

"Not hurt you," it said in Kretan, and Xuthos grabbed her shoulder, startled. The minotaur's voice was higher than she had expected, but still deep. Sort of a light baritone.

175

"I don't mean to hurt you either," she said, speaking in Kretan again. *"We don't."* She stepped to the side so it could see Xuthos. She didn't know how good its—his?—eyes were, but the light was better where they stood than where he was, so he should be able to see them.

"You are new," the minotaur said haltingly, but his words sounded like they came more easily this time. "Not Kretan?"

"Not Kretan," she confirmed. "I'm the daughter of Lord Hephaestus. This is my friend."

*Click, click.*

The minotaur turned. "I should not be here." He bent over, and they heard the scraping from earlier. Koralia ducked, putting her hands over her ears to stop the rattling through her skull. Fortunately, Xuthos, with his human hearing, wasn't affected and leaned over the hedge, trying to see what the minotaur was doing.

"Wait!" a voice cried out, and a smaller person ran past them and threw themselves on the minotaur. "Wait! Don't go yet!"

"I must," he said. "They saw me. She will be angry."

"We won't tell her," the smaller person babbled, and the light shifted enough that they could see she was the young minotaur from earlier. Pasiphae's servant. A female, Koralia thought.

"You won't tell, will you?" the girl begged, seizing Koralia's arm. Her hand was warm and felt soft, like it was covered in very short fur. "He was kind to me earlier, the other one. You won't tell, will you?"

Well, of course they wouldn't tell. But there could be cameras and microphones in any part of this maze, and to be caught on video making this promise could spell disaster.

*Nah, we can invent some story to explain it away.*

She could sense Xuthos's impatience beside her. "We won't tell," she assured the minotaurs. Still, the tall one hesitated.

"By the sacred waters of the Kretan Temple, we won't tell," she promised.

The minotaurs growled, and the younger one flinched.

"Wrong way to swear?" she asked, looking quickly from one to the other. Beside her, Xuthos just seemed confused.

"You talk Kretan," the male said, suspicion back in his voice.

So that was it. "I'm an Amazon. I have been here before, and I speak their language. But by earth, sea, sky, and star—or whatever you hold sacred—I promise that I mean you no harm and that I will not report you to whomever you fear."

"She's right, none of us will." Xuthos backed her up.

"Please stay," the girl begged the male. "I have not seen you for a week."

"The scraping. Underground access," Xuthos whispered in her ear, and she nodded. That made sense.

"I'm Xuthos," he introduced himself. "This is Lady Ko—Skotia. Do you live underground?"

"He does." The girl came closer cautiously, watching them with great wariness. "I live in the palace."

"You're the queen's servant?" Koralia asked. That's what Ariadne had called her, but the best way to break the ice was with a few questions.

"Yes. I'm Tryphosa." The girl put her hands on her hips and stared at them.

The clouds had been shifting for the past several minutes, alternately casting lighter and deeper shadows. Now they broke enough for her to see Tryphosa's face. On anyone else, she would have called that expression belligerent and challenging, but she didn't know this people well enough to know what their body language meant.

"It's an honor, Tryphosa." Koralia held out her hand, and the girl hesitated only a second before shaking it. "Please forgive our ignorance. I didn't know of your people's existence until recently."

"We are quiet people," the male said. "We were."

There was such a wealth of pain in that sentence that even Xuthos winced. "I'm sorry," he said. "I understand you are now slaves."

That was more blunt than Koralia would have gone for, but neither minotaur seemed to mind. Simultaneously, they bowed their heads for a few seconds before looking up again.

"That is true," Tryphosa said. Her voice was higher than the male's but still had a gravelly foundation. "You are from the stars?"

*From the stars?* That was one way to put it. How sheltered were the minotaurs? "We're from out there, yes," Koralia said. "I've been all over the galaxy myself. Xuthos too. And Ky, the boy you met earlier."

"The kind one." Tryphosa nodded.

"Thank him for us?" The male sounded like he was stumbling a little over the words, trying them out under his breath before saying them. "He tried to help."

They stared at him. "How did you know?" Xuthos asked. "Did you see it? I'm just curious," he added quickly.

"She told me," the male said. "We can talk."

So there *was* communication between here and wherever this male lived. Koralia took a half step to the side, trying to see him better. "Why do you live underground, if I may ask?"

He dropped his head and turned away, retreating deeper into the shadows.

"Punishment for something he didn't do," Tryphosa snarled, exposing sharp teeth that looked more like a dog's than a human's, but smaller, like human teeth.

"You talk too much," the male warned.

"One of us has to." She practically flung the words at him and whipped her head around to look between Koralia and Xuthos. "If you are from the stars, from beyond, do you know of..." She came closer and dropped her voice to a whisper. "The rebellion?" She sounded harsh, but Koralia guessed it was merely her normal voice.

"Tryphosa! Stop!" the male growled, and faster than Koralia would have thought possible, he was looming over them, grabbing Tryphosa and yanking her away from them. "She talks silly. I am sorry," he apologized in a gentler voice.

"I'm *not* sorry!" Tryphosa tried to pull away. "Someone has to say it. They swore they would not report us. They might know something. They might be the ones for whom we wait. Our time is—" Her words were cut off by his hand clamped over her mouth. She struggled against him, but despite his firm hold, he didn't look like he was hurting her.

Koralia almost grinned. The scene reminded her of teenagers across the galaxy, including various Amazonian teens: brash, insistent, incautious before the rigorous training hardened them into sensible, balanced warriors.

"By earth, sea, sky, and star, we gave our promise," she said quietly. "We will not report you." But neither was she going to just walk away. "Do you have something with which to write?"

As if on cue, thunder rumbled low on the horizon and rain began to sprinkle. Tryphosa hurried away and came back a moment later, handing Koralia a rock and a piece of smooth bark.

Koralia etched a contact address for the Kallistratus and handed it to the male. "If you are looking for the rebellion, try this."

Xuthos glanced around and said in a low voice, "I don't know if it'll reach through the defense net around the planet. Ours don't."

"Oh, it'll reach," the girl said confidently.

"It will," the male agreed.

She wasn't sure how to reply to that, so she said, "We have to go. We'll be missed soon." Mikon was probably pacing, wondering where they were. Unless he'd actually gone to sleep, which she seriously doubted.

"My thanks to you." The male bowed his head and shoulders, and they returned the gesture. "Be careful. She will..." He hesitated, as if trying to figure out how to say something.

"He means to say I'm a brat and not careful enough but that I can mostly be trusted to not get you into trouble," Tryphosa said for him, her hands back on her hips, her head tilted to the side, the Kretan language flowing easily from her tongue.

Koralia grinned and reached out to put a hand on the young minotaur's shoulder. "Well then, I'll look forward to seeing you again, Tryphosa."

The girl bobbed her head in response. "I have to go too. She'll be wanting me." She hurried off, her footsteps making the clicking sounds they'd heard earlier.

*She*—did that mean Pasiphae?

The other minotaur turned to go, bending over again.

"Wait, please!" Koralia said quickly.

He turned to look at her, his face barely visible in the rain that now fell harder. There were so many questions she wanted to ask him. How did he know the message would get out through the Labyrinth? What had he done— or not done—to earn himself this punishment? How did he live underground, and what could be done about the slavery of his people? But she settled for just one.

"What's your name?"

The shadows shifted enough that she could tell he had leaned closer, as if to see her better. He was silent long enough that she began to think he wasn't going to answer. Then, sounding surprised she had asked, he said, "Asterion."

*Son of the stars.* What an ironic name for one who lived underground.

"It is a pleasure, Asterion," she said respectfully, bowing again.

He turned away, and the sound of soft thumps was followed by the scraping again and then silence. He'd vanished back underground.

Koralia and Xuthos walked around the half hedge and bent down to inspect the stone. It was smooth, as if there had been no door at all.

The rain increased to a torrent, and Xuthos grabbed her hand. Together they raced for the palace as the thunder rumbled louder.

The storm had come.

# CHAPTER 20

"About time!" Mikon exclaimed when they re-entered their suite. "Anyone who might have thought you weren't lovers won't be thinking it now," he added caustically, his eyes storm-blue with annoyance.

"I thought you were going to bed?" Koralia said, halfway across the anteroom to change out of the thin gown that the rain had stuck to her skin.

"Got a message from Command." He waved his comdisk in the air. "Hurry up."

"Bossy, bossy," she returned, but she did hurry. Peeling her soaked gown off, she flung it into the bathtub, yanked a dry tunic over her head, and came back out of her room at the same time Xuthos exited his.

Mikon was waiting impatiently for them, and all three went into the sitting room, where she motioned for them to sit on the same sofa. The closer they were, the more quietly they could talk. And just to make sure they wouldn't start arguing with each other, she sat between them.

"Message?" she asked.

"We have news too," Xuthos interrupted. "On the minotauri."

"Base had news about Pasiphae," Mikon said, propping his feet up on a table. "It was sent hours and hours ago and only came in now. How are we supposed to get an emergency message out if we need to? Did we think about that? And *what* news on the minotaurs?"

"We did think of that," she said impatiently. "We have a slicer, but I won't use it unless I have to. Now what did the message say?"

Mikon grumbled but he spun his comdisk to access it and handed it over to her. She skimmed the message quickly and frowned. It was the report of an old scandal involving Pasiphae and...Daedalus? What good was that supposed to do them?

"No good?" Mikon asked, watching her.

"I don't know." What was she supposed to find significant in the message?

"Tell me about the minotaur," he demanded, as if he couldn't wait another second. "Was it the girl again? And why do I have to miss all the fun?"

"Minotauri," Xuthos said. "Two of them."

"Minotaurs," she corrected. "And you were remembered. The girl—Tryphosa—thanked you for trying to help earlier."

Mikon beamed, pleased.

"Xuthos can fill you in. I want to think."

Mikon leaned behind her to see Xuthos. "Start talking. And don't skip a single detail. I'll know if you do."

She tuned out their bickering over how Mikon could possibly know if Xuthos skipped details and concentrated on the articles. Athanasia—or someone on the rebel base—had thought them important enough to send, but why? Infidelity was as common as breathing among the Kretan royal family. Minos had slept around for years, and it would not be surprising if Pasiphae had too. Even the large family of children was rumored to have had scores of romantic affairs since their mid-teens.

Koralia closed her eyes, trying to remember everything she knew about Pasiphae. News sources generally seemed to agree that the queen had gone insane at least fifteen years ago and had been confined to a different wing of the palace ever since. But some of Minos's children had been born since then, and Pasiphae was assumed to be the mother, and her name was still put on all official documents as queen—a quick search had confirmed that. So she and Minos obviously still had some kind of contact. Unless her name was attached to documents purely for politics, which could be the same reason she was listed as the official mother of the younger royal children.

*And I thought olympian families were hard to keep track of.*

She surprised herself by yawning. *Am I that tired?* Maybe she should go to bed and try to figure it out again in the morning.

Yes, that's exactly what she'd do.

But before she could move, Mikon laid his head on her shoulder, closed his eyes, and stretched his legs out further. "I'm just going to go to sleep right here," he announced. "Wake me when it's morning, Xu."

"I plan to be asleep then; wake your own self up," Xuthos retorted. "And why are you sleeping on the woman I'm having a fling with?"

Mikon cracked open one eye to look at him. "You're the bodyguard; you have to stand watch. And you got her all night; it's my turn now."

"That's not how this works," Xuthos objected, trying to kick Mikon's legs off the table.

"It is now." Mikon twisted, settling himself deeper into the couch.

Koralia rolled her eyes. She really should get up, smack them both, and go to bed. But the couch was just comfortable enough and she was so tired that for a whole minute, she considered not moving at all, just ordering them to stop bickering and telling Xuthos to sleep where he sat.

It wouldn't be the first night she'd slept half sitting up while on a mission.

But if they did that, she would be pretty stiff in the morning, so she made herself wake up enough to slide out from under Mikon's shoulder, ignoring the wounded puppy pout he gave her.

"Bed, everyone. Now. Let's go." She yanked Xuthos to his feet and pushed him toward the door before turning back for Mikon. He was sitting up, regarding her through half-closed eyes.

"Do I have to—" he started.

"You have to," she answered firmly, reaching down and grabbing his arm. For just a few seconds, he thought about resisting and pulling her back down —she saw the impulse cross his face. Then he sighed and came to his feet. Wrapping an arm around her, he walked her to her bedroom door, where he bowed like some parody of a theatre performer and held the door for her.

"Sleep," she told him affectionately, ruffling his hair as she passed him.

"Yes, ma'am," he said and closed the door.

Too tired to even think about changing, she dropped down onto her bed and yanked the covers over herself, once again cursing the filmy sheets and gossamer blankets. The showiness was almost sickening, not to mention impractical.

Thoughts of their mission still drifted through her mind as she relaxed into the mattress.

For their first day's work, they'd done a pretty good job. But the clock was ticking down to the mission's end, and they needed far more answers than they'd received. Like figuring out if the minotaurs had been behind the message in the Labyrinth or whether there was yet another rebel sympathizer on Krete. And discovering what had happened to Daedalus. And why Ariadne had poisoned Xantippos and Heirax...if it really was her.

They needed to try harder tomorrow.

✝

"WHERE IS IT? I want to see it."

The words were half muffled against Talos's shoulder as he hugged the speaker. "Great to see you again too, dude."

Brygos snorted and dragged his bag out of the fighter he'd just landed. "Hi, Talos, nice to see you again. You look terrible."

He really was impossible; Mikon had never been wrong about that. "Like you can talk. Are you even eating at all?" He poked Brygos in the ribs, and the other man tried to dodge but bumped into the fighter. "And when did you sleep last? If you crash because of no sleep, we're all going to kill you repeatedly."

"Sleep is for the weak," Brygos said, impatiently heading out of the docking bay. "And I didn't mean you look that kind of terrible. That shirt doesn't go with those pants."

Talos, shaking his head, lengthened his steps and caught up to his brother. "Sorry I'm too busy fighting a rebellion to pay attention to fashion every single day. I'll make an effort while you're in the area."

"Good. Kynna would have a fit if she saw you. She says hi, by the way. She almost snuck along, but..." Brygos glanced sideways at Talos.

"I'm glad she didn't."

"I'm not," Brygos said.

Talos rolled his eyes. "So you want me to discipline you both?"

"Well, in that case, I'm a little glad she didn't come along." Brygos looked smug, like he'd guessed correctly. "So the memorial is the only free pass we get this year?"

"More or less." They stepped into an elevator, and Talos punched the button for the second floor. Then he stepped back to look his brother over.

As he'd suspected, Brygos was thinner than the last time Talos had seen him, but not by much. So he had to be eating and sleeping some. Not that any of them got what would be called a proper amount of sleep, but some—namely Brygos and Kynna—were worse than others.

His brother shifted from one foot to the other, antsy while filling Talos in on his last few missions, adding a few final details over his shoulder as they entered the bridge.

"Oh, General, our General, best general in the galaxy!" Brygos threw his arms around Athanasia and then hugged Ianessa more gently. "Okay, where's the Labyrinth file?" he demanded, using his foot to propel a chair toward himself so he could sit down.

"Some things never change." Ianessa shook her head. "Barely a hello before you're diving in. The data Talos and Mikon gathered is here." She transferred a virtual file to his screen.

"Where is that little shaz anyway?" Brygos asked, glancing up at Talos.

"Language," Ianessa reprimanded from the opposite side of the table.

Their younger brother frowned. "Talos swore in the elevator."

"Talos has a swearing permit," Ianessa said. "He's allowed to swear here. So am I. You don't have one for this base."

Brygos spun his chair around to find the General. "General, can I swear on this base?"

"Not right now," she answered mechanically, preoccupied with something on a screen in front of her.

Talos snickered.

Brygos shrugged. "Oh, fine. Where is our *darling little brat* Mikon? Did you send him out on patrol? He's been awfully quiet for two days." He frowned suddenly, zeroing in on Talos's face. "Did he get hurt?"

"He's fine," Talos said. Brygos was so full of nervous energy that it was exhausting sometimes. "Cool off and let me get a word in. He's on Krete—"

"He's on *Krete?*" Brygos came half out of his chair, his eyebrows nearly to his hairline.

"—on a mission," Talos continued calmly. "Koralia took a team down to find out more. They're due back in a day or so." He finished gathering up the information he needed to discuss with their mechanics and started for the door.

His brother glowered. "Wait, wait, wait. So not only is Mikon on planet on a mission, but he got to go with the Amazon? *Icarus's* Amazon?"

Talos couldn't resist sticking his foot out to nudge Brygos's chair back. "I think she's her own Amazon, but yes, her."

"There really is no justice in this world," Brygos huffed, sitting back down. But thanks to Talos's little maneuver, he missed the edge of the chair and sprawled on the floor.

Walking away, Talos felt a wadded-up sheet of paper hit him and laughed.

"Mikon thinks it's perfect justice," he said over his shoulder as he left. He would hardly admit it to anyone except the General, but he missed Mikon's bright face around base, even though he'd only been gone a day.

He missed *all* of his siblings. That was one of the hardships of war, especially when you were helping lead it. The Sunfires, who had hardly left each other for several years, were now spread throughout the galaxy on various rebel bases and rarely saw each other for more than a few hours at a time. And almost never were they all together, for security reasons.

But he'd enjoy having Brygos here while he had the chance, especially once Mikon got back and the fireworks started flying between the two.

. +.

No answers had come to Koralia in the night, just dreams of Icarus and the Labyrinth, and she woke tired and heavy. After dressing—she'd be glad when they were back in space and she didn't have to wear formal circlets for a bit—she walked out into the antechamber.

Mikon was just closing the outer door, and when he turned around and saw her, a guilty look spread over his face.

Popping some grapes into her mouth from the bowl on a side table, Koralia raised her eyebrows at him. "Now what have you done?"

He squinted sideways at her, as if trying to gauge how much trouble he might be in. "You sound like Talos."

"Is that because he knows that expression means you did something you probably shouldn't have?"

He twisted his shoulders sideways in a shrug, still not looking directly at her.

"Just tell me. Not telling me or dragging it out is so much worse than having it over with," she told him, trying to look stern.

"Well," he said, sitting down in a chair and clasping his hands between his knees. "I was minding my own business."

"I find that hard to believe, but go on."

"I was!" he protested. "But, well, I might have accidentally met the queen?" he said in a rush.

Koralia blinked at him. It was too early in the day for dealing with potential messes. She grabbed more grapes and ate them one a time. She needed the sweet fruit to help banish the sleepiness left over from the bad night. "How do you *accidentally* meet the queen?"

"She was walking," Mikon explained. "With her minotaur girl—or is it minotauri when it's the race?"

"Minotaur. Keep going."

"Well, I just wanted to see the sunrise in the gardens. It stopped storming, you know."

That she could well understand. Like her, he was a child of the sunsets and sunrises, reveling in whatever glorious colors painted the sky on every planet in the galaxy.

He blinked, as if he wasn't even sure what he'd seen. Koralia looked closer. He was clearly rattled…which was odd. She was pretty sure it took a lot to rattle Mikon.

Grabbing a pear, she crossed the room and pulled a chair over to sit down next to him. "Take your time," she said, putting a hand on his knee.

"It wasn't bad or anything," he assured her. "She asked who I was, and I told her—my fake name," he added.

"Of course." Mikon might be easily distracted, but he wasn't scatterbrained.

He nodded and twisted his fingers together. "Then she said I looked olympian. So I said I was but only part." Frowning, he stared at the floor. "She cackled." The words came more slowly, full of confusion. "And then she said, 'You understand the war my children face.' And she left."

"Going back inside or out further into the gardens?"

"The gardens."

Well, so far, there wasn't anything about the encounter that seemed odd to her.

"What is it?" she asked, keeping her tone gentle. "What's still puzzling you?"

He hesitated and then blurted out, "I thought she was mad. Insane-mad, not angry-mad."

"She is. Has been for two decades, off and on." Koralia had met her in a supposedly lucid moment some years ago, but she was starting to wonder what "lucid" even meant on this planet.

A door closed behind her, which must be Xuthos coming in, but she kept her attention on Mikon.

He shook his head as if trying to make something make sense. "She almost seemed *normal*. Just sad. Right up until the end when she kind of giggled under her breath."

"Sometimes the maddest people are the sanest," Xuthos commented.

Koralia looked up at him in time to catch the sarcastic tilt of his head. "Did you have fortune flowers for breakfast?" she asked. At his shrug, she raised her eyebrows, taking in how wet his clothes were. "And where were you?"

He bowed. "Recon, as your father would've wanted, my lady."

Rolling her eyes, she pushed up out of her chair. "Save the 'what my father would have wanted' lines for when we're in front of others. Time for a meeting. Reset the scramblers, please, and meet us in the sitting room."

When they had first arrived on planet two nights ago, Mikon had set scramblers around their suite, including their bedrooms. The rebellion had an assortment of old equipment and new, but Hephaestus kept new, top-of-the-line scramblers on his ships, and it had been the work of a few minutes to rig up enough to cover their suite. They'd reset them three times a day since then. If Krete did have this room bugged, they wouldn't be able to record anything.

It took Xuthos only a few seconds to reset them and then he followed them into the sitting room. Before the boys could do their usual bickering over who got to sit with her, she sat down in the middle of the larger couch and authoritatively thumped her hands down on either side of her.

Looking pleased, Mikon sat down on her left side and Xuthos on her right.

"We have twenty-four GST hours left," she said bluntly. "We've got to get moving. The minotaur message to the rebellion, the first one, said their contact was in the palace. That could be either Asterion or Tryphosa—the girl —or someone else. We need to figure out which."

"I'm going with the girl." Xuthos propped one foot up on the table in front of them, and Koralia shoved it off again. She wanted them focused, sharp, and lounging would hinder that.

"She's the one who asked about contacting the rebellion," he continued. "They must not know that our messages can't get through the Labyrinth when it's closed."

"What goes out has to come back in," Mikon said, half to himself. When they looked at him, he clarified, "Their messages go out, right? Their secret messages, I mean, not whatever goes through Krete's official communications channels. Somehow they make that happen—Ambrosia or the minotaurs or *someone*. So there has to be a way for messages to come back *in* too, a way that doesn't rely on waiting for the gates to open for the signals to go through, like we are now." He glared at Koralia's comdisk on the table in front of them.

"It's not the disk's fault," Xuthos said, his tone provoking.

"If you wind him up before we finish this, I'm going to let him punch you," Koralia warned.

He leaned closer to her, his shoulder brushing hers deliberately as he stared into her eyes. She couldn't tell if he didn't believe her or if he was taunting Mikon more, but she felt like pinching him either way. Instead, she nudged him to move back.

With a smirk, he did.

"So we have to find out how they get the messages out. You're on that." She pointed to Mikon. "See if you can find Tryphosa again. If you can, try to find out if she's our contact here in the palace. Don't say anything incriminating… you know." She didn't need to give him instructions or even advise caution; he'd been doing this longer than she had.

"Yes." He tipped his head sideways, staring into the distance, thinking. "Cautious contact, ask what she knows about the rebellion and how it could possibly help her. I know." He grinned, and Koralia relaxed. He'd get it done.

"I'm going to keep Ariadne busy," she said, grimacing. "I'm sure I can find more stories to tell her while I try to discover if she's our traitor." *Plus, I have to ask her about Daedalus*, but she wasn't going to tell him that.

187

"Whew." Mikon leaned back and draped an arm over the back of the sofa, brushing her shoulders. "At least I get a break from her."

Xuthos snickered. "You ungrateful little brat. How dare you not enjoy the exclusive attention of the princess of Krete? I think she's almost ready for a ring." Koralia felt him slide closer, looking at Mikon's arm behind her.

"Don't hesitate to reject her advances if she gets too aggressive," she told Mikon, sending Xuthos a warning look.

"She'd be less clingy if you were worse at your job," Xuthos pointed out.

Koralia thought Mikon was about to snap a rude retort, but he grinned. "Okay, fair. I may have been asking for it. But the General *said* to do a good job. All the same, I can only play the mysterious, hard-to-get olympian for so long."

Xuthos laughed, and the brief moment of tension was gone, fading into the morning sunshine, leaving Koralia relieved. Pulling all of this together was hard enough right now without them growling at each other. There was too much to do still and not enough time in which to do it. And she had never been half the strategist that Athanasia had.

Was it even *possible* to pull it all together? She was starting to wonder.

"Keep up the *good work*," she told Mikon approvingly, and he grinned at her emphasis. "I think we've got her just off-balance enough that I might be able to wring some truth out of her."

"Good luck." He meant it, but his undertone made it clear he didn't envy her the task.

She didn't particularly like the thought of doing it either.

"And what is my job, commander?" Xuthos asked. "Guarding your back?"

Koralia rolled her eyes. "My back doesn't need guarding. You'll just be in the way. You go back to the queen's garden and see if you can figure out how Asterion is coming up or if—" She paused. It had seemed last night like Asterion only came up at night. So Xuthos wasn't likely to find anything during the day, but she didn't want him hovering around her, so he needed something to do.

On second thought, having him around when she talked to Ariadne might be helpful.

"New plan," she said, leaning forward and grabbing her comdisk. It wasn't her private com; this one she'd taken off her father's ship. She spun the combination for Ariadne and texted, *What do you have for afternoon clubs around here?*

The reply came instantly. *Only, like, TWENTY!! Want to see some?*

*Yes, something private, if you have it.*

*And by the sea,* she added, after a minute.

*Do we have it???!!! I have just the one in mind!!*

The exclamation points were just annoying, but since that was the way Ariadne actually talked, Koralia had to give her points for staying on-brand.

"So what is it?" Mikon asked, tapping her on the shoulder.

"What?" Koralia stood up and went to check the weather out the window. The morning had been only partly cloudy, but there were more storm clouds rolling in.

When she looked back at the boys, they were both staring at her expectantly.

"The new plan?" Mikon reminded. "You just said we have a new plan."

"Oh, right. Xuthos and I have a new plan. You're still on Tryphosa duty."

Xuthos brought his hands together in a sharp clap. "Do I get to look menacing while I follow your ladyship around?" he asked, bowing.

She was already regretting this. "Yes, more or less. Sorry, Mikon," she added. And she was—he was getting all the boring jobs on this mission.

He had crossed his arms and was leaning back on the sofa, staring at Xuthos with narrowed eyes.

"Don't kill each other," she said, and—ignoring the irritation flowing between the two men—she headed to her bedroom to change.

Kretan fashion was rather more elaborate than she liked, with corseted bodices over tunics and long flowing skirts made up of several gauzy layers of different lengths, but the advantage to traveling as Hephaestus's daughter was that she could wear Vulcani fashion and not be thought rude.

As she changed into something shorter, appropriate for an afternoon club, she wished she could talk to Athanasia. Or Talos. She was used to figuring out a mission as she went. Amazons were taught to work in teams, in pairs, and alone, improvising with whatever they had at hand, whether that was weapons, people, or information.

But there was something so *off* about this palace and the royal family. Like they were constantly wearing a facade but also like they themselves didn't even realize it *was* a facade.

*That's it*, she realized, sitting down in front of the mirror and staring into it for a second before she began applying copper eyeliner. The Kretans felt like they didn't even know they were fake. Not the kind of two-facedness that came from being dishonest with yourself, but a kind of ignorance.

How did you handle that level of oblivion? How did you break through it? Where did truth exist on this gorgeous planet where the opulence choked her and everything seemed only skin-deep...but where she could find no edges to pull the masks off and see what lay underneath?

*Ride the river until you find a rock, and then cling to it with all your might until you can climb onto it and see the shore.*

It was an Amazonian mantra. Battles started out with plans, and so did missions of almost any kind, but plans were only good so far. You had to keep your feet and your head and be able to fill in the holes that opened up as you went. Improvisation was key. Still, she would've given a lot for Talos's relentless planning right about now.

Or maybe she should stop overthinking and get going.

In the antechamber, Mikon and Xuthos waited for her, looking relatively at ease with each other. She studied them for a moment. Mikon looked disgruntled but also a bit pleased. Xuthos's smile carried an edge, faintly resentful under his attitude of smugness.

"Remember what I said," Mikon said under his breath as she crossed the room.

So that was it. Mikon had probably threatened Xuthos, who, stung, had replied that he didn't need the warning.

Sunfires. So protective of their family, which was complicated even further by the little crush both Mikon and Xuthos had.

But they looked like they had settled it between themselves, and she had bigger things to worry about right now. "Formal armor," she told Xuthos, who nodded and went past her to change. Bodyguards had to be able to move quickly when tailing their principals at social affairs, so formal armor was lighter but more durable than everyday armor. The only armor that beat it for strength and maneuverability was battle gear.

Koralia stopped in front of Mikon and held out her hands, palms up. With a smile that was half shy, half rueful, he clasped her hands, long fingers dwarfing hers. "Any questions, Sunfire?" she asked.

His eyes lit as he realized that she'd spoken too quietly for a human to hear. Like they had their own private language, simply because of their exceptional hearing.

*Just how isolated was his childhood?*

"I'm worried about you," he said, speaking in the same undertone. "I'm pretty sure I'll be in less danger than you."

She conceded that with a nod. Anyone who aped olympians as much as the Kretans wasn't likely to offer violence or rudeness to a guest within their palace, especially one traveling under the protection of Lord Hephaestus, who still had a reputation for swift, complete justice on anyone who meddled with him. But she and Xuthos were going out into the town with a probable traitor to the rebellion, who was also a member of the royal family—one who acted like she could get away with anything.

*Well*, she amended, a *potential* traitor to the rebellion. They had no proof yet.

But she smiled, iron hardening in her eyes. "Ah, but I'm an Amazon. Didn't they ever tell you how hard we are to kill? Everyone tries, and no one succeeds. Old age claims us in the end." Sighing dramatically, she shrugged her shoulders and dropped her eyelids in a look of vast experience.

It did the trick, and he laughed, dropping her hands to throw his arms around her for a quick hug.

He was still grinning when he pulled back, just before Xuthos came out of his room.

"And if I see Pasiphae again?" Mikon asked as Koralia pulled a thin daytime cape around her shoulders and adjusted the weapons she wore under her tunic.

"Pasiphae is crazy. Literally insane," she said, pushing her circlet back further on her head. "Try to stay clear of long conversations with her. But if you do see her again..." She paused, thinking.

"Being crazy doesn't mean she can't be of use," Xuthos put in, sliding his guns into their lightweight, streamlined holsters.

"Again with the fortune flower wisdom," she teased him, but he had a good point. "I don't know of anything that might give you any insight with her, but maybe ask her to tell you about her children," she said to Mikon. "If nothing else, it should at least keep her distracted until someone finds out she's out of her rooms and puts her back."

Xuthos stared at her. "Isn't that a little...callous?" he asked cautiously, aware he was on uncertain ground.

Koralia turned away, pinching the bridge of her nose as she finally realized another reason this palace made her so uncomfortable. Mikon's description of Pasiphae reminded her of her mother's more emotionally manipulative moments.

In fact, the whole planet reminded her of Aphrodite's.

"Yes," she admitted, turning back to the clearly confused men. "It is a little. When a whole nation wears masks, it's hard to know what isn't pretend. But he'll be gentle with her."

Mikon's smile flashed out at the trust her words indicated.

"Cheer up," she said, steering both of them toward the door with a hand on their shoulders. "We'll be out of here soon." But strain lined their faces and shoulders. Capture and death weren't their biggest dreads: returning to the rebels with no answers was far worse. And at this rate, none of them would do well on their assignments, including her.

What they all needed was a good speech.

"Listen." She waited until they turned to face her. "I'm the daughter of Lords Ares and Hephaestus. You are both crack pilots in the Kallistratus. You"—she pointed at Xuthos—"were trained in some of the best self-defense schools in the galaxy and are good enough at staying out of trouble that you aren't even on an official watch list anywhere. You," she turned to face Mikon, "are a Sunfire. You've been doing this kind of thing since before you could fly. We've got this."

Mikon's grin was bright, all golden sun and summer evenings. "That speech was as good as Talos's."

"A high honor," she said and smiled involuntarily.

"We've got this," Mikon agreed, tipping his head toward her as he straightened, a swagger coming back to his stance. "Go harrow up her soul and get back so I can hear all about it and we can have a meeting with the minotaurs. And I'm not staying inside this time."

Xuthos's smile was smaller but no less real. "My excellent staying-out-of-trouble skills are yours for the asking, my lady."

And confident once more, they exited the room into the dark-blue halls.

Time to look for rocks in the river.

# CHAPTER 21

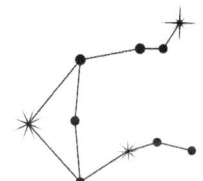

While Koralia conferred with her team in Krete's opulent palace, Athanasia met with her staff on the rebel base among the stars.

The General sat at one end of a briefing table with Xantippos at her left, finally out of medical confinement and looking wan but alert. Talos, Ianessa, and Brygos were ranged down the other side of the table, Talos frowning as he arranged and rearranged something on a diagram in front of him. The other two were engaged in some form of virtual note passing: colored projections flickering between their hands.

"Report," Athanasia ordered.

"Doesn't matter how I figure it," Talos said, looking up. "I can't find the ships to get the minotaurs off of Krete, even if we *were* able to get through the Labyrinth. We don't have the transports, and we don't have the fighters to protect them at that kind of close range, not against the shore defenses."

Athanasia knew deep down that it was impossible, had known it since the minotaur contact had made the request. But she had ordered a complete investigation anyway.

"It's not your fault, Commander," she said. "We tried. We'll have to see if there's some other way of getting the Key."

Talos nodded, but his face was grave. He hated leaving people behind. Knowing Minos had enslaved the minotaurs was enough to light the fuse of every rebel on the base, and most especially his, because of his past on the planet. But if they didn't have the ships to rescue the minotaurs, that was that, and not all the fury in the galaxy could change cold, hard facts.

"I say we blow the shraking thing up," Brygos said, leaning forward with flashing eyes.

"Language," Ianessa murmured from beside him, and then, louder, she said, "And how do you propose blowing up something created out of layers of force fields made from materials we've never seen? Did you forget that Talos threw everything he had at it and nothing happened? And before him, Icarus did the very same thing. We can't. Get. Through. It." Her finger stabbed the tabletop, emphasizing each word.

"We can't, but Kynna's got two new explosives that might be able to." Brygos waved one of the virtual messages around.

So he hadn't just been passing messages between him and Ianessa.

"Talk," Athanasia ordered, pointing at him. "What kind of new explosives? Can she get them in large quantities?"

Ianessa raised her hand, unease settling over her forehead. "Is blowing up the Labyrinth even ethical?"

Xantippos nodded, seconding the question.

"Yes," Athanasia said, hearing Talos say it at the same time. With an approving smile, she motioned for him to explain.

"What's not ethical about stopping the spread of imperialization?" Talos said. "Minos is trying to cut off this area of the galaxy, and we don't care why at this point: it's wrong. Of course blowing it up is ethical."

Put that way, Xantippos and Ianessa agreed. But that wasn't the bigger question right now. *Could* they do it? Kynna knew her explosives, but none of their engineers knew much about how the Labyrinth worked, not yet. They needed time to think and plan and run a test or two.

But they didn't have that kind of time. If Krete found the rebel base anytime soon, the Kallistratus would be forced to evacuate. Not to mention the Labyrinth was spreading fast. In less than a week, this entire sector of space would be barricaded from the center of the galaxy, adding days and days to the routes pilots used to fly supplies in to the nearby colonies. And who knew how much stronger the net would be once it was complete?

They needed to try to deal with it now, before construction finished.

Her decision made, Athanasia called for silence and said, "Brygos, talk to Kynna. Get every piece of information she has on these new explosives. Ianessa, keep working on alternative options for minotaur rescue—and stay in contact with Dione about her communications workarounds for contacting other bases if the Labyrinth cuts us off. I want immediate reports on that project. Talos...you know what to do." And he did. He'd keep the patrols flying and continue trying new weapon combinations against the Labyrinth, buying them as much time as he could. If any.

Hopefully, Koralia's team would find a bargaining chip, some way to make it possible for them to get the Key.

*Hopefully.*

.+.

KRETE'S CLUBS were just as opulent as the rest of the planet: stifling, cloying, but at least offering comfortable seating. The yellow-green, turquoise-blue, and soft-pink color scheme of this one wasn't what Koralia would call pleasant, but at least they had privacy and quiet.

They sat now on the rooftop, in a front corner that overlooked the city. Potted trees and woven screens filtered out the oppressive rays of the afternoon sun, creating a cool haven, and a viewscreen played in one corner, the volume low enough to be unobtrusive. Lounges stood in an L shape, giving them a view of waves crashing against the nearby coastline.

Ariadne turned to the automaton waiter who had followed them and began a long list of drinks, which was recorded with quiet beeps. Koralia had a high alcohol tolerance, so she hadn't bothered to stick to anything milder.

"And you're sure you won't take anything stronger?" the princess asked, pausing to look up at Xuthos again. It was the third time she'd asked him that in five minutes.

"Thank you, no, Your Highness. Her father would want me alert."

Koralia kept her smile to herself. Xuthos was good at playing his part.

Ariadne shrugged like it didn't matter to her either way and sent the waiter off. "You know..." she said to Koralia, back to drawling, an annoying, affected accent that sounded like she was trying to mimic the olympian cadence from Belus. "You know, there's no one here to carry tales. And I don't mind if you sit with your bodyguard." She arched her eyebrows significantly.

Koralia didn't particularly feel like sprawling over Xuthos all afternoon, but as distractions went, this seemed like a good moment to seize, so she leaned forward and looked all around them like she was checking for hidden listeners. "Are you sure?"

"Positive."

"It does look pretty private." Koralia made a show of looking around again before motioning Xuthos to come closer, patting the seat next to her with an inviting look.

"Oh no, my lady, I couldn't." He pulled back. "Your father would never approve."

"I insist," Koralia said, trying not to laugh. Hephaestus wouldn't have cared one way or the other, but neither Xuthos nor Ariadne needed to know that.

Xuthos shook his head, but his eyes gleamed. "Your father would smelt me into butter."

"That's the oddest metaphor I've ever heard." She stood up, stepping closer to him. "But since you went there, *I* have much more *enjoyable* ways of turning you into butter."

His eyes widened, and he grinned. "Are you sure, my lady?"

"Positive." Running her hand up his arm gave her the chance to move close enough to whisper, "Sit down, it'll make her relax more."

She ignored the hitch in his breathing as she backed away and sat down again, moving closer to Ariadne's couch so Xuthos had room to sit down behind her. Ariadne looked like she was enjoying the show. *Voyeur.*

Koralia leaned back against Xuthos, resting her head against his neck. He wrapped his arms around her loosely and lifted one hand to play with her hair.

It was a very good thing Mikon wasn't here.

Ariadne looked outright jealous now, which was perfect. High emotions made people more likely to talk.

"Nice place," Koralia said as the waiter came back with their drinks and then left again.

"Isn't it?" Ariadne looked pleased. "The most important people in Krete come here, like Hybrias and Lucilla and Metagenes. He designed it, you know, him and Daedalus. It was probably the first time they voluntarily got along." She giggled.

*Daedalus.* Koralia tried not to jump at the name. How coincidental that Ariadne had brought them here today—did she suspect why they were here or was it just good fortune?

*Go slowly,* she reminded herself. *Slowly.* "Lucilla?" she asked.

"Head Priestess of my order," Ariadne explained. "Father often consults with her, and she's considered a very wise woman. She's my sponsor," the princess added proudly.

*The head of the order sponsored you joining it?* The position of priestess on Krete must not take many brains or surely Ariadne would have flunked out by now. Or maybe her role and rank had more to do with politics: a token priestess to symbolize the strong relationship between the order and the throne. Either way, it didn't matter.

Koralia sipped slowly from her first cocktail, waiting to ask what she really wanted to know.

Xuthos beat her to it. "Isn't Daedalus the royal inventor?" he asked, his tone careless.

"He is. Well…" Ariadne glanced around like they might be overheard. "He *was.* He disappeared a week ago. Father's had search parties out for days, and..." She dropped her voice, whispering, "*Nothing.* No sign of him. It's like he vanished into thin air."

Koralia hadn't expected to hear that. "Strange," she made herself say.

"Maybe he just wandered off somewhere," Xuthos said with a malicious smirk. "Wasn't he said to be insane?"

Koralia frowned at him. Insanity could be a fraught subject on Krete.

Ariadne made even snorting into an obnoxiously high sound. "It depends on who you ask. Mother never thought so. Father said if he was, it was a useful and brilliant kind of insanity. He built the automatons here and at the palace."

Koralia had noticed those, mostly because building automatons was Hephaestus's favorite way to relax. Most automatons were primitive and simplistic next to her father's, but these were more sophisticated.

"I think it was grief," Ariadne whispered dramatically, her eyes huge.

"Grief for whom?" Xuthos couldn't keep a rough edge from his voice.

"His son." Ariadne nodded solemnly. "And I don't blame him." She choked and fumbled for a corner of her robe to hide her face.

Well, that was a weird reaction.

*How far can I push her?* Koralia debated with herself. Covert information gathering was much harder when you couldn't be sure how smart your source was or how likely they were to guess your motives.

Daedalus missing was enough information to take back to the rebellion, but—if possible—she wanted to learn more. Carefully.

Behind her, Xuthos clenched his jaw quickly, the movement so tense she almost turned around to look at him. He'd been angry since the moment Ariadne had said Daedalus's name. Maybe he needed a few minutes to cool off.

Turning away and trying to seem uninterested, Koralia caught sight of a familiar symbol on the viewscreen in the corner and tapped the control panel at her side to turn the volume up.

The Kallistratus symbol had appeared, a red X through it as the newscaster said, "...has been confirmed that they are not working with the Kallistratus Rebellion, and they have therefore been released." A teenager with blue hair and a pointy nose and chin was escorted out of a station, followed by a sharp-featured woman with red-and-black hair. She could have been anywhere from eighteen to twenty-five, and she grinned and waved cheerily to the crowd gathered around the station. There was a specific kind of defiant air on both of them, the kind that most teenagers wore, the one that said "break all the rules just because." The Kallistratus didn't have a problem employing those kinds of people, but they rarely used them for anything besides information gathering. Such people were just too unpredictable to trust with anything strategically important.

"Ha, amateurs." Ariadne sniffed as she took a sip of her colorful drink and sighed in pleasure at the taste. It was hard to tell if she'd actually been sad a minute ago or had just been pretending.

Koralia turned the volume back down, picked up her drink, and settled herself more comfortably against Xuthos, who went on playing with her hair, before she raised her eyebrows curiously. "Amateurs?"

"Getting caught." Ariadne rolled her eyes. "Probably just took part in a march or something and there's no evidence that proves they're rebels. Cowards. If you're going to rebel, why don't you do it properly?"

If Koralia had doubted that Ariadne had ever worked with the rebellion, she didn't now, not after that tone of voice. Xuthos stiffened again, just when he'd started to relax, and Koralia reached down to entwine the fingers of one hand with his, trying to remind him to stay calm. They were just getting started, and she had a feeling it was going to get worse long before they had all the information they needed.

"I can't argue with that," she agreed. "How would you do it?" Still leaning back, she tucked one foot under her and sipped from her drink as if the answer couldn't matter less.

Xuthos relaxed again, but his hand tightened around hers.

Ariadne was into her third glass of whatever concoctions she'd ordered, drinking with a recklessness that seemed fueled by strong emotion. Something she was feeling or something she was hiding? Koralia couldn't tell yet. She wished Mikon was here to use his persuasion on the princess.

"Subtlety," Ariadne said. "That's the way to do it."

Xuthos bent his head over Koralia's shoulder to muffle a snicker. Ariadne and subtlety were so opposite it was hilarious to hear her talking about it like she was a master.

"That does make sense," Koralia said. Xuthos shook with silent laughter, and she wondered if she'd gone too far with the act, but Ariadne was smiling smugly, preening under the compliment.

"Speaking of the rebels…" Koralia picked up her second drink and sipped from it, then twisted the glass, considering the taste. Not too bad.

"Yes?" Ariadne leaned forward, eagerness in her eyes.

"What? Oh yes, the rebels." Koralia tried to ignore Xuthos laughing silently again, but that was a little hard to do when she was leaning against him. She poked him, careful not to let Ariadne see. "I heard you shot down one of their most famous fighters." The words tasted like vinegar, and she drank from her cocktail again, but the taste remained.

Ariadne's face darkened. "*I* didn't," she said acidly. "My father's gunners did."

"Oh." Koralia hesitated. What else was there to say? That had been a strong reaction from the princess. "You sound like you knew him," she ventured and hoped it sounded natural.

The Kretan girl reached for another drink, her fourth. Did she normally drink that much in so short a time? They hadn't even been here an hour.

"I knew him," Ariadne mumbled.

"Do tell," Koralia invited.

The princess's head shot up, and she stared at Koralia.

"Olympian hearing," Koralia said, tapping her earlobe. "But don't worry." She leaned forward and spoke in an undertone, "I can keep a secret."

Ariadne looked dubious, so as she sat back, Koralia added, "Don't forget who my parents are."

"Oh, that's true." The princess finished her drink, considering, and then sat up like she'd made a decision.

"I knew him very well," Ariadne admitted, half covering her mouth with one hand like she was admitting to a sordid secret.

"Oooh, what was he like?" Koralia tried to lean closer, and Xuthos came with her like he couldn't bear to stop touching her. He was probably as impatient as she was to untangle the mystery of why his captain had been killed, and as long as he kept his temper and she kept hers, she wouldn't refuse him that.

She rearranged them so she was in the corner of the sofa, her legs draped over Xuthos, and she had to turn her head slightly to speak to the princess.

Ariadne's face turned dreamy. "Gorgeous." She sighed. "And so strong." She giggled. "*You* probably see strong warriors every day, but Krete doesn't have many."

That, Koralia knew. It was mostly engaged in trade, and even its few warrior guards were sent elsewhere to train. Usually to Poseidon, before the rift between him and Minos. Then Ares had been asked to train them, but he didn't like Minos and had turned the contract down. Koralia didn't know where they were trained now, but Ares would, if she really needed the information.

Ariadne had always had an eye for a striking face or body. Not to mention Icarus's natural magnetism. So that made at least three totally natural reasons Icarus had entranced Ariadne. It didn't explain why she had betrayed him, if she had.

Talos seemed to think *someone* had.

Koralia wanted to claw the truth out of the girl, but she couldn't, not here, not now.

Ariadne continued to gush about Icarus for several minutes, how bold and bright and brave he'd been and how much she didn't blame Daedalus for his grief, until Koralia could hardly stand it. To hear the princess praising Icarus as if she'd known him intimately sickened her so much that she wanted to throw up everything she'd just swallowed.

Xuthos must have noticed, because he slid one arm around her shoulder and ran his fingers through her hair over and over, caressing, while his right hand grasped hers.

She held on tightly, chanting Amazonian mantras over and over in her head so she wouldn't slip up. Wouldn't snap and beat the woman in front of her to a bloody pulp for what her planet—her *family*—had done to Icarus.

"He was just so bright." Ariadne sighed again, gazing out to sea like a besotted fool.

*Bright.* That was the best she could say of him? Icarus had been so much more than that.

"He sounds like a fascinating person," Koralia said, faking a smile as she started on her third drink.

"Oh, he was!" Ariadne leaned so far forward that Koralia's eyes could barely focus. She motioned for Koralia to come even closer and then whispered, "I asked him to marry me."

With olympian hearing, the sound was too loud, and Koralia yanked her head back suddenly, raising one hand to rub her ear. Fortunately, Ariadne took the reaction for shock and nodded solemnly. "I did."

Now it all made sense, *too much* sense. If Icarus had been betrayed, here was a perfect reason for why.

If it hadn't been for Xuthos still holding her, Koralia might have said something incredibly rash...or just strangled the princess. Simple rejection? *That's* what had brought Icarus down, a spoiled princess miffed at not getting her own way? Of all the ways for him to die, did it have to be so ignominious?

"What did he say?" Xuthos asked, as if he was intrigued by the story.

Koralia thought Ariadne would tell her bodyguard to know his place, but she smiled instead.

Of course. Xuthos was attractive. And Ariadne apparently ran on hormones.

*I...I can't...* Koralia put her drink down with a clatter. "One minute," she said, surging to her feet with one hand over her stomach and heading for the nearest bathroom.

"Hold that thought, please?" Xuthos said, unhurriedly, as if this was normal. "We'll be right back."

She didn't want him there, so she tried to wave him back, but he ignored it. He followed her into the private bathroom and flipped the lock on the door as she leaned against the sink, raw anger surging through her.

"Say the word, and I can make it look like an accident," he growled.

She thought it was a joke, but when she looked up, his eyes were hard. Intensity radiated from him, making him look taller and darker, an avenging erinys. Icarus had been his captain, his leader, and she'd seen enough to know that Xuthos had loved him the same way most people loved Icarus: with a burning allegiance.

"All because he said no," she said aloud, clenching her hands and forcing deep breaths in and out of her lungs.

"And I thought I knew she-devils," he commented, his voice lighter.

She snorted, feeling his gaze on her, a silent reaching out—wanting to help but not knowing how.

Betraying a man because he had rejected you wasn't even she-devilry. It was selfishness, plain and pure and simple.

Koralia leaned back against the wall, still taking deep breaths. Her generals would have smacked her for having slipped up this much, for not mastering her emotion better, but if she hadn't left, she would have punched Ariadne in the middle of her smug mouth and upturned nose.

She sucked in another breath, picturing the rebellion and how badly they needed this intel.

*Okay, I can do this now.*

As quickly as they'd come in, she straightened and moved back toward the door. "Let's go back and finish her—" She halted. "And, no, you can't kill her. Besides, I'm pretty sure I'm better at making death look accidental than you are."

"If you say so," Xuthos said, his eyes sharp on her as he held the door open and followed her back out into the hot sunshine. "*I* was trained on Vulcani."

"I *do* say so," she retorted, pleased he'd argued. It gave her a good pretense for being annoyed. "And you might have been trained there, but I was *raised* there."

"I'm so sorry, Ariadne," she apologized as they approached the princess and sat back down. Xuthos crowded next to her, but she glared at him and pointed firmly for him to back up, to maintain the illusion that she was annoyed with him. "It was so bad of me to run out in the middle of your sad story, but I think that drink had sohni in it."

Ariadne had been on her comdisk, smiling happily, but she looked up when they returned and watched them closely as they sat down again. "Oh, it did; are you allergic?"

"Yes, and my bodyguard is supposed to remember to ask about it." She glared sideways at Xuthos and saw the exact second he realized how she was twisting her annoyance. He ducked his head, looking remorseful, but she was pretty sure he was laughing silently.

"At least he's pretty. That has to count for something." Ariadne giggled, seeming at ease again.

Koralia picked up a different cocktail and took a sip, rolling her eyes. Yes, at least he was that. And thank fires Ariadne was too much of a featherhead to suspect there was anything other than simple annoyance in Koralia's manner. She couldn't afford to alienate the princess right now, no matter how much she wanted to shoot her.

"Please continue. He turned you down, this upstart rebel?" Koralia couldn't quite keep an edge out of her voice, but she could twist it to sound scornful. Ariadne was too thick to realize the scorn was directed at her.

Koralia hated selfish people. Didn't matter who they were or what reasons they gave for what they did. She hated selfish people for the way they wrecked the lives of everyone around them.

Like her mother.

"Ugh, yes. Said he had a girl already." The princess pushed her lips forward in the most ridiculously childish pout Koralia had ever seen. Mikon still looked like an adult when he pouted, mostly anyway. Ariadne just looked like she should be in an asylum...for more reasons than one.

"I could see how you might want him dead," Xuthos said, inching closer to Koralia. She shook her head but allowed him to come closer. She still wanted to kill Ariadne, and he was a halfway decent distraction, a reminder to keep herself in check. Plus, he was too smart not to know that she was using him, which was a relief.

"No, no," Ariadne confided. "I loved him too much to kill him. I would never." She shook her head. "Not *Icarus*." She said the name so quietly it was almost an indistinct groan.

Koralia clenched her teeth and stayed silent.

So Ariadne hadn't killed him—or had him killed—and she hadn't betrayed him. Koralia blinked, not sure how she felt about that other than raw, confused frustration. She just wanted a simple answer: who had betrayed Icarus and why?

It didn't look like there was one. Certainly not a *clear* answer.

"I'm very angry with my father for shooting him down." Ariadne clenched her hands and then made a show of straightening them out, flashing painted nails.

"How did the king take that?" Koralia asked, as if it was something to laugh about. "You being angry with him, I mean."

Ariadne curled her upper lip. "He said the deed was necessary. That Icarus was a menace. Sure, he was a rebel, but he wasn't that bad."

*Well, that shows how little you knew him.* Icarus had been one of the biggest threats to Krete in years, not just because he was a rebel fighting against the very brand of elitism on which Krete's monarchy thrived, but because Icarus had grown up here, surrounded by these same crystalline waters and deep-blue skies and white beaches. He knew details of the government here, the society, the customs and language, and he knew where to hit them so it hurt. Daedalus might not have been much of a threat, but Icarus was most definitely a menace to Krete. Which made Ariadne's whole story about falling in love and her defense of him awfully suspicious, especially the part where she made it sound like she hadn't been a party to his death.

Coincidental…and heartbreaking if it was true.

And Koralia was inclined to think it was. She didn't think Ariadne could have invented the whole story and had it hang together so conveniently without more holes. The princess wasn't exactly stupid, but neither was she the brightest.

Koralia couldn't ask Ariadne about Icarus again without making her suspicious, so she came at it sideways. "You were in the rebellion for a while?"

"I was, until I became a double agent." Ariadne said it so casually, like it was no big deal. "But I'm not now. I have a new alliance, so they had to go. And after the way I left, they won't want me back. I'm disappointed, but it was necessary for my new plans."

*Necessary for her new plans?* Was that how she described poisoning a teenager?

Xuthos's arms slid around Koralia again, and she knew that this time, it was to keep his own control. Heirax had been universally loved by the rebels —it had only taken her a few hours to see how he fit into life on the base. He'd run errands for Xuthos, hovered around the pilot while he worked, and probably helped him with a hundred small tasks, just as he had everyone else. And Ariadne described poisoning him as a *necessity*.

At least, Koralia *assumed* they were talking about the same thing. What else could Ariadne have done recently that wasn't killing Icarus but that was so serious that the rebellion would never want her back?

"Went out with a bang, did you?" Koralia inquired, sipping from her drink again and half closing her eyes, tipping her head back to smile blissfully at Xuthos.

Ariadne laughed, a high, false sound. "A bang is exactly how I went out. A bit of poison, a subterfuge or two, some mysterious messages—that will distract them from me for a while."

They were definitely talking about the same thing. Did Ariadne realize she had killed a boy and almost killed someone else? It took an intense poison to reduce a full-grown kentauri stallion to shaking and looking as pale as death.

Xuthos's hand tightened on Koralia's stomach, and she pried it loose to hold it. They needed to get out of here. If they didn't, either she or Xuthos was going to punch the princess.

So she slid her other hand into the pocket of her tunic far enough to press a tiny button on the bottom of her comdisk. Then she twined her fingers with Xuthos's again and kept drinking.

A minute later, her comdisk rang, sharp and incessant.

"Oh blast," she said as if surprised, pulling it out and reading the screen. "My father wants a conference," she explained in answer to Ariadne's look of inquiry and jabbed an elbow sideways into Xuthos's ribs.

He snapped upright, looking alarmed. "Lord Hephaestus? Why?"

"Oh stars, I don't know, because I'm his daughter?" Koralia stood up, stretched, and smacked Xuthos on the shoulder. "Straighten up. It's not as bad as that. I'll tell him I'll call him back soon and wait until we're back at the palace."

Xuthos slid out from behind her, standing and reaching down to lift her to her feet, his hands steady on hers. When she was standing, he kissed both of her hands, using the movement to slide his comdisk back into a front pocket of his armor.

Smart man. He'd recorded at least some of the conversation. The General would be pleased.

"You two are so cute," Ariadne said, watching them with a little smile. "Are you sure you aren't more than just lovers? Because I think you should keep him around."

Koralia raised her eyebrows and shook her head at Xuthos's hopeful look. "I don't tend to keep my lovers long. I'm an Amazon, you know." It almost made her gag to say the words—as if she was like any other olympian, but they were a handy excuse. "I'm restless. I don't stay in one place long. Or with any one person." *Except one*, of course, but she couldn't say that. Xuthos squeezed her arm, and she leaned back against him slightly, grateful he kept his mouth shut.

Ariadne looked happier than she had since they arrived. "Ah, but when you find the right one, hold onto it. That's what I'm doing."

*I did, you little ker, and your planet took him from me.*

Ariadne was the very last person in the galaxy Koralia wanted to hear talking about relationships. "You'll have to tell me about your someone special," was all she said as they stepped into the shuttle that would take them back to the palace.

"Psiiii, he's wonderful." Ariadne beamed, and while the expression softened the sharp angles of her face, Koralia still felt like ripping her eyes out.

"I've been kind of jealous of you," the princess admitted.

*Am I supposed to be surprised?* Koralia arched one eyebrow and gave her an insincere smile.

"You have this gorgeous man at your back, you have a fallback boy, and you get to travel wherever you want and whenever you want."

Wouldn't Mikon just *love* being called a fallback boy? Koralia could feel Xuthos shaking with laughter.

Ariadne bounced a little in her seat. "But he just messaged me, and I might be getting off planet sooner than I thought. This is my chance to finally see the galaxy!"

"So we're to have an engagement party?" Wouldn't *that* just be lovely.

Panic overspread Ariadne's face. "No! My parents don't know about him. Please don't say anything! We're going to..." The princess dropped her voice. "Well, we might elope. We haven't decided yet."

"Oh, don't worry about us." Koralia motioned between her and Xuthos. "We have no reason to say anything."

Ariadne sank back against the seat in relief as the shuttle started moving.

As they flew through a sky so blue it almost hurt to look at it, Koralia frowned to herself. Who would be willing to risk the wrath of the Kretan royal family in order to help their daughter run away?

That was either one extremely naive boy or an incredibly arrogant one.

And either could be ominous for the minotaurs...and the rebels.

# CHAPTER 22

S he needed Icarus.

Koralia left the talking to Xuthos on their way back to the palace. Whoever special Ariadne had found, it didn't stop the princess from suggesting that Xuthos come to her rooms later that night. He turned the offer aside with a laugh and kept chatting with Ariadne while running his fingers over Koralia's hand, which rested on the seat near him.

She closed her eyes, resisting the urge to pull away and curl up in the corner. He wasn't being rude or obnoxious, and they needed this for their cover, but the pain of Icarus was almost unbearable right now, and this only made it worse.

Over and over in her head tumbled memories of when Icarus would come into a room, see at a glance how she was feeling, and crush her in a hug that didn't let go until they had both relaxed. She longed for just one more moment with him—like when he would pace back and forth in front of her, venting about some problem facing the rebellion until he dropped down at her feet and leaned back against her knees while she ran her fingers through his hair. And when he was calm again, he'd reach up to pull her down and kiss her breathless.

Nothing in the galaxy compared to this pain, like torture wires tightening around her chest.

Krete had to be the reason for the pain being so much worse these last few days. Krete, where he'd died; Krete, where everything was fake; Krete, where his death might have been only an accident or could have been the result of resentment from a selfish princess.

Krete, where truth was as rare as their warriors.

But deep down, she knew that wasn't completely true. Being here made it worse, exacerbated the pain, but she'd have ached whether she was on this planet or on the other side of settled space. Loss hit harder after a little distance, when you pulled free of busyness long enough to look at what lay ahead.

And what lay ahead for her was darkness.

Her only comfort was knowing the Sunfires understood her intense longing for him, because they felt it too. Which was why Koralia wanted to see Talos and Mikon as soon as possible. And Ianessa. Fortunately, their shuttle was almost to the palace, where she could at least see and hug Mikon. But she needed to make sure she was calm before then. She'd have to tell him about Icarus, and the odds were high he'd fly into a rage and she'd have to calm him down, which she wouldn't be able to do if she was still enraged herself.

When she and Xuthos let themselves into their suite, Mikon's voice echoed from the sitting room, raised in laughing protest over something.

A few seconds later, he poked his head out, looking them over. She smiled. "How was your afternoon?" Sliding her shoulder cape off, she tossed it into a chair in the antechamber. Her circlet was bound to be tangled in her hair after all of Xuthos's playing, so she'd leave it for later.

Mikon had been studying her, and abruptly, he asked, "Why do you look so tired?"

She rolled her eyes. "Hello? An afternoon with Ariadne? You of all of us should know what that's like." It was the truth, just not all of it. She'd ordered Xuthos to stay quiet about their afternoon. She would tell Mikon what he needed to know as soon as they had a quiet moment and enough time before seeing Ariadne next that he wouldn't strangle the girl. She wanted to tell Talos and Athanasia first and get an idea of how best to handle it with Mikon, but that wasn't possible right now.

The youngest Sunfire grimaced. "There should be a law against being that exhausting."

That made her grin as she stretched her neck back and to the side, trying to work the stiffness out of it.

"What are you doing?" Xuthos asked, setting his armor on a bench nearby and raising his eyebrows at Mikon. "Why were you laughing?"

As if remembering something important, Mikon dashed back into the sitting room, calling over his shoulder, "Come and see! We can talk to the base now!"

They could talk to base? She could actually speak to Talos and Athanasia after all? She almost tripped over Xuthos as they hurried into the room. Mikon's comdisk sat in the middle of the table in front of the sofa, projecting three people.

"Is that Koralia?" Talos said, twisting around to see her where she'd paused by the door.

"The Amazon?" said an unfamiliar voice as the middle person ducked under Talos's arm, trying to see. He was taller than Talos and had one arm hooked around Ianessa's back, supporting her.

"Kora, come here!" Ianessa waved her over.

Mikon perched on the arm of the sofa, grinning like he'd discovered buried treasure. He jerked his head sideways, motioning for Koralia to sit down in the middle while Xuthos made his way around the table to her other side. "Tryphosa gave me something that allows us to securely broadcast through the Labyrinth," he explained excitedly, gesturing to the almost full-size projection of his siblings.

"Bry, dude!" Xuthos exclaimed, dropping down next to Koralia and holding up his hand for a fist bump. "You got in."

"Xu, man, good to see you." The middle person grinned at Xuthos, returned the fist bump, and then looked back at Koralia, his eyes searching her face.

She smiled. "Hello, Red Arrow."

Brygos—the second youngest brother of the Sunfires and the engineer of the family—looked back at her, his eyes gleaming in satisfaction. "Black Swan. May I just say it is the greatest honor in the universe to finally meet you?"

"How does he eat with his tongue coated in so much silver?" complained Mikon, pointedly moving from the arm of the sofa to sit down next to Koralia.

She smiled at Brygos. "Why, thank you. You're too kind."

Mikon snorted, but before he could argue, Xuthos asked Brygos a question, distracting him.

Koralia nudged Mikon's arm. "Did you find out everything we needed from Tryphosa?"

Mikon nodded, moving so he faced her. "She's not our contact—that's the other guy. I was careful but we might have been followed." He frowned in concern.

"We'll figure it out if you were."

He nodded. "And she gave me these. The minotaurs are apparently really good with tech." He grabbed a small case of something off the table and spilled a tiny gel chip into his hand. "Comdisk?"

She pulled out the one she'd taken from her father's ship.

He flipped it over and showed her where to attach it, then dropped another gel chip into her hand for her private com.

"Thanks." She looked back up into the screen, ignoring the questioning look Mikon gave her. Brygos and Xuthos were still talking about some engineering project—the technical names and terms flying over her head—and Talos was looking steadily at her, waiting. When she met his eyes, he raised his eyebrows, and she nodded, trying to tell him they needed to talk in private. He blinked twice in acknowledgement.

Focusing on the projection, she didn't realize Mikon had moved until she felt hands in her hair. She bent her head to allow him access, and he had her circlet untangled in a fraction of the time it would have taken her. As he handed it to her, he shot Xuthos a smug glance, which was answered with a dark glare.

So they were back to this rivalry, were they? After yesterday morning, they had settled into a truce, teasing each other when off duty and competing to watch her back when they were on duty. Evidently, that wasn't destined to last.

Good thing Mikon didn't know how she and Xuthos had spent the afternoon.

She thanked him with a quick squeeze of his fingers before she took the circlet. Talos was shaking his head, observing Mikon and Xuthos, while Ianessa pursed her lips in a silent whistle—Koralia thought it was sympathy. Brygos looked like a man who had discovered a secret, his gaze gleefully switching back and forth between Xuthos and Mikon.

"Where's Athanasia?" Koralia asked, before teasing could break out.

Talos waved his hand behind him. "In a meeting."

"Which doesn't sound like it's going well," Brygos said, leaning forward and looking her over curiously. She sat back, giving him a better view.

Was that a disappointed flicker in his eyes?

Well, she couldn't expect all of the Sunfires to like her, especially not right away.

"Last-ditch effort to find evacuation possibilities," Talos explained, referring to the General, his tone hopeful even though she could see the truth in his eyes. What they'd all known since the request first came from Asterion.

They wouldn't be able to get the minotaurs off of Krete. Not all of them...if any.

"And Ariadne?" Mikon prompted, looking between her and Talos. "What did you find out?"

"She's a hussy," Koralia said shortly.

"We knew *that*." Mikon rolled his eyes. "Is she the traitor?"

"We're still figuring that out. It's complicated. And if you and Xuthos can manage not to kill each other for the next hour, I need to talk to Talos. Mission stuff," she explained, forestalling the question on Mikon's lips. "Will you still be on base when we get back, Brygos?"

He grinned and brought his hands together in front of him as he wiggled his eyebrows. "Oh, I'm not missing this. I'm *so* going to be here. Especially if I'm seeing what I think I'm seeing."

Mikon made a disgusted sound. "What does that even *mean*?"

"It means *you*"—Brygos pointed at his younger brother—"have a *crush*."

"You're crazy." Mikon snorted.

"Well, he is sometimes," Xuthos agreed, "but not about this. And I have the stories to prove it."

"Oh, hot *wires*," Brygos said, clearly gleeful.

Koralia rolled her eyes and pinched the bridge of her nose. "I mean it. You had both better be alive when I get back." She narrowed her eyes sternly at Xuthos and then ruffled Mikon's hair as she stood up. "No punching, Mikon."

He reached up and caught her hand, long fingers tightening around it as his gaze zeroed in on her face. "You aren't telling me something."

"I'll tell you later." She pulled free and patted his curls again, giving Xuthos one last stern look for him.

"Oh, I like her. I *really* like her. She fits right in," Brygos was saying as she left.

So maybe it wasn't disappointment she'd seen earlier. That made her feel better, especially because she liked what she'd seen of him so far. He was a Sunfire. They were hard to *not* like.

In her bedroom, she leaned against her door for a minute, just breathing, trying to pull the most important facts out of her afternoon so she could give them to Talos. Then she applied Tryphosa's gel chip to her private comdisk and dialed his com. The display flickered to life, but he wasn't in sight.

"Just a sec," he called, his voice muffled. He ducked back into view, his jacket hanging over his arm. Tossing it over the back of a chair, he sat down.

Looking around, she could tell he sat in his office, which was on the same floor as the command bridge. She'd gotten the impression earlier that he barely spent any time there, too busy running between stations and pilots and personnel, but whenever there was enough room in a base, Athanasia assigned offices to her senior staff so they had a place to handle interviews and more clerical duties. That came in handy at times like this.

Without preamble, she launched into a report of everything she and Xuthos had just discovered. Talos didn't blink at her account of Ariadne, but his eyes darkened when she told him what the princess had said about Daedalus.

"Who knows what the actual truth is," she finished.

"Oh, Daedalus up and disappearing is the least surprising part. Coward." Talos scowled. "The thing that has me confused is her account of the battle. Icarus being an accident?" He sat back in his chair and shoved his hands into his hair, pulling at it in frustration. "An *accident.*"

"Yeah." Not very eloquent, but what else was there to say? War sucked. All the stories and poems that called it glorious were wrong. The cause for which the rebels fought was right and just and worthwhile. But war itself was ugly and bloody, raw, sweaty, painful, and it left gaping holes when it took people.

She should know; war was Ares's business, and she'd lived with it since before she could remember, growing up knowing blood and fighting as naturally as food and drink.

"But we were right," she continued. "Ariadne—Ambrosia—is a traitor."

"And I was right that whether she betrayed Icarus directly or not, it did have something to do with love." He frowned and reached out as if he could touch her shoulder through the transmission. "You know he didn't love her, right?"

That was something she'd never wondered about. "Oh, Talos, of course I know." Shaking her head, she smiled. "Would he have kissed me like that if he did? Of course I know."

She almost laughed at the look on his face, eyebrows raised high, one slow blink, and an expression that looked like it didn't know whether to be a grin or an uncomfortable grimace.

"Too much information?" she asked lightly.

"I'll get back to you on that," he answered, and she couldn't help snickering. "How are the boys doing?"

Rotating her neck from side to side again, she kneaded the muscles in her shoulder and along the back of her head, but the knots in her neck stayed. "They haven't killed each other yet. Came close yesterday morning. Xuthos got caught by a servant while he was sending the morning check-in, so he said he was looking for a spot for us to rendezvous for an affair."

Talos's mouth hardened into a straight line. "And?"

"You Sunfires." Koralia shook her head, but her voice was fond. "I *have* done this before, you know. It's been excellent cover, and he's been more than decent about it. Mikon tried to strangle him for it, literally..."

Talos was grinning now, pride beaming in his face. "That's our boy."

"...shouting that I'd just lost Icarus, which Xuthos apparently didn't know." She eyed him questioningly; how hadn't the pilot known about her relationship with Icarus? *Wasn't it mentioned in briefings? I can't remember.*

But Talos shrugged, so she kept going. "And whether it was respect for Icarus or compassion for me, I don't know and I don't much care; he's been behaving." Granted, he had been pretty hands-on with her that afternoon, but she didn't tell Talos that. She had allowed it, after all, even encouraged it. She didn't exactly want it, not so soon after Icarus, but a mission was a mission, and they needed their cover story to hold. Besides, it wasn't like Xuthos was exactly *distasteful.*

"Well, good. But don't hesitate to let Mikon take a swing at him if he steps out of line." Talos leaned back, linking his hands together behind his head.

Koralia rolled her eyes, but the family loyalty felt wonderful. "How badly is Brygos going to torment Mikon about his crush?" she asked.

"Ohhh, I'd say he won't let up on him for a month at least, and then only a little bit." He spread his first finger and thumb about half an inch apart. "Mikon is way ahead in the sibling tally right now. Not only did he get to meet you first, he had a few days on base with you, and now he's on mission with you. Nah, Brygos isn't letting up on him for months. Especially not if Mikon lies about it. He shouldn't; his feelings are visible from *here*, so there's no use trying to hide them."

She had to smile at that.

"Does it bother you?" Talos asked quietly. His voice was hard to read, like he was intentionally going for neutral.

"No." She rested her chin on one hand, watching him. "No, it doesn't bother me."

"Oh good." He sounded relieved. "It's not..." He hesitated, looking unsure.

"He's used to hopeless crushes," he said after a minute, searching her face. "Mikon, that is. It's not the first time he's crushed on a girl someone else in the family had their eye on. It's not even the first time he's gone for someone Icarus had." He trailed off and sat there for a minute, his face dark with worry.

*About Mikon?* From what she had seen, the boy was well used to handling himself—in life, love, or war.

Talos dropped his voice lower, confiding, "His longest crush was an ex-Amazon Icarus was with for a while. His crush came after they broke up. She didn't understand Icarus, and she definitely didn't understand Mikon, so he never really had a shot. She was pretty but too practical for either of them. And kind of a hellcat in all the worst ways."

She snorted. "Hence the *ex*-Amazon."

"Really?"

"Sure. If your attitude is that bad, you don't last long in our ranks, doesn't matter how good of a fighter you are. Who was it anyway; do you have a name?"

He narrowed his eyes for a minute, mentally sorting through something. "She was a bit younger than you. A blonde when we knew her. Slight and short, smile that always looked like a sneer. From a Central world. Polydora, I think?"

Oh, *her*. "Hellcat is a nice word to use for her." Koralia scowled. "We were pretty thrilled to see the back of that stygere siren."

He chuckled at the insult. "It was before the General assigned us to different bases. We were still mostly operating out of the same area, and we all met her, so at least we were there for both Icarus and later Mikon. She worked him over." A dark shadow crossed his face.

Koralia understood. Just the *thought* of Mikon in Polydora's vicinity made her want to growl.

"That's where Icarus first heard about me, you know," she said lightly, trying to take his attention off of the memory. "From her. I was part of the mission that ended in her getting kicked out, and she didn't take it so well."

Talos threw back his head and laughed. "So not only were you olympian and full-fledged Amazon, he'd heard trash talk from a former comrade? How typical of Icarus." He shook his head. "Now that you mention it, I remember him saying something about that. Of *course* he'd hear that and think you were someone he needed to meet."

That was Icarus, all right. "It was hilarious when he figured out I was *the* Koralia she used to talk about."

He grinned. "I just bet."

An alert of some kind rang, and his face, which had looked relaxed for just a minute, hardened again, strain carving lines in his forehead. "I don't have much longer. The minotaurs…we can't take them all off. We haven't been able to find a way."

It had been a tall order. "I figured. I'll break it to the minotaur and see if there's another way."

"Can Mikon talk to Pasiphae again?" he asked. "Question her more about the minotaurs? This whole thing about servants and slaves sounds murky."

"Maybe. We can't exactly *ask* to talk to her; we have to wait until she turns up. And I'm betting we'll get better information out of Asterion tonight anyway." She glanced out the window, ducking her head to see more of the sky. The sun was beginning to touch the horizon, so night would fall soon. "I should go tell the boys to get some sleep."

"And lie down yourself," he told her, leaning forward with a smile that was half caring, half exhaustion. "Hurry back. We miss you, you and Mikon. I wouldn't even mind seeing Xuthos again."

"Now that *is* high praise," she teased. "And I've only been gone two days; how can you miss me?"

His exasperated look said he couldn't believe he'd heard that. "It's been *three days*, and you're family, and we've barely had a chance to really talk."

She swallowed hard, refusing to cry at the fondness in his voice.

"Plus," he added, "if you were here, Brygos would quit pestering me about you, and my com would stop ringing twenty times a day with everyone demanding more details about you in the group chat. I've told them to fortify up and contact you themselves, but did they? No." He rolled his eyes.

That was a flattering thought, that all the Sunfires were that curious about her. "If they're intimidated, tell them I only bite olympians."

He burst out laughing. "I'm definitely not going to repeat that to them. You'd never hear the end of it from Siromos. He could make an innuendo out of a hymn."

"They're the same thing for some olympians," she said seriously.

He laughed again just as his com started chiming like crazy, and he looked at the screen before shaking his head. "Mikon sent replies, and they just now decided to come in. Ohhh, Siromos and Dione are going at it again. Brygos must have told them about Mikon's crush." He snickered. "The torment won't end for a long time."

She started to speak, but an alarm on her com cut her off. What she wanted most right now was to sit and talk with him, to soak in the companionship that wrapped naturally around them as fellow commanders and because of Icarus, but that would have to wait.

"I need to go brief the boys. You'll tell Athanasia? About Icarus?"

Talos's jaw clenched, and he nodded stiffly. "She'll hate it."

"She'll understand it." Not just the frustration they felt but also the bittersweetness that came from knowing he hadn't been betrayed.

*Probably* hadn't been betrayed.

"Yeah. Yeah, she will." Talos rubbed his eyes and flexed his hands, stretching, and she wondered when he'd last had a full night's sleep.

Likely not since Icarus's death, same as her.

"And Talos?"

"Yeah?" He paused, his hand hovering over his comdisk.

"I wish you were here." And she did. She wished all the Sunfires were here. They were used to winning impossible situations; maybe somehow they could together figure out a way to take the minotaurs off Krete.

And even more, she wanted a contingent of Amazons.

But she didn't have time for useless wishing.

Talos grinned. "I wish I was there too. Stay safe."

"Audeamus."

# CHAPTER 23

When Koralia came out of her bedroom and looked into the sitting room, Mikon was sprawled across the sofa, his eyes closed. Xuthos was nowhere in sight.

Quietly, she moved toward him. He looked like he was dozing, but maybe he just had his eyes closed. She listened for a minute. Regular breathing, completely relaxed body—he was definitely sleeping. None of them had gotten much sleep the previous night, and she hated to wake him, but they needed to have this meeting.

Still, she paused. Maybe she could go get Xuthos first.

Then Mikon moved, and Koralia held her breath. He looked angelic in the golden rays of the setting sun. Not adorably cherubic, but burning with a fire that was otherworldly, one that set worlds ablaze and healed with a touch.

"Icarus," he mumbled. "Don't do it."

On second thought, Xuthos could wait.

"Mikon," she called softly, poised to step back if he was startled when he woke. "Mikon."

He snapped awake instantly, coming half off the couch, alert gaze sweeping the room, identifying where he was and what was happening. When he saw her, he dropped back down onto the seat and moved over, leaving room for her.

Cautiously, she sat down. "I didn't want to wake you." She paused and then asked hesitantly, "Were you dreaming of Icarus?" She felt like she'd known the boy-man beside her for years, but really, she'd only met him a little over a week ago, and she had a lot to learn about him still. Was he volatile in his just-awakened state, or did he switch from sleep to full awareness instantly, like most Amazons?

"Yeah," he muttered. "It's this rotten planet. I can't get away from it."

"I know," she whispered. "I can't either."

Restlessly, he turned his head from side to side, blue eyes darkening with... resentment? Irritation? She couldn't tell. She slid her hand over his, and he gripped it so tightly it almost hurt.

"You said something earlier...about how weird this planet is and everyone on it." He turned his head far enough to see her and squinted. "Pasiphae is weird. Ariadne is really weird. And *did* she kill him?"

She'd planned to wait, but now was as good a time as any to tell him. "I don't know. I really don't know. She loved him. She proposed; he turned her down; she left the rebels. But she swears she didn't kill him."

He clenched his teeth together and ground out a single sentence. "Do you believe her?"

"I believe she didn't mean to kill him," she said cautiously. She really did believe it, but she didn't want to inflame him. "Talos believes it's possible the firefight was accidental, that Icarus was simply spotted and the guns were already hot because the gunners were at their posts day and night while the Labyrinth was finished. Like you discovered on the scouting mission."

His face twisted, and he laughed once—short, sharp, harsh. "Icarus, brought down by an accident."

She felt it too, the ignominy of the rebellion's best and brightest falling to an accident.

But that was the reality of war.

They still had no evidence to back that theory up yet, so she would keep looking. There were giant holes in Ariadne's story, and she wouldn't be happy until they were filled. Talos's suggestion that they get Mikon to talk to Pasiphae again was a good one, but she didn't want to go that route unless they had to. Insane people could be hazardous.

"Brygos thinks we might be able to blow it up, did he tell you?" she asked. When they were back in space, they could fume about Icarus, but she was walking a knife's edge herself, and she wasn't sure she'd have the control to help Mikon if she didn't stop thinking about this. The mission had to come first. They had to talk to Asterion. Then they could get out, be angry, and maybe...maybe even strike at the heart of Krete's too-beautiful world.

Revenge was not encouraged in the Kallistratus, but justice for the mino-taurs was a worthy cause, wasn't it?

"He did. I hope we can." He sounded exhausted but in control, to her relief. "Do we have to do dinner with the king tonight?"

"I'll decide as soon as we hear your report on your mission."

"There isn't much to tell." He shrugged, letting go of her hand and bringing his knees up, resting his arms on them and laying his head down on them, still facing her. "Xuthos went to lie down. Do you want me to go wake him up?"

Did she? No, if anyone was going to wake Xuthos up, it should probably be her. But if Mikon didn't have much to report, it made no sense to call a team meeting.

"No." She shook her head. "Just tell me."

"Tryphosa was waiting for me. I think she followed me out of the palace."

Followed him...like she had been *waiting* for him? That could be dangerous for all of them. But Mikon was still talking.

"She said she could get us a meeting with Asterion tonight, at the hour after midnight, and then Pasiphae came up." He stared out the window at the lavender sky darkening to purple night, his forehead lined with confusion.

"And?" She nudged him. "Don't keep me in suspense here. Did you have to use your power?"

"A little, once. I asked her to tell me about her children, and she just replied in riddles. All about shining jewels of Krete, dawn of a new age, children of the sun and sea, and how she would be the—" He broke off and grimaced. "The mother of a new race of gods."

Were all the Kretans obsessed with godhood? Koralia rolled her eyes. The thought of Ariadne as a goddess made her gag. *She's more annoying than the Charites. Mother might like her...no, actually, she's a little too fake even for Mother. She prefers real emotion, not melodrama.*

It made her feel strange to admit that even to herself. But it was the truth. Whatever her mother's myriad faults—her stupid excuses, her selfishness, and her twisted perspectives—at least her emotion was genuine.

"And your afternoon?" he asked, pulling her out of the unpleasant thoughts.

"Long," she said, pondering how much to tell him. Teams ran better when there was as much communication as possible between most of the members, at least when a team didn't contain anyone likely to take information and use it to be impulsive. Despite the tightrope she and Mikon were both walking, he'd stayed in control well, and he did deserve to know.

"Xuthos and I pretended to be close to get Ariadne to relax, and she blathered on and on about how much she'd loved Icarus."

"Well, Icarus never loved her," he declared. "Who could love such a fake-ass—" he appeared to be searching for a word. "Well, a fake-ass person," he finished. "Which sounds stupid, but I can't think of a better word."

"Fake-ass mormo," Koralia said, relaxing into the sofa. "Empusa, strix...no, she'd have to have a personality to be any of those. I've been calling her a ker, but I don't know, death-demons are at least committed—"

Mikon snickered.

"—and Ariadne's just *annoying*. And not that special or distinctive. She's *common*. Boring. Let's call her what she is: a bitch."

"That's unfair to dogs," he objected.

"A little, but only if you use it like you are comparing her to a dog. If not, if you're just using it as a descriptor, that's different."

He thought for a minute. "Okay, fair."

"GSL is dumb," she said, wrinkling her lip in disdain. "Olympian has different words for it."

"Mmmhmmm," he hummed, his eyes shut.

Tucking her legs under her, she laid back against the corner of the sofa and closed her eyes too. She wanted to sleep before their nighttime meeting, but she wasn't sure she could relax enough. Over and over it pounded in her head that they wouldn't be able to take the minotaurs off of Krete. That was their main bargaining chip with Asterion. Without that...

Mikon toppled over, half onto her. Sitting back up, he shook his head and rubbed his eyes. "Sorry," he said, his voice clouded with sleep.

"It's fine. Sleep." She pushed his head gently back against the sofa. "We don't leave until midnight. I'll text Xuthos and set alarms."

He cracked open his eyes and peered sideways at her. "Are you going to sleep?"

"If I can."

Still looking at her, he shoved his legs toward the other end of the seat and then lay down and rested his head on her legs.

Startled, she dropped her comdisk on him. He caught it and handed it back to her, smirking up at her in a way that made him look like a teenager again. "This *is* a comfortable way. Now you can't go anywhere and have to sleep too."

Staring down at him, she raised her eyebrows. "And what if I get up and leave?"

"You won't," he said confidently, closing his eyes, to all appearances immediately asleep again.

The little punk. For a minute, she watched him, then she shook her head and chuckled softly. He was right. She wouldn't. There wasn't anything else she had to do right now.

But there was one question she needed answered first. She poked him in the shoulder until he opened his eyes.

"Is this another competition between you and Xuthos?"

"*Him?*" Mikon grinned contemptuously. "No. If it was, I'd be winning anyway. You're a Sunfire, so I'll get to see you long after he will."

She blinked. That…kind of made sense. "Unless I start a romantic relationship with him for real," she said, sending Xuthos a text updating him on their nighttime plans.

"You won't," he said, closing his eyes again, his voice complacent. "He'll never hold a candle to Icarus."

Right again. Xuthos was a decent guy, even a good one under the bad-boy demeanor. But he wasn't Icarus, and he wasn't even anyone she'd look at a third time. He fought loyally for the rebellion, but he lacked the core of living flame that had attracted her to Icarus. The same core all the Sunfires shared.

But Mikon hadn't answered the deeper question.

Koralia set alarms on all three comdisks and set hers down nearby. She wasn't sure how to ask this, but she needed to know, especially after what Talos had said.

"And this doesn't bother you?" she asked in a whisper so low it was barely audible, squeezing his shoulder. "I know what you feel—some part of it. I know you aren't neutral to me. I can't…it's too soon for me to even think… missions, I can do; family, I can do. But Mikon—"

"Like I don't know that?" he demanded, his voice intense enough that she would have called it snapping if it wasn't so sincere. He sat up abruptly, avoiding bumping her head. Twisting so that he faced her, he took her by the shoulders and leaned closer, his eyes locking on hers. "I would never, ever ask that of you. You aren't responsible for how I feel. I'm okay, I promise, I'm used to handling this." He pulled her into a hug that was at once platonic, comforting, and most importantly, *understanding*. When he let go, he was grinning. "Friends, Sunfires, rebels, yeah?"

"Friends, Sunfires, rebels," she answered. "Now let's get some sleep."

Without another word, he lay back down on her legs, and she stretched out so she could rest her head on the back of the sofa. Any hesitation she'd had about lying next to him was gone now.

And, really, she did need to sleep.

Smiling quietly, she closed her eyes and settled back. It was good to have a family.

+

KORALIA DIDN'T EXPECT to actually fall asleep, but when the alarms rang a few hours later and she sat up, she realized she had slept better than any night on Krete so far.

Mikon was awake too, sitting up. Blinking, he shoved his hands through his hair to straighten it.

"Can't wait to be off this planet," he grumbled. "Eating without looking over my shoulder, sleeping on a proper bed, and not being tied to the ground."

"Last I checked, cots weren't proper beds, at least not compared with the mattresses here," Xuthos said, coming into the room. "It's like sleeping on a cloud."

Mikon shuddered. "Cots on base are the only proper bed," he declared. "Do I have to dress up for this meeting?"

"No, wear whatever you want," Koralia spun through the new messages on her comdisk. She fired off a quick reply to Athanasia and a notice to the base that they were about to meet with Asterion.

When she looked up, Xuthos was frowning at the floor. Now what had him annoyed? Unless it was her and Mikon in here together...

"What's wrong?" she asked.

He looked up quickly, startled. "Oh, uh, nothing really."

"Doesn't look like nothing," Mikon put in, stretching.

Xuthos shrugged. "I have a weird feeling about this. Tonight," he clarified. "I welcome any chance to pretend with you," he gave Koralia a half bow, "but the air feels weird tonight."

She thought about that for a minute and nodded. She'd been feeling the same way all day, like they were on a doomed mission. But they'd actually made progress with Ariadne this afternoon, and whether they came to a compromise with Asterion tonight or not, they'd at least know if they could take down the Labyrinth.

"I actually agree." Mikon scowled at the dark sky out the window. "It does feel weird."

All three of them feeling it? Never a good sign. "It could be coincidence," she suggested.

The men swung to look at her with matching looks of disbelief.

"Okay, I don't think it is either," she said, standing up and straightening her tunic. She needed to switch it out for a light gown before she left, but that would be the work of seconds. And no stupid circlets. "But," she looked from one to the other, "we have to get this done. One more night. That's all. We can go home tomorrow." Their departure time was already set for shortly before dinner, which would give them time to be back inside rebel space before the night watch began.

"I hate this planet," Mikon muttered, striding past her and Xuthos and into the antechamber. "I'm going to get some water."

"You good to go?" Xuthos asked her, and she knew he wasn't asking if she was physically ready.

"I'm raring to go," she answered. Despite the strange heaviness in the air, she was impatient to have this meeting, deliver the bad news, and hear what Asterion had to say. Not to mention being intensely curious about the minotaurs. She had so many questions still.

"You?" she checked, moving closer to him and tipping her head so she could see him better in the dim lighting.

A slow smirk spread on his face, and he leaned his head down close to hers, eyes roving over her face with evident enjoyment. "Oh, *yes*. I'm ready."

Rolling her eyes, she smacked his shoulder and left, going to change.

When she came out, Mikon and Xuthos were standing in the antechamber, checking to make sure their comdisks were synchronized. They finished and slid them back into their pockets.

"We good, man?" Xuthos asked Mikon.

"Sure, we're good." Mikon shrugged like they had never not been fine, and Koralia turned her head to hide her smile. *Impossible boy.*

The movement made both men turn, and Xuthos whistled, looking her up and down. She was used to that, but from these two, it carried a different feeling. It made her feel wanted, needed, without any of the complications that came when you mixed love and war.

It felt amazing.

Mikon grinned and held out his arm to her. "My turn tonight?"

"Don't you wish, but, no. You need to go ahead of us and wait in the maze...connector...passage thing." What *did* one call it anyway? It wasn't easy to define. Too short for a maze, too distinct to be anything less.

"Mazeway?" Xuthos suggested.

"Yeah, that. Wait for us there."

Mikon saluted her and turned to go, but she held up her hand for them to wait. "What are we?" she asked.

"Rebels," Mikon answered with no hesitation and then remembered he wasn't supposed to say that out loud and looked around him nervously.

"Warriors," Xuthos said and then tipped his head smugly at Mikon.

"And what are we fighting for?"

"Freedom," Xuthos insisted.

Mikon's eyes flashed, answering her challenge. "Justice."

"And healing," she added, "in this galaxy being torn to shreds. So let's go get this information so we can get back to those fights. And to hellraising."

Mikon threw back his head and laughed while Xuthos's eyes gleamed. "Why didn't the General bring you on a long time ago?" he teased as he took her arm.

"Because she was doing important work on Akwila, idiot," Mikon retorted, but his voice was joking instead of caustic. "Don't take too long." Then he was gone, vanishing into the darkness in the hallway.

She and Xuthos waited, counting out five eternally long minutes before following. Outside, the air tingled with salt and a wild spark blowing in off the sea. Clouds rode the horizon, rolling higher but not yet approaching the half moon that lit their path with pale blues and silvers.

It was a night for devilry, Hephaestus would have said. Ares would have called it a war-cry night. Normally, Koralia loved those, relished the electric air raising tingles on her skin, adored the breeze tugging at her hair, reveled in whatever mission she'd been assigned. Nights were always her favorite for missions. But not tonight.

Tonight, she felt heavy as she and Xuthos strolled down the paths to the queen's garden. They were intentionally a little early for the meeting, so they'd have time to settle in before Asterion arrived. The walk to the mazeway seemed to take forever tonight, the moments stretching out until she felt the urge to hide in the shadows and watch while she caught her breath.

But there wasn't anything *to* watch. The garden seemed deserted, the soft thump of their footsteps the only noise around them. To all appearances, it was a peaceful night perfect for meeting with a new rebel contact.

So why did her tension keep rising? Xuthos felt it too, because he clutched her hand tighter as they walked.

Two more paths and three more turns, then they'd be at the mazeway, hidden from the nonexistent eyes she could feel watching.

"Hold right where you are!" a voice screeched.

They jerked to a stop, Xuthos pressing close to her side as both of them stared around for the source of the voice.

Maybe the eyes hadn't been nonexistent after all.

"Don't move!" the voice screeched again, and this time, they both shuddered. It sounded more albatross than human, and she knew at once that this was what their premonitions had been about.

"I'm calling the guards." The screech was menacing now, more of a croak with a chilling high note threading through the words. "You are trespassing and will be prosecuted to the fullest extent of the law!"

A female voice in the queen's garden, a voice with authority to call guards and dictate punishments.

Queen Pasiphae.

*The mad queen.*

Holding up her hands, Koralia called out quietly. "Your Majesty, I meant no har—"

"Silence!" the voice shrieked. "I did not give you leave to speak!"

"Please, Your M—" Something landed with a clatter at Koralia's feet, and Xuthos pulled her back a half step.

A rock. Another landed in front of them, somewhat larger than a pebble, big enough to do some damage if they were hit. And if Koralia was injured, it would provoke an international incident with at least one of her fathers, if not all three of her parents. Cold desperation started to swell in her stomach, rising to choke her.

Maybe if she couldn't talk, she could *show* Pasiphae they meant no harm. Acting on the impulse, she turned toward Xuthos as running footsteps came from the direction of the maze. Mikon, coming to their rescue.

Another rock landed near her, and Xuthos winced as something hit him in the leg.

Even if Pasiphae would listen to Mikon, there was no time to wait for him. Only two things might move Pasiphae, and Koralia never begged if there was another option.

Sliding her arm around Xuthos, she pressed her body to his, silently willing him to understand as she lifted her face to his and kissed him full on the mouth.

There was no need to tell him to keep it real. After one frozen, shocked second, he put his arms around her, pulling her tightly to him and kissing her with all the pent-up energy of a man who had been wanting to do that very thing for a while.

She didn't let it continue long, breaking it but staying close, leaning into his shoulders. When he bent to kiss her again, she reached her hand up to his forehead and pushed him back gently, whispering, "Resist what I'm about to do."

For the second time in as many minutes, shock screamed in his face right before she closed her eyes and drew a deep breath. "Your Majesty!" she called, flooding the words with as much power as she could muster.

It was as if an invisible wave had left her, washing over Xuthos, beyond the trees to wherever Pasiphae was, and…and Mikon, freezing ten steps away, his eyes locked on her.

Time stopped around them as they waited, hardly daring to breathe. Then slow clapping came from the same direction as the voice, and the queen herself stepped out of the bushes beyond the path.

Mikon was moving before Koralia could even step away, striding toward the queen with his hands clasped respectfully in front of him.

"Madam queen," he said, and the pulse of power from him hit Koralia with such force that her head would have snapped back if it had been tangible. There was no room for subtlety tonight.

But Pasiphae was looking at Koralia and Xuthos, and her smile could only be called gleeful as she clapped again. "Young love," she cooed.

What was it with the Kretan women and their voyeuristic behavior and their obsession with forbidden love? They had problems.

With a quick bow, Koralia advanced on the queen, Xuthos at her heels. "Your Majesty, I apologize. I didn't mean to disturb you. I thought the garden was deserted at night, and we—" She ducked her head as if she was blushing and hoped Pasiphae couldn't see the lie in this light. "We have to go home tomorrow. It was our last chance to be alone for a while."

"No, no, my dear, you are right. Love is a reason to break every rule." Pasiphae came closer, still grinning gleefully, the expression definitely maniacal but sophisticated at the same time.

The *wrongness* of the expression made Koralia want to throw up.

"You must not leave," Pasiphae insisted. "Stay. Enjoy each other." Her smile sent shivers up Koralia's spine. "There are many private places in this garden." The queen gestured around her. "They have been used for affairs often. I once declared this garden hallowed to love." Dreamily, she stared into the trees behind them. "It will be so again tonight. It has waited years for you. Under these skies, it will protect you."

*Definitely insane. Especially that smile.*

"Thank you for your pardon and your courtesy, Your Majesty," Koralia said. "But we should be going."

"No," Pasiphae snapped, the words turned demanding. "You must stay. Go. Kiss your lover while you have time. He will be taken from you soon enough." The albatross tone was back. "Stay," she said, her voice matching her dreamy look. "And this beautiful boy will talk to me." She reached out and patted Mikon's cheek. Koralia felt like ripping the woman's hand away. *Don't you touch him,* she wanted to say, but Mikon was no child in need of a guardian. He smiled benevolently down at the queen and stepped to the side, offering her his arm.

Had Koralia's power not worked? Why wasn't Pasiphae a little more open to listening to her? If she kept insisting on having her way, it would throw their entire night into chaos. They needed this meeting with Asterion. They didn't have time for this.

So Koralia readied herself for another use of power, reaching deep inside, calming herself so she could access her reserves. But Mikon beat her to it.

"Madam queen," he said again, his persuasion more subtle, drawing attention magnetically instead of sweeping in like an ocean at high tide. "I would like to hear more about your children."

Koralia didn't want to leave him there, but she didn't have another option. Asterion would be at the meeting place within five minutes, and if they weren't there, he couldn't wait long. The risk of discovery was too high.

Leaning close to Xuthos, she whispered, "Go to the maze and wait for us."

"Sure," he said easily. *Too* easily.

*No*, she wanted to scream.

He hadn't resisted her use of power.

But she had bigger problems to worry about, like Pasiphae's possessive looks at Mikon.

Xuthos went past them and was gone, disappearing into the shadows.

"Your Majesty?" Koralia said, walking toward her, holding Pasiphae's gaze steadily with her own. "If I may talk to my friend for a minute before I leave?"

The queen looked mildly annoyed, but waved for Mikon to go.

"What are you doing?" he asked in a rapid undertone when she had pulled him off to the side. "Go! This is our ch—"

"Shut up, would you." She cut him off. "Are you armed?"

"Yes, of course."

"She's mad, Mikon. Literally insane. Promise me that you'll defend yourself if you have to. I'll get you out of whatever follows, but I can't do that if you're dead." Her voice shook on the last word, but it was justified. The look in Pasiphae's eyes had been horrifying: gleeful and powerful under the roving eyes and blank stare. As if the queen knew exactly what she was doing.

"I know," he whispered, sounding miserable. "I know she is. I..." He bent his head and closed his eyes as if steeling himself. "I promise," he said firmly, when he looked up.

The thought of walking away from him, leaving him in the presence of a queen who still had authority despite her madness...for a minute, Koralia didn't think she could.

But the mission came first.

She gripped his hand so tightly it probably left marks and walked back toward the queen. Just before they reached her, several pairs of footsteps ran toward them, half a dozen guards slamming to a halt, surrounding them.

Then someone gasped. "Mother?!" Ariadne's disgusted shout echoed through the night.

Just when Koralia had started to think the night couldn't possibly get any worse.

# CHAPTER 24

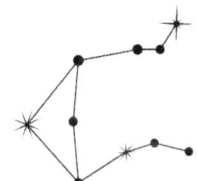

"What is going on?" Ariadne demanded, stalking up to her mother, her thin dress fluttering around her. "What have you done now?"

"Don't you take that tone of voice with me, girl," hissed the queen. "I am your mother, and you will treat me with the respect I deserve."

"And these are *my friends*." Ariadne stepped between her mother and Mikon and Koralia, her hands on her hips, lips curled into a sneer. "You said you were going to bed."

Pasiphae put her hands on her hips too, glaring at her daughter. "I don't answer to traitors, girl."

Ariadne didn't even flinch. "And I don't listen to tyrants," she shot back. Turning on the guards, she ordered, "Leave my friends alone. Go back to the palace. And take my mother with you."

"You have no authority here! This is my garden!" Pasiphae screamed, the high tone of insanity back.

"Nonsense," Ariadne drawled. "I might not have authority here, but let's just ask Father to make sure." Taking her mother's arm, she led her from the gardens, winking at Koralia and signaling for the guards to fall in around them.

Koralia didn't breathe until there was silence again, with Ariadne and her mother well out of earshot.

Then she gasped in a shaking breath, and so did Mikon, steadying himself on her shoulder.

Without a word to each other, they darted into the shadows of the trees, running toward the maze as quietly as they could. They didn't stop running even inside the maze, hurrying through the twists and turns until they reached the center and dropped down onto the benches there.

Xuthos had been pacing, and Asterion sat in one corner, hunched over as if trying to make himself as small as possible. When they came in, he looked up and then back down quickly.

She couldn't tell in the half-light, but he looked like he'd been *worried* about them.

"Well, that was fun." Mikon tried to laugh, but it came out as a wheeze.

She choked on a laugh, grinning at him. It *had* been fun...now that it was over. Flipping her hair over her shoulder, she waved to the minotaur. "Asterion. I'm sorry if we kept you waiting."

"No sorry," he rumbled. "She hurt you?"

The queen? "Pasiphae didn't hurt us. And Ariadne saved us, kind of." She'd have to thank the girl later.

"Good." He sounded relieved...and that's when she realized there had been real fear in his voice.

*What has he been through?* And was he more scared of the queen or Ariadne or being discovered collaborating with the rebellion?

Koralia had her breath back now and moved over to sit in front of him. "Is it safe to talk here?"

"Safe," he said. "I will know if not. If it *is* not," he corrected himself. "You are here now. I will set sensors."

Mikon and Xuthos gathered around, Xuthos sitting down next to her. While Asterion did...whatever it was, Koralia tried to study Xuthos without meeting his eyes.

He had barely taken his gaze off her since she'd entered the area, and when he did, it was only to glance at Mikon with a confused look. Dread and frustration wrapped around her as he put his hand possessively over hers, watching her like he was waiting for an order. If she had any doubt about him having felt her persuasion, it was gone. He had to be feeling *ridiculously* high levels of loyalty right now. She hadn't used her power in at least two weeks... or was it three now? She couldn't remember, but even diminished by stress, it had been extra strong.

It was no wonder Xuthos was looking at her like she was his whole world. He'd be feeling it for a while.

She had *hoped* he'd be able to withstand her, withstand *them*—she'd felt him shake slightly when Mikon's power hit and knew he'd been affected by that too. Had she not given him enough warning? Or had it been too strong for him to resist?

Maybe he didn't *want* to fight it.

That, she didn't want to think about. That, she'd rather not think about. Some people in the olympian courts loved feeling the pulses of persuasion, chasing the thrill of the power in the same way adrenaline junkies chased extreme adventures. Was Xuthos one of them? He'd never seemed to be that kind, but she barely knew him.

This was part of why she hated using her power around friends.

"I'm here," a loud whisper carried through the maze, and Tryphosa dashed into view, pulling up short when she saw them. "Am I too late?"

"Stand guard," Asterion said. It didn't sound like an order, more like a request, but when she made a face and he lifted his head slightly, facing her down, she tossed her head and spun around. They could hear her footsteps thunking down the path for a minute until she took up her position, huffing loudly enough that Koralia easily heard it.

*Teenagers.* She tried not to smile, not wanting to be disrespectful.

"I am ready now," Asterion said, looking at Koralia. "I am sorry for—" He hesitated, seeming to search for a word. "For my talking. I learn slowly."

"We can talk in Kretan if that's easier for you," she said. "My friends have translators." They'd worn the earrings most of the time since arriving but hadn't needed them much because the royal family spoke Galactic Common as easily as their native language.

"Thank you." Asterion switched into Kretan. "I am ready now."

She'd been waiting to ask this question for hours. "What do you know of Kretan double agents with the rebels?"

"Princess Ariadne?" he guessed. "I know she worked with them for a while. I tracked her messages, and I followed them the day your people tried to get the Key again. I tried to warn you. I am sorry."

So that had been the message later in the day. Too late to help.

"And the day of Icarus's death?" Mikon asked eagerly. "What do you know about the transmissions then?" He fidgeted, cracking his knuckles and shifting around on the bench, too worked up to sit still.

"There was one," Asterion said slowly, "to all the fortresses. It said to be alert. That was a few minutes before the battle." He spoke Kretan more easily than Galactic Common, but he still sounded rusty with it, like he wasn't used to talking much. His voice had a pleasant cadence, mellow and deep, relaxing.

Koralia could feel some of her stress slipping away as she listened.

"Was it Ariadne?" Xuthos asked, and Koralia translated it.

"I do not think so." Asterion shook his head, his horns and headtails making odd shadows on the hedge behind him. "I think it was the watcher?"

"The...watcher?" She wasn't sure she'd heard that word right.

"A...a guard," he said. "I do not know if that is the right word. The person who watches the radar."

A radar tech who had spotted Icarus and had alerted the fortress. Which meant his death had more or less been an accident. She'd still had one slim hope that it wasn't, that Asterion would know something she didn't and could give them a traitor's name.

She saw her disappointment mirrored in Xuthos's and Mikon's faces and changed the subject. But not fast enough, because Mikon got up and punched the tree that marked the center of the maze. Xuthos clenched his fists tightly before settling back with a growl and leaning against Koralia. She let him, and when Mikon sat back down on her other side, she put her hand on his arm, sliding her fingertips to his wrist so she could feel his pulse. Olympians were often more volatile for an hour or so after having used their power. This way, she would know if he started to flare up.

"My general wants me to ask you how you can help the rebellion," she told Asterion.

"A good question," he said. The moonlight had shifted as the moon rose higher, and they could see his face better now. Koralia had no idea what was typical for minotaur looks, but Asterion was a handsome man. His face was less angular and a little more rounded than the woman she had talked to with Chryse, but he had similar full lips and a square chin. His lower face, arms, and neck were tawny-colored, but around his eyes his skin began to darken to medium-brown at the top of his head. Sparse dark-brown hair covered the base of his ears and horns, which were almost black. His headtails were broad, slightly flattened, and faded from medium brown to tawny at the tips. It looked like tufts of hair hung from the bottom of the headtails, but in this light she couldn't be sure. Now that she could see him close up, she guessed he was close to six and a half feet tall, since even seated, he was taller than Mikon.

His eyes were the most striking thing about him, large, deep-brown, and hugely expressive. Right now, they were gentle and sad.

"I can give you the secrets of the Labyrinth," he said, sitting straighter. "I built most of it."

"You built it?" Mikon exclaimed. "Wow."

Asterion ducked his head, shy. "Yes, I built it," he repeated. "My people love mazes. We made them for fun, for games. Then the king asked us to build one for him. My father did, for his private home in the mountain country. He did not want the queen coming there."

Minos had walled Pasiphae off from his vacation house? That would irritate anyone, let alone a queen.

"Then he wanted us to build a bigger one, for his planet." Asterion pointed downward, to the tunnels that ran under the garden. "We refused. But he forced us. It has taken us many years."

"How old are you?" Mikon asked.

Koralia frowned. That question wasn't considered polite on some planets.

But Asterion didn't seem to mind. "In human years, I am twenty-five."

That was somehow surprising and unsurprising at the same time, like she had consciously expected him to be younger but unconsciously realized he couldn't be.

"Have you been down there all your life?" Mikon asked, leaning forward on the bench and tucking one hand under his legs. He left his other hand in Koralia's grasp.

She wanted to know too, wanted to ask Asterion questions about his life, so she was pleased someone was asking them. But time was winding down, clouds were starting to reach higher in the sky, and they hadn't yet gotten to the worst part of the discussion, so this would have to be cut short. If they got him off, they would have time to talk backstories.

"Most," Asterion said. His ramrod-straight posture eased slightly, and she realized Mikon had put the barest hint of power into his question.

*Working with him has a lot of perks.*

Suddenly, she felt like yawning. The reaction from using her power was starting to set in, not just the shot of satisfaction but the tired feeling. When it was used regularly, the energy draw and replacement evened out better, but her power use had been erratic for a month.

"Asterion." She waited until he was looking at her and then went on slowly, hating the words. "We cannot find the ships to take all of your people off at once."

He was silent for a full minute. Then he said, "What if not all at once?"

"If we could make it past the Labyrinth and past Minos's fortress guns, we could arrange to do it in phases. But I'm sorry, so sorry," she said, wishing they had any other answer. "We tried—our people have been looking for days —but we can't even do that yet. Not with the Labyrinth in the way."

"Thank you that you tried," he said, his voice subdued as he slumped down on his seat and leaned back against the hedge.

She let him absorb that for a few minutes. "I have to ask—if you were not here on Krete, would Minos still be able to operate the Labyrinth?"

Asterion looked at her, as if trying to figure out her reason for asking. "Yes, if he has a minotaur. It would not work well. *As* well. It would not work as well. But. Yes, he could still."

"Can you destroy it?" Xuthos asked. "The Labyrinth—can you destroy it?"

He'd spoken in rapid Galactic Common, but the tone of his question, the simmering anger in it needed no translation. That, or Asterion was getting better at understanding Xuthos's accent, because he answered right away.

"Yes," he said decisively. "I want to."

Destruction would solve so many problems. It didn't always, but it would this time.

"You can destroy it *and* you want to?" she double-checked.

"Yes. I need help. But yes."

"Can you blow—" Mikon started to ask, but she tightened her hand on his arm in a silent request to wait.

She needed to get the hardest question out. "Would you be willing to leave the planet and your people?" She rushed straight into an explanation before he could answer. "If you come with us and we bring it down, then we have a chance to get your people off of Krete later, and we'll be saving this whole sector of space. You could do so much good," she added. As tempting as it was to use her power to nudge him to agree, this had to come from him.

"It would be hard," he said at last. "The king knows I have made the Labyrinth perfect. He wishes to sell it to other people. He knows some already."

Minos already had buyers lined up? That was news, especially after how he'd dodged her questions at the table the other night, questions which she had worded to sound like they came from Hephaestus.

If Minos was willing to annoy Hephaestus by being evasive about the Labyrinth, he was an idiot...or whatever he was getting from these other buyers was well worth angering one of the most powerful olympians in the galaxy.

"If you destroy the Labyrinth, will he still be able to sell to other people?" she asked.

"He will still have pieces. He will have to wait, but he will fix the pieces to sell six months. *In* six months."

Six months would buy them a lot more time than they had right now. It was a gamble, but the risk seemed worth it.

"We can use those six months to figure out another way to stop Minos," she said. "What is the worst that could happen to your people here in that time?"

He was quiet for several minutes. She couldn't tell if he was just thinking or if he couldn't figure out how to say something. Or maybe he didn't want to tell them.

"He will work them harder," Asterion said at last. "But the worst will not come then. That will come later." He lifted his head and stared straight at Koralia. "The king will make one of my people go with a Labyrinth every time he sells it."

Silence fell as she stared at him, running the words over and over in her head, trying to see if she'd misheard them, if there was an alternate translation.

There wasn't.

Xuthos *snarled*, his voice angrier than she had ever heard it. "Are we talking slave trading?"

At least he'd remembered to keep his voice down. Under her fingers, Mikon's pulse jumped slightly and then settled down, and she realized he was looking between her and Asterion, waiting for her lead.

"Yes," Asterion agreed simply, looking relieved at their reaction.

Had he thought they wouldn't care? They cared. It just didn't change what they could do about it.

Xuthos swore, long and colorfully, his shoulders stiff with outrage.

Athanasia would be livid when she got this report. Especially after her years of running Amazonian anti-slavery patrols on various planets.

"So we'll have to stop him before then," she said. "I'm sorry, Asterion, we still don't have the ships to take your people off. But we do have to get you off or your people will have no chance at all. I think we can do it. Krete will think we've kidnapped you to use the tech ourselves, and their anger will fall on us."

She hoped.

"And hey, when you're safe, you can try to sell the tech yourself," Mikon suggested. "It would go for high prices and then you can have money to help your people start over."

"*If* you ever want to build another one," Koralia added quickly, not sure he'd want anything to do with Labyrinth tech once he was free, not after what he'd confessed earlier. The nerve of Minos, taking what this people loved and twisting it into slavery. He wasn't just rotten, he was a monster.

"I will think about it," Asterion said slowly. "My people—many of them do not want to build mazes any longer. It is ruined for them." His growl was so deep it vibrated right through her, and her own fury flamed higher. "But I still love mazes. They are still my home." He frowned. "That word is not right but I do not know the right one."

Given the shine in his eyes when he talked about the Labyrinth, she thought *home* might be exactly the right word.

Mikon put his other hand over Koralia's and squeezed it in silent reassurance that he would be okay before standing up and starting to pace. She felt like doing the same thing, but there wasn't room here for both of them.

"We will try to help you find a way to keep what you love *and* be safe," she said, holding his dark eyes so he could see how serious she was. "Will you come with us, away from Krete? Not today or tomorrow, but very soon? Maybe the next day?" *How long will the rebels need to plan the mission?*

"I will come," he said. "I will come, but if the king starts to sell my people off this world, I must come back."

"You have my word that I will bring you—*we* will bring you back if that time comes," Mikon promised, coming to stand behind her. Both Koralia and Xuthos nodded agreement.

Asterion bowed his head, looking at the ground. "Thank you." His voice went almost as deep with gratitude as it had with anger.

Koralia reached out her hand to him, and he took it. Instead of shaking and dropping it, she held it until he looked at her again. "Hear me, Asterion. This is not the end for your people. I swear on your Labyrinth that I will not leave your people to Minos's mercies."

Mikon put his hands on her shoulders, leaning forward over her, and Asterion raised his head further to look at the Sunfire. "And I swear by the fire of my family that I will do whatever I can to save your people." Mikon's words echoed solemn and hollow in the moonlight, bouncing off the marble around them.

"By the earth below, by the sea beneath, by the sky above, and by the stars beyond, I promise to help them help you," Xuthos said, the words quiet but as serious as theirs.

Asterion bent his head, sliding his foot along the ground as he cleared his throat. When he spoke, his voice was husky with emotion. "I looked to the rebellion for aid. I did not expect to find such care."

Mikon grinned, squeezing her shoulders as if he needed an outlet for his feelings. "Dude, you're in the Kallistratus now, so get used to this."

Asterion sounded like he was struggling to find words again, and that made her feel just a little better about this whole rotten mess.

Xuthos stretched his legs out in front of him. "What I want to know is: what does Minos have against your people that he's selling you with the Labyrinths?"

"Partly, it is that we have a natural...*knowing* for the mineral that powers the force fields," Asterion explained.

"Natural affinity?" Koralia translated.

"Yes. That. His humans can mine the mineral with machines, but only minotaurs can..." He frowned, puzzled.

"Put it into place?" Mikon guessed.

"Yes." Asterion sounded relieved and a little frustrated but not at them. "Many races cannot touch it without heavy protection."

"What mineral?" Xuthos asked, and when everyone looked at him, he shrugged. "If the mineral is native only to Krete, Minos is about to build a monopoly. And Asterion'll have a harder time selling the tech on his own."

That was an excellent point.

"Anogbey," Asterion's pronunciation lingered over the G, almost rolling it. "I have heard reports of there being more elsewhere, not just here."

"Uhhmmmm," Xuthos kicked one toe against an urn at his feet, and she remembered that his personnel file claimed he'd been a fuel engineer for a short while before joining the rebellion. "Yeah." Xuthos nodded, still thinking, and then nodded again. "Yeah, I think there are a couple asteroids in the Outer Arms where it's found. There are other places that might have some, but I don't think they've been tested."

"There's that problem solved then," Mikon said, sounding pleased. He started walking around the clearing, checking behind hedges to see if their exit was clear.

Asterion started to say something and then stopped. Three times he did that before he finally spoke, his voice so low it was almost an indistinguishable rumble. "May I ask one thing?"

"Of course." Koralia motioned for him to go ahead.

"If it is possible, can you take Tryphosa out too? She will suspect it is Tryphosa who helped us, and she will have her killed."

*She?*

"Ariadne?" Xuthos asked.

Almost at the same time, Mikon asked, "She who?" his tone sounding like he already knew but dreaded confirmation.

Oh. Oh, *no.* She knew the answer a split second before the minotaur confirmed it.

"The queen." Asterion wrapped his arms around his chest, hunching into himself.

"The queen?" Xuthos looked puzzled. "Pasiphae?"

Solemnly, Asterion nodded. "She is one of the most dangerous people on this planet. And she will be very angry when I leave."

And then it all came together for Koralia. Pasiphae's heated words to Ariadne about being a traitor, the queen calling the guards on them, her treatment of Tryphosa, Ariadne's mocking of her mother, and what Asterion had said about a watcher. There was another translation for that word: guardian, as in a singular protector of a place.

"Pasiphae is the spy. She's your radar watcher." She turned, looking for Mikon, but he was staring at Asterion, his eyes wide with comprehension and an empathy that could only come from some shared horror.

"She's your *mother*," he murmured, understanding aching through the words.

Asterion flinched like he'd been slapped. "Yes. How did you know?"

Cold slid around her shoulder blades as she processed that. Pasiphae wasn't just the queen of Krete, she was his mother... Asterion was half-human.

Mikon shrugged, sitting back down and resting his elbows on his knees, his chin in his hands. "I know what it's like to be a child of two worlds. You have the same look in your eyes. And Pasiphae's weird riddles from this afternoon—they make sense now. Well, as much sense as they can. They weren't random, they *weren't*. When she said I'd understand her children, when she talked about a new race... It wasn't total nonsense."

Koralia felt for the lonely child Mikon had been. How far he'd come—how far they'd both come. And she and the rebels would now give Asterion the final piece of his freedom just as Talos and Icarus had for Mikon.

Well, almost the final piece. Asterion would never feel truly free until his people were safe too.

"We have to get off this planet," Xuthos said, standing up as if he could take them all off that very minute. "What?" He held his hands out, palms up, and shrugged when they looked at him. "You're all thinking it."

"You don't have to be so obvious." Koralia rolled her eyes and turned back to Asterion. "We'll take Tryphosa too. So this—*you* are why the king hates you and your people so much."

He nodded.

Which was stupid. Why blame a whole race of people for the choice of your own queen? The entire Kretan royal family was mad, that's all there was to it.

"And the queen will see your leaving as betrayal." Mikon swayed back and forth, fidgeting again. "She could flip on you."

"Yes," Asterion said, with a slow nod. "Yes, and it is why you must be careful. The queen could already suspect you. She has already delayed me once, the day your friends met Ariadne."

"*No one* will suspect them after the show they put on earlier," Mikon grumbled, glancing sideways at her and Xuthos.

"Jealoooous," Xuthos said in a casual tone without any heat.

Mikon snorted. "Oh, you bet I am."

"Boys," Koralia warned.

They stopped, giving her enough quiet to think. She had a nagging feeling that she was forgetting something, but no, they had achieved their main objectives. Asterion would be coming with them, and the rebels now knew more about Krete's secrets than they had even expected to learn. Plus, rescuing Asterion would give them a major source of information on not just the Kretans but also the minotaurs.

Athanasia would be so pleased.

"We should head back," she said, reluctant to leave. There was so much more she wanted to ask Asterion, but that would have to wait.

They stood, and Asterion rose with them, finally giving them a chance to see his full height, which was impressive. Mikon was the only one of them tall enough to look the minotaur in the eye.

"Tryphosa will take you back," Asterion said, and somewhat awkwardly, he reached out his hand to shake theirs. Xuthos shook first and stood back, waiting for them. Mikon went next, and impulsively, he threw one arm around the minotaur and thumped him on the back.

Koralia's eyes widened in alarm, but Asterion returned the gesture and... was he actually *smiling*? Letting out the breath she'd been holding, she smiled too. Mikon had been the perfect person to have along for this whole mission; he kept proving it every minute.

*Icarus knew how to pick his family.*

When it was her turn, the minotaur clasped her hand with both of his. "Thank you."

"You're welcome." And she meant it.

"Will you stay one minute?" he asked.

About to leave, she stopped, looking over her shoulder at him. "Yes? Is there something else?"

He pointed upward. "No, but in one minute the moon will be shadowed and your path will be more secret."

She couldn't see any clouds close enough to the moon, but he seemed so sure of himself that she agreed. And in a minute, the moon was indeed completely covered, a thin cloud sliding over its face and growing thicker with every second, until the light was almost gone.

"How did he do that?" Mikon wondered, turning to look for Asterion, but he had vanished, and Tryphosa stood in front of them, motioning for them to hurry. She took them a long and circling route through garden paths, hedges, and shadowed archways until she led them through a back door of the palace and down the halls to their rooms.

Mikon brought up the rear, frequently checking behind them to make sure they weren't being followed. Xuthos kept close beside Koralia, his hand brushing her arm every time they stopped, until Koralia wanted to hit him for touching her.

They needed to have a conversation about what had happened in the gardens, and somehow, he needed to break out of the persuasion...but all of that would have to wait. First, they needed to get off Krete and back to the rebel base.

And then the Labyrinth was coming down.

# CHAPTER 25

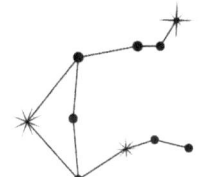

Athanasia had thought that one advantage to having the Sunfires posted with different generals throughout the galaxy was that they wouldn't suddenly be dropping in on their siblings anymore, riling them up and inciting pranks and chaos for a day or two before disappearing.

Obviously, she had been wrong. Radically wrong. So wrong that she couldn't believe she'd ever even thought that in the first place.

The bridge doors hissed open, and the short, sturdy blonde Athanasia had been watching on the security monitors entered, looking around her with satisfaction. Flinging her arms wide, the blonde announced, "Hey, bitches! I'm back."

"And that's a no swearing permit for you too!" Ianessa called as she pushed back from her station and went to hug her sister.

But Brygos beat her there, leaping up and across the bridge. He and Kynna met in the middle of the room, throwing their arms around each other, laughing and talking at the same time—something about bombs and had she packed the material properly and what did he take her for, an amateur?

"Since when does one offense mean I don't get a permit?" Kynna demanded good-naturedly as Brygos stepped back. She ruffled his hair, and he pulled on her jacket to straighten it.

"Since you two started sneaking around the rules, remember?" Ianessa pushed Brygos to the side so she could hug Kynna.

Kynna wrapped her arms around her older sister, squeezed gently, and then pulled back, holding Ianessa by the waist and looking her over anxiously.

"I hardly feel any pain at all now," Ianessa assured her. "It's a lot better."

"Bet you're lying." Kynna gave her an extremely skeptical look. "It still hurts at night, doesn't it?"

Ianessa's raised eyebrows were answer enough. "Speaking of lying..." She shook her finger at Kynna. "What are you doing on this base?"

"Like she was going to pass up the chance to meet Koralia if she was anywhere nearby," said Talos, coming into the bridge. He grabbed Kynna from behind and spun her around in a hug.

"Ugh, put me down!" the blonde insisted, pushing against his shoulders. "Face me when you do that, how many times do I have to tell you?"

Athanasia laughed as Talos complied and ruffled her hair. With a glare at him, Kynna crossed the deck to Athanasia, who had been watching fondly. She hadn't seen the girl in three months, not counting her breezing in for Icarus's memorial and leaving again almost right away.

Kynna saluted. "Reporting with the explosives you need, General. I was told you're running out of time, and it was faster to bring them myself. My general agreed."

"Faster to bring them yourself, eh?" she said. That was probably stretching the truth at least a little, but what could Athanasia do but smile? Kynna hated being left out of things—it had probably been torture to know Koralia was on base and she had missed meeting her.

"I want a full report first thing in the morning," she said, smoothing Kynna's hair, which was a tousled mess from greeting her siblings. "But for right now, go get some sleep. *All* of you."

"Why is everyone still up anyway?" Kynna asked, looking around the bridge at her siblings working side by side with the night duty watch.

"Weird readings on the boundary sensors," Talos said briefly. "Night patrol will do a sweep in two hours, and Brygos and I will go out at first dawn."

First dawn meant 0500 hours GST. Which gave them all four hours to sleep, if they left right now. But they wouldn't do that without proper motivation.

Athanasia snapped her fingers, and as one, the Sunfires and other techs turned to face her. "You, you, you, and you"—she pointed to each of the Sunfires and used her sternest voice—"get off this bridge right now and go straight to your beds. Don't you dare do anything other than read your messages, if that, until the dawn alarms ring."

"Uh, yes, ma'am!" Brygos and Kynna said at the same time, turning to leave. Ianessa smiled at the General, and Talos saluted her before both followed their siblings.

"Does Talos have a swearing permit?" Kynna asked as they left.

"Damn right I do," Talos said, their voices starting to fade as they turned the corner toward the elevators.

Athanasia could hear Kynna protesting and Brygos declaring he and Kynna could be delinquents together, since he didn't have one either.

*Just like they do everything else together,* Athanasia smiled, watching them on the security monitors until they were in their quarters.

If anyone could figure out how to blow up the Labyrinth, Kynna could, especially working together with Brygos. They were the go-to team for whenever the rebellion had a so-called impossible problem of science.

And if Koralia could buy them enough time, maybe, just maybe they could break Krete's stranglehold before it got properly started.

. ✝.

KORALIA'S last thought before sleep had been wishing they didn't have to endure hours more of the following day until leaving. Then the world faded around her, and despite restless tossing and turning, she didn't wake until someone slammed into her room the next morning and threw themselves on the bed, wailing about how unlucky their life was.

Blinking, she sat up and tried to understand what crisis Ariadne could possibly be having before breakfast.

"And I just really need your help!" Ariadne pleaded.

Koralia closed her eyes, restraining the urge to hit something. She'd been grateful to the princess for saving them from Pasiphae the night before, but now she was back to wanting to strangle her.

"Can you let me breathe for just a second?" she asked in her most sarcastic tone.

Ariadne either missed the sarcasm or ignored it. "Oh, of course! Here, have some water." She shoved a full glass from the bedside table toward Koralia and watched impatiently as she drank.

"Yes?" Koralia said finally, setting the glass down with a sigh.

"I need you to run interference." The words tumbled from her lips, and Ariadne got up, gesturing nervously.

"What kind of interference?" Koralia asked. Behind Ariadne, Mikon appeared in the doorway, sleep-rumpled and raising his eyebrows at the commotion.

She shook her head and waved for him to go away. Ariadne being distracted by a pretty face was the last thing Koralia needed right now.

"I told you I met someone special?" Ariadne was saying. "And that we're going to leave? Well, he got here early, and I need someone to distract the palace while I sneak off to meet with him."

*This is going to be a disaster. I don't need to hear anything else to know that.* But she could hardly refuse to help after what Ariadne had done the night before.

Speaking of whom—she could hear Xuthos in the antechamber, asking Mikon what was going on.

"How should I know?" Mikon responded, sounding grumpy and tired. "She stormed in here like a tornado, and she's blathering on about distractions."

Fortunately, Ariadne didn't have olympian hearing.

Koralia raised her eyebrows as Ariadne stopped explaining and looked expectantly at her. "Wait," the princess said, looking from Koralia still in bed to the clock to the mid-morning light outside the window. Her hands flew up to cover her mouth. "You did it, didn't you? With both of them? You bad girl! Now there's something I didn't think I'd see, the Amazon spicing things up." She giggled, and Koralia wanted to throw the water pitcher at her. "We need to get you away from your dad more often—just look at how much more fun you are!"

Koralia tried to laugh and couldn't, so she settled for a wide, fake smile, and a vague, "Yes, well."

Clapping, Ariadne sat back down on the side of the bed, looking like she was going to keep teasing for a while.

Koralia cut her off before she could start. "So you just want me to distract the palace? When?"

Ariadne looked taken aback, like she hadn't even considered when.

It really was almost shocking that such a scatterbrain had managed to first be a spy and then a traitor.

"In an hour?" Ariadne guessed. "In an hour, yes." She clasped her hands together and turned an imploring look on Koralia. "Well? Can you do it? Please say you can. This is so important, and I can't wait to see Theseus. It's been so long..."

Theseus?

Ariadne was dating *Theseus*?

Dread swept through Koralia, and she swung her legs over the opposite side of the bed, hiding her face and keeping her back to Ariadne. Theseus was Ariadne's "someone special"? The same Theseus who Koralia knew as a war-mongering Athenian brat?

Several thoughts raced through her mind at once, none of them good. "Sure," she said casually over her shoulder as she walked toward the bathroom. "So his name is Theseus?" Maybe it was a different man than the one she knew.

"Oh, thank you!" Ariadne leaped up, practically dancing in the middle of the floor. "And oops, I didn't mean to say his name, but you'll keep my secret, right?"

Brushing her teeth, Koralia nodded.

"He's the most gorgeous, wonderful man ever," Ariadne exclaimed. "I've known him for years, ever since—oh, you know him too, don't you? From school?"

Well, there went the hope that it might be someone else. Koralia pushed the toothbrush to the side of her mouth and said, "Mmmhm. Wasn't that such a long time ago?" She couldn't let Ariadne guess how recently she'd actually seen Theseus.

"Yes! Aren't we just the perfect match?" Ariadne could hardly stand still, she was so excited.

"Yes." It was the most sincere thing she'd said to Ariadne since arriving. "Yes, you really are."

The traitor princess and the arrogant prince. A match made by angels...if there were such beings. Eros and Aphrodite themselves could not have done it better.

"So you'll do it?" Ariadne asked again. "I need to go get ready, but you'll do it?"

Koralia rinsed her mouth out and turned around, all friendly reassurance. "Of course. Now you'd better hurry. I'll text you when I'm ready."

"Yes, oh, yes!" Ariadne sped out of the room, and a few seconds later, Koralia heard the outer door close.

She hurried out into the antechamber, where Xuthos and Mikon waited for her.

"What was that all about?" Xuthos asked immediately, winking at her short tunic—she hadn't bothered to dress just yet. This message couldn't wait.

"No time for questions. Xuthos, send a code crimson scarlet to the base, right now, and use Tryphosa's gel chip. If they don't respond in fifteen minutes, use the slicer and send it again."

"What the hell? Why?" he asked even as he ducked into his room for his comdisk.

"I'll explain later! Mikon, how fast can you get us off the ground?"

Eagerness lit his face. "In that ship? Come on, sixty seconds, if I have to."

"You might have to. Get ready to go, both of you. We're getting off Krete now." Spinning around, she shut her bedroom door and went to work packing, pausing only to throw on a gown and circlet.

243

"It went through!" Xuthos yelled not five minutes later.

Perfect. Every moment they stayed was a minute too long. Theseus eloping with Ariadne could only end one way, and she intended to be far away from Krete when it did. Stuffing the last of her belongings into her bags, she grabbed them and lugged them into the antechamber.

A distant alert screeched, and she grinned. That would be Hephaestus, requesting his daughter's immediate return.

*Thanks, Dad.*

A servant knocked on their door a few minutes later and handed her a formal message that allowed them clearance through the Labyrinth.

**You have your distraction,** she texted Ariadne. **Dad sent for me so I'm going home at once.**

Mikon and Xuthos were gathering their bags and handing them to waiting servants to take to the ship when Ariadne burst through the door, fully dressed and with her makeup on.

"What's going on?" She took in the servants, the packed bags, and the men doing a final check of the rooms. Grabbing Koralia's arm, she asked again, breathlessly, "What's happening?"

"Like I said, Dad called me back. Some kind of emergency," Koralia said, calmly shaking off Ariadne's hand and putting on a long shoulder cape.

"But what about my distraction?" Ariadne wailed. "What do you mean I have it?"

*How stupid can she be?* Given that she was dating Theseus, that kind of answered the question right there.

"The palace is focused on Lord Hephaestus calling me away suddenly," she explained patiently, feeling like she was talking to a child but trying not to sound like it. "They won't be paying attention to what you're doing. And if you walk with me to the landing platforms, who will notice you slipping off?"

"Ohhhh." Ariadne's eyes gleamed. "Yes! I'll meet you outside." She rushed off down the hall, and Koralia sighed in relief, echoed by Mikon somewhere behind her.

She turned, and they grinned at each other. Ariadne was such a wisphead.

Outside, Minos waited for them with a few attendants. The formal goodbye was mercifully short, and then Koralia was walking toward the shuttle that would take them to their ship, Mikon at her side, his arm in hers, Xuthos walking slightly ahead of them. Ariadne danced up on her other side, and Koralia hooked her arm through the princess's to keep up her cover.

*Just a little longer.*

Every step closer to the landing platforms, every minute they were in the shuttle, Koralia expected for them to be stopped, called back, for something to happen that delayed them.

Something that would keep them on Krete.

But nothing did.

And in the end, leaving was almost anti-climactic. At their ship, Xuthos loaded their bags while Mikon warmed up the engines. Ariadne hugged Koralia and kissed her cheek, and then Koralia was walking up the ramp, forcing herself to keep going as her back tingled with the sensation of something about to go wrong.

Inside, Xuthos waited for her to be seated, and they both strapped in. Then Mikon was taking off, soaring through the brilliant blue sky with sunlight sparkling on the waters below, until clouds blotted out their view as they flew through the atmosphere.

The tension in the ship smothered any sounds, like they were in water, drowning as they floated away from each other, unable to call for help or speak at all.

The mechanical voice of the gate control tower broke the stillness. "You are cleared to cross through the gates. Thank you for visiting Krete."

Mikon increased engine power slowly, easing them through the force fields...and then Krete was behind them and the Labyrinth gates crackled back into place.

Koralia gasped, sucking in air as her heart raced, reminding her that most humanoids shouldn't hold their breath unless they had to.

"We did it." Mikon turned around in his seat to grin at her, relief and excitement turning his eyes a brighter blue than normal. "We're going home."

*Home.* The base. Where General Athanasia waited for them. And Talos's proud grin. And other Sunfires.

The relief in the air was tangible, washing the tension out of each of them.

Until Mikon opened up to full speed, and Koralia saw a row of ships off to the side of the Kretan system, far enough out that they didn't register on planetary sensors.

*Is that...Poseidon?*

"Stardusting what?" Mikon muttered, swinging the ship around to get a better look.

The cold hand squeezing her stomach was back as she stood up and moved behind him, leaning down to get a better look out the window.

"Drop speed," she said, but he was already doing it, maneuvering as close as he dared while still having the space to escape if something went wrong.

"That's a whole fleet." Xuthos stared, blinking as if he couldn't believe his eyes.

And then the command ship came into view behind two other ships, its emblem blazing out against the blackness of space, a golden wreath surrounding an owl.

She closed her eyes, but she felt calm now that the blow had fallen. "Holy titans."

Mikon whipped around for a second, staring at her in horror before he focused again on his piloting. That was not an oath anyone used lightly.

Koralia didn't even raise her eyebrows as she stared at the ships. "Damn, Ariadne, you really do know how to screw everything up."

"What do you know?" Xuthos asked, his voice wary.

"That's not just a fleet. It's an armada." Still calm, she shook her head and sat back down. "Take us back to base, please, Mikon."

"Sure," he said, but he sounded uncertain, like he'd really like to know what was going on...or like he was worried about her.

She wanted to tell him, but she didn't want to repeat herself. It would be bad enough briefing Athanasia and Talos.

"How do you know it's an armada?" Xuthos asked, leaning back in his chair and propping his legs up on the dashboard, ignoring Mikon's glare at him for doing so.

"Because I trained them."

# CHAPTER 26

"You're really not going to tell us anything until we get back to base?" Xuthos asked, ten minutes into their trip. Mikon had barely said a word since they'd left Theseus's ships behind. Occasionally, he glanced back at Koralia, seeming more worried about her than the ships that had just become a threat.

"I'd rather explain it all just once," she said. *I'm too tired for this.* "I train armies for a living, or I did. Use your imagination."

"No, please don't," Mikon grumbled. "That's the last thing you want him to do."

"Jealous spoilsport," Xuthos retorted with a smug look.

Which reminded her that there was another important conversation she could and should have right now. It was a thirty-minute trip back to base on a normal day, but they had to circle around and meet Talos on the backside in order to avoid Hephaestus's ship being spotted by anyone that could identify it, and that added an hour to their trip.

So now was as good a time as any. And better than waiting until they got back to base.

"Xuthos, can I talk to you?" She pointed to the back of the ship. His eyes gleamed, and he jumped up, practically swaggering to the back room.

This was going to be so much *fun.*

Gritting her teeth for a minute, she slid into the co-pilot's seat and waited for Mikon to look at her. "Has he ever been affected by olympian power before, that you know of?" she whispered, knowing he'd still pick up the words over the engine noise.

"Other than mine once or twice, not that I can remember." He shrugged, like he had no clue what the other pilot got up to in his spare time. "I say just leave him like that," he suggested. "It'll be good for him to follow you around base like an adoring dog and then get taunted for it later."

Despite the heavy weight that had settled in her chest and stomach, she grinned. It *would* be hilarious, yet she should at least *try* breaking Xuthos out of the persuasion for his sake and for the sake of whatever missions he'd be on in the near future. But first, they needed to discuss that kiss.

Mikon flipped a switch to put the ship on autopilot and swiveled his chair until he was facing her. "You okay?"

This family. Hearts so big they put the rest of the galaxy to shame. Putting one hand over his, she squeezed. "I'm okay. Worried about how the rebellion will pull out of this mess."

"Eh, we're Sunfires." He lifted her hand and kissed it, grinning playfully. "We'll figure it out."

*We'll figure it out.* Their mantra. Like there was nothing in the galaxy they couldn't fix when they put their minds to it. Which wasn't actually that far off, now that she thought about it. *Here's hoping that holds true.*

She stood up and ran her hand over his hair, letting it linger a minute as she bent down to whisper in his ear, "You were amazing down there. Thanks for having my back."

"No," he said, grabbing her hands and holding them tightly, his words choked and husky. "Don't do that. Don't thank me like it's something extraordinary. We always, *always* have your back. *You're* a Sunfire too, don't forget."

She squeezed his hands again and gently pulled away. "Get us home, flyboy."

"Don't spoil the fun with Xuthos," was his flippant rejoinder as he turned back to the controls.

She smiled as she left.

✦

"I'm going to guess you aren't here for more kissing," Xuthos said when she entered the back room and shut the door. His voice was equal parts teasing, respect, and wistfulness.

"First of all"—she jerked her thumb toward the cockpit—"if you say that around Talos or Mikon and they rip your throat out, I'm not responsible."

He didn't answer that directly, watching her like he couldn't tear his eyes away. He'd been doing that since last night.

"I never thought you'd do it," he said, wonder in his voice, his dark-orange eyes, and the way his hand reached for hers. "I wouldn't have—"

"Wouldn't have thought to kiss me, mission or no mission?" she finished, avoiding looking directly at him for longer than a few seconds at a time. It was uncomfortable to see so much adoring loyalty in his eyes. From anyone else, it was easier to see—but not the rebels. Not when…it wasn't supposed to be like this.

"Well, yes."

"Just because Icarus is dead doesn't mean I am." Her tone was sharper than she'd intended.

"Good point," he said quietly, serious now.

"Please don't get any ideas," She finally looked at him. "I did it for the mission, and the mission is done now. Are we going to have problems?"

"No," he said, and she believed him, trusting the sincerity in his tone. "No, we won't."

She leaned back against her seat and pinched the bridge of her nose in relief. She meant what she'd told Mikon on the planet: it *had* been for the mission, so she had done it without a second thought. And she would have done it all over again, if need be, but it still hurt. Deep inside, she had bled at being kissed like that by someone else. Especially when all she wanted was to feel Icarus's arms around her again and hear his voice whispering in her ear.

Even the persuasion she would do again if given the choice, because it had worked and gotten them out of the queen's stupid game or trap…or whatever it was. She almost shuddered every time she thought of Pasiphae's strange laughter and the high, weird tone to her voice.

It wasn't Xuthos's fault he was looking at her like that—at least, she didn't think it was. Maybe he really hadn't been able to resist her persuasion.

"Didn't you hear me tell you to resist?" she asked.

"Well, yeah, but I didn't know what you were going to *do*," he said. "And I was kind of…" He coughed. "Well, recovering from that kiss. It's not every day I get kissed like that."

Like what? "That was…not normal for you?"

"Not for my first kiss with someone."

Oh. *Well, awkward. Maybe I should have listened to Mom.*

When Koralia was a teenager, she'd been given a long lesson-slash-analysis about kissing various galactic races. Her mother had even included a list of her personal favorites: humans and olympians and satyrs. Marsh nymphs were her least favorite.

Being thirteen and more interested in passing her upcoming Amazon test, Koralia had promptly ignored the lesson.

"Sorry," Xuthos said, his lips twisting up in a winsome grin.

"Not your fault." She waved the apology away. If anyone's, it might be hers, for just letting her power flood out and not shaping it first. *I can be damn glad there were no olympians or Amazons around to catch that lapse.* Had her generals seen that, Koralia would be—well, she flinched at the memory of the punishments in store for anyone who was careless with their power.

*I've got to get my head back on straight.*

"I might be able to dull it later," she told him. "Just not here."

"I don't care if you do." He put his arms behind his back and smirked at her. "There are worse fates."

Shaking her head, she changed the subject. "You have experience with slave trading, don't you?" she asked, tucking her legs underneath her. Hephaestus's ships flew smoothly enough—and Mikon was a good enough pilot—that she could do that without worrying about being shaken loose and falling on the floor.

Xuthos shrugged, uncharacteristically silent as he dropped his gaze and stared at the floor, tapping his foot lightly.

She let him sit. He'd talk when he was ready.

The ship banked at the same time her comdisk chimed with a message from Talos. It didn't carry an urgent code, so she pushed it aside for later.

"Yeah. Yeah, I do," Xuthos said at last, his voice low, blending with the sound of the ship's engines. When he looked up, his face had lost its usual lazy look. Shadows spilled out of his angled eyes, and his cheekbones looked sharper, like he hadn't eaten in a while.

Whatever memories she'd nudged were extremely traumatic, then. She almost told him to forget it, but he was speaking.

"I grew up in a mining colony."

Near Vulcani, she remembered Athanasia saying. There were dozens of mining colonies around Vulcani, humans and automatons digging out some of the precious metals her father used in his work. It paid well enough for those colony leaders willing to take hold and stick out the time and labor it took to set up a good operation. Some were under the direct jurisdiction of her father; others were in unclaimed space and sold to the highest bidder.

"Life there is…even with machines, it's hard work. It's cheaper to ship in slaves than pay full wages to legitimate workers." His forehead was deeply lined, and his hand flexed as if he was remembering those days. "And a lot of pirates will take kids from one colony and secretly sell them to another."

That, she also knew. She'd raided some of those ships herself, freeing the slaves and taking the pirates in for trial...and shooting the ones who tried to run. And she'd sat in on some of the trials when her father judged the criminals. Usually, the pirates and slave traders were sentenced to the same kind of hard work they'd sold people into—with no pay other than food and board. It was hard but more than fair.

Unfortunately, it didn't really *stop* the trade. There were always colony leaders looking to cut corners and ship in cheaper labor, even with strict laws against it.

"To this day, I think Lord Hephaestus's surprise raids on his colonies are what kept me from being snatched as a kid. I had friends who were, before your father shut down the ring on Jabal al-Nar."

She remembered that incident. It had happened during Vulcani's winter. Phobos and Deimos had dropped her off at her father's palace to recover from a wound she'd taken during an Amazonian mission. They'd hung around long enough to help Hephaestus clean up the pirate nest, and since she couldn't join the raid, she had run communications for it.

Life took odd twists sometimes. The galaxy was huge, with trillions or more people in it, but right now, it felt small to her. "We might have met as kids, you know," she said. "I visited Dad's mining colonies several times."

"I thought about that." He grinned. "But I think I would have remembered you if we'd met then."

*Flatterer.* "So that's why people trafficking and slavery are so important to you."

"Yeah." His hands gripped his knees, and he stared into the distance, seeing something far away, a memory that made his lips tighten. "Yeah," he said again, shrugging. "And about the loyalty...I *really* don't mind, you know." His mood lightened, like a switch had been flipped, and he leaned closer, tipping his head to the side to whisper, "You can use it on me anytime."

"Flirt." She pushed his head away. "Not going to happen unless I have to."

"So..." He reached for her hand again, and she pulled it away, narrowing her eyes at him. "I suppose this is over the minute we step on base?"

"It's over now."

"Makes sense." He grinned, but there was a sad undertone to it. "Icarus is a hard act to live up to."

Hidden in the folds of her skirt, she clenched her other hand. This conversation was hard enough; if he brought Icarus into it, she would feel like crying again. "True. But that's not it. You're a good man, when you let yourself be. I'm just not the woman for you. I'm flattered, but there's nothing for you with me." With a tired sigh, she raised her eyes to his. "Please understand that. I'd like to be able to work with you still, but I won't if this is going to be too hard for you."

"I get it," he said and shrugged.

They were quiet for a few minutes, and she was just about to suggest they go back to the cockpit when he spoke again.

"The Sunfires were always so *whole*, together or apart. Confident. 'We'll figure it out,' they always said, and somehow, you knew they would. The rest of us envied it as much as we admired it. They were *ours*, they belonged to the rebellion, all of them." He rubbed one finger across the edge of the table next to him. "Icarus—he was larger than life. You hear people say that and you think it's nonsense." He chuckled. "But he really was. When he was with the Sunfires, they moved as one. On his own, he outshone everyone, but in a way you didn't even mind, because he really *saw* each person around him. They mattered to him."

"I know," she whispered. It was part of why she'd loved him, heart and soul. He was one of the few people to look at her and see *beyond*, past her olympian blood, beneath the mantles of her fathers and her mother, through her Amazonian rank to the woman underneath.

Xuthos's smile was definitely sad this time. "Brygos recruited me. But Icarus *accepted* me. Without a question." He swallowed hard. "And I just want to make his death mean something. I was there—on the mission. Lasthena and I were his other wingleaders. I *saw* him go down." He breathed in and out quickly and closed his eyes for a second. "He died to save me as much as anyone. And I want that to *mean* something."

She stood up, putting one hand on his shoulder and lifting his chin so he was looking at her. "You will. Your time will come. He'd be proud of you for how you handled this mission."

And he would have. Despite plenty of opportunity to take advantage of her, despite Mikon's goading and annoyance and teasing, Xuthos had been courteous, respectful, and had even grounded her when she'd wanted to tear into Ariadne.

"He would have been so proud of you," she repeated.

"Coming from you, that means a lot." Xuthos said, his voice thick. "Thank you."

"Thank *you*. Now let's go before Mikon comes to check on us."

He grinned, slipping his arm around her shoulders and squeezing once, then stepping back. "Okay," he agreed. "Let's go meet Talos."

+

BUT IT WASN'T Talos who met them. His message to her said that Cleon would pick them up since Talos was still elsewhere.

Koralia didn't know Cleon well—she'd barely met him before leaving—but he seemed quiet and friendly. Still limping, he turned down Mikon's offer to pilot.

On the return trip, Cleon and Xuthos swapped stories about the mission, Xuthos doing more than his share of bragging. She tuned most of it out. The last few days had started to take their toll on her, and she wanted to curl up and sleep.

Mikon sat next to her, gripping her hand. She couldn't tell if he was excited, nervous, tired, or picking up on her apprehension, but it didn't really matter. He needed the touch, and she gave it until the ship docked in the bay and the doors hissed open to reveal the Sunfires.

+

TALOS HAD WANTED to meet Koralia's ship himself, especially since the base hadn't had many reports from the team. Short messages was all they could manage while on planet, aside from one day. So he had no idea how the last eighteen hours had gone. Between that and what he and Brygos had seen on patrol that morning, he wanted very much to talk to Koralia and her team the instant they were back in rebel space. Then he went out on a second patrol and a delay meant Cleon had been assigned the pickup.

But he and his siblings were waiting in the docking bay when the ship landed. Brygos and Kynna were standing so close together that he almost teased them about it, until he recognized that they weren't just excited, they were nervous. They didn't need to be—Koralia would like them—but it was understandable. Icarus's girlfriend had loomed large for them, almost a goddess in their eyes...in the eyes of every Sunfire aside from him, actually. Well, and Siromos, probably.

She *looked* like a goddess too. *No, nope, not going there.*

Ianessa looked tired, but eager. And it hit him that she probably enjoyed talking to another woman her age and rank. As much as Ianessa loved Dione and Kynna and they adored her, she was always the big sister. She was friendly and knew plenty of female rebels, but hadn't ever seemed to click with any as close friends. Maybe because she was so wrapped up in the Sunfires?

He'd ask Loxias. His brother would know.

Either way, Ianessa was as eager as any of them to see Koralia again. She probably should have been resting, since she looked like she was staggering on her feet, but he wouldn't suggest that now. He just moved closer and slid his arm through hers, pulling her to lean on him. With a grateful smile, she did, putting her head on his shoulder as Cleon's shuttle swept into the docking bay.

The pilot extended the landing struts and shut off the engines. Popping out of the cockpit, he saluted Talos and made the signs for "all okay" and "I'll report later" before he hurried out of the bay as fast as his limp would allow.

Giving the Sunfires room for their reunion.

Xuthos was the first one out of the ship, and he stopped to salute Talos.

"Briefing in half an hour, command bridge," Talos informed him. That didn't give them much family time, but they'd have to make up for it later. Athanasia had been clear that she wanted the Kretan reports as soon as possible.

Xuthos saluted again and clapped Brygos on the shoulder as he went to leave.

"Did you behave?" Brygos called after him.

"I did, but you'd better ask Mikon that question," Xuthos said over his shoulder.

"You're the one who kissed her!" Mikon accused, still inside the shuttle.

"Yeah, but I'm not the one who slept with her!" Xuthos retorted maliciously, and the door of the docking bay closed behind him.

"What?" Brygos and Kynna demanded, looking at each other like they couldn't have heard correctly.

Talos took a deep, patient breath and repressed the urge to punch Xuthos while Ianessa laughed silently. Those words had been a tactical error on Xuthos's part. Whatever Mikon had done couldn't have been inappropriate— they all knew him too well for that. Whether he'd wanted to or not, he had behaved.

So Xuthos had to be feeling pretty irritated to have thrown that last shot.

Great. Just what he didn't need right now, touchy pilots. *What happened down there?*

"All we did was take a nap!" Mikon yelled, glaring at the door as he bounded down the ramp. He threw his arms around Talos and Ianessa at the same time, hugging Talos hard but being gentle with the arm around his sister.

"It's good to have you back," Talos said. "And no, you can't go shoot Xuthos."

"I'm going to kill him just the same," snarled Mikon, turning to Brygos and Kynna, who threw themselves at him, hugging him and yelling at him in the same breath. For a few minutes, it was all jumbled laughter and arguing and catching up.

There was movement on the ship again. Talos looked up...and time paused around him for just a second.

Koralia stood in the doorway, watching with such wistfulness and grief in her eyes that fiery agony ripped through him again. He knew exactly who she sought: the same laughing face and sturdy figure that Talos still expected to see gathered with the rest of the Sunfires, striding down the halls of this base, or coming to meet him when he landed.

She still wore olympian robes: a long-sleeved black gown accented with cuffs and a wide corset of finely chained copper. Her red-and-yellow hair spilled down her back, bright against her gown, and a copper circlet rested on her head.

"Icarus knew how to pick them," Ianessa said quietly, like she understood what he wasn't saying and a lot more besides.

Talos yanked his thoughts back into their proper place. *Sister. She's your sister...practically.*

Koralia turned to look at him and smiled. As she started down the ramp, a hush fell over the rest of the bay. Brygos and Kynna stared with wide eyes, suddenly shy again. Well, Brygos was. Talos wasn't sure Kynna actually knew *how* to be shy, but even she was hesitant.

Ianessa walked forward, and Talos stepped back, letting her go. She met Koralia at the bottom of the ramp and hugged her, whispering something in her ear.

Laughing at whatever Ianessa had said, she nodded, and Ianessa turned to her brothers and sister, tugging Koralia closer.

"Isn't she great?" Mikon said proudly as they came up.

That broke the barrier, and Kynna leaped forward, ignoring Koralia's outstretched hand to throw her arms around the Amazon, rocking her back on her feet.

"Let me look at you," Kynna demanded after a minute, pulling back and holding Koralia by the arms as she searched her face. "You're every bit as pretty as he described."

Koralia laughed. "I'm glad I live up to the expectations."

"Actually, you're better than we expected," Mikon put in, his arms crossed as he grinned at her.

"Not a word from you." Kynna glowered up at her younger brother. "You got to spend three whole days with her. Three days! And I hadn't even gotten to see her! So you just shut up and stand there."

Mikon complied, but it wouldn't be for long.

Talos snickered, watching them.

Brygos was next in line, and Koralia held out her hand to him as well, but he brushed it aside with barely more politeness than Kynna had used. "You're in the Sunfires," he said with disgust. "We don't do that. In this family, we hug, and we hug properly." Which is exactly what he did, but she was better prepared this time and met him halfway.

"Hmmm, I can see why Mikon's got a crush," Brygos observed when he stepped back, looking her over critically.

Koralia raised her eyebrows at him as Mikon kicked Brygos in the heel. "I'm not sure what to say to that, but excuse me." She held out both hands to Talos, and grinning, he came forward to wrap his arms around her.

"I'm glad you're back," he said, feeling her lay her head on his shoulder briefly.

"So am I," she said. "Glad and relieved."

"Can't wait to hear all about it." He squeezed her. "I really hate to rush you, but we now have a briefing in"—he checked the time—"seventeen minutes, so if there's anything you need to do before then?"

"Seventeen minutes?" Mikon looked at Kynna and raised his eyebrows. A crafty look came into her eyes, and she cackled as they set off toward the door.

"We'll meet you on the bridge!" Mikon called over his shoulder.

"Hey, hold up, you think you're going without me?" Brygos hurried to catch up with them.

Sighing, Talos offered Ianessa his arm. "I don't want to know."

"Yes, you do." Ianessa jabbed him in the side.

"Okay, fine, I do, but if they piss the General off right now, I'm going to ground all three of them." He shook his head.

Koralia was watching the younger Sunfires exit with a puzzled look.

"Here." He grabbed one of her bags while she shouldered the others. "Ignore them. If I had to bet, I'd say they went to do something to Xuthos, but that's just a guess."

"That's exactly where they went," Ianessa said. "And if they make a mess or go overboard, I'm *also* going to ground them. It's the only way to keep them in line," she explained to Koralia as they left the docking bay, heading for the Amazon's quarters.

Walking the gray halls, Talos drew a deep breath, soaking in Koralia's presence and the bright auras of his siblings. They were home. Back with him. Not in danger...any more than all rebels were at any given moment. And they'd get some family time with Koralia once battle planning was done.

*If* three of them weren't grounded to their quarters.

# CHAPTER 27

"**W**hat do you mean *you* trained the armada?" Xuthos asked Koralia the instant she stepped through the door onto the bridge.

General Athanasia rolled her eyes and cleared her throat. "Lieutenant."

Xuthos snapped to attention and saluted.

"If we could possibly let everyone get through the door and seated before we start the question bombardment?"

Grinning, Xuthos walked over to the briefing table to wait.

Koralia, standing by the door, came toward Athanasia. "General."

Athanasia hugged her, patting her shoulder. "It's good to have you back."

"It's good to be back." Koralia looked around the bridge with a satisfied smile. She must not have had time to change, since she still wore her formal gown and circlet. Well, if the Sunfires had ambushed her as soon as she stepped off of the ship—and Athanasia was positive they had—of course she wouldn't have had time to do anything other than be hugged and talked at.

"You look good," she told the younger woman. And she did. A little strained, but good. It was easy to forget Koralia was anything but an Amazon until you saw her in olympian robes, which she wore with an unconscious confidence and grace that only came of being born to them. "Still haven't mastered the trick of wearing your circlets without tangling your hair, hm?"

Koralia grinned. "Not yet."

"I hear you have a willing pair of hands to help with the untangling now." Athanasia looked sideways at her, and Koralia rolled her eyes.

"Brygos was talking, was he? Or was it Xuthos?"

"Brygos. Did you expect him not to?" Athanasia motioned toward the table as Talos and Ianessa came in, followed by the younger Sunfires, whose faces were too innocent.

Mikon hadn't even been on station for an hour and they were making mischief already. She wondered how long it would be before someone was yelling down the halls in outrage over having been pranked.

One by one, everyone took their seats at the table, Athanasia and Xantippos at one end, facing Talos and Koralia at the other. Down one side, Ianessa sat next to Talos, with Xuthos beside her and Tisandros between him and Xantippos. As Talos's new third until Lasthena recovered, Tisandros had a seat at all planning meetings. Plus, he'd been the one flying the night patrol that had discovered the Athenian armada.

On the opposite side of the table, Mikon tried to seize the chair next to Koralia, but Brygos pushed him to the side, and while the brothers wrestled, Kynna slipped the chair out from under them and sat down, flushed and triumphant. Seeing that, Brygos dropped into the chair next to her, and with a smug comment about being magnanimous and another about "you left me the seat of honor anyway," Mikon sat down between Brygos and Athanasia.

She raised one eyebrow at him, and he gave her his most charming smile.

*Little brat.* Under the table, she squeezed his knee in welcome.

"Okay, *now* can she tell us about the armada?" Xuthos asked in the voice of someone who had waited a long time for something important.

She sent him a single small glare, and he quieted, sitting back in his chair.

"Actually, Xuthos, you're first up. Fill me in on the minotaur situation." Athanasia flicked on a recording app.

He did, only glancing twice at Koralia to confirm a detail and once at Mikon. One reason Xuthos was such a valuable rebel, aside from his piloting skills and his engineering knowledge, was his nearly perfect memory for things he'd heard.

After he finished, she nodded, motioning for him to sit again. "While you were flying in, I've been in contact with Asterion about blowing up the Labyrinth. I've sent him specs about the new explosives, and we're waiting for him to tell us if they'll work. Kynna is pretty sure they will." She looked at the blonde, who stood up and nodded.

"And I think we'll get a cleaner, faster destruction if we mix it with this one." Kynna brought up a diagram on the projection. "I really want to test them out before working up a firing pattern, but…" She looked from Talos to Athanasia.

"But we might not have that time," the General said, motioning for Kynna to return to her seat. "Mikon, report on the palace situation."

He did, his voice flat as he got through the parts about Pasiphae. At one point when describing the gardens, Talos shot Koralia a quick, keen look, but she didn't seem to see it, focusing on Mikon's account. Athanasia made a note to ask Talos about it later.

"And I thought olympians were bad," Brygos commented when Mikon finished. He looked his younger brother over, his brow furrowed, obviously worrying about something, but whatever his question was, he didn't ask it.

"Tell me we're taking them down." Brygos leaned forward to look between her and Talos. "The whole rotten royal family."

"We're not, not at the moment," Athanasia said, shooting the idea down before anyone else could jump on board. She loved the thought of taking down the Kretan royal family and installing a better government, but that wasn't their job. "We don't meddle in internal politics unless the planet wants us to. Remember? This is only a small subsection of the planet that's unhappy. We'll do everything we can to help and relocate the minotaurs, but we're not —" She paused and raised her eyebrows, looking sternly at Brygos, Kynna, and Talos in turn. "We are *not,*" she repeated, "going to Krete to take down their king. Or their queen."

She looked at Mikon. "Well done," she told him, and his bright smile flashed out as he sat down again.

Then she paused, double-checking her list. Was there anything else they needed to cover before going into planning? *No, that's everything.*

Athanasia stood up and rested her hands on the table. "To recap…" Closing her eyes, she drew a deep breath. "Icarus."

A long, low hum ran around the table, anger and grief stirring.

Athanasia spoke before the mood rose to the surface. "Krete's shore defenses were hot the day of the Key Mission, and some vigilant radar tech spotted our ships even though they were in stealth mode. The gunners fired, and we lost three pilots. Ariadne did not betray Icarus, and to our knowledge, he was a casualty of hyper-vigilance where we expected laziness. Yes or no?" She looked at Koralia.

Her face impassive, Koralia didn't even blink. "Yes, ma'am."

"Somehow, that doesn't make it any better," someone muttered, Tisandros, she thought.

"You prefer treachery?" Xuthos snapped. "You think that's better?"

"Neither is better." Talos's gaze burned into both men. "Accident, random casualty, bad information, treachery, it's all hell. Now shut up and let the General finish."

Ianessa put her hand on his arm, and for a second it looked like he would shake it off. But he let it stay, and Athanasia waited a minute until everyone had calmed a little.

"But since Icarus was such a threat to Krete and they have an excellent propaganda team," she continued, "the planet broadcast his death as a major victory."

Koralia nodded, her voice emotionless as she said, "Not just for the planet —they spun it as a major victory for the law and order of the olympians over the ragtag rebels. They expect you to crumble after this."

"Then they're about to be surprised, aren't they?" Talos smiled, but it was an expression of savage glee that echoed in every face around the table.

Even Athanasia's. She wanted to see Krete humbled as much as the rest of them.

"Daedalus," she said, and waited for the Sunfires to stop swearing under their breath. "He reported that Ariadne—codename Ambrosia—was dead and the Key was in his possession. Then he disappeared from Krete, about a week ago?" She glanced at Koralia for confirmation, and the girl nodded.

*Idiot.* Athanasia really should have expected that; it was so typically Daedalus. Sign up for a mission, but the instant your son goes down, leave. If she knew him as well as she thought she did, he'd hidden himself in some out-of-the-way place to grieve. She knew how he felt—Icarus was as much her son as he was Daedalus's. But there were people depending on her; she didn't have the luxury of just falling apart. And neither did Daedalus, but that didn't stop him.

"Ianessa, when we're done here, you and Dione refine the alert on his name and broaden the search. Anything you hear I want to see at once, no matter how unimportant it seems."

The redhead dipped her head. "Ma'am."

"Heirax." Athanasia steeled herself for the fresh wave of irritation that rolled around the table. Not even halfway through the recap and she felt tired. "Ariadne gave a fake, poisoned Key to our team. Asterion tried to warn them but Krete's Watcher delayed the message, he thinks?"

Xuthos nodded. "Something like that."

This past month had just been one messed-up mission after another. Athanasia frowned down at the table. They needed a win.

"Ariadne," she said, and tried not to smirk at the dark looks Mikon and Koralia exchanged. "In love with Icarus…Brygos, Kynna," she raised her voice in warning, "there will be time for that later."

Glaring at no one in particular, the Sunfires hunched down in their chairs, fuming silently.

*Where was I?* "Ariadne proposed to Icarus, he turned her down—" And really, why had he never told Athanasia that? Probably because Icarus got proposals all the time and he thought the princess was just Ambrosia, a random Kretan palace worker. "But she didn't betray us until she took up with Theseus."

"Morons that they both are," Koralia agreed.

Mikon snickered.

Athanasia studied Koralia for a minute. She said she'd trained Theseus's military, but her tone there sounded...personal. *Another story I haven't heard yet.*

She double-checked her list. "Pasiphae. Mother of Asterion, Krete's Watcher—and some kind of radar technician or supervisor?" At Mikon's nod and shrug, she went on. "Presumably knows Ariadne was a traitor but we don't know when she found out or how long she knew Ariadne worked for us."

Mikon, Xuthos, and Koralia all nodded.

That was worrying. As soon as they finished with the Labyrinth, she would shift her headquarters far away from Krete for a while.

"What I don't get is what was up with the Daedalus and Pasiphae rumors you sent us." Mikon pointed to Ianessa.

Talos snorted. "A smoke screen for Pasiphae's affair with the minotaur. It couldn't have been anything else, not with that timing. Daedalus sleeping with the queen? Yeah, right." He gave Ianessa a smug look. "Told you so."

"You don't have proof," she countered.

"Don't need it," he muttered. "I know these things."

"Now you sound like Mikon."

"Ahem." Athanasia cleared her throat, and silence fell again. "I'm assigning Pasiphae a threat level of orange." She and Xantippos had discussed that in a few words over text while the Kretan team was debriefing. The queen might only be a yellow, but better to be safe than sorry. "And that brings us to the minotaurs."

Everyone sat up or leaned forward, most interested in this part.

"Asterion sent the transmission warning us about Ariadne and lured Talos and Mikon into the Labyrinth to communicate with them. Minos forced the minotaurs to build the Labyrinth, and now he's going to sell them as slaves to operate other Labyrinths around the galaxy."

Xuthos swore but stopped at a look from Koralia. Talos looked impressed and amused.

Athanasia felt like snickering too. She'd never seen Xuthos stop so fast.

"We can't take them all off right now, but we'll try to get Asterion and the girl off and blow up the Labyrinth."

She looked at each person around the table,. One at a time, they nodded.

"Then let's start planning. Koralia? Theseus and the armada?" Athanasia sat down and sipped her water. She'd expected more explosions about Icarus, but fortunately, everyone was focused on the upcoming battle.

"Right." Koralia stood up, folding her hands behind her back, Amazon-style.

Athanasia smiled. *You can take the girl away from the Amazons but you can't take the Amazon out of the girl.*

"Should I start with the history lesson or the fact that, yes, I trained part of Theseus's armada because I'm the daughter of the Lord of War and my day job used to be training armies?" She arched an eyebrow at Xuthos.

"I think we have that fact covered," Athanasia said before Xuthos could answer and start flirting.

"Why do we need a history lesson?" Brygos asked, not looking up from scribbling a note. "Is it the boring kind?"

Mikon must have kicked him under the table from one side and Kynna from the other, because Brygos suddenly winced and jerked back from the table, glaring at the siblings on either side of him.

Honestly. None of the Sunfires were under twenty-five, but they still acted like teenagers.

Koralia ignored the question, focusing on Athanasia and Xantippos. "I got to thinking, why is Theseus here? And there are at least three potential answers, but after the kind of training he requested for his armies, I think it has to do with a feud from a decade ago or so."

*Ohhhhh. Oh, now, that might just be it.* Athanasia herself had thought it was the Labyrinth, but maybe just for once someone *didn't* want it. "The one about Krete's former crown prince?" she asked, and Koralia nodded.

"That's the one."

"*I'm* listening, whatever everyone else is doing." Mikon slid his chair back and stretched his legs out under the table, dodging Brygos's punch to his arm.

Ianessa was tapping on the screen in front of her, no doubt pulling up some research they'd need or double-checking Koralia's story.

"Everyone knows Aegeus is king of one of the Athenian planets, right?" Koralia waited for the answering nods around the table. Tisandros apparently hadn't known that, but he was from the opposite side of the galaxy, so that wasn't surprising.

"He's king of Athens Six. That's Theseus's native star system. Megara is the capital planet of the system." She shoved her hair back over her shoulder. "Ten years ago or so, there was a summer games event on Megara. Krete's crown prince at the time—Androgeos—decided to enter these games. He won big, one event after another. Someone didn't like that, and he had an 'accident,' crashing his shuttle into a monument late one night." Koralia snorted. "No one believed that story, even other citizens of Megara. Androgeos was badly injured and lived disabled for a year before dying. Or maybe it was two years. Anyway, he's dead, that's the important part."

"Okay, I might have liked history if she had taught it," Brygos remarked to the room at large.

"Shut up or I'll tip you out of your chair," Mikon threatened.

One more word out of either of them, and Athanasia was going to put them on cleaning duty. There were acceptable interruptions and non-acceptable ones and they were getting awfully close to the line.

Koralia was trying not to smile at the byplay, the General could see it in the twitch at the corner of her mouth. *Don't do it. Don't encourage them right now.*

Talos nudged for Koralia to continue, so she did. "Krete swore revenge and cut off all trade with Megara. At that time, the two were major trading partners, so naturally, the economy of Athens went crazy for several years. I think they only pulled out of the slump recently, but I don't remember for sure."

"And you think"—Talos motioned between Athanasia and Koralia—"this Theseus might be here for revenge on Krete?"

"Yes." Koralia keyed in a projection of an armada, glancing at Talos. "How many ships do you estimate?"

"Less than sixty. I'd say around fifty."

"You?" she asked Tisandros.

"I estimate between fifty and sixty too, but he got a more complete circle than I did."

"That's his advance guard, then." Koralia removed half the ships from the projection and spun it, studying it from all angles. "Theseus came to us six months ago with a contract to train five hundred men in three months' time and then another three thousand over a period of six months. So if he has all five hundred on these ships…" She trailed off, thinking.

"Then those are some lightly manned cruisers." Talos said what every pilot and general at the table was thinking. "So…a show of force?"

"You know Theseus," Athanasia said to Koralia. "What do you think?"

"About Theseus himself or what he's planning?"

"Both," said Talos and Athanasia at the same time, echoed by half the people around the table.

"Well, Theseus is that one person you always knew was going to be horrible trouble, and almost nothing they do surprises you." Koralia wrinkled her nose. "This isn't the first time he's had a relationship with Ariadne either. It's been, oh, a decade." Koralia smiled to herself, rather deviously, the General thought.

*Yet another story I want to hear.*

"Is that why he's here now?" Ianessa asked. "Because they rekindled their relationship and he's just here to pick her up?"

"Not with those ships," Talos scoffed.

Koralia spun the projection again and shrugged. "Yeah, agreed. With those ships...he wants a show of force for some reason. Could be it's just so he can get Ariadne off Krete and they can run." She frowned at the ships blinking in the projection. "If that's it, then they should be leaving already, because Ariadne left the planet the same time we did. The palace *has* to have discovered she's missing by now. So why haven't they moved? It doesn't make sense."

Athanasia shook her head. Something about that just didn't add up.

"Maybe it does go a little deeper," Koralia mused. Sitting back down, she swung her chair gently from side to side for a minute while everyone else looked at the map projecting from the table.

"Hellstars," she swore, standing up and extending the projection, overlaying Theseus's ships with the route from Krete to Poseidon's territories.

"Yes?" the General said after a few minutes. "What is it?"

"Could be nothing. Stupid blood," Koralia said, disgusted. "What most people don't know is that Theseus is adopted. He came to Megara as a child, and the king treated him like his own son right away. But," she looked around the table, "Poseidon is rumored to be his real father."

Well, that complicated things. Athanasia rested her chin on her hand. *Couldn't anything be simple? Olympians and their ridiculous sleeping around. Most of them should be neutered—then the galaxy wouldn't be in this mess.*

"So is he here for his adopted father and Megara or because of his possible-biological father—Poseidon?" Xantippos asked, sliding his chair back from the table and stretching. He looked pale but waved off Athanasia's concerned look, his ears flicking back for a second in impatience.

Koralia shrugged. "I have no idea. At school, the Jupiterians were his favorite people to challenge in anything—sports, academics, you name it. That should give you some idea of his arrogance."

"Or his stupidity," Talos said.

Mikon straightened in his chair. "What if he really is here for the Labyrinth? Or the Key at least?"

Koralia looked at him and squinted in thought. "It would be a fine revenge."

Talos stood up, turning the projection slowly, looking at it from different angles. "You're thinking he's going to use his ships to bluff his way in, get the Key, and run to Poseidon to show it off?"

Koralia rubbed the back of one finger along her jaw in concentration. "Maybe? Problem is: there are at least five ways this could go, and we don't have enough clues to guess which way is most likely, much less deduce anything."

"Yeah, but look at where the ships are." Talos pointed, turning the armada bright pink. "No one but an idiot puts their ships in that formation unless they're planning some kind of distraction for a stealth mission or a kidnapping or something. Did you say he was going down to the planet to meet Ariadne?"

"Wait, wait, hold on, *kidnapping*," Mikon said slowly, and several things happened at once.

Koralia swung to face Mikon, horror growing in her face.

The Sunfires froze in their chairs, staring at their youngest brother.

Xuthos jumped up from his chair, swearing as he stared at the ships.

Athanasia sighed heavily.

And Talos flipped the projection sideways so that flight paths for the armada blinked red, pointing to the secondary entrance for the Labyrinth.

"Asterion," Mikon and Koralia said at the same time.

"That's where Ariadne fits." Xuthos swore again.

"He wants to kidnap the minotaur." Talos sat down hard, like the weight of the world was suddenly on his shoulders.

Athanasia shook her head, wanting to curse every olympian in the galaxy and drag Minos to hell with her bare hands. "Between Scylla and Charybdis," she said into the silence.

IT HAD BEEN a long time since he'd been in a meeting as glum as this one. The rebels weren't idiots, even if they looked like it sometimes. They knew going up against the Labyrinth was more high-risk than most of their missions, but they were still willing to do it to stop Minos from taking over this sector of space and making innocent settlers pawns in his and Poseidon's game of empires.

And if going up against one olympian army or an olympian-allied planet was hard, being caught between two of them was like a mouse deliberately walking between two lions. Not even the Kallistratus was that stupid.

*But we can't just leave the minotaurs and the Labyrinth.*

"Well." Talos squared his shoulders. "We're just going to have to beat them there, that's all. Come on, this isn't over yet."

That broke the hush, and his siblings leaned forward in their chairs, their eyes gleaming. He grinned as the tension in the room eased, dissolving as the battle fire rose in his siblings. This was Sunfire territory.

"*Now* we're talking," Mikon said excitedly.

Kynna clenched her right hand into a fist and slammed it into her open palm. "Hel—er, yes, let's do this." She darted a quick look at the General, who didn't look up from her screen, though the corners of her lips tilted up in a small smile.

Everyone turned expectantly to Athanasia. She finished reading something and settled back in her chair, looking at Koralia.

"What do you think he's going to do with the Labyrinth technology?"

The Amazon narrowed her eyes, staring at the table in thought. "If I had to guess, I'd say he's going to take it back to Megara and use it to protect their borders and possibly expand them. Plus, that gets it out of Poseidon's way for a little while, long enough for him to make a move on Krete, if he's going to, or at least take over this sector so his territory comes right up to Minos's front door."

Talos drummed his fingertips on the table, trying to separate out the most important facts. "But whether he takes it to Megara or Poseidon, that doesn't really change that we have to get Asterion out, does it?"

Koralia shook her head. "He can't operate the Labyrinth without Asterion or another minotaur," she said. "And they won't go voluntarily, which makes it kidnapping."

"Then, no, whatever Theseus plans to do with it doesn't change that we have to get him out," the General said. "So he's going to kidnap Asterion and Ariadne's going to help him. How soon?"

That was the big question. Talos grimaced at the clock. *If it was me, I'd do it as soon as possible so the whole thing was a two-for-one shock for Krete. Elope with Ariadne, kidnap the minotaur, get off before Minos's lazy ass could figure out what to do.*

Mikon and Xuthos both looked at Koralia like she should know, but she shook her head. "Ariadne was supposed to meet him this morning, but they wouldn't try something like this in broad daylight. There is a Kretan festival in two days, so I would guess probably then or right before then."

In that case, maybe they weren't eloping quite yet? Talos rubbed his forehead. Figuring out how these people thought was a headache.

"So if the festival is the day after tomorrow..." Ianessa kept typing, and the word *festival* appeared in glowing letters at the top of a list on the projection.

"I could try to contact Ariadne again, see if I can get information from her." Koralia held up a bronze comdisk.

Talos recognized it as non-standard Kallistratus issue. "Is that Hephaestian?" he asked.

Koralia handed it over, and he ran his fingers over it admiringly. "I hear these are top-quality for signal receiving."

"Only the best for Dad," she said, her eyes softening for a second.

Now that was one olympian he'd like to meet. Hephaestus intrigued him. Talos had seen a few videos of him at public olympian events, and the Lord of Fire had been reserved but undeniably charismatic, an occasional smile hinting at the strong personality beneath. Hephaestus stayed out of olympian politics, seeming content to build weapons and automatons for everyone else. It was a wonder how the olympian managed to stay neutral and hold contracts with multiple factions at the same time. It was a skill Talos wished he had—it would come in handy with the Kallistratus.

Koralia had her father's reserve, but her fire sat closer to the surface. Come to think of it, she looked a lot like him too.

The General held up her hand for attention. "*Don't* try to contact Ariadne. We can't be sure how much she knows, and I don't want to risk it unless Asterion can't get us the information we need to make the rescue."

"Yes, ma'am." Koralia took the disk back and slid it into her pocket, but Talos sensed her annoyance. He thought it was worth the risk, because the princess might let something else slip, but the General's word was law.

"If he's smart," Xantippos said, "he'll do it the night before, while everyone is feasting. Then the uproar will happen when everyone is tired the next morning or getting started with the festival. Any earlier, and he runs too many risks of being caught."

Koralia curled her upper lip. "I don't know, sir. That seems like the common-sense way to do it, but he never had a lot of that. He's smart and canny, but I just don't know."

Talos groaned quietly. Enemies without much sense were the worst.

"Let's say he will do it then," the General said. "That gives us about twenty-six hours, a full day."

"Then we go in first thing tomorrow morning," Talos said, planning it out in his head. The rebels preferred early morning missions anyway, and the

Kretans tended to sleep as late as the olympians, from what Mikon had said. This played right into their hands. "Yeah, let's do it then, General."

She considered the projection for a minute and nodded slowly. "Alea iacta est."

Chairs scraped around the table as everyone sat up and cleared the virtual notepads in front of them. Talos grinned to himself. This was one of his favorite times of any mission, when ideas were put into solid form and organized into a plan of action.

"Before we get started, can I please have something to eat?" Mikon pouted, looking sideways at the General with a pleading smile. "I've barely eaten all day."

Talos began sketching out attack vectors, waiting for Ianessa to spit out whatever big-sister speech she had ready.

Sure enough, she answered before Athanasia could. "You should have been eating before the meeting instead of making mischief." She leaned back in her chair with a merciless arch of her eyebrows.

That was his cue. Ignoring Ianessa's frown, Talos pulled three energy bars out of one pocket and tossed them down the table to Mikon, who caught all of them with one hand. Stripping the wrapper from one, he shoved it into his mouth and held the other two up in silent thanks. Talos nodded in welcome and then tossed a bar to Brygos and another to Kynna. They snatched them out of the air without looking, concentrating on a readout on the screens in front of them.

Always hungry, these three.

Koralia watched him, looking curious. "Do you always carry snacks around with you?" she asked, leaning closer and dropping her voice.

"They always need them," he said with a shrug. He'd started doing it when he and Icarus were preteens, because Icarus would get so involved in adventures that he'd forget to bring food and then they'd be starving after two hours. As more siblings joined the Sunfires, especially growing teens, he'd kept doing it, and now it was old habit. Mikon especially still needed the food, since he was still growing and regularly forgot to eat, not to mention having a high metabolism.

"I'll have food brought up," the General said, looking at Mikon with a fond smile. "Now, if we can begin?"

Mikon nodded, shoving the last of the energy bars into his mouth.

A message chime rang through the bridge, and Ianessa bent over her screen for a few minutes. "Asterion says those explosives will work, but to mix them with...here, you decipher it." She flipped the report across the table to Kynna, and it copied onto everyone else's screens.

Talos's eyes sparkled as he read it, feeling the usual pre-battle adrenaline start to rise. Perfect. They had plenty of the second explosive on base from a mission a few months ago.

"Tell him everything we know about Theseus and that we have to move up the rescue. See what he thinks and what he can do from his end," the General said, and Ianessa nodded, bending over her screen again.

Athanasia stood up, pushing the button to darken the room until just the table glowed with projector light, swept clean of previous elements.

Talos placed Theseus's armada in the position he'd last seen it while Koralia made an overlay and used it to arrange the ships into the attack patterns she thought Theseus might follow. Ianessa added the specifications for the Labyrinth's current boundaries, the purple line winding around and through the projection like a snake making its way through underbrush.

Then they all sat back, and Kynna and Brygos—who'd had their heads together, quietly discussing—started dropping in yellow and orange dots for where they'd place the explosives to blow up the Labyrinth. Surreptitiously, they placed several dots on Theseus's ships, but Talos had been watching for that and quietly removed them.

Koralia was laughing silently next to him; he could feel her shoulders shaking when he brushed up against her, and he smiled. It was a game the Sunfires had played for years, one that kept battle planning from feeling too heavy.

"There's one thing we haven't talked about." Xuthos rested his elbows on the table, leaning to one side so he could see the projection better. "See, the Labyrinth takes a certain mineral to run. Does Megara have anogbey? I looked it up, and it doesn't look like they do. So are they going to take it from here?"

Ianessa tapped something into her screen and then said, "There are some asteroids nearby that have trace amounts."

"Hmmm." The pilot shook his head. "That's not enough to power a network around the whole system or even the planet for long."

"So they'd have to get more from somewhere else." Brygos sat back down. "Do they trade with anyone else who might have it or will they have to find some way to get it from Krete?"

His sister was already tapping another search into her screen. "I can't find that information," she said after a minute.

"Let's deal with what we *do* know," the General said. "Done, Talos?" At his nod, silence dropped over the bridge, broken only by the humming of control panels as the rebels all studied the projection.

"If we take Asterion now," Xantippos said into the quiet, "won't Ariadne just kidnap another minotaur—minotauri?" He looked at Koralia for confirmation of which word to use, but she was absorbed in the projection and didn't seem to hear him.

"Minotaur," Mikon said quietly, and Xantippos gave him a quick nod and smile.

Talos felt a brief moment of relief that the younger general worked so well with Mikon. It was hard to find generals who appreciated his brother's brilliance or would even be comfortable around a half-olympian—Sunfire or no Sunfire—but Xantippos had liked Mikon the moment he met him. As a kentauri, he was used to being underestimated or judged, and he brought that understanding to working with Mikon. *Good men, both of them.*

Apparently, Koralia had been listening after all, because she looked at Xantippos and said, "I've been thinking about that." Her tone had all of the Sunfires and Xuthos sitting up straight while the General raised her eyebrows. "And I might just have an answer to it"—the Amazon smirked down at the table—"as well as an answer to our problem of not being able to take the minotaurs off Krete."

Talos twisted to face her, but she was looking at Athanasia.

"Well?" the General said, "What are you waiting for?"

"Athina." Koralia leaned back in her chair.

Talos blinked, wondering how the Lady of Justice could help.

Mikon leaned forward in his chair, looking eagerly at the Amazon, and Talos almost laughed. If the youngest Sunfire could be said to have a celebrity crush, it was Athina. Whatever Koralia had in mind, Mikon would support.

A slow smile spread over the General's face. "Do it."

# CHAPTER 28

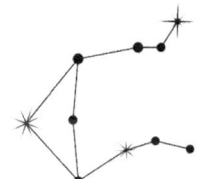

It was so simple that Koralia couldn't believe she hadn't thought of it earlier. Athina could solve most of their problems in one sweep, protecting the minotaurs and complicating the lives of the Kretan royal family to such an extent that reprisals against the rebels would be limited for a while.

And she'd probably be able to find a planet for relocating the minotaurs faster than the rebels. So when they could round up the ships, the minotaurs would be ready. She jotted down a quick note to find out later whether Hades had a planet that could support the minotaurs.

It was almost *too* perfect. *If* Athina wasn't too busy.

Koralia looked at Ianessa. "Can we get a secure signal to Athens—Athens Prime, I mean?"

Ianessa swept her display clean and began to dial addresses. "With the new boosters Dione sent, I can get a secure signal a lot farther than that. One second, please."

Koralia put up her hand to brush hair out of her face—it kept falling down, and her fingers touched her circlet. *Oh, right. I still haven't changed.* Well, at least that would make it harder for Athina to guess her location.

When she looked around the table, most of the rebels were staring at her, the Sunfires with glee, the generals with approval, and Tisandros with suspicion. "You know Athina?" he asked.

Koralia wasn't the only one who rolled her eyes.

"Of *course* she knows Athina," Mikon said, his tone implying that had been a really stupid question. "She's an *Amazon*."

That was just one of the reasons she knew Athina. "She often visits Akwila," Koralia explained, but didn't go into details. She didn't know Tisandros well, just that he'd been one of Icarus's wingleaders and didn't seem to think very highly of her.

At the other end of the table, Athanasia was laughing quietly. She had known Athina for years, so she knew how this conversation was likely to go.

Which reminded her—she hadn't talked to Athina in a long time. *Great. She'll probably grill me about what I've been doing.*

"Do you know *everyone?*" Xuthos asked, grinning at Koralia.

*Please stop looking at me like that.* "If you're one of those idiots who thinks that olympians are the only ones worth knowing, then yes, I know almost everyone. Olympians are in and out of Akwila and Vulcani all the time." She kept her tone mild, but Xuthos caught the note of warning in it and sat back in his chair.

*Good. Still, I better try to break him out of the persuasion.* Or was he finding it hard to switch from pretending to be in a relationship with her to being only coworkers again? She didn't know how much practice he'd had being undercover.

There was more than one reason it was easy for her.

*Icarus.*

"And somehow, what you saw there made you decide to join the Kallistratus?" Tisandros asked, his tone wary.

The Sunfires bristled, more felt than seen, except for Kynna and Mikon, who both glared at the pilot. Talos started to speak, but Koralia put a hand on his arm and shook her head.

"Yes," she answered the pilot. Tisandros's suspicion was normal; he'd have to learn for himself that she was fully loyal to the rebels. Even if she sat everyone down and gave them her life story, or at least the facts that had led her to join the rebellion, it wouldn't necessarily make a difference. It would take some of them a long time to trust her, and she refused to use her power to shortcut that. She didn't need their trust to work with them—she just needed to know that the General and the Sunfires trusted her, and they did.

"Your link is set up," Ianessa said. "I've keyed it to be just your face at first, but I can widen it later."

"Thanks."

Everyone stayed quiet while Koralia tapped in Athina's personal code and started the call connecting. Ianessa did something on her control panel, and small screens popped up in front of everyone so they could watch the call.

When Athina's face appeared, she looked as though she'd been sleeping. A nap, probably, given that she was in full makeup. "Sko—Kora!" The lawyer's smile was warm, welcoming. "What trouble have you gotten into now?"

Now that was just unfair. "I don't only call you when I'm in trouble," Koralia protested indignantly. "I only did that twice!"

"Ah, right. So which of my cases have you called to discuss?" The olympian folded her arms expectantly.

"Can't I call you just because I want to?"

"My *favorite niece* certainly can. But since *you* haven't for the last..." Athina pretended to spin through a calendar disk. "...eleven months, I thought maybe you'd decided you were too old for that. Especially since I called Akwila a week ago to talk to you and was told you'd disappeared." She said it laughingly, but Koralia could hear the undertone of disappointment.

She almost felt like she should apologize, but Athina had been joking—mostly. So she smiled and said, "Well, I'm calling now, and I have some fun for you, if you're interested."

"I'm always interested." Athina leaned to one side and then the other, looking behind Koralia. "Why is this call high security? Where are you?" The question was a combination of aunt-voice and lawyer-voice, with an added layer of "I need to know so I can get you out of trouble in the future."

"I'm helping some people out with something."

"*Really.*" The word dripped with skepticism. Athina folded her arms again. "What's this *fun* you have in mind?"

Talking to Athina usually made Koralia feel like she was on the stand being cross-questioned. The olympian would ask one thing and while she was thinking about the answer she'd been given, she'd ask another question. Despite that and how bossy she was sometimes, she was high on the list of olympians Koralia actually liked.

"You feel like meddling with Minos of Krete for a while?"

"You know I always feel like meddling with Minos. What's the gambit this time?"

"Personal rights violations."

Athina's casual demeanor dropped, her gaze sharpening. "Start talking."

"It's about the minotaurs, ever heard of them?" At Athina's nod, Koralia laid out the problem quickly, trying to hit all the important points while keeping it concise. "Do you feel like helping out?" she finished, keeping a blank face.

"Don't be a brat," Athina said. "Of course I'm coming, and you know it. How soon do you need me?"

"How soon can you be here?"

"Let me check."

While Athina was gone, Koralia covered the projection point with one hand so the screen went dark. "Mikon, do you want to meet her?"

"Do I?" he exclaimed. "*Can* I?"

"Sure, come here." Glancing at Ianessa, she added, "You can widen the camera, but keep the background blacked out, please? Gives her plausible deniability."

"And yet *another* olympian we're trusting," Tisandros muttered, but no one acknowledged it.

"When you're done, I've got more specs from Asterion," Ianessa whispered, and Koralia nodded.

Mikon came to stand behind her chair, and Koralia uncovered the projection just as Athina sat back down in front of the camera.

"I can be there in twenty-nine hours."

It was longer than Koralia had hoped, but sooner than she'd feared. It meant Athina would arrive before the festival but after the rebel attack. They'd have to hope that the Kretans would be too stunned to move against the minotaurs in the meantime. Which was a hell of a lot to leave to hope, but there wasn't much else they could do.

"That's great," she said sincerely.

"I'll leave as soon as I can." But Athina wasn't looking at Koralia; her gaze was focused on Mikon, and she raised her eyebrows while her lips quirked in interest. "Who is he, Kora? With the face of a teenager, the body of a man, and the aura of a young god—if there were such things—you have to be olympian," she said to Mikon. "Poseidonian line? Apollonian? Mercurian? No, no, you have the wrong build for Mercury. So Apollo or Poseidon."

Athina was one of the few who could actually tell the difference between Mercurian and Apollonian olympians. She'd told Koralia years ago that it was all about the torsos: shoulders, pecs, and waists. Mercurians were slightly slimmer in all those places, noticeable when you knew to look for it.

"Uh, neither, actually, ma'am." Mikon stumbled a little over the words, smiling shyly.

Koralia came to his rescue. "You don't really expect us to talk about that over this line, do you?"

"Of course not," Athina said, shrugging one shoulder in a deliberately casual manner, clearly enjoying herself. "The security of the Sunfires is high priority."

Mikon was staring into the screen in surprise, but Koralia snorted. "Precisely, Aunt, precisely. How long did it take you to put that together?"

Athina smirked like no one else in the galaxy, and Koralia always enjoyed seeing it. "I suspected last week, but then you said Krete. Half the galaxy knows there are rebels near Krete, fighting with Minos."

Koralia didn't want to ask this question but it was necessary. "Do you... does that change anything?"

"If you were any closer, I'd be smacking you upside the head."

Grinning, Koralia saluted her. "I promise I wouldn't dodge it this time."

"You'd better not. By the way, I hear your mother stopped by Akwila recently. How did that dinner go down?"

Koralia stiffened a little. She tried not to, but the reaction was automatic. Mikon put one hand on her shoulder, squeezing it a little, while on her other side, Talos nudged her arm.

"I wasn't on planet," she said, unable to keep the irritation out of her voice.

"Your fathers apparently weren't either," Athina remarked, one eyebrow raised. Her manner still seemed casual, but Koralia could *feel* Athina studying her.

She widened her eyes innocently. "Well, you know. Dad has a lot of contracts in the general area, and Tata is busier than ever right now."

"Mmmm, yes, I do know." Athina raised both eyebrows this time. "Do your generals know where you are?"

This was the part of talking to Athina that she didn't like quite so much—all the questions, as if Athina felt a need to make up for her sister's deplorable mothering. She might be the fun aunt, but she was still an aunt.

Koralia sidestepped the question. "They know *who* I'm with. The important ones do, anyway."

"Ah." Athina crossed her legs and leaned back as if she was done, but Koralia knew she wasn't. It was one of Athina's favorite interrogation tricks. Sure enough, the next question came a few seconds later.

"And which ones would those be?"

Koralia sighed. It mattered to Athina because then she knew whom to contact if something went wrong, and while there was sense in that, it was also annoying. The Amazons would contact *her* if something went wrong, and wasn't that enough?

Not for Athina it wasn't.

"You know who," Koralia replied, intentionally vague.

"No, I don't." Athina's response was immediate. "It could be any one of seven. So again, which ones?"

"I can't answer that on the grounds of security." Koralia raised her chin slightly, daring Athina to contradict her. She could feel Mikon and Talos shaking with laughter on either side of her, while others around the table snickered.

"Give me a break." Athina snorted. "If I needed any more confirmation that you're with the rebels, you just gave it to me. What's wrong with talking about your generals? Everyone knows the Amazons are neutral."

Koralia tried not to fidget, feeling like a teenager again. "I'm something of a curiosity," she said.

"You've always been that," Athina waved one hand in the air dismissively. "What is it now, your mother?"

No, because of Icarus, but she wasn't going anywhere near *that* with her aunt. Some of the rebels looked oddly at her because she was the first full-blood olympian to join them. But most of them acted awkward around her because no one was quite sure how to treat the woman who had been engaged to Icarus. That news had spread through base while she was on Krete, Talos had told on their way to the bridge earlier, explaining the curious looks and ducked heads of base personnel.

"Ohhhh," Athina chuckled, "they don't know who your mother is, do they?"

With a wince, Koralia realized the olympian had been watching Mikon's face. Okay, reason number two she disliked video calls with her aunt. Athina missed very little, her sharp gaze constantly reading the faces of the people around her.

"I'm going now," Koralia said firmly. "Contact me when you're close to Krete, please."

Athina laughed. "I'll do that. I'd like to see Athanasia again."

*Won't that just be a delightful meeting.* Koralia closed her eyes for a second and sighed as she opened them again. She didn't need to see the General's face to know Athanasia was amused. "She wants to see you too. I'll make sure to be absent when that happens."

Athina's laugh rang out, her face gleaming with anticipation.

"And, Aunt?" Koralia paused with her hand over the button that would end the transmission. "Thanks."

"Don't be a goose." Athina winked at Mikon and blew Koralia a kiss before disappearing.

Mikon squeezed her shoulder again before returning to his seat, and Koralia looked around the table with a little dread as the lights came back up. Xuthos was staring at her in undisguised admiration and curiosity while everyone else looked indifferent or confused. Except the Sunfires, who grinned at her.

"So," she said, holding up both hands in a "what can you do?" gesture, "that's Athina."

"I like her." Mikon folded his hands on top of the table, grinning.

"You would. She likes you too." That had been obvious from her wink at the end. Athina only winked for two reasons: she approved of someone or she hated them and was being sarcastic. For a lawyer, she was almost shocking in her extremes; she tended to be either all love or all hate. Koralia was just glad she was on the *love* side.

"Well done. Now let's get this mission mapped out." Athanasia darkened the room again to highlight the projection. "Start tearing into the plan and let's get the flaws solved."

Koralia breathed a sigh of relief that she didn't have to answer any more questions. As much as she loved Athina, it was uncomfortable to be questioned about the olympians. Well, to answer questions from anyone who wasn't a Sunfire. She was here to fight a war, not be a freak.

She'd known the weird looks would happen eventually. It was hard for the rebels to look past the olympian reputation. But just because *most* of the olympians were arrogant sybarites didn't mean *everyone* was.

It would take time, but they'd see that. Mikon had made headway; she would too.

Eventually.

# CHAPTER 29

"Three teams then," Talos said half an hour later. They'd finished working out most of the flaws, and he was confident they had a solid plan. "Explosives." He pointed to Brygos and Kynna. "Rescue team." He nodded toward Koralia. "And distraction-slash-fighting, led by me." He pointed to himself.

"Which means we'll *definitely* be fighting," Tisandros said, looking as if he didn't care one way or the other. That was a lie. He wanted to fight. They all did. Talos would bet that everyone in the room, including him, was secretly hoping Theseus did something that meant they'd have to fight.

"We need three more people on our team," Kynna said, pointing to the orange and yellow dots on the map. "To get it right so we blow it up without damaging the planet, we need more insertion points." She zoomed in on the explosives map. "I'll go in here, Brygos can cover here, and then there's these." She tapped the projection, marking three other places with silver dots, and looked expectantly at Talos.

He motioned around the table. "Go ahead." Standard operating procedure for the Sunfires meant each team leader got to pick their own team. As long as they didn't poach from his pilots, they had free rein. Athanasia still had veto power, but she rarely needed to use it.

"I speak for Xuthos," Brygos said. "I want him on our team."

Xuthos snapped his fingers and shot finger guns at Brygos, who responded the same way.

"Good," Mikon said with a disgruntled flash of his eyes. "'Cause I don't want him on my team, whatever that is. I had him for three days."

"Hey, you already saw me make out with Koralia." Xuthos propped his foot up on his chair and grinned at the youngest Sunfire. "The worst is behind you."

Talos shot Koralia a quick look. She rolled her eyes, but other than that, she acted like she hadn't heard, focusing on her calculations.

"First of all," Mikon said, in the voice of a person prepared to throughly verbally destroy another person. "*She* kissed *you*. You did not *make out*. And secondly, you're in enough trouble as it is. I'd watch yourself."

The way Mikon said it confirmed to Talos exactly where he and Brygos and Kynna had been earlier. Xuthos would be in for an unpleasant surprise when he got back to his quarters.

And the pilot apparently knew it too, because he tensed, staring at Mikon with suspicion.

"Well, anyway, he's ours," Brygos said, rubbing his hands together. "Get over here so we can finish planning, dude."

"No," the General said, barely raising her voice. Xuthos had been walking around the table, but he stopped and turned around.

"Ma'am?" three or four voices said at once, including Xuthos.

"Rescue team will be Koralia as leader, plus Mikon and Xuthos. You can have anyone else for your team, except for Talos's pilots, of course."

"Oh, holy ashes," Mikon muttered, slumping down in his chair and glaring at the table like he did whenever he wasn't thrilled about something.

Xuthos's eyes gleamed, and he gave Brygos an apologetic shrug. "Sorry, man, but duty calls."

"You are *not* sorry." Mikon snorted, throwing Xuthos a look that was both bored and dark with annoyance.

Talos leaned forward, ready to pull Mikon back if needed, but he looked to be well in control of himself.

"You're right, I'm not." Xuthos smirked. "No offense, Bry, but you just don't hold a candle to Koralia."

Brygos heaved an exaggerated sigh. "I see how it is," he said glumly.

"So do I." Kynna tilted her chin up so she could look down her nose at Xuthos. "I'd want to be on her team too, but at least it's nice to know how we rate these days."

Talos glanced at Koralia, wondering what she thought of the bantering.

But she still looked like she wasn't listening, conferring quietly with Ianessa and mapping out routes around the information Asterion was sending.

The General looked like she was trying not to laugh. It had probably been a while since her briefings had been interrupted to this extent. Icarus was a tease, but he had been all business in battle briefings or any kind of planning meeting. He wanted the facts and then he wanted to be done and off doing something. Mikon was bad enough on his own but he usually confined himself to sassy comments. When you added Brygos and Kynna to the mix, you might as well resign yourself to meetings taking three times as long as normal. If the rebels had been really crunched for time, everyone would have been quiet and listening, but as it was, they still had a few hours before evening, and the attack couldn't begin until morning. A lot of time stretched between now and then.

Still he almost snapped at the Sunfires to stop being disgraceful and behave, but the General caught his eye and smiled. It was small, understanding, and he closed his eyes and took a quick breath.

Everyone was on edge because this was *it*. They were finally about to take down what the Kallistratus had been fighting against for well over a month now. The thing that had indirectly been the cause of Icarus's death. Not to mention they were going into *battle*. And it was a fight that would end in some deaths. When the rebels climbed into their ships, they'd level out and be fine. But before, during planning, that was when they let themselves be restless.

So if the General was willing to tolerate the chatter and interruptions, he wasn't going to be the one to stop it.

"Ahem." The General cleared her throat, and everyone fell silent immediately. "Koralia, Mikon, and Xuthos are the rescue team," she repeated. "Koralia leading."

"Understood, ma'am." Koralia glanced up and nodded before going back to reading the messages from Asterion.

Talos turned his chair a little to the right, looking sideways and trying to study her unobtrusively. She seemed completely at home in the organized chaos the meeting had become, her head bent as she crossed something out and added a line of numbers.

She went to move around him, looking up to say, "Excuse me," but he watched the words die on her lips as she caught his gaze.

"You don't think I can do it?" she asked quietly, misinterpreting his scrutiny.

"No!" he said a little louder than he intended. Mikon glanced their way, and Talos lowered his voice. "No. It's not that. It's...you just seem so at home right now. My idiot siblings won't stop teasing each other and joking around, and it's like being in a room with balls of paper being thrown in all directions.

Most people hate their first Sunfire briefings until they get used to them. With your hearing, how is it not giving you a headache?"

She blinked and looked around like she hadn't realized it was so crazy. "It doesn't *feel* chaotic," she said, looking back at him. "Chaotic is...confusion. It's conflict. People not being sure what they should be doing. I've seen my fair share of that." Her lips twisted in a half smile. "New armies are crazy before they settle down. But this?" She shook her head. "This isn't chaos. It's...kind of fun," she admitted quietly. "It's just...people thinking."

He nodded, his mouth twisting in a quick smile. She'd understood—that was *exactly* what was happening. The rebellion was up against an almost staggering amount of unknowns with this mission. Any other time, the General wouldn't have even considered mounting a mission until they had more information about Theseus's fleet, about where he was going to strike and when. And Talos would have backed her completely.

But they were out of time. They *couldn't* wait anymore. They had to go, and they had to go *now*.

Fortunately, the Sunfires had made a career out of sudden strikes. Talos tuned back into the discussion, leaving Koralia to finish drawing her lines and boxes on the projection.

"It's because of the oaths we swore," Mikon was saying, as if it was a given that the same three people who had been down to Krete would be flying the rescue mission.

Which made sense, but the General folded her arms and gave Mikon a look that shut him up, at least for the moment.

"No, you would be fulfilling those oaths no matter how you helped in the rescue," the General said. "You're going on the mission because you're the best fit for it, since you know the minotaurs. None of us do, and from what Asterion is saying, time will be tight. Familiarity will help."

Mikon tipped his head to the side as if he was considering that, and then he added, "Also we're deadly. Well, two of us are."

Athanasia rolled her eyes, and Talos shook his head. Xuthos must really have pushed his buttons on Krete; Mikon had never been so antagonistic toward the pilot before, in fun or seriously.

Everyone knew exactly what Mikon meant, and Xuthos squared his shoulders, more than ready to take up the challenge. "In case you've forgotten my incredible record, I can be just as deadly as you."

"I doubt it, but whatever keeps your lonely bed warm at night." How Mikon managed to sound both dubious and cheerful at the same time, Talos had no idea, but somehow, he did.

"Keep winding him up, Mikon, and he'll be second-in-command on the mission," Athanasia said. Her voice was mild, but the warning was clear, and Mikon folded his hands on the table in front of him, straightening into the perfect picture of innocence.

Talos was laughing so hard under his breath that he had to turn away from the table to calm down. Beside him, Koralia turned away for a minute too. Trust Mikon to lighten the mood.

"How come he gets to be in charge over me?" Xuthos asked. The question wasn't belligerent; it sounded bored.

"Because he's slightly higher ranked as a pilot," Xantippos answered. He finished reading the list in front of him and slid a sheet of scrip over to Brygos and Kynna, who were still conferring.

"Oh, right," Xuthos said as if he'd forgotten, which Talos knew he hadn't. The question had been asked purely to mess with Mikon.

Mikon glowered, but Xuthos clasped his hands together and wiggled his thumbs back and forth, pretending to be completely absorbed in getting it right. It looked ridiculous from where Talos was standing.

Who was or wasn't in the chain of command didn't matter much one way or the other to Xuthos—in the field, he went with the flow and tended to operate by his own rules. Talos was actually impressed Koralia had managed to keep him following her orders on Krete even *before* he'd been hit with persuasion. He didn't have the full story yet, but from what Mikon had said, Xuthos had worked better with Koralia than he'd ever worked with Talos.

Granted, Talos wasn't beautiful or an Amazon. Xuthos always worked better when there was a gorgeous woman involved. But Talos really didn't want to think about that right now...not in connection with the woman at his side.

"Speaking of deadly..." Mikon tapped his fingertips together, looking sideways at Talos and then at the General. "How much force are we authorized to use?"

"Up to lethal," Athanasia said. Looking at each person around the table in turn, she added, "That goes for everyone. Leaving Asterion in their hands to be sold into slavery or as a target for every bounty hunter and princeling with grand ideas is worse...*far* worse for the galaxy."

*Worse than a few Kretan lives* is what she didn't say, but Talos heard it anyway. The General was a diplomat at heart; she always had been. Talos knew it was why she'd joined the Amazons—as a way to channel both her aggression and her diplomacy. She didn't *want* to kill Kretans, and she didn't give this order lightly. But Minos was exploiting an entire race, and if Athanasia had to sacrifice a few lives to stop him, she would.

And Koralia was an Amazon, while Mikon had been thoroughly trained by

Icarus in when to kill and when not to kill, so there was little danger either of them would go too far. Xuthos might be a different story, but with Koralia on the team and her persuasion still in his head, he'd be fine.

"I've got our other team members," Kynna said, putting three pictures up on the planning board that hovered over the map. If Talos remembered correctly, one young woman had been bomb defense in a planetary police force for six months before joining the Kallistratus. The other two he'd just met when coming back to this base, but Kynna and Brygos were used to picking out people just from personnel files.

"So we're ready to go over the final plans?" Talos asked, checking with each person around the table.

Koralia nodded. "I am, but our schedule is going to be even tighter than we thought. Asterion can get himself and Tryphosa up to an orbital maintenance station, but they'll have at least twelve guards with them, and we'll only have thirty minutes from the time they arrive until they leave. And if that's not enough, the coastal defense guns will be hot during that time so that they can protect the planet during maintenance."

That chilled the mood in an instant. Talos clenched his hands at his side to shove back the voices and images suddenly repeating in his head. Screaming, swearing at Icarus, a flash of light...he'd seen the video of that fateful day too many times.

Glancing around the table, he knew he wasn't the only one thinking of it. Koralia had caught her breath next to him with a quick hitch, and he wanted to pull her close and reassure her. But this was no time for being sidetracked by feelings.

"Guess what, everyone." Mikon stood up like he had an important announcement to make, and even the General turned to look at him. He let the silence stretch out for a minute, looking grave. "I officially hate the Kretan mess." Dusting his hands together, he sat back down, leaned his head against the back of his chair, and closed his eyes.

Ianessa threw a wadded-up sheet of scrip at him, hitting him dead center in the forehead. He reached out and caught it as it fell and opened his eyes to throw it back at her.

Talos grinned. Mikon had broken the gloom again, not much but just enough that everyone was sitting up straight, ready to dig in and add the final details. He'd have to make it up to the little brat later. He needed to give him some positive attention anyway. It had been a while, and if Mikon didn't have family time regularly, he got off-balance and his moods were harder to regulate.

*All of us need a break and some proper family time*, he corrected himself. But this was war, so they would have to settle for what they could get.

With a quick shake of his head, Talos yanked his attention back to the discussion.

"It all looks pretty solid to me," Xantippos said. "But I still have a question." He made an overlay of the projection, shrank the original, and used the overlay to move Theseus's ships so they surrounded the gates of Krete. "What happens if he moves in closer overnight? It's what I'd do if I was going to grab the kid then—move in closer and sit there all day so if anyone was scanning beyond the immediate boundaries, they'd notice the ships and start thinking, maybe even get spooked. Then I'd strike."

Talos had the answer to that. "Then we trap him between us and the planet and let Krete know they're planning something. Perfect cover for our own rescue." Part of him hoped Theseus would make that exact move. It would simplify things for the rebels—they'd have no compunction about attacking him then.

Xantippos grinned, slow but eager. "I like it."

"So do I." The General moved the fighter fleet further out into the projection. "But either way, you're going to need a distraction for Theseus if he notices our ships. What do you have?"

Koralia raised her hand. "I've got that covered."

"How?" the General asked. "You'll be leading the rescue team. How do you plan on doing both?"

"We"—she pointed to a radio tech who had been clustered with her and Ianessa—"think we can bounce my signal off of the base to a drone. Theseus will think we're trying to slip around his fleet and go straight for the gates, but Talos will instead trap him between the gates and us. Then our team will go straight to the station and pick up the minotaurs."

"Will you get there in time if you have to distract him?" Talos asked. That was a lot to put on one person in an attack.

He conveniently ignored the times he'd taken at least that much on himself, if not more.

"I can't go in until after you're in place anyway, right?" Koralia pointed to the green line that showed the rescue team's flight plan. "So I distract him while you get your ships into position. Then you pester his fleet while we head for the rescue point."

It was a sound plan. He grinned. *I could get used to working with her.* "You're sure he'll listen to you?"

She looked down at the table, a smirk twisting the corners of her mouth. "Oh, he'll listen long enough for you to get your ships into position. I'll make sure of that." There was venom and malice behind the statement, enough that more than one person at the table turned to look at her.

"Do I smell a scandal?" Kynna whispered loud enough for the room to hear.

Koralia tipped her head further down to hide her widening smirk. "Let's just say I know how to hold his attention."

"Draaaama," Mikon whispered, as loudly as Kynna. "This is going to be fun."

"Won't you be discovered though?" Xantippos objected. "It's a good plan, Lady—"

The Amazon held up both hands. "Just Koralia, remember?"

"Koralia, no offense, it's a good plan, but how are you going to manage it so that your secret isn't out?"

Talos had been wondering the same thing.

As if she knew that, she turned to look at him, her gaze holding his as she said, "Maybe it's time more of the galaxy realized this war isn't about everyone else against the olympians. I think it's time to show them that this is about power and arrogance and empires, not to mention fear." The words fell softly into the silence, and it seemed the whole room waited.

It was as if something had reached out from her spirit and touched his, a tiny but glittering brush of invisible fingertips.

He had only one response to it. Gripping her shoulder with one hand, he grinned. "Damn right. So let's go fan the flames of the rebellion."

Her own smile spread slowly, but it was bright when she turned back to the table.

Time for the Kallistratus to rise and shine.

# CHAPTER 30

T*he guns will be hot.*

When Koralia read Asterion's message, she felt as if a light mist had fallen over the room.

The haze had persisted through the rest of the meeting, clearing only for a moment near the end when she had looked at Talos. But it returned as she left the bridge with the radio tech so they could run some tests.

It still hovered around her when she left the communications room an hour later.

Xuthos had bolted from the bridge the instant Athanasia had closed the meeting, and now he was loudly complaining about something in the distance, but he was too far away for her to make out the words. That or the haze was clouding her hearing too.

Mikon and Talos came down the hall toward her, grinning.

"We're going to eat and then we have our usual pre-battle drink," Mikon said, practically bouncing with eagerness. "You are coming, right?"

"The General gave orders for everyone to be in bed early," Talos explained. "So if we want to do this, we have to start soon." He waited until she looked at him before adding, "We want you there, but if you need space, it's okay."

She did want to be there this time, she really did, but there was something she had to do first. "I'll join you soon."

"Sure," Talos said, his gaze holding hers for a few seconds, understanding gentle in his normally hard brown eyes. He lifted one hand in a small wave as she turned away.

The haze in her mind seemed to fill the hallways, not so thick to be smoke or fog, but enough that sounds felt a little fuzzy. She needed to think. Meditate. Clear her mind for the upcoming battle. Her team needed her clear-headed. She'd seen her restlessness echoed in Talos's eyes, and she knew the entire base was thinking about Icarus. Team leaders would need to be even calmer than usual for tomorrow's battle so they could keep their people in check.

There weren't many empty rooms on this particular base, but the docking bay with her fighter should be quiet right now, so she turned in that direction.

As she climbed onto the nose of her fighter, she realized that she still hadn't changed out of her formal wear, but long skirts were hardly an obstacle to her. She just tucked the skirt into the crook of her elbow and scrambled up.

Lying back, she closed her eyes and breathed out, picturing the tree houses of Iskyra, home of the Amazons. Platforms wound around thick trunks, and roofs sloped under wide branches heavy with sky-blue and turquoise leaves. Carven steps led up and around, and braided ropes hung within easy reach. The younger Amazons never climbed steps when they could swing from tree to tree.

Nowhere else in the galaxy had technology been so perfectly blended with natural resources—the Amazonian tree houses were the envy of many.

"Find your center," Hippolyta said when teaching every new recruit how to meditate. "Find an anchor point, a home, and return there."

Her treehouse on Iskyra was where she'd first found herself as a person, separate from the three olympian bloodlines into which she'd been born. It was also where she'd grown to adulthood, where she'd been tempered and trained, not just for battle but for life.

And it was where Icarus had told her he loved her.

"After your center, look for your guiding lights," Hippolyta had said.

Mentally, she reached for the faces of her Amazon generals. Hippolyta. Antiope. Menalippe. Penthesilea. Athanasia. Ares. Hephaestus.

Each in some way had pulled her out of herself, shown her the wider world and what she could do to find her place in it. But only Icarus had ever truly *surrounded* her with that place.

The memories gave her the calm she needed, the light to push back the fog in her mind and center herself, looking ahead to the battle with determination and awareness.

And with it came a rush of missing the Amazons. *It's been...how many months since I went back?* Ares had needed her for a while, and then she'd stayed on Akwila because she was most useful there, at least for the rebellion.

*I want to go home.*

That was it, she realized now. Part of the ache in her heart these past weeks had been because she longed for Iskyra, for the beautiful houses and the warm laughter of her generals. Home, where she was safe and where she could grieve the man she loved and relax into the familiar rhythm of Amazonian life.

But she couldn't leave the Kallistratus, not now. And the Amazons would join the rebellion. At some point. They couldn't yet—they had to look out for their people and their homes first, but she knew with unshakable confidence that there would come a day when the Amazons would agree that they had the same goals as the rebellion.

And how the galaxy would burn then with the fires of justice.

A door closed somewhere below her, and quiet footsteps came toward her. The person paused at her fighter, watching her, and asked, "Should I go away?"

It was Mikon, his voice subdued, as if he too understood what mood had driven her here.

Of course he did. He was Icarus's brother and had been almost as close to Icarus as Talos had.

*My little cub,* Icarus had called him.

She opened her eyes and smiled down at him. The haze was gone now, everything clear again. Mikon stood as tall as the nose of her fighter, his auburn hair level with the blue-tinted metal. His eyes, usually so bright, looked gray in the shadows of the bay, dull with exhaustion and grief.

"Come up," she invited, sliding over. Eagle fighters were wide enough to handle as many as three people sitting on their nose at once.

He leaped up and stretched out next to her. They lay that way for a few minutes, just staring up at the ceiling, two siblings resting in the calm before the storm.

"Thanks for letting me meet Athina," he said after a while. "I've wanted to for a long time."

She turned to look at him. He was close enough to reach out and touch but not so close that she felt crowded.

"I know. But wait to thank me until after you've seen her in person. Let's see if you still like her after she relentlessly interrogates you about everything in your life."

He grinned, and they were quiet again for a moment.

"*How* did you know…oh. Icarus?" he asked, barely above a whisper.

"Icarus," she confirmed in the same tone. "He said you really wanted to meet Athina and more Amazons—especially the generals—and he was quite angry at fate or whatever kept him from being able to take you to Iskyra."

"Yeah. And you're like all of it wrapped up in a package and tied with a shiny bow." His gaze still rested on her face.

It was a genuine compliment, and she could feel her smile brighten.

"I've met a few Amazons," he continued, looking back at the ceiling so far above their heads. "Lone warriors or rangers or...what do you call the ones who go out to check on situations and report back?"

"Rangers works." Few warriors had an official title among the Amazons. They had a rank, but that was about it. Who you were, what you'd done, and what rank you'd earned were more important to the Amazons than a formal title.

"Yeah, those. Icarus made sure I got to meet them whenever he could make it happen. Talos too."

"You'll meet others," she assured him. "Amazons much better than Polydora."

He winced, and she wondered if she should have kept quiet after all.

"So you heard about her, huh?"

"Yes, and she was an ex-Amazon for a reason, you'd better believe. Most Amazons are nothing like her. My generals will scold you and boss you and feed you...and give you a galactic perspective on justice, if you didn't already have it."

He laughed then, the sound echoing from the walls around them. "I'd like to see that."

So would she. Mikon should meet Ocyale, her former second. Tall, with gorgeous dark hair and golden skin, the girl was a fully ranked Amazon now, smart and brilliant and polished, dashing around the galaxy scouting for the generals. It had been a few weeks since Koralia had heard from her—from any in her squad. She should check in with them...but that could wait until after the battle.

Her Amazon generals would like Mikon. Hippolyta would itch to train him to harness his anger better. Penthesilea would shove a sword into his hand and drag him onto the dancing grounds, testing him on his reflexes through one of her favorite sword dances...and getting him to loosen up at the same time. Melanippe would take him gliding over the Iskyran plains and get him involved in the missions she staged to keep the younger Amazons from getting bored. And Antiope—oh, Antiope would take one look at him and her eyes would gleam like she'd found a new weapon. Then Koralia wouldn't see him for hours, and when she did, he'd have a tree house all his own and be engaged to help them on their next seven missions.

Yes, she definitely needed to take Mikon to Iskyra sometime.

"I've always been curious about olympian life." Mikon broke into her thoughts, the words no longer whispered but just above it, husky. "I guess because it almost *was* my life."

She twisted so she was lying half on her side, facing him. "Do you miss it? What you knew of it anyway?"

"No." He turned too, so he could see her. "No, I'd never give up the Sunfires for life with my mother. Never. Not even for a minute." He traced a random pattern on the fighter with one finger. "I just wonder sometimes about the life I could have had."

"Icarus understood that," she said. That had been clear from their conversations.

"Icarus understood *me*." He closed his eyes against the tears that glimmered there. "How long does it take to stop hurting?" he whispered.

Reaching between them, she put a hand on his cheek. "I don't know."

She wished she did, that she could tell him—and herself—how long the gaping holes inside them would bleed. But grief didn't work like that, especially not when you had loved someone as much as both of them had loved Icarus.

Easing herself into a sitting position, she slid closer to him so she could rest her hand on his head.

Some griefs healed slowly.

So she just sat there with him, stroking his hair while he cried, and she cried a little too, for the bright light that Icarus had been.

"Do you believe in a god?" he asked, after he'd been quiet for a while.

"What do you mean?"

"An all-knowing power in charge of the universe. Greater even than the olympians or the titans."

She considered that. "I don't know. It all seems a little too cohesive for random chance. But an all-seeing power? I think if there was one, it would have put better checks and balances into place for the olympians." The fact that the galaxy's rulers did what they wanted with little to no consequences...surely any actual god in charge would restrain that...wouldn't they?

"Hmmm." Mikon pondered that, still curled into her hand running through his hair.

Koralia lost track of how long they sat there, deep in their thoughts.

"We should get back to the others," Mikon said at last, picking his head up and giving her a tired smile. "Someone is going to come looking for us. Probably Talos. And we have to go to bed in, like, half an hour or something."

"Closer to an hour," she said, checking the time. Athanasia had said curfew would be at 2300 hours and it was just before 2200 now.

Mikon covered her hand with his and squeezed it before sliding down the nose of the fighter and holding out both hands to help her down. She slid down and was letting go to move around him when he put a hand on her arm to stop her. Then she felt something on her hair and smiled.

He was untangling her circlet again.

When he handed it to her, she looked at it for a second before tipping her head back to see his face. He topped her by a full head, but standing this close, it felt like more.

"Why do you keep doing this?" she asked, holding up the circlet.

A slight frown crinkled his forehead as he shrugged. "The first time...you glared at it like it was so frustrating, and I just wanted to help. And now?" He shrugged again. "You're so quiet. Contained—all the time. But you're hurting. It bleeds from you like it does from Talos, me...all of us. I just want to help." He hesitated, twisting his mouth like he wasn't sure he should say anything more. "You feel like you're so far away." His voice dropped even lower, until she could barely hear it. "I just want to remind you that we're here. You're family now. You have been since Icarus fell in love with you. And now we're here for you like you have been for me. And Talos. And Ianessa. The same way I know you'll be there for all of us when we need you."

She swallowed hard against the tears burning her eyes. This golden family and their loyalty glowed so radiantly that it almost hurt, in all the best ways, touching the deepest parts of her soul.

"Thank you," she said, but the words felt lame and inadequate. So she wrapped her arms around him, holding him tightly.

He sighed and relaxed against her, his head bent over her hair as he pulled her closer.

"He's right, you know," a different voice said when she pulled back. Talos stood several feet away, leaning against his own fighter.

Mikon grinned. "Told you he'd come."

With a smile that included both of them, she gathered up her skirts so she could move more freely and started toward the doors.

"Brygos and Kynna are in the middle of some drinking game that makes no sense. He says there won't be anything left unless you get up there right now," Talos told Mikon, who detoured to the light switches.

"We'll just see about that." Mikon made a face, and the bay went dark as he turned out the lights.

He was back to normal, something Koralia didn't even realize she'd been listening for in his voice.

291

"The boys wouldn't let up on Icarus when he told them about you," Talos said conversationally as they left the docking bay. "It was just like him to go and fall for someone forbidden."

She raised her eyebrows. "You make it sound so *scandalous*."

He stopped for a second to stare before catching up to her again. "Lord Ares and Lord Hephaestus wouldn't care about their daughter loving the most notorious rebel in the galaxy?"

Oh, they cared. They just couldn't stop her when her mind was made up. "I make my own choices," she said, straightening her chin haughtily. "They can either accept them or else."

Both brothers snickered at the same time. "And that's why Icarus picked you," Mikon said.

"Obviously." Talos was still chuckling when footsteps thudded down the hall, and she looked up to see Xuthos striding toward them, glaring at Mikon.

"See you in a few minutes," Mikon said, escaping down a side hall.

Xuthos switched his glare to Talos. "They glitter-bombed. My. Quarters," he ground out between clenched teeth.

"And?" Talos asked.

Xuthos floundered for words, and Talos shrugged, thumping him on the shoulder in a way that was probably supposed to be sympathetic but just looked like he couldn't care less.

"You implied Mikon had done something inappropriate," he said. "Maybe don't do that again."

"It was a joke!" Xuthos snapped.

"Brygos and Kynna are a little weird when it comes to what jokes they allow and what they don't, especially when it comes to their younger siblings."

"It doesn't look bad on you," Koralia said, trying to smooth his mood. And it didn't, with his dark-tan skin, angled eyes, high cheekbones, and black hair. He actually made the glitter look good...except for the gaudy pink chunks caught on his sleeves.

Xuthos looked pleased for just a second, and then, still huffing, he stormed off down the hallway.

Koralia kept walking for two steps and then stopped. "You...go on. I'll be there in a minute."

Talos turned, looking at her and then down the hallway where Xuthos had gone. "Going to try de-programming him?"

She smiled at the term. "Essentially."

"Eh, I'm with Mikon. Let him be. It'll do him good."

But she couldn't. Not with what they were going into tomorrow. This might not work anyway, but she had to try. "I'll be there soon," she said, and started down the hallway after Xuthos.

"Forward observation deck," Talos called after her.

She lifted her hand in response, already thinking about how to do this. It had been a long time since she'd tried to modify persuasion. It wasn't dangerous, usually, but it rarely worked, so olympians didn't bother most of the time.

*I can do this. I just have to go slowly.*

First, she had to find Xuthos.

+

WHEN KORALIA CAUGHT up with the pilot, he was standing outside the mess hall, joking with Cleon and Tisandros.

Cleon saw her first and tipped his head to her before clapping Xuthos on the shoulder and disappearing into the mess hall. Tisandros and Xuthos saw her at the same time.

Xuthos gave Koralia what he probably thought was a charming smile, but which had no effect on her. Bending low in a bow, he took her hand and kissed it. "To what do I owe the pleasure, Lady Amazon?"

Tisandros made a sound that could have been exasperation, disgust, or confusion—Koralia didn't know which. "Don't be late," he said over his shoulder as he went into the mess hall.

"Can you spare me fifteen minutes?" Koralia asked, trying to move back a step. He was too close for comfort, especially when he looked at her like *that*.

"You never have to ask me that. Lead on." At least his voice was teasing, not obnoxiously fawning.

She led the way around the corner to a medium-sized storage room and pushed open the door, hunting for the light switch.

A long arm reached in front of her and flicked on the light. When she turned around, Xuthos had closed the door and leaned against it, smirking at her.

"I know what comes next," he said, his voice low and inviting. "And here I thought you said we couldn't do this anymore."

"We're not, this isn't..." She stopped and bit her lip. How long had it been since she'd felt *nervous* about something? It felt foreign.

Xuthos's eyes darkened, and he came toward her. "Koralia? Are you okay?"

"I want to try something," she said quickly, reaching out to put her hands on his shoulders.

But he was faster, grabbing her wrists and holding her off. "No. I don't mind it, really." He waited until she looked up at him. "I don't *care*, Koralia," he repeated. "Don't… Just leave it be."

"Why?" she whispered. She didn't have to ask if he knew what she was going to do; somehow, he did. And in this small room, her skin prickled with how close they stood.

"Because I like you, and it's a cool little tie between us for a little longer. The Sunfires get you forever, it's nice to have this for a few days." Then he winced and closed his eyes, looking like he couldn't believe he'd said that.

Koralia tried not to laugh. Obviously, Mikon's power was still wearing off too.

But it had eased the tension a little, enough for her to move closer and say, "I have to. If I go down tomorrow—"

"No," Xuthos growled, stepping closer to her as his grasp on her wrists tightened.

"If I go down tomorrow," she repeated, her voice hard, and she locked eyes with him, "you have to be able to follow other orders. That's going to be hard unless I do this. Please…*please* don't fight me."

Defiant stubbornness swept over his face, and for one long moment, he looked like he would refuse. Then he capitulated. "Fine. Do whatever you want."

Grudging agreement was better than none. *I'll take it.*

"Relax," she said softly. She slid one wrist out of his grasp and set her fingertips on his shoulder where it met his neck. He dropped her other arm, and she lifted her hand to his cheek, her thumb stroking his jaw.

"Relax," she whispered again. Closing her eyes, she visualized a handheld firework. Lighting it, angling it just right so it burst where she wanted, feeling it leave her hand, and then, there, exploding into a flash of colored sparks. She filled her lungs with as much air as she could and began a slow exhale, visualizing the whole thing again, this time pushing power through it. When she reached the explosion point, she let go.

A shudder rippled over Xuthos.

Koralia opened her eyes. He was staring at her, stunned.

"What…" He coughed, clearing the gravel from his voice. "What was that?"

"Talos would call it reprogramming."

He mimed gagging at his commander's name, and she rolled her eyes.

She wouldn't know until tomorrow how much of it had worked, but his dark-orange eyes were clear of the adoring puppy look, so that was improvement.

"Thank you," she said. "Now let's get out of here before anyone gets any ideas about what we're doing." She turned toward the door, not wanting to see his flirtatious smile after that charged moment.

"Wait." His arms slid around her waist and he hugged her, quick and hard, backing out of the room before she could react. When she came out of the room and closed the door, he was standing on the other side of the hallway.

"Goodnight, Koralia."

He clearly didn't want to talk about any of it, so she just gave him a small smile. "If you're hungover tomorrow morning, I will punch you so hard you won't wake up until next year," she threatened.

Xuthos threw back his head and laughed, saluting her and then blowing a kiss from his fingertips.

Her shoulders lighter, Koralia turned toward the observation deck and her new family.

✦

WITH NOTHING TO do while waiting for Dione and her general to call in, Athanasia sat down in front of the security monitors. They were the easiest way to check on all her people and stay informed about the mood of the rebels. She knew her command team looked forward to tomorrow, but she hoped to get a feel for how everyone else on base was reacting.

So she saw Mikon, Talos, and Koralia come out of the fighter bay and head toward the lounge. And she laughed when Xuthos stalked up to them, furious, and then marched away again. But when Koralia went after him, the General leaned forward, watching closely. Koralia didn't have to work too hard to persuade him to follow her—no surprise there. The storage rooms didn't have security cameras, so Athanasia watched the clock as it ticked off minute by minute and she grew more and more impatient waiting.

She'd expected Koralia to take a little longer with the re-persuading, but they came out after only eleven minutes. Xuthos walked like a man just waking up, but if he was aware enough to laugh and salute, he couldn't be feeling it too badly. Athanasia had no way to tell if the process had worked or not, but when Koralia smiled as she went toward the observation lounge, the General relaxed in her chair.

Koralia wouldn't be smiling unless she was relieved or confident. It had worked.

*One more problem fixed.*

Whatever losses faced them tomorrow or in the future, there was no place Athanasia would rather be than here and now, surrounded by the rebels.

*Her* rebels.

# CHAPTER 31

W hen she arrived at the observation lounge, Kynna and Brygos both rushed over to her, and before she'd taken a full breath, she was sitting between Kynna and Ianessa with a goblet of hyacinth nektar in her hands.

The lights were dim, so everyone had a full view of the stars beyond the base. A dozen chairs had been dropped in front of the giant observation window. Ianessa had said these chairs were common on Kallistratus bases. Made out of waste material, they sat low on the floor and could be squeezed into almost any shape. They were easy to transport and store, and they were actually comfortable. So she sat back, took a deep breath, and sipped her drink.

"Talos, does Xuthos hate being under my command because I'm younger than him?" Mikon demanded as if he'd been in the middle of an argument with someone and wanted support for his side.

Talos poured himself a glass of nektar and sat down on the other side of Ianessa, turning so he could see everyone. "How should I know? I'm not an expert on the guy."

"He probably hates it because you needle him about it," Ianessa admonished. "Stop rubbing his face in the fact that you're a Sunfire, and he'd be fine."

Sitting up quickly, Brygos pointed at Ianessa, "I'm telling Loxias you're thinking about other men."

"Oh, lay off her." Kynna used her foot to shove him back down.

"Mmmm, I think Xuthos is just being an ass," Talos said, but his eyes glinted in the low light, and Koralia realized he was teasing Ianessa.

"Probably to make up for having been so good down on the planet," she agreed. Talos's smile when he realized she'd backed him up was...*intense* was the only word she could find.

Ianessa sighed. "Do *not* encourage him, Kora. As for Xuthos, maybe it's hard for him because his head is all messed up right now." She held out her cup for Talos to refill.

Mikon's snort was particularly eloquent. "Well, if you ask me, that doesn't mean he gets to be a jerk about it. *Or* complain about his assignment."

"He does it for attention," Kynna said. "I like the guy—"

"Because you have awful taste in men," Mikon interjected.

"—but he's an attention whore," Kynna finished and then kicked Mikon, not seeming to care whether she spilled his drink or not. "There's nothing wrong with my taste in men, thank you."

"There is," Mikon retorted. "It's hideous."

"Hate to agree with him, but your taste in men does kinda suck," Brygos said, dodging the kick he knew was coming.

"The only reason I'm not getting up to deal with you is that one of you will steal my seat next to Koralia," Kynna threatened Brygos, who shrugged, grinning and saluting her with his nektar.

"He isn't totally wrong," Talos said. "Your taste in men is one-third decent and two-thirds 'he's hot enough to kiss, I'll go with it.'"

Kynna glowered at her older brother while Ianessa laughed. "He's right, and you know it."

"Well, his taste in girls isn't any better." Kynna pointed at Brygos. "He dated that shiny piece of straw at our second to last base, and there wasn't anything between her ears but"—she blinked, like she couldn't find a word empty enough to describe the girl's brains—"well, more straw."

"Very eloquent." Mikon taunted, dodging another kick from Kynna.

"That," Brygos said with a dignified huff, "was for a Reason."

"I date some of mine for Reasons," Kynna argued.

Ianessa leaned closer to Koralia and whispered, "In case you can't tell, this is normal. Any minute now, they'll start in on Mikon and Talos and then circle around to me."

"I think it's hilarious," she whispered back and knew Mikon had caught the exchange by the way he grinned.

Which reminded her of something she'd been wanting to know. "Exactly how old are you, Mikon?"

Kynna and Brygos suddenly stopped their bickering and leaned forward eagerly.

"In human years or olympian?" Mikon asked.

"Olympian."

He shrugged. "Thirty."

She blinked. Thirty? That was...that made him only three years younger than her. He was *thirty*? Looking at him, that was hard to believe. She'd known he wasn't a child, wasn't even a teenager, but she'd put him at least five years younger than her.

"Twenty-four in human years if you need the conversion," Mikon added, his eyes gleaming.

The little brat knew he'd startled her and was enjoying it.

"Then I'm with Ianessa," she said, her tone supercilious. "Don't torment Xuthos, and he might not resent you so much."

Brygos and Kynna burst out laughing as she watched Mikon's blue eyes flash surprise and then respect, raising his glass in salute.

With a sassy half shrug, he went back to taunting Kynna about something, and Koralia sat back, still trying to absorb his age. He acted like he was just out of his teens, and she'd just accepted that he was. She should have known better. That young, he wouldn't have had quite the level of power he did now.

Talos leaned back, his eyes half closed as he watched his family, his gaze flicking often to her. Koralia wondered what he was thinking, but his face didn't give anything away.

Being in the middle of the Sunfires was totally different from anything she'd ever experienced, but it was fun. Maybe it went back to how the Sunfires had grown up in the rebellion. Most of them had spent half their lives here, moving from base to base, harrying the olympians when they got too greedy for conquering.

Perhaps that was why she understood them so well. She, too, had been fighting wars since her teens.

"Oh, I meant to ask." Mikon abruptly stopped wrestling with Kynna and sat up, looking at Koralia. "Who is your mom? Unless you really don't want to tell us."

She swallowed, trying not to wince. No, she didn't mind if they knew, but... "You don't know already?"

They shook their heads. "Icarus said that was for you to tell us," Ianessa said. "And believe me, we tried to figure it out. Dione searched every olympian family tree, but there were so many possible names, and Hephaestus and Ares had theirs locked...she couldn't figure it out."

"I've been imagining someone scandalous," Kynna said, taking advantage of Mikon's distraction to wiggle out from under her brother's legs and prop herself up on her elbows. "Like Juno. Or Amphitrite."

Amphitrite. Koralia laughed at the thought of either Ares or Hephaestus sleeping with Poseidon's haughty wife.

Talos knew the identity of her mother; she could tell by the way he poured himself another drink and sat back to watch the conversation.

Icarus had told them so much about her but not her mother? With a shrug, she finished the rest of her nektar and said, "Aphrodite."

"Aha," Ianessa said, like everything suddenly made sense.

Mikon didn't say anything, but his eyes widened and then softened, and he smiled sadly at her.

"The Lady of Love?" Brygos gasped.

"Try the lady of damnation." Koralia curled her upper lip in a grimace, forcing herself not to think about what it had meant to have her for a mother, their arguments, their estrangement.

"Nah, that would be my mom," Mikon said, decisively, trying to pull Kynna back down onto the floor.

"Who is?" She raised her eyebrows. She'd been meaning to ask him that for a while.

He stopped wrestling, looked at the floor for a minute, and then rolled back up into his chair. "Eris." He hunched his shoulders and ducked his head, shrinking himself.

*Since when did Eris have kids? All this time, and she never mentioned that.* "I'm sorry," she said, knowing the words didn't do much against the shame and pain from years of growing up with a mother who treated you as less than human.

Eris being Mikon's mother explained so much. His tension around conflict but the keen enjoyment he took in riling people up. How quick he was to go into rages around conflict or grief. Why he shook himself after crying, as if he felt ashamed. And how quickly he'd understood what she didn't say about her mother. He, too, understood broken homes, parents who only loved you for what you could do for them or bring to them.

Yes, it all made sense, including why Icarus had left it to him to tell her who his mother was…and why he hadn't told anyone other than Talos about hers. He had wanted them to have this moment.

"Your moms suck," Kynna said, lying back on the floor. "I'm glad you guys are here with us now."

Koralia wasn't sure what to say to that, so she just nodded. Mikon's answer was to slither sideways off of his chair to trap Kynna between himself and Brygos, putting her in a headlock.

Talos handed Koralia another glass of nektar, his brown eyes warm, and she settled deeper into the chair, watching the tussle on the floor.

She was glad she was with them now too.

✛

KORALIA HAD HANDLED tonight very well, Talos thought as he watched the Amazon. She was even more relaxed than she'd been in the bay after talking to Mikon.

He'd noticed his brother slipping away earlier and knew he'd gone to talk to Koralia. Talos had given them an hour before going to check on them, arriving in time to hear Mikon's worry about her distance.

That didn't worry Talos yet, but the haunted look in her eyes did make him want to hold her until it went away.

Except that it wouldn't vanish with a hug. Just like his wouldn't.

*Damn you, Icarus.* He had no other words. What *did* you say when the brightest light in the family went out so suddenly?

Brygos stretched and yawned, and Talos looked at him for a moment. He really should send them to bed, but he didn't want to break this up. It was the first time they'd been able to relax together since Icarus's memorial, and that time hadn't lasted longer than an hour.

They were all having trouble sleeping. As per Athanasia's orders, they'd go to bed early tonight, but he thought they all dragged out these moments because no one actually *wanted* to sleep.

Sleep was full of loneliness and nightmares and memories—some good, some bad.

Brygos yelled something, and Talos blinked, focusing on the tangle of people on the floor. Mikon had both Brygos and Kynna pinned to the floor and was holding them there, looking like it was barely an effort.

That would teach them not to underestimate him in a fight again. *He's improved*, Talos thought proudly. *I'll have to spar a round with him when we get back.*

"Xuthos said you were a jealous hoe on Krete. Tell me more," Brygos said, breathing hard from the weight of his brother on top of him and thus trying to distract Mikon.

"Sure, just stand up so I can punch you," Mikon snapped cheerfully. "That will tell you everything you need to know."

Koralia laughed quietly. Having gotten the full story from Mikon earlier, Talos thought Brygos's description was pretty accurate.

Ah, Mikon, always falling for the wrong woman.

Not that Talos was any better this time.

"Ow!" Brygos yelled suddenly and wrenched Mikon's arm away, finally tackling him to the floor.

Ianessa looked over at Talos like she expected him to do something.

"What?" he tried to ask, but she shook her head in exasperation.

"Okay, that's enough, get up and settle down," Ianessa called. "Geez, seems like all I do anymore is tell you guys to behave. When did that become my job?"

Activity in the room stopped so abruptly that Talos looked around to see if the General had come in. She hadn't; everyone was staring at Ianessa in disbelief.

"Oh my gosh," she said, realization dawning on her face. "That's always been my job, hasn't it."

"Uh, yeahhhh." Brygos snorted. "It has. Hello, *big sister*? That's what you've always done."

"You're lucky you're pretty," Kynna said, vaulting to her feet and plopping back into her chair, reaching behind Koralia to pat Ianessa's shoulder. "At least you have that to fall back on when your brains don't work as fast."

Talos whistled. "Shots fired."

Koralia grinned and drank the last of the punch. He knew he should stop watching her, but it was hard. And not just because she was pretty. Icarus had talked so much about her that he found himself looking for his brother in her. Feeling closer to Icarus when he was with the woman Icarus had loved.

How long would it be before he stopped thinking about his brother constantly?

Ianessa's voice broke into his thoughts, raised to carry over the sound of Brygos and Mikon laughing over something. "Well, as your big sister, I'm ordering you to bed."

Talos glanced at the time. They had five minutes to get to their quarters before the General checked up on them. "You're not *my* big sister," he said, but he got up and used his foot to nudge their brothers.

"Maybe not in age, but you need as much bossing as they do." Ianessa shook her head.

Koralia was already on her feet, gathering up the cups and putting them on a side table. "If I wasn't older than you, *I'd* take you for a big sister," she said as she took Ianessa's cup.

"Oh, good, someone appreciates me." Ianessa held out her hands to be helped up, and Talos reached out to her, but Koralia beat him to it, helping the redhead up without putting strain on her arms.

Ianessa dropped one arm around Koralia's shoulders and squeezed. "You're my favorite new sibling."

"She's your *only* new sibling," Brygos objected as he got to his feet, dodging Kynna's attempts to pin him down so she could stand up first. "So I think you mean she's your new favorite."

"And here I thought I was the favorite." Kynna pouted, her eyes twinkling as she came up on Ianessa's other side and draped Ianessa's arm over her neck, taking her sister's weight.

"The favorite is clearly me." Mikon loomed over them, his hands shoved into his pockets as he smirked down at them. He was at least two inches taller than Brygos, making him the tallest person in the room, and he used that to his advantage, moving in front of the lights so his shadow dwarfed everyone.

Talos grinned, switching off the lights as he shoved Mikon in front of him and followed them all out the door and down the halls toward their quarters. "At least I'm the General's favorite."

"Ha! You wish," Mikon jeered. "Pretty sure that's Koralia. And I don't blame the General."

"Cruuush," Brygos whispered from ahead of the girls.

Mikon returned a rude gesture.

"Koralia's her favorite *girl*," Talos argued. "I'm her favorite guy."

Mikon tapped his chest. "Nah, that's me, for sure. I'll ask her tomorrow and you'll see."

*Tomorrow.* The word cast a cloud over them all until Kynna rallied, tossing her head. "She won't answer you," she informed Mikon. "She never does."

"I can persuade her." Mikon grinned, and Talos smacked him on the shoulder.

"Don't even think about using your power on the General."

"I wasn't going to." Mikon looked horrified, but Talos knew it was fake. "I was going to *charm* her."

"Which has never worked in the history of Athanasia," Koralia said in an undertone, and everyone laughed.

They were still laughing when they paused at Koralia's door, the first in the hall.

"Welcome to the Sunfires," Talos said, his tone sarcastic as he motioned to his siblings. He needed to say something to get his mind off how adorable she looked while tired, her freckles stark on her face in the harsh overhead light. Red-and-yellow hair tumbled about her shoulders, highlighted by the black gown she still wore.

"Thank you." She smiled, a world of meaning in the short phrase, and he understood what she didn't say. Thank you for the love. For the evening.

"Until tomorrow." She slipped into the room, and with a quick round of hugs, the Sunfires also dispersed, going to their own rooms.

*Tomorrow.* The shadow that had stalked them all night, daring them to think about the high stakes they faced. The danger of the mission.

What had happened the last time.

Talos shut his door and leaned against it, letting the fire of anger and the rebellion flame inside him even as he flung himself on his bed and yanked his blanket up. There were a hundred things that could go wrong, but they would force this battle to go their way.

Krete had already claimed one Sunfire; it would not claim another.

✝

"MELAINIS. GOOD MORNING, LOVE."

Koralia turned over in bed, pushing the familiar voice away. It couldn't be morning already; she was too tired.

"Come on, my black swan, wake up for me."

Sleepily she blinked her eyes open, seeing blue eyes and a laughing smile above her. Then wakefulness crashed over her, and she sat up abruptly, pushing herself backwards so she wouldn't crash into Icarus.

"What are you doing here?"

"Well, that's a fine welcome." He stood up and crossed his arms. "I thought you'd be happy to see me. I am here to see you, of course. Nothing else brings me to this forsaken desert."

"Liar," she answered automatically. "Missions take you to the desert."

"Not *this* desert," he said, leaning over her and brushing her hair back from her face.

She blinked again and shook her head, trying to clear away the image of him in front of her. It had to be another dream. She'd dreamed of him so often lately.

"You slept in your clothes again?" He clicked his tongue, but the question was fond. "Too busy to change into nightwear?"

"Huh?" She stared up at him for a second before rolling her eyes. "I always sleep in my clothes when I'm at an encampment. It saves time."

"It's got to be uncomfortable," he observed, looking her over.

She blushed at the raw appreciation in the smile he gave her. "Not as much as you might think. The Amazons do it all the time," she defended herself. "And they're clean clothes." Leaning back against the wall, she yawned. "How are you even here?" she asked again.

"Your father let me in."

That couldn't be true, but she wasn't sure why. Sleep still clouded the edges of her brain, the exhaustion of the past few weeks starting to take its toll on her body. "How did you persuade him to do that?" she asked, swinging her legs over the side of the bed and wiggling her toes on the sun-warmed stone.

"My natural charm." He grinned at her mocking snort.

The last fuzzy edges of sleep vanished, and she narrowed her eyes at him. "You didn't see Tata at all, did you? He's not here." She'd been the only trainer at this encampment for six days.

Laughing, he reached down to pull her up. "Nope, he's not. I told your guards I had a message from the General."

He looked so incredibly good that she ached to throw her arms around him and kiss him breathless, but she needed to get ready for the day first. Like put a proper shirt on over the thin top she wore.

"Get out." She shoved him toward the door. "I'll be there in a minute."

"I'd rather stay here." He crossed his arms and leaned back against her push.

"I need to get dressed."

"I thought you were already dressed." He motioned up and down her body, grinning again.

She let go suddenly, but he only swayed a little on his feet and kept his balance. "Go stand outside the door," she insisted, grabbing a pillow from her bed and throwing it at him. "Now."

"I'm going, I'm going." Laughing, he went back out into the hall, closing her door behind him.

It took her less than a minute to be ready for the day—exactly the reason Amazons slept in clean clothes every night and didn't bother with sleepwear, at least on missions.

When she opened the door and Icarus was still there, still present in the flesh and not some phantom of the night, she almost threw herself into his arms. But if she was still dreaming, she didn't want to wake up yet, so she held back.

Icarus grabbed both of her hands, the pressure of his fingers finally convincing her that he was real. He tugged her along with him, down the long hall.

Ares always sent half a dozen guards with her, and she knew at least two of them had spotted her by the time she and Icarus had reached the end of the hall. She wished he wasn't so bloody overprotective. *I'm an Amazon. None of these new recruits, no matter how strong or cunning they are, can possibly hurt me.*

"Is there a balcony or window around here to watch the sunrise?" Icarus asked, looking around at the dark-gray walls.

"A watchtower. This way."

Then they were running hand in hand and laughing, the summer morning swirling warm air around them. Down the stairs, across the courtyard, and back up another short flight of stairs to the watchtower and into the elevator that would take them to the top.

The door had barely closed behind them when he crushed her in his arms, holding her so tightly against him that she could barely breathe. But that didn't matter because she was hugging him back just as hard. It had been so long since she'd touched him—there were days his absence ached so much that she felt like her entire body was hollow.

She lifted her face to kiss him, but he shook his head. "Wait, Black Swan."

Startled, she backed up half a step, but he pulled her back into his chest, tucking her under his chin. "I want to kiss you under the sunrise."

She couldn't help but roll her eyes. "Who would ever guess the big, bad rebel is a romantic at heart?" she teased, the words muffled by her head being pressed into his shoulder. She eased her hands up and down his side, and he grabbed her arms and pulled them around him.

"Mikon would," he said, laughing. "He says I talk like a third-rate florist."

"How is the boy?"

"Less and less a boy with every day."

"And everyone else?"

"Still going strong. I'm going to see Talos after you. It's been too long, and I hate it. But y'know. Everything for the rebellion."

She did know. Sliding her fingers up his neck, she was going to run them through his hair, but the elevator door was opening and he was pulling her down the short hall to the observation deck, which towered many stories over the desert on this side of Akwila. This was where Ares came to watch troop movements, to analyze new units and catch any flaws that indicated the trained armies still needed practice moving well as a unit.

The dawn sky flushed saffron and lavender as Icarus closed the door behind them, still holding tightly to her hand. She tugged him toward the edge, but he pulled back.

"You know I adore heights, love, but I can't kiss you *and* sit on the edge at the same time."

"At last, something the great Icarus can't do," she teased.

He just grinned and sat down against the tower, pulling her down next to him and wrapping his arms around her again.

As the first edge of the sun crested the horizon, dark pink stained the sky, blending into sunny yellow, dark lavender, and pale blue.

Icarus turned her head to face him and kissed her.

It had been well worth the wait. He breathed against her skin like a parched man drank in water, like he couldn't get enough, his hands both gentle and hot on her face as he pulled her closer.

When she pushed away to breathe, he pressed her face to his, as if he couldn't stop touching her, feeling her skin on his.

She understood—she'd felt that too when she ached in the long watches of the night, or at random moments through the day. Like at midday when work stopped so everyone could eat and the warriors she'd been training gathered around, laughing and joking, while she was left to eat on her own. Or when she saw a young couple kissing before training started.

So she held on tightly, kissing him again and again until the sun was above the horizon and starting to beat down on the dry plains.

Then he leaned back and she snuggled against him, her head on his shoulder and his arm around her with her hands clasped in his.

"I thought you were dead," she said, tucking her head under his chin so his breathing ruffled her hair. "They said you died on Krete."

His chest moved with his chuckle. "Oh, love, they can't kill me, don't you know that? I'm immortal."

She grinned, snuggling closer. "No one is immortal. Not even olympians."

"Mmmm." He lifted her hand to his mouth and kissed her fingers one at a time. "Let's be the first. Let's promise to live forever."

Tipping her head up, she kissed his chin. "I don't think it's that simple."

"Maybe not." He closed his eyes, leaning his head against hers. "But let's try it anyway. We'll get married, and we'll live forever—you, me, the Sunfires."

It was a ridiculous thought, but right now, she felt like she could fly if she only tried and if he was there beside her. "I love you," she murmured.

"And I love you, my Amazon warrior."

And then something was falling, shadows streaking across the sun. She looked up to see comets hurtling across the sky, leaving blood-red trails in their wake.

She turned back to Icarus, but his face was blank as he stared at the sky, explosions mirrored in his suddenly black eyes, yellow and red and white dancing across her vision until she blinked.

That quickly, he was flat on his back, his eyes closed, gasping for breath, bleeding out around her, her hands wet with his blood as she hunted for the wound.

Red, red blood. Soaking her clothes, dripping from her hands.

"Icarus!" she cried, the word half scream, half gasping sob. "Icarus, no!"

+

"KORA. Koralia, wake up. It's a dream."

Gasping, Koralia sat straight up in bed. Talos waited until she blinked and gasped in another breath, until he was sure she was awake enough to know he was there. Then he touched her, sliding his hands up her arms until he was grasping her shoulders.

"Nightmare?" he asked unnecessarily. It couldn't have been anything else.

"Yeah." She sucked in another breath. "Did I scream?"

"No. Not really. Just gasped at the end."

"Then how did you know?" She peered at him. He'd flipped the lights to their dimmest setting earlier, and now he could just make out her face.

"I have a sixth sense for when my family is having nightmares." It sounded stupid when he said it aloud.

"And I'm a part of that now?" she asked, her voice tired, so tired.

"Apparently." He tried to keep his tone light. It felt weird and a little wonderful and *right* that she was a part of that now.

She looked down at herself and shook her head.

"What?" he asked.

She motioned to her clothes, but he couldn't see anything wrong with them.

"He was so close," she whispered, her breath growing short again. Talos reached out and grabbed her hands, shaking her a little to pull her out of whatever emotion was sweeping over her.

She closed her eyes, and worry knifed through him, but she opened them again, blinking back tears. "The worst ones are when it's half memory."

He knew those, when the dream felt so real you could reach out and touch it. And then you remembered the nightmare every time after that when you thought about the memory.

"Just a dream," she said, her voice steady now.

"Do you want to tell me about it?" he asked.

"No. Not really."

He sat back and nodded.

She slipped off the bed and joined him on the floor, pulling a blanket with her. Drawing her legs up to her chest, she leaned against her bed and covered herself with the blanket, offering one edge to him.

He took it, crossing his legs and putting his back against the bed, close

307

enough that she could lean on him if she wanted but not so close he was crowding her.

The silence wasn't uncomfortable, but it was heavy, weighed down by the memory of Icarus, his laugh, his smile, the way he raised his eyebrows—*him*.

"He was the brightest of us," Talos finally whispered, feeling like he'd choke if he didn't say something, wanting desperately to talk to her about the man they'd both loved. "I don't know how the hell I'm supposed to lead them now. I'm trying, but—" He shook his head.

"He trusted you implicitly, with everything," she said, reaching out for his hand and holding it tightly.

He grabbed the offered comfort gratefully.

"It was always Icarus for Mikon." Talos stared at the floor in front of them. "We rescued them close to the same time, Dione first and Mikon a few months later. I went in after her—Dione—and she didn't let go of me for hours." He smiled, remembering the young Oread's death grip on him as he carried her battered body into the base where the Sunfires were staying.

"She was my baby from that moment on. Brygos and Kynna were tight already, and Loxias, Siromos, and Ianessa had always been a close trio."

He realized there were tears on his cheeks and dashed them away with the hand not holding hers. "When Athanasia told us about Mikon, Icarus was the most insistent about getting him out. It was one of our hardest missions, and just the two of us went in because no one else was ready yet."

Her fingers tightened on his, as if she was seeing the danger too. How much had Icarus told her about that? Had he told her how they almost didn't make it out?

"But he was right." Talos pulled his knees up and rested his chin on his arm. "We thought our family was complete before, but we didn't realize how much it wasn't until that little brat came along. If Icarus was our heart and soul, Mikon was our crown." He choked on the last word and paused to breathe in deeply for a minute.

"It was no wonder that Mikon followed Icarus around like a shadow for the first year. Dione did the same to me. We were already in the Kallistratus then, but Athanasia found a way for us to stay close to base or take the kids along." He smiled at the memories.

"And without him..." Talos shook his head. "Without Icarus, Mikon's adrift. Alone. That's part of how he recognized you feel the same way."

"I didn't mean to push you awa—" she started to say, but he squeezed her hand.

"No, it's okay. We're all like that right now. Shadows. Half alive. Looking for our center in everything we do." He laughed, a hollow sound. "If his eidolon showed up right now, we probably wouldn't even think about questioning it. We'd just hug it."

She choked. "Yeah."

"Mikon…" he said again, needing her to understand why the boy was so jagged-edged these days, why he clung so tightly to her, why his volatility was so close to the surface.

Needing to know she saw their family the way he and Icarus did.

"We're here, and we're doing everything we can," he said. "Brygos and Kynna—that's part of why they're teasing him both more and less. It's less savage than usual, but there's even more of it. Dione messages him at night whenever she can. Her night and his aren't always the same—she's posted halfway across the galaxy—but whenever possible, she texts him when it's night for him. Siromos sends memes. Loxias and Ianessa check up on him. He knows we're here, but we're also trying to give him space because otherwise he feels like we're hovering, and that makes it worse." He sucked in a breath and rushed on. "It does for all of us—we need space and we need family at the same time. And it's not like he doesn't see us too; he understands what it's like for each of us, and he's trying to help."

Talos sighed, feeling like he wasn't making any sense, wondering if she was even listening at this point. "I think that's why the General assigned us both to the same base for right now." Athanasia had known he needed Mikon as much as his little brother needed him. And both of them needed the General's steadying presence, her familiarity with loss, her understanding smile that preceded kicking them into action.

"I know," she whispered. "It isn't just Mikon. You're not the laughing commander Icarus described. Your shoulders are heavy, and you don't smile like he said."

He couldn't speak for a minute, just gripped her hand, swallowing down tears and marveling again at how well she understood. This, *this* was why Icarus had loved her so much.

"I'm not Icarus," he choked out. "I can't *be* Icarus. But we're doing what we can."

He closed his eyes, and then he felt her fingers on his face, brushing away the tears. "That's all he would want," she said gently. "Don't you realize that, Talos? He wouldn't want you trying to be him. He wanted you to be *you*. You can't replace him, but you can lead just as you always have. That's all he ever wanted."

Her words crashed into him with the force of a battleship. That was exactly what he'd been doing: trying to be both himself and Icarus at the same time. Instead of just being himself and letting the Icarus-sized holes in all their hearts match as they grieved. He put his head down on his arms and let his tears fall for a minute.

"Thanks," he said when he could speak again. "That...*thanks*."

"Thank *you*." She squeezed his hand again and pulled away. "I thought it would be hard for you to see me. To be reminded of him like that. And you've all welcomed me with open arms. So thank *you* for letting me in and for holding onto me."

He hadn't even considered that it might be hard to see her. That wasn't the way the Sunfires worked. "Always. You're one of us now. I'm never letting go."

She made a soft sound like a cross between a smile and a sigh.

"And Talos?"

"Yes?"

"Mikon will be okay."

He nodded, even though he knew she couldn't see it. "Yeah. Yeah, he will. You've anchored him too, you know. I can tell. He looks at you, and he sees olympian, and he needed that so *badly*." He wouldn't admit that he had secretly wondered if she and Mikon would even get along. Icarus had been positive that they would, but for an instant after Talos figured out who she was, he'd envisioned how horribly wrong it could go if the two of them clashed.

That worry had been swept away when Mikon had grinned at her and claimed her as his kin.

Sister, crush, Amazon, fellow olympian—Talos wasn't exactly sure how Mikon saw her right now. Whether he liked her for herself, for Icarus, or because she'd been a comfort to him, he did like her, and for Mikon, that was vital right now.

Icarus's final gift to the Sunfires: the love of this woman.

"It's the first battle tomorrow," she said, looking closely at him through the darkness. "The first actual battle since him. Are you going to be okay?"

"Oh yeah. We all will once we get out there. We always are. You?"

"I'll be fine. As long as I can keep Xuthos in line."

He chuckled. "The persuasion will help."

"True."

Cold terror shot through Talos. He stiffened as hot fury and then the urge to scream followed.

*Mikon.*

Talos flung the blanket off, diving through the door and racing down the hall to his brother's room.

Mikon had thrashed all his blankets off, his shirt soaked with sweat. Talos dropped down next to the bed and covered Mikon's mouth with one hand before he could scream.

His brother jerked, almost throwing Talos off, and sat straight up in bed. He shook violently, his eyes wide with panic as he stared from Talos to Koralia, who had followed him.

The Amazon sat down on the other side of the bed, taking one of Mikon's hands in hers, rubbing her thumb over it. Talos pulled his brother close until Mikon put his head down on Talos's shoulder, still shaking. Mikon's other arm pulled Koralia closer until he was holding tightly to both of them while he tried to breathe.

Koralia hummed low in his ear—reciting a poem, Talos realized, though he couldn't make out the words. It helped, and Mikon's breathing became more regular until it leveled out.

When his brother grew calmer, Talos pulled him up out of the cot and rummaged in a drawer for a dry shirt. Mikon changed, still looking shell-shocked, and Talos handed him over to Koralia, whispering, "Same place as last night."

Kynna was waking from a nightmare too; he could sense her sobbing, and he hurried down the hall to his sister's room. Brygos arrived only seconds after Talos, and both of them hugged Kynna until she stopped crying. Then Talos pulled both of them up to follow him.

In a few minutes, they were all gathered on the observation deck, huddling close together in the chairs still in front of the window. There was no fighting over positions. Koralia and Talos sat in the middle, Mikon leaning on Koralia and Ianessa sitting on Talos's other side. Kynna rested her back against Ianessa's knees, and Brygos sat on the floor nearby with his arms wrapped around himself, rocking back and forth slightly while he stared out the window.

The nightmares had been worse for all of them tonight. Talos knew they should be trying to get more sleep, but what was the point when they'd just wake up screaming again?

Ianessa started braiding Kynna's hair, humming a poignant melody. Talos recognized it as an old nereid song she only sang when deeply upset. The sound wrapped itself around the little group, somehow full of both grief and belonging at the same time.

Had the azure waters of the Kretan sea called out to Icarus as he fell? Did they welcome his ashes, whisper that he was home again?

There was such bitter irony in Icarus dying over Krete.

His throat tightened, and he must have made some sound, because Koralia covered his hand with hers and squeezed. He turned his hand, clasping her fingers.

As the hour passed and the base lighting came on dimly before morning, most of them did drop off to sleep—Ianessa with her head on Talos's shoulder, Brygos and Kynna pillowed on each other, and Mikon with his head in Koralia's lap.

Now and then, he and Koralia would turn to check on each other and nod. For a little while, there was no war, no rebellion, no imminent olympian or Kretan threat. There was just them, the Sunfires, wrapped in their own little space, holding onto each other.

They sat that way until the dawn alarms rang at 0500 hours.

# CHAPTER 32

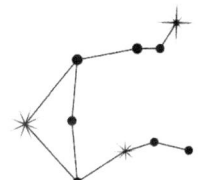

One thing the Sunfires were good at was being early to briefings, no matter what hour of the day they took place. Athanasia never knew if they'd picked up the habit from her, from Talos and Icarus, or if it was something they independently liked doing. Whatever the reason, it was handy, since it meant she always got a few minutes alone with them before meetings started.

"Bad night?" she asked when the Sunfires came through the door to the large bay where she would be briefing everyone. All of them looked some shade of exhausted, and each clutched a cup of coffee or citrus nektar.

"Yeah." Talos rubbed his hand over his face, and she looked closer at him. He looked like he'd barely slept, but fire burned as brightly as ever in his eyes.

It was a wonder how the boy kept going some days. He was burning himself out, or he had been. This morning, despite his fatigue, he seemed a little lighter, like he'd found some closure.

*Maybe he has*, she thought, looking at Koralia, who moved in sync with Talos. They'd obviously found their harmony.

*Good*. They'd need that before the day was done. She wished she didn't have to send them out this tired, but it was unavoidable.

"Can you still do the mission?" she asked, looking at each Sunfire in turn.

"What a stupid question," Kynna said loudly.

"Very stupid," Brygos agreed.

Talos smacked them both on the shoulder. "Respect," he hissed. "Do it right."

"Yes, General, we can still do the mission," they said in almost perfect unison. Athanasia bit back a laugh.

"I'm in." Mikon's eyes glowed with eagerness.

Ianessa gave the General a wry look in answer.

*Objective accomplished.* Athanasia knew nothing would keep them from the fight, but it psyched them up to hear themselves say the words out loud.

In small groups, everyone else filed in, pilots clustering around their wing-leaders and Talos, while Koralia's team and the explosives team gathered closer to the projector table.

"Everyone is clear on their roles?" the General asked when everyone was quiet. She flipped a switch, and the map came to life, glowing white underneath the colors that showed flight plans, battle movements, and Theseus's ships.

Talos pointed one at a time to the commanders around the table, and they rattled off their designations and assigned jobs.

"Team Boom. Plant explosives," Brygos said. "Make sure the triggers work so they can be detonated from outside the Labyrinth."

Kynna raised her hand before anyone else could speak. "We are not calling it Team Boom."

"You're Team Drakon," the General said, cutting off the impending argument. "And Brygos is lead." If she didn't designate that, Brygos and Kynna would be arguing about it right up until they went into action. When just the two of them were on a team, they didn't need a leader, because they worked together seamlessly. But with five people on the team, there had to be a chain of command.

Brygos smirked at Kynna, and she muttered something obscene, which got her smacked by Talos again.

"Lasthena, Cleon, and I are wingleaders for Team Khimera," Tisandros said when Talos pointed at him. "Support the other teams, keep everyone safe, and don't engage with the enemy unless they fire on us." Tisandros would also be flying as Talos's second-in-command today, since Xuthos was on the rescue team.

Athanasia had almost held Lasthena back, especially since Talos was torn between needing the woman to fly and wanting her to fully recover first. Lasthena had solved that for them by telling Talos she'd ask for immediate reassignment if he didn't let her fly.

When Talos pointed to the rescue team, Mikon jumped in before Koralia could speak. "Team Pegasus. Get in, get the minotaurs, get out, make everyone else look sluggish." He grinned smugly at his older brother.

Before Brygos and Kynna could taunt him, Koralia raised one eyebrow at Mikon and he settled down.

*Impressive*, Athanasia noted.

"And distract Theseus if need be," Koralia added.

"You know there's no going back from that?" Talos reminded her. "If they find out..."

"If Theseus opens his big mouth, it will be fine," Koralia said, her tone firm. "I'll deal with it then."

A hush fell over the rebels, everyone turning toward the General.

Athanasia looked from Talos to Koralia to Brygos to the rest of the pilots and techs gathered around. Some of these people would not be coming home today. Everyone in this room knew that. And still they went forward into death bravely, trusting that their sacrifices would light the way to a better future for the galaxy.

She looked at Talos and caught her breath against a sharp stab of grief. Before she released any team to battle, she waited for her fleet commander's nod. She was used to blue eyes and a golden smile nodding steady assurance, not dark-brown eyes burning to get going.

"Audeamus," she said. "Dismissed." She nodded at Talos.

Without a backward glance, their heads up and their shoulders straight, the rebels filed out of the briefing, pounding footsteps echoing down halls as they raced for their ships.

The final Labyrinth Mission had officially begun.

. ✝.

"Can I go now?" Mikon hollered across the docking bay that held his fighter and those of the other Sunfires.

Talos, busy running the final check on his fighter, turned away, shaking his head. "No, you can't; stop asking stupid questions!" he repeated as usual. He grinned. Mikon was so cheery, as if last night hadn't happened.

"Yes, Mo-o-om." Mikon dragged the word out.

When Talos looked up, Mikon flipped him off, and Talos laughed out loud. *Little brat.*

All around them in the bay, the other Sunfires were gathering, their flight checks complete. When going into a mission together, they never left without a final farewell to each other.

"Are we going to leave sometime this year?" Mikon complained, sliding down from his fighter as Koralia joined the group.

Kynna moved to punch Mikon in the shoulder but was yanked back by Brygos.

"Come back safely." Talos kept the goodbye brief. No sense prolonging it. That would put everyone on edge, which is the last thing they needed right now.

He gripped Mikon's shoulder a moment, then kissed Kynna on the forehead. Brygos shifted impatiently, and Talos kissed his forehead too.

Then he held out his arm to Koralia, feeling it was safer than kissing her today.

She clasped it Spartan-fashion. "Audeamus," she said, her face impassive but not indifferent.

"Audeamus," he replied, echoed by the Sunfires.

Then they went to their ships.

*

KORALIA LOOKED OVER HER TEAM, doing a final examination before climbing into her fighter. They'd be flying eagle ships today. She was most comfortable in one, since it was what she usually flew. But Xuthos was used to a falcon, and she couldn't help wondering how he'd do, despite his assurance that he'd be fine.

Xuthos and Mikon gathered around her. Glitter still dusted Xuthos's hair and skin, glinting in the light whenever he moved.

"You know what you're supposed to do," she said. "Let's get it done."

"Not big on briefings, Amazon?" Xuthos teased. Loyalty still shone in his eyes, but it had faded since last night. Today, he looked the same as everyone else who had been at the briefing.

Which was a relief. Thirty minutes wasn't much time to get in, rescue two people held under heavy guard, and get back out. They wouldn't have time to deal with any problems caused by residual persuasion—like him being over-protective or refusing to leave her side.

"I'm big on getting the job done, *Lieutenant*." Her voice turned sober. "And staying alive." She kissed his cheek. "You said a kiss gave you luck. Well, there."

Mikon groaned as Xuthos strutted to his fighter, almost bouncing off the floor. "Why did you do that? He'll be insufferable for days. Ugh, and so unfair."

She looked up at him, noticing the tired lines in his forehead had faded. Adrenaline, probably. It blocked out a lot, and it would keep them all going until the end of the mission. "Why, Mikon, does that mean you want one too?"

The battle fire was flowing now; she could feel it sliding through her, tingling down her arms and legs, up her spine, curling around her neck and jaw.

"Well, of course I want one." He narrowed his eyes speculatively. "But does it have to be on the cheek?"

Laughing, she pulled his head down and kissed his forehead. "Get in the fighter, little manticore. We've got a war to win."

He blinked at her for half a second before throwing her his brightest smile, blue eyes so brilliant it almost hurt to look at them.

As she strapped herself in, she thumped her clenched fist against the side of the fighter three times.

"For you, Icarus."

TALOS'S keen eyes swept the darkness before them, his hands steady on the cockpit controls. As always, his nervous energy had faded the instant he'd left the base, settling to focused determination.

"Coming up on Krete now, Commander," radioed a pilot from the front row of ships.

Finally. The journey to the planet had never seemed so long. "All teams, report in," Talos ordered.

"Team Pegasus, reporting in," said Koralia's voice, as impassive as when she'd left.

"Team Drakon, reporting in." Brygos sounded excited, which was normal.

That just left Talos's team. "Khimera wings, sound off." He checked off his wingleaders in his head as they reported in.

"Team Khimera, Beta Wing." *Tisandros.*

"Team Khimera, Gamma Wing." *Cleon.*

"Team Khimera, Delta Wing." *Lasthena,* defiant still, making him grin.

That was everyone. "Listen up," Talos said, his eyes tracking the fleet on his radar display. "You all know that we've lost people to this planet and its damned Labyrinth. We're taking it down today."

His pilots cheered, and he waited for them to stop.

"Icarus would have said to remember how he lived. To remember what he fought for. So today, we are not here for revenge. We are not here to make Krete pay. We are here to prevent a planet from selling a people into slavery, to stop a princess from kidnapping a brother whose only crime is that he was born, and to block a king from grabbing an entire sector of space to enlarge his empire, totally ignoring the problems he causes in the process."

There was no cheer when he paused this time, just a low hum, resolution taking hold of everyone in the fleet.

"And *so*," Talos raised his voice to make sure it carried clearly, "our battle cry today is not for Icarus. It is not for Heirax. It is for what is in front of us, for the galaxy and for justice. Are you with me?"

The roar that filled the radio was almost deafening. "For the Kallistratus!" his pilots chanted. "Audeamus!"

*Hell yes, we dare.* Talos clenched his hand for a minute, sucking in a deep breath of the defiance emanating from every rebel here.

"Pegasus Captain to Khimera Captain," Koralia said over the radio. "As far as inspiring speeches go, that was top of the line."

Grinning, he twisted his switch to clear the static that had clouded her last word. "Khimera Captain to Pegasus Captain, shouldn't you be focusing on your distraction?"

He could hear Koralia's smile. "And do only one thing at a time? You have a lot to learn about Amazons, Commander."

Something flashed in the corner of his vision, and Talos lifted his head with a smile. There, just ahead, sparkled the boundary lights of Krete. "Khimera Captain to Khimera Wings, drop to half speed. Teams Drakon and Pegasus, you're clear. Go...and audeamus."

Leading the way, he eased their speed to slow as Theseus's ships came into view.

*For the Kallistratus.*

⁺

*"Teams Drakon and Pegasus, you're clear. Go...and audeamus."*

Koralia leaned forward, searching for Theseus's lead ship as she laid in her course.

A young woman's voice came over the radio. "Khimera Delta Wing to Team Pegasus. Lieutenant Koralia, the drone is in position."

"Acknowledged," Koralia said. "Team Pegasus to Base, do I have a clear field?"

"Base to Pegasus," said Ianessa. "You have a clear field in three...two... one...and connected." She had insisted on running the radio for this mission since she still couldn't fly.

"Acknowledged, Base." Koralia twisted in her seat, making sure her jacket was straight. "Captain Theseus of Megara," she spoke crisply, projecting the arrogant tone that most olympians used. "I have an important message for you."

318

There was garbled sound for a minute and then Theseus's voice. "Unknown ship, I am receiving you. Do you have visual?"

A red light on her dash blinked, and Koralia pushed the button next to it. "I have visual."

"Well, hello, beautiful." Theseus whistled when he saw her.

Koralia sniffed when his face filled her screen. He hadn't grown any more attractive in the few months since she'd last seen him. He was still short, and he'd dyed his hair white on top and black on the sides, which made him look like an exotic rooster.

"Theseus," she clipped out the name.

"I'm sorry, do I know you?" he asked, peering at her.

"No, but you like to pretend to."

He looked doubtful. "I really think I'd have remembered such a pretty face."

Koralia rolled her eyes as her wingmen snickered over their coms. "Save it, little hyena," she said, and Theseus frowned at the familiarity in her tone. "Summer camp, nine years ago, you were trying to win a test set by Hermes Mercury. For some strange reason, you thought you'd have a better chance of winning if you were dating an olympian." She clicked her tongue. "You really should remember. Ariadne stepped in and filled my place when I turned you down."

"Lady Skotia, *darling*!" His voice was so full of sugar it was sickening. "What a propitious meeting. I told you then that we were fated. Can you deny it now?"

Fated? She wasn't even going to try answering that.

"Don't *darling* or *fate* me, you backwoods orangutan," she snapped. "I know why you're here, and I know your army's capabilities. If you attempt to move into the Labyrinth or take its operators by force, I will open fire."

She had missed this, the rush of battle, of stalking the enemy, of bringing it to bay.

"You and what army?" Theseus made a show of searching space through his viewscreen. "You don't have Daddy's fleet behind you—either of your father's fleets. Neither is likely to make a defense pact with Krete. And rumor has it you haven't spoken to Mommy in five years. Besides, your mother doesn't have any armies to speak of, does she?"

Aphrodite did, actually, but since their existence was a secret, of course Theseus wouldn't know about them. And she *had* spoken to her mother in the last five years, so Theseus definitely needed to update his sources of information.

A message flickered across her text screen. Talos and his fleet were almost in position to start harrying the Athenians. She needed to keep Theseus talking a little longer.

"I am the daughter of three of the most powerful olympians in the galaxy," she said with a casual wave of her hand. "Do you really think I'm sitting here with no navy?"

Talos's ships made their move, firing along the edges of Theseus's fleet. Missiles arced over the ships that sat closest to the Labyrinth.

"Who is that?" a feminine voice asked behind Theseus. He beckoned to someone out of visual range and waited until the woman joined him.

*Ariadne.*

"Why, Skotia!" she exclaimed. "What are you doing here? Come back to visit?"

"No, I'm here to prevent you from kidnapping your half brother and taking him off-world," she said coldly.

Ariadne's face first showed shock and then turned ugly. "You—you—" she sputtered. "How did you know?"

"You aren't as subtle as you think you are, Princess. My midnight meetings with my bodyguard led me to the minotaurs forced to maintain your planet's defenses."

"Serves them right," Ariadne snapped petulantly. "It's all they're good for. And you have no authority to stop us."

"Oh no?" Koralia curled her upper lip. "You will be violating at least seven galactic laws if you take any minotaurs from this planet, and I know three lawyers who would back that up—two of whom are olympian."

Ariadne actually hissed like a snake, and Theseus pulled her back from the viewscreen. Ariadne disappeared from view, only to reappear a moment later and whisper frantically to Theseus before looking straight at Koralia.

"Tell me, Skotia," she sneered, "how is it that the great Aphrodite's daughter is with the rebellion. Did you get bored of playing with your bodyguards and Daddy's toys?"

"Aphrodite's daughter?" at least half a dozen voices exclaimed over the radio.

"Focus, pilots!" Talos snapped.

Ariadne whispered to Theseus again and turned back to Koralia. Tipping her sharp nose in the air, she demanded, "And how does such a fleet even follow you? An olympian with the rebels who are fighting to kill olympians? What rebel did Daddy or Mommy pay off to let you play around for a while? The great General Athanasia herself?"

"The Kallistratus is an organization fighting for justice in the galaxy," Koralia said in a bored tone as another message scrolled over her screen.

Asterion had left the planet, heading to the orbital station, and Team Drakon had finished placing the explosives along one side of the Labyrinth. She needed to wrap this up.

Time for some drama, in true olympian fashion.

"Theseus of Megara." She used her best parade-ground voice. "You have five hundred men on those fifty light cruisers. The ships are woefully under-manned, not even at half strength, and those are mostly new men fresh out of training. Against a veteran fleet even one-fourth your size, you'll be crushed. There are at least thirty fighters waiting between you and freedom. They can and *will* outmaneuver you if you try anything. Before you can blink, your ships will be space dust and Krete's palace will receive a transmission stating that you have kidnapped their princess."

Ariadne screeched in outrage, but Koralia ignored it. "As for you, traitor princess"—she bared her teeth—"you want to know who I am? By what authority I command in the Kallistratus?"

Slowly, never taking her eyes from the screen, she opened her black jacket to show her red shirt. The two colors that had surrounded her from her birth. Black for death, for darkness, hatred, cold metal. Red for flame, war, determination, passion.

Black for battle. Red for blood.

"Is this what you wanted to see?" she challenged. Her voice rang back from the metal of her ship, and she drew the sound into herself, used it to fuel her.

"By what authority do I command this army, these ships, these men and women?"

Talos would forgive the stretch of truth there.

"By my own. Authority I earned by proving myself. Not given to me through the soft smiles of the Lady of Love and Beauty. Nor by Hephaestus's name or money, not by an ounce of the metal or a spark of the fires in his forges. And not by the fury or battle cries of my father Ares. I command these ships in my *own* name: Koralia Nikephoros, now of the Kallistratus Rebellion."

She paused for effect. Ariadne looked stunned, and Theseus goggled at her.

"It is my rebellion as much as it is anyone's, for the same reasons they fight: to bring truth and justice and liberty to this galaxy that runs too deep with the pain of those the olympians have trampled and oppressed. I have bled for this rebellion; I have sweated and cried and ached for it as much as anyone."

She took a quick breath and snarled, "And if you doubt that, little princess, if you think I am just playing or that I will not do everything in my power to stop you and your puffed-up rooster boyfriend, ask the Sunfires the name of the woman Icarus loved."

The silence was so still, so deep that she heard her own heartbeat thundering in her ears over the hum of her ship and its instruments.

Hellstars, that had felt good.

Ariadne reeled back from the projection, her hand going to her mouth, but whether it was in horror or some other emotion, Koralia didn't know. She didn't care either.

"Daaamn," Theseus drawled, his voice admiring. "If you ever get tired of playing rebel, Lady Skotia, look me up."

"Khimera Captain to Pegasus Captain," Talos said, his voice a little hesitant. "We have control of the situation. Repeat, we have control of the situation."

And just in time too. Koralia wanted to keep going, to verbally tear Ariadne to metaphorical shreds, but that wasn't their mission.

"One final thing," she said. "Theseus, if you doubt whether my fleet is a threat, remember who you contracted to train your men." She jabbed her finger down on the button, cutting the transmission.

"And I thought *my* speeches were dramatic," Talos teased. "By the battle cries of my father Ares?"

"Oh, shut up," she retorted, laughing. "That was the most cathartic thing I've done in a month."

"Well, you got him good and worried," Talos reported. "He's heading for the gates. Thanks, Pegasus."

"Anytime, Khimera." Koralia swung her fighter around. "Pegasus Captain to Team Pegasus, let's go get the minotaurs."

And angling her flight path toward the Labyrinth, she dove for it at full speed.

# CHAPTER 33

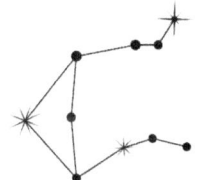

I f ever there was a time Talos felt super-human, it was when leading a fleet of fighters into battle.

He double-checked the position of his wings and barked, "Delta Wing, you're getting a little too close; fall back. Remember, we're only here to keep the Athenian fleet distracted. Push them toward the planet but not close enough that the guns can rake them." He made a minor course adjustment. "Delta Wing, come from underneath, Beta and Gamma Wings, hit them from the sides. Alpha Wing, cover the top. Fire across the bows and at non-vital areas."

Personally, he didn't care if they crippled Theseus's fleet. It would mean one less olympian to worry about for a while. But Athanasia's orders had been clear. They were running low on goodwill in the galaxy; there was no sense in making the situation worse unless they had no other choice.

Theseus's gunners finally went into action, shooting back at the rebels. As Koralia had predicted, they weren't very good at their job. Sure, Talos's pilots were good, and falcon fighters were easy to maneuver, but it should not have looked like they were facing toddlers in a snowball fight.

This was a joke, not a battle.

But his pilots were doing great, harrying Theseus without getting too close or firing lethal shots. Most had fought with Icarus, so they had as much reason to want revenge as he did. But they held off, diving and ducking and wheeling enough to confuse Theseus and keep his mind off the Labyrinth and the other teams. Koralia's team had disappeared inside the Labyrinth, but

Brygos's team raced around the planet, firing explosive packs into the force fields. The Labyrinth force fields would trap the bombs until they were detonated, crumbling the walls.

As long as his fleet didn't run out of fuel, they could do this all day. It was almost too easy. And whenever things were too easy, Talos got nervous.

He kept checking the Kretan fortress. Why hadn't it gone into action, even to scare off the fleets? The guns were primed, glowing red and orange and yellow. So why hadn't they fired? Theseus's fleet was close enough that they should have seen it by now, especially with the missile flashes from Talos's ships.

Maybe they were focusing on the Labyrinth. That had to be it. Their job was to protect the Labyrinth right now, while it was vulnerable, so they'd ignore anything that wasn't a direct, immediate threat.

Which was handy for him but not so much for Koralia's rescue team. If they were spotted...

"Team Drakon to Khimera Captain. We're done."

"Get back here," Talos ordered. "Cross under Krete and come up behind us. Team Pegasus, where are you?" They should have reported in by now. They were supposed to drop down on top of the station five minutes ago.

"A little busy!" Mikon yelled. "We're almost at the pickup point!"

"Khimera Captain to all wings, increase fire." It wasn't likely to distract the fortress, not if Krete already knew people were in the Labyrinth, but it couldn't hurt to try.

That was when Krete's shore defenses fired their first broadside, the explosions falling just short of Theseus's fleet. Either they had decided the fleets were worth taking out after all, or they were no longer worried about protecting the Labyrinth—which meant the Labyrinth was online enough to be dangerous.

"Team Pegasus, report in."

Silence.

"Team Pegasus?"

Still silence.

*Dammit.* "Mikon? Koralia? Talk to me, you guys!"

Still nothing. Talos swung wide of his fighters, scanning the entrance to the Labyrinth where the rescue team had disappeared. The force fields undulated with their usual blue and green, with no sign of a ship anywhere.

"Beta Wing, can you see anything of Team Pegasus?"

"Negative, Commander. We'll keep looking."

*Stay with us, Mikon, Koralia.* He'd even be happy to see Xuthos right now.

Another broadside rippled from the planet, and Talos dove back into the fight. He needed to concentrate on his part and trust Koralia. Her team was good—and she was an *Amazon*, for stars' sake.

*They'll make it. They have to.*

.+.

"TEAM DRAKON to all other units, the explosives are in place. You're clear."

*Finally.* Koralia had tried not to show her impatience, but it was hard when all around them towered the walls of the Labyrinth, shimmering green and blue, marked by scattered dots of yellow and red as the guns on the planet below fired into space.

Into the Kallistratus fleet.

No, she couldn't think about that, not now.

"Base to Pegasus," Ianessa's voice crackled. The coms had held up so far, but the static grew thicker as they pushed further into the Labyrinth.

"Pegasus here," Koralia answered.

"Asterion has landed. You have thirty minutes from right now before he'll be forced to leave again."

"Roger, Base. Xuthos, start the countdown clock," Koralia ordered as they flew through the last of the Labyrinth paths, guided by the same pulsing purple string that had once guided Talos and Mikon.

Xuthos had the ability to accurately count down time in his head, which was another reason Athanasia had picked him for the rescue team.

There, just ahead, was the docking platform. They banked and slid into an empty emergency docking bay at the top of the station.

*Nailed it.* Koralia felt a rush of thankfulness for Asterion and his maps.

She waited for alarms to scream and guns to turn on them, but nothing happened. Asterion must have taken care of that too. Minos definitely did not deserve the minotaur's brilliance.

Leaving the fighters running—they'd need a fast getaway, and even one minute to warm up was too long—they vaulted down to the floor and raced through the access door.

Asterion had told them where to find him, but he hadn't been able to tell them where all the guards would be. Her team would need to clear the station completely before they could leave, killing or stunning every guard, or they wouldn't stand a chance at getting out. All it took was one guard to raise an alarm.

"Mikon, you take the left wing; Xuthos, you take the right; I'll take the center. Meet at the server room." That was where the minotaurs should be.

Xuthos and Mikon were already hurrying through the halls, sweeping the darkness ahead of them and then turning around to check behind them. She'd have preferred to stay together—there was strength in numbers, and she liked a triangular formation for clearing an area—but that wasn't practical this time.

*Three right turns, two left, down the stairs,* she chanted Asterion's directions silently as she went down the central level, which had three floors. The server room was on the bottom.

There. Just ahead, a guard patrolling. She circled around, coming up behind him and pressing the muzzle of a stun gun into his neck. Two blasts, and he was unconscious on the floor before he knew what had happened.

One down.

No other guards appeared until she crept down the final set of stairs and into the hall that led to the server room. Four guards paced there—probably too many for her to take on alone without one of them raising the alarm, especially without her knowing how many were in the server room. But at least she knew the minotaurs were there. There was no other reason to have that many guards outside it.

*Stardust.* She'd either have to wait for Xuthos and Mikon to get back or... she might be able to lure them out.

Drawing back into the shadows around the curve of the hall, she tapped on the wall, trying to make it sound like someone was going down the hall in the opposite direction.

"What was that?" a guard said in Kretan.

"Probably the scouts coming back," another answered, sounding bored.

"Go look," ordered the first one.

Footsteps came toward her—two sets, she thought. She pulled back further into the shadows, holding her gun with her right hand and withdrawing a stun dart from her belt with her left.

The two guards came around the corner, sweeping their lights from side to side. Before she could deal with either, Mikon and Xuthos came up behind them and stunned them at the base of their necks.

*Whew.* While she hadn't expected them to have trouble, it was still a relief to have them back. She grinned, and Mikon gave her a thumbs-up sign.

Xuthos held up three fingers, pointing down the way he'd come. Three stunned—or killed.

She held up one finger, signifying the one she'd gotten rid of earlier. Then she pointed in the direction of the server room and held up two more fingers.

Four guards down and two in front of them...that meant there were at least six guards in the server room with the minotaurs.

*I hoped for less.* This would be tricky.

Touching Xuthos's shoulder, she raised her eyebrows and made the sign for *time*.

*Seventeen minutes*, he signed.

If it took them ten minutes to get back to the top of the station, that left only seven minutes to get the minotaurs out of the server room.

*Go, now.* She pointed down the hallway, motioning for Mikon to lead since he was tallest. She would bring up the rear.

He stepped in front of her and then turned back, pointing to Xuthos and frowning.

She raised her eyebrows at him.

He glowered, pointing at the glitter that still stuck to Xuthos's skin, wiggling his light to show her how it flashed.

*Well, you shouldn't have glitter-bombed him before a stealth mission*, she wanted to say, but Xuthos beat her to it, holding up his fist like he was going to punch Mikon.

*Just go.* She pushed Mikon ahead of them and shook her head warningly at Xuthos, rolling her eyes. He could at least have dusted his face with something that would cover the shimmer. But they'd be in and out too quickly for glitter to matter.

Mikon sneered silently at the pilot, and then they were moving around the corner and down the hall. She had a brief moment to appreciate how well the rebels were trained and how easily they fell into step with each other. Their teamwork didn't have the graceful unity of the Amazons, who moved like fighting was a dance, but it was smoother than many an army she had trained.

Before either guard in front of the server room could react, Mikon had stunned them both, firing one blast into the guard on the left, two into the one on the right and swinging back to shoot the one on the left again. Two blasts apiece was pushing the limit for what most humanoid bodies could stand at any one time, but it would keep them down for a while, which made it worth the risk.

In front of them was the door that led to the room where Asterion and Tryphosa were supposed to be replacing a section of mineral that had mysteriously malfunctioned overnight.

Those who could build could also destroy, and if Minos had remembered that, he might have been suspicious at the Labyrinth suddenly needing maintenance.

Fortunately for them, he hadn't.

Mikon went left and signed that there was a door on that side. Xuthos stripped the guards of their key disks and pointed up and to the right. Koralia followed his finger to where three steps led up to a half door.

*Stay here.* She pointed to Mikon and then the side door. If any guards came out, they wouldn't immediately see him. They would see their fellow guards lying stunned on the floor, but the team had no time to hide the bodies.

*Time?* she silently asked Xuthos again.

*Thirteen,* he signed.

Okay, scratch recon. They'd have to go in hot.

Xuthos tossed Mikon one key disk and handed her another before swiping a third through the swirled slot at the side of the door at the same time Mikon opened the door on the other side.

The server room was harshly lit and hot enough that the stench of sweat hit her as the doors swished open. One whole wall was open, bricks of semi-translucent material fitted into geometric patterns beside blocks of a solid color, probably conductors.

Asterion stood in the middle of the room, bending over a control panel, his wrists bound with some kind of rope that glowed a sickly greenish-white.

Tryphosa knelt in front of the wall, wiggling a brick back into place, and her wrists were bound with the same glowing rope. As she worked, she tried to stretch her arm to push the brick harder but jerked her hand back with a little cry. Whatever the material of the bindings, they had obviously sent a shock of some kind through the minotaur.

That was too much for Xuthos's self-control. Sliding under the low door and straightening in the same motion, he threw himself at the guards standing behind Tryphosa. For once Mikon didn't have a sarcastic remark or even an eye roll as he ducked through the doorway to their left and charged the two Kretans standing by Asterion, leaving the door guards to Koralia.

The first one was easy, too surprised to resist when she hit him, stunning him with two blasts to his shoulder. That would keep him down for at least twenty minutes. The other guard was raising his com, frantically pushing the button. She jabbed the stun dart into his hand, and he dropped his com, yelling. To be on the safe side, she shot another dart into the side of his chest.

Mikon had dispatched one guard and was grappling with another. Asterion stood over the still form of the fifth, but Xuthos...

Xuthos had his hands around the neck of the sixth, strangling him.

"No!" she yelled, speaking out loud for the first time since coming on board. "Xuthos, stop!"

"He deserves to die," the pilot snarled, squeezing tighter. The man's skin was starting to pale, and his eyes bulged.

"If he dies, you're a murderer," Mikon said sharply. "Which I'm sure is exactly how you'd like to be known to the rest of the rebellion." The sarcasm lashed through the room like a whip, and Xuthos faltered.

Koralia crouched slightly, ready to spring. She could command Xuthos to stop, but she didn't know if the remaining loyalty in his system would kick in fast enough. And if she pushed him too hard...

Xuthos stared at the Kretan for what felt like five minutes but couldn't have been more than a few seconds. Indecision hovered almost tangibly around him, and the way he tensed showed just how badly he wanted to kill the man in front of him.

Abruptly, he swung to the side and chopped the man in the neck with his hand, enough to knock him out but not kill or cripple him. "Let's go," he said shortly.

Koralia breathed a quick sigh of relief and turned to look at the minotaurs.

Mikon was pulling Tryphosa to her feet and yanking the binding rope off of her.

"Time?" she called to Xuthos as she started to work on the rope around Asterion's wrists. It was tied too tightly for her to pull it off, and the knots seemed to have glued themselves together.

"Eight minutes."

That wasn't enough.

"Get her to your ship now, Mikon! Don't stop!" The rope around Asterion's hands would have to wait. She shoved the minotaur in front of her. "Let's go. Xuthos—"

"I've got your backs! Just go!" he called, gathering up the coms and key disks from the other guards in the room.

Nudging Asterion forward and into a run, she kept turning around to sweep the corridor behind them until she saw Xuthos racing toward her. He held up his hand, palm out, closing it and opening it again.

Five minutes. Which meant four minutes to get to their ship and one to take off.

"There you are!" Mikon yelled, poking his head back around a corner. "What the hell are you doing, stopping to paint the walls?"

"I told you to get clear!" she snapped. "Get her out of here!"

"You run slower than I do!" he shouted but kept going, half dragging Tryphosa, who was leaning on him like she'd been injured.

The sound of pounding feet echoed behind them, too many to be Xuthos. Some of the guards must have woken up, at least two by the sound of their shouts.

Skidding into the docking bay, she grabbed Asterion's arm and pulled him toward her fighter. Mikon had Tryphosa in the second seat of his ship and was climbing in, and Xuthos raced into the bay and leaped toward his own fighter just as alarms began to scream.

Koralia shoved Asterion half up the ladder and into the back seat before springing up and swinging herself into the pilot's seat. The bay doors were closing over them—closing too fast. They wouldn't make it out.

Then an explosion rocked the station, and the blackness of space yawned above them. As Koralia took off, she could see Xuthos's guns pointed at the opening. He had shot the doors open.

If Krete didn't know they were here before, they sure did now, but that didn't matter since the rebels were on their way out.

Mikon flew out first, and she followed, turning to check that Xuthos was behind her. Pushing their ships to full speed, they soared through the wavy force fields of the Labyrinth, following the purple string that still shone above them.

"Pegasus to Base, come in," Koralia called into the radio as she flew through another turn, almost bumping the force field.

No response.

"Maybe we just have to go out further," Mikon suggested. He swore, and she saw his fighter swerve hard. "The Labyrinth is back online! The traps are armed!"

So much for getting out before that happened. Koralia pressed her lips together, blocking out everything but the string and the flight.

"I've got you," Xuthos said for the second time in half an hour, and his ship fell further behind. "Hurry up, both of you."

"What do you think we're *trying* to do," she growled, concentrating on dodging a net trying to drop over her. It clipped her left wing, and she barely rolled her fighter in time to avoid another one coming from below.

"Hellstars. Guys, speed up." Mikon sounded anxious, which didn't bode well for what lay directly ahead of Koralia.

Like *that*. Yanking her fighter to the side, she narrowly avoided crashing into another wall. Asterion's hand came over her shoulder, pointing, and she angled her fighter up to follow the direction he indicated.

And at last, her radio crackled with Ianessa's worried voice. "Base to Team Pegasus, can you hear us?"

She felt like shouting in relief but kept her tone calm. "Pegasus to Base, I read you."

"Finally!" Ianessa exclaimed. "Where are you?"

"We're clear of the station and heading out of the Labyrinth."

"I'm out!" Mikon shouted, exultant. "Well, I guess Krete isn't sleeping anymore."

She could see it now too—ahead stood the Labyrinth's side gates, and black space lay beyond, lit with the flashes of exploding missiles from the shore fortress. As she shot through, she glanced over her shoulder to check on Asterion.

He was staring around him with wide eyes, in awe of the sight before him.

Was it the first time he'd ever seen open space? Her throat tightened.

"Take that, Krete!" Mikon yelled, even as he dodged a pair of shells headed for him.

"Told you we'd be back!" Xuthos's shout was savage in its glee.

She laughed out loud, relief and satisfaction crashing over her. Xuthos's ship was still inside the Labyrinth, but she could see him now, and he'd be clear in a moment.

"Pegasus Captain to all units, we're out of the Labyrinth."

*Mission accomplished.*

✝

CHEERING ECHOED over the radio as the pilots heard Koralia's announcement. Talos grinned fiercely, baring his teeth at another broadside from the Kretan guns.

They'd done it.

Almost.

Just one thing left.

Talos glanced around, trying to see any of the third team. "Khimera Captain to Drakon Captain, blow the charges."

"Yes, sir, Captain!" Brygos answered.

For a moment, everything seemed frozen in space, and then green-and-blue light curved up from beyond Krete, the far side of the Labyrinth going up in flares of shimmering fire and smoke.

"It's gorgeous!" Mikon's awed voice said over the coms.

It really was, Talos agreed. But it was most gorgeous because it was being destroyed.

"Drakon to Big Captain, I can't detonate the side bombs!" Kynna's voice rasped through the radio. "Something's interfering with the signal! I can't detonate it!"

Big Captain? If Kynna was forgetting codenames, her agitation was strong.

"We'll have to do it manually," Brygos said, and Talos saw his fighter swing toward the side entrance.

"No!" he yelled, automatically moving away from his fleet to track his brother. "You saw how fast the far side went up. If you go in now, you will not survive when the bombs blow. Stay clear!" They could destroy the rest of the Labyrinth another day. It wasn't worth losing more people.

"This could be our last chance," Brygos argued. "If we leave it up, Minos will rebuild too fast."

"Damn it, Brygos, it's not worth your life." Talos put as much command as he could muster into his voice, wishing for a fraction of olympian power. "This is a direct order from your commanding officer. *Stay clear.*"

He almost didn't. Talos saw the fighter hovering in mid-space and clenched his hands so hard they ached. If Brygos went any closer, Talos would disable his brother's fighter.

Then Brygos pulled back, and Talos nearly gasped in relief.

But it didn't last long.

"I'll do it. I'm still inside," Xuthos said.

Bullshit. Talos had seen his ship exit two minutes ago. But when he dove down and brought his fighter around to see the side entrance, Xuthos's ship was slipping back inside the opening.

Ice clawed through Talos's shoulders and stomach. "Xuthos, get back out here." He hadn't saved Brygos just to lose Xuthos. "As your captain, I'm *ordering* you to turn back." Talos waited for him to snap a reply about how Koralia was his captain at the moment, but nothing came.

Above him and off to one side, Koralia's fighter turned to face the Labyrinth.

"Xuthos, please," she said. "Don't make us lose you too."

*Listen, you idiot*, Talos begged silently. *Listen to her.* He wished Koralia could *force* him to turn back. But her power didn't work like that. It could only influence, not coerce.

"Who says I'll be lost?" Xuthos retorted, a grin in the words. "Give me some credit, Amazon."

"Xuthos, this is a Black Order," Talos said, even as he knew it was hopeless. "Get back here."

"Sorry, sir, can't hear you," Xuthos said flippantly.

"You're already a hero!" Koralia pleaded. "You don't have to do anything else today."

There was a burst of static, and then Xuthos's voice came through again, fading in and out. "Ah, Amazon...that's where you...you're wrong. We need to bring this...down now or else...sold into slavery, and...and I'm already...inside."

Talos swore.

"That's not—" Koralia said.

Brygos tried too. "Xu, man, don't—"

Xuthos cut them all off, his voice clear for a minute. "You know it's what he would have done."

Talos winced. Icarus would never have let his pilots sacrifice themselves when they could live to fight another day. But the Labyrinth against one pilot's life—Xuthos was right, Icarus might just have made that sacrifice.

Krete fired again, the missiles falling just short of the fighters as another plume of blue-and-green fire flared up into space.

"Koralia." Xuthos was interrupted by a burst of static. When his voice came back, it was distant, as if he was speaking from a long way off. "Thanks. For the fun. And for understanding."

"No," she said hoarsely. "Xuthos, you idiot. It was an honor. And…you'll…" Her voice faltered. "You'll see him before I do. Just tell him…tell him we're okay."

"I'll tell him so much more than that." Xuthos laughed, the sound full of exhilaration as he fired into the Labyrinth wall again, igniting more of the bombs. Blinding white surged up followed by a sickly green.

"Hey, Commander," he called through the radio. "Sorry to disobey orders." His voice was flippant, taking Talos back to their first meeting after Icarus's death, the laughing scorn in his face as he mocked the Sunfires' attachment to their fighters.

Talos wanted to shake him and drag him out of the Labyrinth by force—anything other than sit here watching the bombs go off one at a time, knowing Xuthos was in the middle of them. "It was an honor to fly with you," he choked out.

"The honor was all mine." Xuthos's voice crackled. "Bry, Kynna, Kallistratus, see you on the other side."

"Audeamus," Talos whispered as half the Labyrinth crumbled in on itself, erupting into smoke and a cloud of teal-colored dust.

"Pegasus Captain to all units," Koralia's words were a flat monotone. "We're heading back to base."

Talos took a deep breath, steadying his voice. "Khimera Captain to all fighters, return to base. Repeat, return to base."

He hovered until the rest of his fighters had turned for home, but he wasn't really watching them. Instead, his gaze remained riveted on the Labyrinth, its remaining walls incandescent in the light and glitter of the explosions.

And then they were swallowed in a ball of fire so bright he closed his eyes as the explosions rocked through space, the shock waves pushing gently at his fighter even at this distance.

Krete's Labyrinth was no more.

Xuthos did not emerge from the fireball.

# CHAPTER 34

I t didn't matter in what army you fought: as a warrior, you had to accept that sometimes you lost people. And some losses hurt more than others.

Koralia leaned back against the windshield of her fighter. It had been several hours since the attack, but she hadn't had a chance to sit down since getting back. It had been all hurry and debriefing and reports and—

"Lost in deep thought?"

Her head snapped up and around toward the door as heels clicked across the floor. "Aunt."

"Kora." Athina reached the fighter and swung herself up easily. Seated on the nose, she looked her niece over for a few minutes. "You look good," she said at last.

"So do you." Athina always looked well put together. No matter how dusty or wrinkled her clothes got, she still seemed immaculate. It was a trick Koralia had never been able to learn.

"Did you see Athanasia?"

"Sure did." Athina settled back against the fighter's windshield, next to Koralia. "She's in her element."

"Yeah. The rebellion would be lost without her."

Athina hummed a response, and they just sat there for a while. Koralia was grateful for the silence. She really didn't feel like talking right now. Xuthos's last words played on a loop in her head over the memory of the final explosion.

To distract herself, she glanced at Athina. "When—"

"Who was he?" Athina turned so she could see Koralia's face.

Koralia winced, seeing Xuthos's mocking grin. "A pilot. And a good man."

"No, not him, although I'm sorry for your loss." Athina tilted her head, studying her niece. "The boy who took your heart and then left you. Who is he?" She might as well have said, *Who do I need to destroy?* Her tone said it, even if her words didn't yet.

"Who says there was a boy?" Koralia asked. *Do we have to do this now?* Weariness dragged at her. She wanted to lie down and sleep for a month.

Athina raised one perfectly groomed eyebrow. "Do you think I'm blind? I know your eyes. You glowed the last time I saw you, and you're hollow now. So who is he? Do I know him?"

Who *was* he. But Koralia couldn't bring herself to say that, not now. "I don't know if you ever met him," she said, closing her eyes. "He was Icarus."

There was such complete silence that Koralia opened her eyes again. Athina was looking at her with so much sympathy that she winced and turned away.

"Skotia Koralia Melainis Nikephoros," Athina said, settling back beside her again. "Why must you *always* choose the hard road?"

The way she said it told Koralia that Athina *had* met Icarus before, long enough to feel his charisma, his magnetism, and to understand how completely Koralia had fallen for him.

"I don't know," she whispered. "I don't. Know. Aunt."

Athina tactfully changed the subject. This wouldn't be the last time they talked about Icarus, but she at least wouldn't push right now, and for that, Koralia was grateful. It was too raw still. Especially after Xuthos's sacrifice.

"So where's the beautiful Sunfire hiding out?"

Koralia shrugged. After his mission report, Mikon had stormed out of the bridge, and she hadn't seen him since. She'd been in briefings while Ianessa helped the minotaurs settle into their new quarters. And afterwards, she knew she would only inflame Mikon, not help, so she had come here to be alone. But Talos had disappeared an hour ago, and she knew he'd gone to find his younger brother.

"I don't know that either. We just got done with a battle, so it's been a little..." She shook her head. "Do you want me to go find him?"

"No." Athina pushed her sunglasses further into her hair. "I'm heading down to the planet to see just how enraged Minos is. I'll see the young god another time."

There was something oddly comforting in that. *Another time.* It was said casually, like Athina hadn't even thought about it, but it was still a promise.

She'd see Koralia again, and she'd meet the Sunfires when the time and place were better for it.

Mikon would be ecstatic when that happened.

Athina swung her legs over the fighter and slid down, managing to be totally graceful about landing in high-heeled boots. "Talk to you later, kiddo."

"Give Minos hell," Koralia said, remembering just in time that she didn't need to raise her voice to be heard.

Athina was halfway to the door but turned back with a grin and a wave. "Oh, you know I will."

She did know. Athina was perfect for smoothing ruffled feathers on Krete...and then ruffling them back up again as soon as she had Minos right where she wanted him.

Lying back again, Koralia closed her eyes, breathing in and out slowly, centering herself. She heard the door close behind her aunt, but footsteps were still coming across the bay. They stopped by her fighter, and Talos said, "I like her."

She opened one eye. "Athina?"

"Yeah. She's cool."

"She is." Koralia pulled herself up and dropped down onto the floor, bending her knees to absorb the shock. If Talos was looking for her, other people probably were too.

Athina's visit had helped—Koralia felt more like herself. She could hold out a few more hours now and then meditate before bed.

Talos looked as exhausted as she felt.

"You okay?" She tipped his chin toward the light so she could see his face better. Stress lines were heavy in his forehead, and under the calm command in his eyes lay dull grief.

He held her in place, doing the same thing to her, his fingers gentle on her jaw. "I will be. You?"

She nodded. "And Mikon?"

Talos grinned, quick but genuine. "Come see for yourself, before he comes in here to drag you out."

She smiled as she left the bay, walking shoulder to shoulder with him. They'd lost a man today, but they'd won a huge victory, and that was something to celebrate.

Xuthos would have agreed.

+

336

"WELL, IT'S ABOUT *TIME*," Mikon said when Koralia and Talos walked through the door into the observation lounge. Anxiously, he searched their faces. They'd both been ragged earlier, like they couldn't take one more thing, but now they looked closer to normal.

*Thank stars.*

"Come on." He waved them toward the chairs in front of the window and held out cups of punch. "I have the most delicious cocktail so we can celebrate."

Koralia held back a little, looking around the room. Talos took a cup and frowned down into it suspiciously. "Did you mix this?"

*Rude.* Mikon scowled down at him. "No," he said sullenly. "Kynna did."

"Oh, okay." Relieved, Talos took a sip. "Mmm, it's good."

Instead of taking hers right away, Koralia rested her fingers over Mikon's —a silent signal to stand still—and looked up at him with a question in her eyes. *Are you okay?*

He nodded, not moving his gaze from her gorgeous, fascinating eyes, which started as pure golden amber around her pupils and then shaded to dark golden-brown at the edge of her irises. Did all Akwilan women have eyes like that?

Koralia tipped her head, and he realized she was still waiting for an answer. "I'm okay," he murmured, too low for anyone else to hear.

After the battle, he had screamed and punched things for a few minutes, sparred with Talos, and then just sat with him for over an hour. It helped, and he felt more in balance than he had in days. Especially since both Talos and Koralia looked better. Tired still, but not like they were carrying the galaxy on their shoulders. That probably wouldn't last long, but right now—right now, it was *good*.

She smiled, taking her glass...and his breathing stuttered for a few seconds. He'd known her for days now, but every time she smiled at him, he felt like he was seeing it for the first time: all beauty and intrigue.

"Much better than Mikon's horrible concoctions," Kynna said smugly, watching Talos and Koralia drink.

"My cocktails aren't horrible," he muttered, throwing her a look that promised revenge later. "You all just have terrible taste."

"No, your cocktails *are* horrible." Brygos got up and held out his empty cup for more. "Sorry to hurry this along, but me and Kynna have got to leave in fifteen minutes."

About to take another sip, Koralia paused. "You're heading out already?"

"Yeah, as soon as our fighters are refueled." Kynna unfolded her legs and stood up, also holding out her cup for Mikon to refill. "We've already stayed longer on the base than the General likes. Too many high-ranked rebels in one spot—" She chopped off the words, looking disgusted with herself.

Mikon's least favorite rule. It made sense, but he hated it.

Ianessa put an arm around Kynna, and Talos motioned for everyone to gather around. "Final drink," he told Koralia.

"It's tradition before we leave," Ianessa explained.

Wincing, Mikon turned away so they wouldn't see his disappointment. She'd said *we*. Of course she'd be leaving too. Athanasia would be moving them all to a new base again soon. After that victory, it wasn't smart to stay so close to Krete. And the Sunfires were about to disperse again.

But having so much of his family around had been *fun* and...healing.

*All good things end*, he could hear Icarus saying like he had so many times before, his voice encouraging as he hugged Mikon goodbye.

He blinked, trying to compose himself.

"C'mon," Talos said, his voice quiet.

The Sunfires closed up into a circle—Brygos and Kynna on either side of Ianessa, Talos next to Brygos, and Mikon beside Kynna. Koralia slipped into the empty space between himself and Talos as if she'd always been there.

Mikon felt like she had.

"Icarus made us," Talos began, his voice husky but his eyes clear and steadfast as he looked at each of his siblings, tipping his head back to look up at Mikon last. "He was a huge part of all of us, including Koralia."

Talos's smile was especially warm when he looked at her, Mikon noticed.

"We're not even sure who we are without him," Talos continued, "but he'd want us to figure it out. Find ourselves again. And stay strong together. So that's what we're going to do." He paused and nodded to Ianessa.

"To the best pilot in the galaxy," she said, her eyes warm.

"To a mediocre swordsmanship teacher at best." Kynna's mouth twisted, trying to keep her smile in place.

Brygos grinned. "To the man who took three months to learn how to hotwire a fighter."

Mikon snickered, remembering. That had been hilarious. "To the galaxy's greatest older brother," he said fiercely and felt Koralia lean against his shoulder.

Talos smiled down into his punch. "To the Sunfires. And to finding ourselves again."

"To Icarus," Koralia said softly.

Raising their glasses, they drank, looking out at the stars.

# AFTERWORD

This book was something I'd unconsciously been preparing to write all my life.

I'd been obsessed with Greek mythology since I was, oh, seven maybe? No, closer to nine. Like plenty of other geeky teens, I spent several weeks as a teenager making a family tree of the Greek gods. Then I moved on to trying to catalog all the different kinds of nymphs. I never finished either project, for the record, though I came close with the nymphs.

After a few months, something else—probably another ancient queen, if we're being honest—grabbed my attention, and I was off on another research journey. After that, Greek mythology was only occasionally an active part of my life, but it always hovered in the background or sideground. It came out when I needed to argue that ancient peoples weren't stupid, when I was making a point about mythologies and religions, when I was bored and felt like interjecting something shocking into my family's table conversations, and when I felt like being especially dramatic.

Hilariously, through all of this, I'd never liked the story of Icarus. Literally never. I thought he was an arrogant twit, and I didn't appreciate or sympathize with the Tumblr perspectives that made him out to be a tragic hero or an icon of teenage independence.

Until this story idea burst on me fully armored, like Athena herself (Athina in this book). I'd had a difficult day, starting with my horse of twelve years dying of cancer. That night, so tired and sad I could barely think, I went to shower. For years, showers have been my best inspiration: when I have writer's block, when I've been staring at the page for too long, when I'm not sure about titles or scenes or lines, I take a shower.

That night, inspiration was the last thing I was expecting, but by the time I got back to my room, the first scene was burning through my fingers. I pounded it out, sent it to my best friends, received an enthusiastic response...

And the rest is history.

Fast-forward a few months to a difficult October, deciding almost last-minute to do this story for NaNo, and a somewhat brutal month of November—which included getting the flu for the first time in a decade. Still, this story continued to pour out, and in 33 days I had a 115,000-word first draft completed and knew this would be the first book I published.

And here we are.

For those of you who don't know much about Greek mythology, I hope you still enjoyed this book. If I've inspired you to look up more about mythology, I'm delighted. If you're content to just read this story, I'm still delighted. If you hated this story, well, I hate plenty of books too, so I get that.

If you want to know more about the myths I incorporated, you can visit my blog or sign up for my newsletter. I'll have several posts on the mythology behind this series.

The story doesn't end here, in case you're wondering. There are least eight other books, plus a prequel, and probably a side story or two. You can look forward to the appearance or reappearance of a lot more olympians (oh yaaaay), including: Koralia's fathers, Athina, Hermes Mercury, and the son of Hades and Persephone. Other characters who will show up (or show back up) at some point include: Medusa, Ariadne, Helen of Troy, more minotaurs, a bunch of kentauri, and—of course—the Amazons.

Until then, readers.

# THANKS TO...

All the amazing friends who have supported and encouraged me on this journey.

My siblings: Froggie, Bluebird, and SillyMilly, for enthusiastically loving this book, and yes, for the furious stomping and glaring at me. I would apologize for making you cry + get mad at me, but Mom always said lying was bad. Plus, I'm planning to do it again next time, sorrynotsorry.

And more siblings: Shark-son, Shark-brother, and Shark-daughter, my first-round proofreaders, who helped me work out technical details and clear up confusing wording. And who told me they wished this was a movie. Shark-brother, your versions of the falcon and eagle fighters are magnificent. All of y'all are superb.

My brother Giraffe: I did not expect you to love this book as much as you did (maybe stupid of me in hindsight, given how much you adore Star Wars), and I smile so hard every time you talk about this story and these characters. Love you, bro.

My sister G, who stormed and raged at me over this story and who was the first person to ship anyone in this book. You enthusiastically greet every single idea of mine, even the bad ones, and that's heartwarming. You should have been in bed at least one night of this process, but you stayed up late finishing your proofread so I could get this out in time, and your questions helped me refine several tricky areas. Thank you.

Mom, staunch supporter of the Koralos ship and of Xuthos—to be honest, I did not expect you to love my bad-boy pilot that much, but I'm beyond delighted you did. Thank you for the time several years ago when I off-hand-edly mentioned writing as a career and you looked at me seriously and said, "Yes, I think you could be a great author." Thanks for the love, for believing in me, and for eagerly reading every book I hand you. Thanks for taking time to remind me that I was already good and would get better. And thank you for using your superb grammar eyes on the manuscript in these final days.

Michelle, fantastic lady, for freely offering her help, encouraging me through all of this, and being willing to honestly and courteously discuss all the aspects of publishing, even when we disagree on things.

Lucy and Emma and Angela, terrific authors in their own right, for greeting this idea with squealing and excitement when I first talked about it. Lucy for the laughing conversations about mythology and languages and cultures, and Angela for the enthusiasm every time I post about this book, plus how down she is to talk fairy tales and retellings most hours of the day.

Kat, for her encouragement, excitement, and the Instagram snickering about Greek Mythology.

Eli, who has been incredibly supportive of my writing for years and especially this book. Your sharp eyes in the final stages helped a lot. And for the intense side-eyes and dubious looks when I was "angelic" did a lot to brighten the final stressful stage.

Mel, who squeals about what I send her even when I haven't included any context. And both her and Randi, for the long conversations in the car about what makes good writing and what helps people connect with characters.

My Fairy Tale Central girls—Faith, Christine, Hayden, Tracey, and Kiri—plus Deborah O'Carroll: for the applause you gave this book every time it was mentioned. You cheered me on during writing, and you celebrated with me when I was done. All six of you are awesome, and I'm so glad to know you.

My beta readers: Carolyn, Micaela, and Jess—for asking to read the book and for the conversations about it.

Nathalie Kemp, whose feedback on another book really helped me see my writing with a different (and much-needed) perspective.

Larissa, you amazing girl, who read this even though it wasn't your usual genre and gave me invaluable feedback. Thank you so much.

My ARC readers: Christine, Deborah, Eli, Kiri, Kat, Hayden, Heather, and Tracey. You kept me going in the final stages. Thank you. And Christine, for screaming at me whenever this book was mentioned.

Emma. You ROCK. Thanks for enthusiastically pouncing on this concept the instant I first talked about it, all the nudging to get it DONE so you could read it, our conversations tearing apart books and movies, and the amazing above-and-beyond-a-proofread you did on this book. You brought your A-game to help me with the final polish, and I'm so *grateful* for all the comments, the yelling, and swearing at me at the end of That Scene. (No kidding, I laughed out loud and beamed so hard.) I can't wait to meet you in person whenever you come to town next. (Hint, hint, hurry up.) Or whenever I make it to your current location.

Lauren Richard for the support + honest critique over the years. It pushed me to improve a lot, and I hope this book is finally easier to follow. You couldn't be with us this past NaNo, and you were sorely missed, but I like to think you were there in spirit anyway through this book's creation. You're always down for the most bizarre random questions and for talking "monsters" at any hour of the day, and I appreciate it so much. I'm particularly impatient to know what you think of my minotaurs and my kentauri.

Alisa. You were the very first person to suggest I could be a published author some day, and I've never forgotten it. I laughed at the idea then, but you kept suggesting it, through our co-writing attempts, our story discussions, our serious-eyed teenage discussions about people and the world, and our numerous late-night phone calls. Well, here we are now, and I bow to you, dear friend. You were right. I *could* be a published author. Thank you.

Morgan G. Farris: awesome author, client, manager of Epic Faerytales, creative brain behind Minor 5 Emporium, and good friend. Thanks for having my back through all of this, especially the beautiful formatting and the gorgeous cover designing. For the long hours ranting about books, the passionate discussions about the world, the egging each other on to do more in the world of business, and for offering your help so freely and generously. You're a great woman, and it's been an honor. Here's to many more years of friendship and working together.

To Jenny for the warm encouragement and the faith that she didn't even have to speak—it was *there* around me. And for years ago, during the first word war we did together, pointing out something I could improve and saying, "I wouldn't say anything if I didn't think your writing was worth it." That meant a lot and still does.

To Kate for the long hours of encouragement, the many emails and texts, the reminders that I would find what I sought, I would improve, I would pull free of the drought, and for staying up way too late most nights to comment on this book. I probably would have drowned in grey before now if not for you. You should have been in bed sleeping off your brutal month of hospital wards (not just once, but *twice*), yet you made time for me as much as possible. That helped me SO MUCH in writing this. *Thank you.*

To Mirriam, my yang, my MuseTwin, my magnificent cover artist, and the captain of the Mikalia ship. I might never totally understand how you managed to fall in love with one character after THREE PARAGRAPHS, but boy, am I glad you did. And so is Mikon. This book would not have been possible without your overwhelming support, including the times you glared at me and wanted to shake me (or punch me? yeah, you definitely wanted to punch me) because I couldn't see my writing the way you did. Thank you for all the word wars, the screaming encouragement, the incoherent keyboard smashes, and your constant enthusiasm for this book, these characters, and this world. Ad astra per aspera, parabatai.

And thanks to every reader who picks up this book.

# ABOUT THE AUTHOR

*Arielle Bailey taught herself to read at age four, and words have been her primary passion ever since. In her day job, she edits other people's books and writes blog posts analyzing TV shows and movies. The rest of the time, she brainstorms, plots, and writes her own books. At night, you can usually find her outside, staring at the moon and stars.*

*Her favorite genres to read and write include contemporary fantasy, court intrigue, and space fantasy—because what is better than fantasy among the stars?*

*To learn more about her fiction (and that of her writing buddies), sign up for the Citadel Fiction newsletter: https://www.subscribepage.com/b1h5v9*

Blog: http://thesplendorfalls.blogspot.com/

Photo credit: Daze Passed Photography

[f] facebook.com/citadelfiction
[twitter] twitter.com/ArielleMBailey
[instagram] instagram.com/ariellemelodybailey

www.ingramcontent.com/pod-product-compliance
Lightning Source LLC
Chambersburg PA
CBHW071749110726
47908CB00006B/1748